"I WANT YOU TO CALL ME LUCIEN," HE COMMANDED.

Ariel automatically bristled at the order. "I prefer to call you Mr. Morgret."

Something dark and dangerous flashed through his eyes, and she experienced a shaft of fear as she watched his hand rise slowly to the crystal on a chain around his neck.

"Say it," he murmured.

His voice, deep and mellifluous, shimmered through her, setting off sparks. His piercing eyes were riveted on her, causing her heart to race and her pulse to pound. When he gently caressed the length of that damnable crystal, she felt as intimately connected with him as if they were in the throes of lovemaking. She was horrified by the sudden heat that spread through her. He leaned toward her. If she'd felt pierced by his eyes before, it was nothing compared to the invasion she now experienced. "Say it, Ariel," he coaxed as he lazily traced the curve of her bottom lip with one long, graceful finger.

"Lucien," she whispered breathlessly.

"**A wickedly exciting tale of eerie suspense and blistering passion ... Ms. Rafferty delves into some of our deepest, most erotic fantasies with an irresistible intensity.**"

—*Romantic Times*

TOUCH
OF
NIGHT

~

by

Carin Rafferty

A TOPAZ BOOK

TOPAZ
Published by the Penguin Group
Penguin Books USA Inc., 375 Hudson Street,
New York, New York 10014, U.S.A.
Penguin Books Ltd, 27 Wrights Lane,
London W8 5TZ, England
Penguin Books Australia Ltd, Ringwood
Victoria, Australia
Penguin Books Canada Ltd.,
10 Alcorn Avenue,
Toronto, Ontario, Canada M4V 3B2
Penguin Books (N.Z.) Ltd, 182-190 Wairau Road,
Auckland 10, New Zealand

Penguin Books Ltd, Registered Offices:
Harmondsworth, Middlesex, England

First published by Topaz, an imprint of Dutton Signet,
a division of Penguin Books USA Inc.

First Printing, February, 1994
10 9 8 7 6 5 4 3 2 1

 Topaz is a trademark of Dutton Signet,
a division of Penguin Books USA Inc.

Printed in the United States of America

PUBLISHER'S NOTE
This is a work of fiction. Names, characters, places, and incidents either are the
product of the author's imagination or are used fictitiously, and any resemblance
to actual persons, living or dead, events, or locales is entirely coincidental.

To Debra Dixon and Lisa Turner

Good friends are hard to find. Good writing friends are even harder. You two are the greatest! Thanks for putting up with me.

Prologue

THERE was only the faint glimmer of starlight when Armand Dantes slipped furtively out the front door. This was the part of being an investigative journalist that he liked best—the stealthy exploration of the unknown, the flirtatious game of tag with danger—and soon he should know if the cult he was investigating was dangerous.

He couldn't see into the thick Pennsylvania forest surrounding the old stone house, but as he took the path leading into the trees, he was alert to every sound. For two weeks he had searched the woods for the cave that supposedly housed the coven's altar. He'd hoped to inspect it by day, but from sunrise to sunset the coven children gathered before it, the smaller of them at quiet play and the older ones sitting in a silent circle, as though engaged in communal meditation.

During his three years of reporting on dangerous dissident groups, Armand had found that it was always the children who bothered him the most. They were often the pawns and frequently the victims of twisted adult minds. These children, however, were disturbing in their own right. They looked at—or, more accurately, probed—him with silvery eyes that had a tendency to grow opaque. And regardless of their coloring, they all had the same eyes—the same eyes that Lucien Morgret possessed.

The thought of Morgret, the self-proclaimed warlock

who had told him about the coven, made Armand
shudder. It was obvious that Morgret was crazy, and
Armand still hadn't figured out why the man had
sought him out and confided in him about this place.
But whatever Morgret's reasons, his story was compelling.

When Armand finally reached the cave, he saw a
spectral light emanating from its mouth, bathing the
clearing in front of it in a moonlike glow. His first
thought was that the coven must be meeting, but the
ponderous silence was too acute.

Curiously, he approached the cave. Its entrance was
a small circular passage that angled to the right, hiding
the interior from sight. He had to crouch to enter, and
shortly after he rounded the bend, he was in the cave
itself. As he stood upright, he gazed at his surroundings in awe.

The floor, the walls, and the ceiling were covered
with luminescent quartz crystals that glowed without
any visible light source. The chamber appeared to be a
perfect circle, about twenty feet in diameter. A large
block of gleaming wood stood in the center, and a collection of objects rested on its surface.

He approached the wooden altar to study the items.
There were two obviously old double-bladed knives—
one with an ornately carved black hilt and the other
with an unadorned white hilt. Beside them sat a small
dish that was so blackened from smoke he couldn't tell
if it was metal or pottery, though it gave off the pun-
gent odor of incense. Beside it was an unpretentious
gold chalice that looked old enough to have come out
of an archeological dig. Next to that was a stone pen-
tacle the size of his hand and carved with runic symbols. Finally, there was an ebony wand about two feet
long, winged at the top, with entwined snakes carved
along its length.

Armand recognized the items as a set of witches' tools used in rituals. Fishing the small camera out of his pocket, he took pictures of the tools, the altar, and the magnificent crystalline interior of the cave. Then he tucked the camera back into his pocket and tried to figure out a way to photograph the cult in action. There was no place for him to hide, and though his camera was equipped with a timing device, its black box would stand out in the room. He would have to find a way to disguise it, so there was no way he could set up the camera tonight. He would need to come back another night.

With a resigned sigh, he turned toward the mouth of the cave. He'd taken half a dozen steps before he saw the three white-robed figures blocking the entrance. Their robes were hooded, hiding their faces, and they stood so still that they resembled statues. It was their stillness against the crystal background that had made them nearly invisible.

Instinctively he began to back up. He didn't have a weapon, but if he could get to the knives on the altar, he'd be able to defend himself if the need arose. The figures didn't move, even when he reached the altar and made a grab for the knives. But before he could touch them, he was hit with a jolt of pain so intense that it made him stumble away from the altar. Before he could regain his balance, the crippling energy hit him again, and he fell to his knees.

Who sent you here?

It was a clear, angry demand, but it hadn't been spoken. It had been mentally communicated, and suddenly Armand believed everything that Morgret had told him. These people were witches and warlocks, and now that they considered him a threat, they would combine their powers to read his mind. He never should have told his twin sister, Ariel, about the coven;

if they learned that she knew about them, she also would be in danger.

But he had told her, and he was faced with two choices. He could take a chance that these men really couldn't read his mind, or he could drink the potion Morgret had given him to use if he was caught. According to Morgret, the potion would bring on instant amnesia, and right now, amnesia seemed the lesser evil.

He jerked the chain holding the vial out from beneath his shirt, popped the cap off the tiny container, and lifted it to his lips. The robed man in the center of the trio emitted an enraged scream and sprang toward him, his hands reaching for the vial, but it was too late.

An instant lethargy overtook Armand. As he felt himself losing consciousness, he suddenly realized that when he woke up he wouldn't remember anyone—not even Ariel, who was his sister, his best friend, his *twin*! For the first time in his life he would be utterly alone, and that panicked him.

Ariel, help me! his mind screamed as the darkness began to overtake him.

Even as he lost consciousness he heard that unspeaking voice demand, *Who is Ariel?*

Chapter One

Double, double toil and trouble;
Fire burn and cauldron bubble.
　　　—William Shakespeare, *Macbeth* 4.1.10

ARIEL Dantes shuddered as she stood before the door of the Witches' Brew, a bar located in a dilapidated neighborhood of downtown Philadelphia. The door was black with a red stained-glass inverted pentagram centered at eye level. Delicately etched in the glass were indecipherable, demonic-looking symbols. Below the pentagram were teardrop-shaped chips of red glass that ran to the bottom of the door. Like the pentagram, the chips glowed, giving the impression that the door was bleeding from an open wound. Ariel couldn't believe that her brother had been headed here when he bussed her on the cheek six weeks ago and told her he'd be in touch.

Though she knew she had to go inside, she couldn't bring herself to open the door. She turned away from it and nervously studied the street. A dozen motorcycles were parked in front of the bar amid the overflowing garbage cans whose stench turned her stomach. Most of the crumbling three-story brick buildings on the block were boarded up and had Condemned signs posted on them.

She watched an old woman push a shopping cart filled with junk up the middle of the street with one hand. She was talking and gesturing wildly with the other hand, as though in passionate conversation with some unseen companion. An emaciated woman, with a wraithlike child in tow, crept furtively down an alley. Two men wearing tattered clothes and obviously drunk or high on drugs were staggering up the block toward her. An equally tattered man stood across the street, staring at her with such absorption that she stuck her hand into her jacket pocket and took a firm hold on the Mace canister she'd placed there earlier.

It was dusk, and she cast a quick glance up and down the street, confirming that all the streetlights had been shattered. In a matter of minutes it would be so dark that she wouldn't be able to see her car, which was parked a block away. She should have parked closer, but it had been the only spot on the street that hadn't been covered with broken glass or garbage cans.

Common sense told her that she wasn't safe here, that she should hurry back to her car and leave. She could return tomorrow and confront Lucien Morgret in the daylight.

But even as she offered herself the chance to escape, she dismissed it. Her only clue to finding Armand was behind the macabre door of the Witches' Brew. It was here that Armand had met Lucien Morgret, the owner of the bar, who also claimed to be a warlock. It was conversations with Morgret that had sent Armand on his ridiculous search for a coven.

That had been six weeks ago, and she hadn't heard from him since. At first she hadn't been concerned. Armand was an investigative journalist who specialized in dangerous, dissident groups. It wasn't unusual for him to go underground, but no matter how far underground he went, he always called her once a month to reassure her that he was safe. For him to go this long without contacting her could only mean he was in trouble. She wasn't about to let another day go by without trying to find him. Drawing in a deep breath to bolster her courage, she turned back to the door and pushed it open.

When she entered the bar, she came to an abrupt halt. There were only half a dozen light bulbs illuminating the room, but even dimness couldn't disguise its shabby interior. She eyed the customers warily. Although the crowd—all male—wasn't large, enough chains, leather, and tattoos were displayed to make her grip the canister of Mace more tightly. But the men weren't as intimidating as the engraved images of devils and demons that populated the room were. They glared at her from the frieze that circled the ceiling. They scowled at her from the wooden booths and sneered at her from the arms and legs of chairs. She couldn't help feeling that when she stepped into the Witches' Brew, she had taken a step into Hell.

Again her common sense urged her to leave, but again she reminded herself of Armand. She hurried toward a scarred mahogany bar, which was also populated with demonic countenances, and slid onto a barstool, trying to decide how to approach Morgret. Armand had said the man was suspicious and wary of strangers. Should she just tell him who she was and why she was here, or should she be subtle? Her first instinct was to be direct so she could leave, but Morgret might be involved in Armand's disappearance. She had to be subtle.

The bartender was serving a customer at the other end of the bar, so Ariel surreptitiously studied the crowd. Armand had told her that Morgret was so distinctive that the moment you saw him you knew who he was. To her chagrin, everyone in the bar looked distinctive. As a dealer in rare and antique books, she usually dealt with a clientele that ran more toward pipes and tweeds. She doubted that there was a chain or tattoo among her customers.

She started when a deep voice suddenly asked, "What'll it be?"

She glanced up at the bartender and her jaw dropped. Armand hadn't been joking. Morgret was definitely distinctive, and she had no doubt that the man standing in front of her was Morgret. Though she didn't believe in warlocks, she could see why people would believe that he was one.

He was dressed in black jeans and a black shirt, unbuttoned halfway down his chest, with the cuffs rolled to his elbows. There was a small drawstring pouch at his waist, and an extraordinarily long transparent crystal was suspended from a heavy silver chain around his neck. He wasn't a handsome man. Indeed, the best description she could come up with was threatening. His shoulder-length black hair was shaggy. His features were sharp planes and angles. But it was his eyes that gave him a sinister presence. They were such a pale blue that they were almost silver. They didn't look at you; they pierced you.

She had to clear her throat to find her voice. "Do you, uh, have white wine?"

"I don't have wine, nor do I make mixed drinks," he answered tersely, staring at her with the same malevolence as the gargoyles framing the bar mirror behind him. "Our customers prefer their liquor straight and hard."

"Beer?" she suggested, intuiting that if she wasn't drinking, he wasn't going to talk to her.

"Tap or bottle?"

"Bottle," was her quick response.

His mocking smile said that he knew she was questioning the sanitary condition of his glassware, and Ariel cursed herself for the blunder. She couldn't afford to alienate him. She considered changing her order, but he had already pulled a bottle of beer from beneath the bar and twisted off the cap.

"Two bucks," he said, setting the bottle in front of her.

Ariel retrieved her wallet and handed him a $10 bill. While he got her change, she tried to think of a topic of conversation that would get him talking without making him suspicious.

She was still floundering for an icebreaker when he returned with her change and demanded, "Why are you here?"

The blunt question, delivered angrily, caught Ariel off guard. Again she had to clear her throat. "I, uh, came in for a drink."

He arched a disbelieving brow. "Fine. Finish your beer and get out. This isn't the type of crowd to pay for what they can take."

With that, he turned and walked away, leaving Ariel staring after him in bewilderment. What in the world was he talking about? A customer from a table at the back of the bar hailed him, and he grabbed a bottle off the shelf behind him and carried it toward the table.

While he served the customer, Ariel became aware that two burly men with long, greasy hair and tattoo-covered arms were leering at her. When one of them waved a handful of bills at her, the meaning of Morgret's words sank in. He thought she was a hooker!

It was obvious that the leering men thought so too, and she quickly turned her back on them. Lord, what *was* she doing here, and how could they possibly mistake her for a hooker? She was dressed in a pair of faded jeans, a baggy T-shirt, and a shapeless windbreaker. The women she'd seen strolling the streets during her search for the bar had been dressed—or rather *undressed*—for work!

"I thought I told you to get out," Morgret muttered, appearing in front of her silently and suddenly.

"I haven't finished my beer," Ariel said, giving him her friendliest smile.

He fixed her with an unblinking stare, and it took all her willpower to keep from squirming beneath his disturbing scrutiny. She took another swig of beer, hoping the action looked nonchalant but suspecting it looked as awkward as she felt.

"Why are you here?" he demanded again, his brows drawing together in a menacing scowl that caused gooseflesh to spring up on her arms.

"I told you. I came in for a drink."

Something flared in his eyes, making them seem even more silver, and he suddenly raised his hand toward the crystal. Ariel instinctively perceived the gesture as a threat.

Before he could touch the crystal, she said, "I'm looking for someone." She was relieved when he dropped his hand back to his side.

"Who?" he questioned in a voice so soft it was almost inaudible. It was also the most menacing sound Ariel had ever heard. The hair on the back of her neck prickled, and she decided to hell with subtlety. The faster she confronted Morgret, the faster she could leave.

"I'm looking for Mr. Morgret. Is he here?"

"No."

"No?" Ariel echoed in confusion. She'd been positive that he was Morgret. Had she been wrong? Even as she asked the question, she knew the answer. He was Morgret, and he was wary of strangers. "Do you know when he's expected?"

"No."

"Are you sure? It's important that I speak with him."

He shrugged dismissively. "I can't help you. Now finish your beer and get out."

Ariel was so stunned by his order that she automatically lifted the bottle to her lips. Even if he wasn't Morgret, he should have been curious enough to ask who she was.

She set the bottle back on the bar and said, "If I leave my name and number, would you make sure Mr. Morgret gets it?"

"I'm a bartender, lady, not a receptionist."

"Was that a yes or a no?" she shot back sarcastically. She knew she was baiting him, but she'd been pushed to the limit today. She was frantic about Armand, and she'd been patronized by both his boss and the police. She wasn't going to be stonewalled by the very man who got him into this mess in the first place.

He crossed his arms over his chest and eyed her with an expression that was devoid of emotion, which made him all the more threatening. Even as fear vibrated at the base of her spine, anger and pride made her meet his daunting gaze head on. She was here to find her brother, and she'd be damned before she let the man know that he scared the daylights out of her.

"What do you want with Morgret?" he asked after they'd stared at each other for what seemed an eternity.

Ariel sighed inwardly in relief. Finally she'd made some progress. "It's a personal matter that I prefer to discuss only with Mr. Morgret."

"If you want me to give him a message, you'll have to do better than that."

"All right. I'm Ariel Dantes and I need to speak with him about my brother, Armand."

She watched his face closely for any sign of recognition, but she didn't see even a muscle twitch. Suddenly he raised his hand and caressed the crystal. The moment he touched it, Ariel felt a tiny jolt. It left her with the unsettling feeling that she'd been invaded.

That feeling intensified when he narrowed his eyes consideringly and announced, "I'm Morgret. What about your brother?"

"He's missing, and I'm looking for him."

He gestured toward the room behind her. "As you can see, he's not here."

"I know he's not here," she said impatiently. "I want you to tell me how to find him."

"Do I look like Lost and Found?"

Ariel's temper began to stir, but she ignored it. She was too close to getting what she wanted to succumb to his taunting. "Mr. Morgret, Armand told me about you. I can understand your reluctance to speak with me, but my brother is missing. You're the only lead I have to finding him."

"What makes you think he's missing?"

"I haven't heard from him in six weeks."

"I wouldn't think that's unusual. From what your brother told me, it's common for him to go underground for months at a time."

"You sound just like the police!" she said in exasperation. "And I'll tell you exactly what I told them. No matter how deep underground Armand goes, he always calls once a month to let me know he's okay."

"You've been to the police?"

His voice had a chilling edge, and without warning, he gripped the crystal, causing Ariel to start. The feeling of invasion was back, creating a strange tingling sensation that quickly spread from the top of her head to the tips of her toes.

It was just her imagination, she told herself. But the reassurance didn't alleviate her anxiety, because Morgret's eyes had grown almost opaque and the crystal seemed to be taking on an unearthly glow.

She sensed danger and gulped at the realization that she'd been so eager to speak with Morgret she hadn't told anyone where she was going. How could she have been so stupid? Armand didn't investigate anyone unless he thought they were dangerous, and Morgret had belonged to the witchcraft cult he was inquiring into. The man could probably kill her right where she sat, and from what she'd seen of his patrons, she was sure none of them would lift a finger to help her.

She glanced around anyway, looking for some person with a friendly face who might come to her rescue. All she discovered, however, was that the men who'd been leering at her had left the bar. She returned her attention to Morgret.

"I didn't tell the police about you, Mr. Morgret," she said, hating the quiver in her voice but unable to control it.

"Only because they didn't take you seriously."

His reply startled her. How had he known that? But again she knew the answer. If the police had taken her seriously, they'd be sitting here instead of her. So why did she feel as if he was reading her mind?

It was those eyes—and his hand lingering on the crystal.

"Regardless of the reason, I didn't tell them. And if you tell me where Armand is, there won't be any need for me to tell them in the future," she pointed out.

One corner of his lips lifted, as though he was amused, but Ariel sensed his underlying rancor as he drawled, "Are you threatening me?"

She started to deny his assertion, but then recognized that she was issuing a threat, albeit a feeble one. "I suppose I am. But I don't want to complicate your life, Mr. Morgret. I simply want to find my brother."

He released his hold on the crystal. "I have no idea where your brother is at the moment."

Ariel frowned at his evasiveness. "I'm not asking where he is at the moment, Mr. Morgret. A general vicinity will do just fine."

"I can't tell you that."

"You mean you *won't* tell me," she countered.

"Arguing semantics doesn't change anything, Ms. Dantes."

"Look, Mr. Morgret, we're talking about my brother. If he's in trouble, then I have to help him."

"I can assure you that Armand is safe."

"If he's safe, then why hasn't he called me?"

"Maybe he's busy and forgot to call."

"No," she denied with a firm shake of her head. "Armand would never forget me. The only reason for him not to call is because he's in trouble. You have to tell me how to find him."

"I can't help you."

"You mean you *won't* help me."

"You're arguing semantics again."

"Dammit!" Ariel cried in frustration. "My brother is in trouble because of you. Don't you feel the slightest bit of responsibility."

"You have no proof that he's in trouble."

"I feel it in my heart, and that's proof enough for me. You have to tell me where he went."

He tilted his head and regarded her for a long moment. "And what if you're wrong, Ms. Dantes? What if you go rushing in to save the day, only to blow Armand's cover? How will he respond if you destroy six weeks of hard work?"

"In the first place, I'm not wrong," she stated emphatically. "In the second, I have enough sense not to go rushing in. I'll come up with a plan."

"A plan to deal with an entire coven?" he scoffed. "You have no idea what you'd be getting into."

"So you can tell me what I'd be getting into. I have to find him. Please, Mr. Morgret. Help me."

Something flared in his eyes, and for a moment Ariel thought she'd reached him. But then his expression became harsh, and he shook his head. Tears of frustration burned her eyes, but she blinked them back. She wasn't defeated. She'd find Armand without Lucien Morgret's help.

She rose to her feet, stating stiffly, "Good-bye, Mr. Morgret."

"Where are you going?"

"To find my brother."

"Stay out of this, Ms. Dantes. If you don't, I'll . . ."

"You'll what?" she demanded when he fell silent.

"I'll have to stop you."

He delivered the words without inflection, but Ariel only had to look into his eyes to know that the threat was real. Oddly enough, instead of frightening her, it made her angry.

"It's obvious that you have no sense of family, Mr. Morgret. If you did you'd realize that I'll do anything to help my brother, and that includes fighting you." With that, she stalked out.

But the moment the door closed behind her, her anger dissipated and her fear returned. Night had indeed arrived while she'd been inside, and it was even darker than she'd anticipated. There was no illumination from the bar, and a quick glance toward the window revealed that it had been painted over. Reluctantly she looked over her shoulder at the door and shuddered in revulsion. The eerie appearance of dripping blood was even more pronounced now, reminding her of Morgret and his parting threat.

Retrieving the Mace canister from her pocket, she walked briskly toward her car. The street was silent, except for unidentifiable rustling sounds. Afraid of stumbling over the disintegrating sidewalk, she fought the urge to break into a dead run. If someone was following her, she wouldn't be able to defend herself if she tripped and fell.

She was halfway down the block when she heard a footstep behind her. She cast a nervous glance over her shoulder, but except for a very faint reddish glow from the door of the Witches' Brew, she couldn't see anything.

Panic sliced through her. Someone was there. She could feel eyes watching her, and suddenly Morgret's words flashed into her mind: *This isn't the type of crowd to pay for what they can take.* She began to walk even faster.

She had almost made it to the corner when she heard a bellow of fear. Even as her common sense told her to run like hell, she spun around in time to see a man lifted into the air by some unknown force. She watched in disbelief as he was thrown backwards by an unseen assailant. He landed on the sidewalk with such force that Ariel could hear bones breaking.

"What the hell!" another man yelled as he also was lifted into the air and thrown. He hit the side of the building and slid down it, landing in a crumpled heap.

Instinctively she looked in the direction of the Witches' Brew and then began to shake uncontrollably. All she could see was the silvery glow of Lucien Morgret's eyes and the bottom half of his face, cast in a macabre, pulsing light emanating from the crystal on his chest. Obviously he'd saved her from being attacked, but that didn't make him less frightening.

With a low moan of terror, Ariel spun around and ran for her car. When she reached it, she hurriedly unlocked the door, leaped inside, and fumbled her key into the ignition. Thankfully, the engine started on the first try, and she pulled away from the curb before she even turned on the headlights.

As she turned the corner and stomped on the gas pedal, she whispered, "Oh, God, Armand. What have you gotten us into this time?"

Lucien cursed as he watched Ariel's car disappear around the corner. Then he glanced down the sidewalk toward the two men who had been intent on raping her. He could hear their groans, and he cursed again. He'd probably have to call an ambulance, which would bring official attention to him and the bar. Why had he gone to her rescue? If she was stupid enough to come here at night, then she deserved what she got.

But sexual violence was a behavior he didn't understand in mortals. Of course, there wasn't much about mortals that he did understand. They were a mass of contradictions, the only predictable thing about them being that they were unpredictable.

The men were easier for him to deal with than the women. The average male functioned at a base level. Regardless of his intellect, he seemed to be driven by ego and libido. The mortal female, on the other hand, seemed controlled by emotion and exercised little common sense. Those two traits made her extremely dangerous and abjectly helpless at the same time.

He touched the crystal to determine the injuries of Ariel's stalkers. One man was merely dazed and would soon regain consciousness. The other had suffered a broken leg, some cracked ribs, and a concussion. His condition wasn't critical, but he definitely needed medical help.

Lucien grasped the crystal more tightly and inserted himself into the men's minds. He wiped out their memory of Ariel Dantes and re-created a scene in which they'd attacked each other in a drunken brawl.

When he was sure that he had firmly implanted the image, he clutched the crystal with both hands, seeking contact with every mortal who had seen Ariel enter the bar. The number was greater than he'd imagined, and it took all of his concentration to erase their memories. She'd already been to the police. He couldn't afford to have her connected with him in any way.

By the time he was done, his body was weak and trembling. It had been a long time since he'd had to exert such effort. He found his exhaustion exhilarating. Finally, after three long years, he was functioning as a warlock!

He went back into the bar and called 911, summoning help for the injured man. As he waited for the ambulance and the police to arrive, he tried to decide what he was going to do about Ariel Dantes. He had to either stop her or help her, but whatever his decision, he had to make it before the witching hour. Why had he believed Armand Dantes when he'd sworn he wouldn't tell anyone about him? He should have known he couldn't trust Armand. He was, after all, a mere mortal.

He heaved an irritated sigh. As much as he wanted to dismiss Ariel's claim that her brother was in trouble, he couldn't. When he'd probed her mind, he discovered that she and Armand were twins, and from what he'd read he knew that twins often held a strong mental link. If she felt he was in trouble, then it probably meant that the coven had become suspicious of him.

If that was true, however, then Armand must have been able to drink the amnesia potion that Lucien had given him or Galen would have been here by now. It also meant that Galen must have chosen to keep Armand prisoner, because if he had let him go, Lucien would have connected with him the moment he stepped off coven land.

Lucien raked a hand through his hair as he again tried to decide what to do. If his suspicions were true, then the potion could wear off at any moment. When that happened, Galen would get his answers, and Armand, Lucien, and Ariel Dantes would all be in serious trouble.

As he heard the wail of sirens, Lucien pulled a coin out of the cash register and tossed it into the air. When he caught it, he slapped it to the back of his hand. Heads, he'd help Ariel. Tails, he'd let her deal with Galen on her own.

Chapter Two

'Tis now the very witching time of night,
When churchyards yawn and hell itself breathes out
Contagion to the world.
            —William Shakespeare, *Hamlet* 3.2.413

B Y the time Ariel reached the entrance ramp to the
interstate, her terror had receded. As her nerves
calmed, she couldn't decided which of the evening's
events distressed her the most. She knew instinctively
that those two men had been stalking her, and she suspected that they'd had more than a simple mugging on
their minds. Then there was the bizarre "assistance"
she'd apparently received from Morgret, though why
he helped after threatening her was beyond her com-
prehension. But for whatever reason he had decided to
help, she was grateful. It had taken all her nerve to go
to the bar in the first place. To have faced potential violence had her on the verge of collapse.

Damn! She hated it when Armand put her into a position where she had to be brave, and since she was a
full-fledged coward, he was the only person who could
arouse a feeling of bravery in her. But even Armand
was asking too much when he pitted her against a man
like Lucien Morgret, she concluded with a shudder.

She still didn't believe in warlocks, but she was
willing to concede that Morgret might have some kind
of ESP powers. That was the only logical explanation
she could come up with to explain what he'd done to
those two men.

Her conclusions about Morgret made her more worried than ever about Armand. Unlike her, he wasn't receptive to the possibilities of psychic phenomena. He considered it trickery and would go out of his way to prove it was all a hoax. If the remainder of the "coven" were psychic and as ill-tempered as Morgret, they might choose some very nasty ways to convince him otherwise. Was that what had happened to him?

Impulsively, she bypassed the exit to her home and headed for Armand's apartment. He might have left some clue there as to where he'd gone. If he hadn't, she didn't know what she was going to do. Her intuition was telling her it was critical that she find her brother as soon as possible.

When she entered his efficiency apartment, she gave a distressed shake of her head. Though the room was small, it looked large because of the lack of furnishings. There was a worn sleeper sofa, a broken coffee table with a portable television set on it, and a battered chest of drawers.

Her own home was so important to her that she was perplexed by her brother's Spartan lifestyle. She understood it was a holdover from the nomadic life they'd lived with their mother, who had been a career naval officer. The constant moving hadn't bothered Armand, but Ariel was a nester. The happiest day of her life had been when she left for college, knowing that she would never again be uprooted at the whim of the United States Navy.

She walked across the room, dropped her purse on the sofa, and absentmindedly brushed the dust off the top of the television set with her hand. Then she headed for the chest of drawers.

It didn't take long to search it or his closet. Armand was disgustingly neat, another holdover from their life as military brats that hadn't rubbed off on her. Finally she inspected his kitchen cabinets finding nothing more than a couple of dozen cans of ravioli, a single pot, a package of paper plates, and an unopened package of plastic utensils. At least Armand had one failing. He was a lousy cook.

With a despairing sigh, she crossed to the sofa and sat down. She hadn't really expected to find a clue here. Armand was positively paranoid when it came to his stories. He worried that the people he was investigating would find out what he was up to. He worried about the competition stealing his ideas. He would even be suspicious of Ariel until she became so exasperated that she threatened never to speak to him again. Then he would finally open up and give her a few details. That was how she'd learned about Morgret.

So what was she supposed to do now? When she talked with Armand's editor, he all but patted her on the head while telling her it was silly for her to worry about Armand. The police had been just as patronizing, pointing out that he hadn't actually said he would call her. She tried, to no avail, to make them understand that the very fact that Armand hadn't called was why she was so worried.

She and Armand were closer than most siblings. Part of the reason was that they were twins, but that connection had been amplified by their family's constant moving. They learned early that the only people they could truly rely on were each other. They were more than brother and sister. They were best friends, and they adored each other. Neither would ever purposely cause the other distress, which was why Armand always found a way to call her when he was undercover. He knew how much she worried about him.

She closed her eyes against the sting of tears. She wished her mother was still alive. She was sure she would know what to do. But her mother wasn't alive.

Armand was all the family she had, and if anything happened to him . . .

She wouldn't let herself finish the thought, because just the thought was enough to fill her with panic. Instead she again considered the options. The only conclusion she reached was that Morgret was still her only hope if she was to rescue Armand, but she'd have to be crazy herself to go near him again.

With a morose shake of her head, she rose, grabbed her purse, and headed for the door. It was almost midnight, and her day had started at 5:00 A.M. She'd try to get some sleep and then decide how to proceed from here.

When she finally got home, she was so exhausted that it took her a moment to remember the security code for her alarm system. As she punched the numbers in, she concluded that the system was more trouble than it was worth. Her neighborhood, which consisted of old Tudor houses like her own, was quiet and respectable. There hadn't been a single robbery in years. Unfortunately, her insurance company wasn't appeased by those statistics. Since she often kept rare and expensive books in the house, they refused to cover the house unless the alarm was in place.

She walked into the house and tossed her purse onto the small entryway table. Then she reset the security alarm and reached for the mail in the basket on the back of the door. She sorted through it quickly, hoping there'd be something from Armand. When there wasn't, she cursed and threw the mail onto the table beside her purse.

"Damn you, Armand," she muttered as she shed her jacket and hung it on the antique coatrack beside the table. "When I finally get my hands on you, I'm going to strangle you for doing this to me!"

"Why, Ms. Dantes, I'm shocked. I would have never suspected that you were the violent type."

With a yelp, Ariel spun toward the archway leading into the living room. Lucien Morgret was sprawled on her sofa. She blinked, telling herself she was imagining him. It was impossible for him to have gotten past the security system! But there he sat, bigger than life and looking as menacing as ever.

Anger coalesced into fear, and she demanded shrilly, "How did you get into my house?"

His lips curved into a slow, diabolical smile. "I'm a warlock, Ms. Dantes. I can go where I wish and take what I want. Nothing as mundane as a security system can stop me."

She couldn't decide which rattled her the most—his answer or the predatory way he was watching her. Regarding him warily, she wondered if he'd followed her, but realized that wasn't possible. If he had followed her, he couldn't have beat her into the house.

So how *had* he found her? Her phone number was unlisted. The only other possible way he could have known where she lived was if Armand had told him, and Armand would never willingly reveal her whereabouts. Indeed, only his editor and a handful of his friends even knew he had a sister. He insisted on keeping her a secret to protect her from the people he investigated, claiming that they might try to use her to get to him. It suddenly occurred to her that by approaching Morgret tonight, she may have played right into his hands and put Armand in serious jeopardy.

Damn! Why had she acted so impulsively? Why hadn't she taken time to analyze her actions and consider the possible repercussions? Why . . . She stopped herself. It was too late for recriminations. She'd gotten herself into this situation, and now she was going to have to figure a way out of it.

"Why are you here?" she asked, trying to buy some time while considering her options for escape. If she could get out the front door, it would set off the alarm and summon the police. Could she unlock it before he could get to her? What if he came after her, or worse, what if he tried to do to her what he'd done to those men outside the bar?

Morgret shrugged at her question. "I decided to help you find Armand."

She edged closer to the door, "Why did you change your mind?"

"My reasons aren't important."

"That's not good enough, Mr. Morgret."

"Call me Lucien."

"I'll stick with Mr. Morgret," she replied dryly. "I tend to be formal with a man who is prone to breaking and entering."

"I didn't break a thing."

"I could call the police and have you arrested."

He laughed. The sound was as sinister as he looked. "You could, but you won't."

"You're awfully sure of yourself."

"I have reason to be. If you want to find your brother, you need me."

It was the truth, so Ariel didn't even attempt to deliver a comeback. Instead she massaged her temples. The stress of the day had given her a pounding headache. All she wanted to do was take some aspirin and tumble into bed. Unfortunately, she was going to have to deal with a crazy man who not only thought he was a warlock but also had some kind of power that allowed him to beat men up without touching them and bypass top-of-the-line security systems.

"Let me," Morgret murmured.

Ariel glanced up, startled to find him standing right in front of her. He had moved as silently and swiftly as a cat, answering one of her questions. She would never make it out the door before he overtook her, regardless of whether he used physical or mental means.

Before she could speak, he placed the tips of his fingers in the center of her forehead and caressed the crystal with his other hand. Her headache miraculously disappeared.

"How did you do that?" she asked in amazement, momentarily forgetting her suspicions.

"I'm a warlock," he answered simply.

As she gazed up at him, Ariel became aware of his height. She was five-foot-ten, and it was rare for her to have to look up at a man. Why hadn't she noticed that he topped her by a good six inches? The only reason she could come up with was that he moved with a fluid grace that didn't diminish his size but somehow camouflaged it.

"Look, Mr. Morgret, it's late and I'm beat. I'd appreciate it if you'd just tell me where Armand is and let me call it a night. That way, I'll be fresh when I start looking for him in the morning."

He regarded her for a nerve-rackingly long moment. "I didn't say I'd tell you where he is, Ms. Dantes. I said I would help you find him. If I decide he needs help—and I'm still not convinced that he does—we'll go after him together. If you can't live with those terms, I'm out of here."

Ariel opened her mouth to object, but closed it when she realized she wasn't sure what she'd be objecting to. She did know, however, that she didn't trust Morgret. At the bar, he told her to stay out of this and threatened to stop her if she didn't. Now he was stating that he wanted to help. If he was setting her up, cooperating with him was out of the question. But what if he was sincere? He was her only lead to Armand, and if she refused to conspire with him, she might never find her brother.

As she searched his austere face, looking for some clue to his true purpose, she concluded that whether or not she trusted him was immaterial. He had exhibited a power that she was incapable of fighting, which meant he could do anything he wanted with her. If she appeared to be cooperating with him, she might have a chance to outwit him.

"All right, Mr. Morgret. I accept your terms. I'll meet you at your bar in the morning and we can decide what we're going to do."

He shook his head. "The coven may be able to connect with you through Armand. If they find out I'm helping you ... Well, let's just say that we can't let that happen. I need to cast a spell over your house, and I need to do it before the witching hour is over."

That pronouncement brought Ariel up short. Her house was her pride and joy. There was no way she'd stand by and let a crazy witchcraft cultist vandalize it!

"If you expect to run around doing weird things to my house, you can forget it. I'll take my chances with the coven," she stated staunchly.

He shrugged away her protest. "You can watch."

If he expected his statement to reassure her, it hadn't. She also had no idea how to handle him if he did start doing something weird. A moment ago she'd become aware of his height. Now she was becoming aware of his breadth. She'd seen smaller shoulders on fully padded linebackers! He wouldn't need psychic powers to overcome her. He could probably knock her off her feet with a flick of the wrist.

When he reached for the pouch at his waist, she resisted the urge to wring her hands, asking instead, "Is that your charm bag?"

He glanced up at her, his eyes narrowed warily. "How do you know about charm bags?"

"I'm a dealer in rare and antique books. Old witch-craft publications tend to be popular."

"You sell rare and antique books for a living?" he said disbelieving.

Ariel nodded. "Why does that surprise you?"

"I don't know. I guess I would have thought some-one in that profession would be . . . older."

"That's a common misconception. So, is that your charm bag?" she asked again.

"Yes, it is." He fished a small vial from the pouch and held it up to her. "Nothing weird here, Ms. Dantes. It doesn't even have an odor."

Ariel caught her lower lip between her teeth as she eyed the clear liquid. She was dying to ask him what it was, but even if he would tell her, she suspected she'd be better off remaining ignorant.

He popped open the cap. While clutching the crys-tal and muttering some indistinguishable chant, he sprinkled a few drops around her front door. He re-peated the process at every door and window on the first floor.

When he started upstairs, it dawned on Ariel that he was going to see her bedroom. She didn't let *anyone* see her bedroom. Not even Armand. As much as she loved it, she was also embarrassed by it, because it was so out of character for her.

"Do you have to go upstairs?" she asked nervously.

He was standing three steps above her, and if he had towered over her before, he now seemed like a giant. To make matters worse, there was a strange glitter in his eyes that was as alarming as it was spellbinding. No matter how hard she tried, she couldn't break loose from his compelling gaze.

"What's the matter, Ariel? Have you got something to hide?"

His taunt shattered the spell. "Of course not. It's just . . ."

"Just?" he prodded when she fell silent.

"Nothing," she mumbled. "You go do what you have to do. I'm going to make myself some tea. Would you like some?"

"Why not?"

When she entered the kitchen, she glanced at the clock. It was twenty minutes after midnight—the witching hour—and she had a man who thought he was a warlock casting spells on her house. It seemed impossible that just a few weeks ago, she'd been bemoaning how boring her life was and wishing for some excitement. She ruefully acknowledged that it just went to show that the old adage was right: Be careful what you wish for. You just might get it.

Lucien waited until Ariel disappeared down the hallway leading to her kitchen before he brushed his hand against the crystal. It was obvious that she was upset and he was determined to know why. He was startled to learn it was because she was embarrassed by the way her bedroom was decorated.

He frowned in puzzlement. If she was embarrassed by it, then why did she have it decorated that way? He shrugged off the perplexing question and started up the stairs. He had more important matters to attend to than trying to figure out a mortal woman's decorating schemes.

When he entered her bedroom, however, he was so shocked he could only gape. The rest of her house was tastefully decorated with neutral colors and an eclectic collection of antiques. This room, however, was a veritable bordello. Red and shocking pink vibrated in striped wallpaper. The carpet was a deep, plush pink that butted up against red floorboards. The furniture was the shimmering ebony prevalent in the Orient, and mirrored closet doors reflected the entire room back at him.

But even more remarkable was the huge canopied bed. The canopy was red silk, and a matching silk bedspread was folded neatly at its foot, revealing shocking-pink satin sheets that matched the pink stripes in the wallpaper.

He walked to the bed and curiously lifted the pale-pink nightgown that had been tossed onto the sheets. It was so diaphanous he couldn't help wondering why Ariel even bothered wearing it. As he envisioned what she'd look like in it, he felt himself becoming aroused, and he muttered a curse.

He was a warlock, and warlocks were not attracted to mortal women!

Except you're not a full-bred warlock, his conscience was quick to point out.

Lucien scowled at the detestable reminder that his mother was a mortal, which made him a half-breed. It was that heresy of life that had cost him everything— his home, his friends, and his preordained right to the leadership of his coven.

Knowing that if he let himself think about the past he'd just work himself in a rage, he tossed the nightgown on the bed, pulled a small vial out of his charm bag, and sprinkled the contents on her pillow. Then he went back to work on his spell.

When he joined Ariel in the kitchen a short time later, she refused to look at him. He pulled out a chair and sat down at the table, studying her as she carried a china teapot to the table and then retrieved two teacups. He didn't have to touch the crystal to know she was still embarrassed, and now that he had seen her bedroom, he could understand why. For some inexplicable reason, however, he wanted to reassure her. "You have a nice home, Ms. Dantes."

"Yes, well, thank you. This place means a lot to me. Do you take sugar or milk in your tea?"

"A slice of lemon if you have it." When she nodded and crossed to the refrigerator, he asked, "Why does your house mean a lot to you?"

"Armand and I were military brats," she explained, slicing a lemon and put it on a small plate. She carried it to the table and sat across from him.

As she poured the tea, she continued, "We spent the first eighteen years of our lives moving. It didn't bother Armand, but I hated it. It seemed as if I'd no more than get settled in when we'd be pulling up roots again. I always felt homeless, I guess. Does that make sense?"

"Perfect sense," Lucien answered, as he accepted the cup she handed to him. Before he knew what he was saying, he added, "For the past three years, I've felt that way myself."

"Why is that?" She propped her elbows on the edge of the table and rested her chin on her palms as she waited for his answer.

"It's too long and complicated a story to go into," he replied, annoyed with himself for revealing his feeling of homelessness to her.

He took a sip of the tea and was surprised to discover it wasn't the revolting, bitter brew mortals seemed enamored with, but an herbal blend with an apple flavor. He studied Ariel over the rim of his cup, fascinated by her eyes, which were a deep, rich green. He'd never seen green eyes before. All the children in his coven were born with pale blue eyes, the color of his own. At the age of sixteen, they changed from blue to various shades of brown. He was the exception to the rule. His eyes hadn't changed, another curse from his hated mortal heritage.

As he felt the surge of bitterness rising, he broke the silence between them by asking, "Did you find anything at your brother's apartment?"

Ariel's elbows slid off the table at his question. "How did you know I was at Armand's apartment?"

"I keep telling you that I'm a warlock. I know everything. So did you find anything?"

"I thought you said you know everything," she countered.

He gave her a diabolical smile, making him look even more sinister. Ariel shivered and wrapped her arms around her middle, deciding that he was creepy enough to be in a Stephen King novel.

But if she found his smile unsettling, it was nothing compared to the fear he evoked when he said, "If I want to find out, I can, Ms. Dantes, but I don't want to invade your mind needlessly. One never knows what deep, dark secrets one might stumble over in the process." His voice lowered to a soft, caressing level that was downright menacing. "Do you want me to know all your deep, dark secrets?"

He was baiting her, Ariel told herself. There was no way he could read her mind. But as she watched his hand rise toward the crystal, she experienced a surge of doubt.

"I didn't find anything," she admitted irritably.

He dropped his hand back to the table. "So, without me, you're at a dead end."

Ariel would have rather bitten her tongue than admit he was right. But he was right, and he knew that she knew it. "Without you, I'm at a dead end."

"How much did Armand tell you about the coven?"

"Just that they think they're witches and warlocks."

"You sound skeptical. Don't you believe in witches and warlocks?"

"I believe there are people who practice witchcraft, so I suppose in that sense of the word I believe in them."

"Very tactfully put, Ms. Dantes. So you don't have any idea where the coven is located?"

She looked at him askance. "If I knew that much, I wouldn't have come looking for you."

"Why, Ms. Dantes, it sounds as if you don't like me."

"You said it, I didn't."

Lucien placed the teacup on the table, leaned back in his chair, and said, "Good. Keep it that way, Ms. Dantes. I'm as dangerous as you think I am."

Ariel knew he'd just thrown down the gauntlet, and though her common sense told her to leave it alone, she couldn't stop herself from picking it up. "And I'm more dangerous than you think I am, Mr. Morgret."

He nodded. "I guess we understand each other."

"I guess we do. Now that we've gotten that out of the way, I'm exhausted. If you're finished with your tea, I'd like to call it a night."

"You go on to bed," Lucien said magnanimously. "Now that the house is secure, we can both get some sleep. I'll just stretch out on your sofa."

Ariel blinked as her tired brain assimilated his words. He had to be joking. There was no way she'd let him spend the night!

"You can't stay here, Mr. Morgret."

He crossed his arms over his chest and announced, "I am staying, Ms. Dantes. The spell I cast needs a few hours to fully take hold. I'm not going to risk negating it by opening the door."

"You are *not* spending the night," she asserted. "If you break the spell by leaving, so be it."

Lucien braced his forearms on the table and leaned toward her, those silvery-blue eyes piercing her with an intensity that she felt all the way to her toes. Ariel wanted to jump to her feet and run, but she knew that she didn't dare show any sign of weakness. Instead she met his gaze head on. This was one battle of wills she had every intention of winning.

When he suddenly caressed the crystal, however, she gulped, because she felt his touch as intimately as if he were caressing her body. It was the most erotic sensation she'd ever experienced. She kept telling herself that her response was nothing more than a figment of her imagination. The man could *not* turn her on by touching a damn crystal. Besides, she didn't even find him attractive!

Only that wasn't true, she realized with a start. There was something about him that appealed to her on an elemental level. Perhaps it was the danger surrounding him, the sense of carefully controlled savagery. There was something wild and reckless about him, and she'd always yearned to be wild and reckless. Unfortunately, she'd been born with a reticent nature, which, she supposed, was a diplomatic way of admitting that she was a coward.

"What's the matter, Ms. Dantes? Are you afraid that I'll crawl into your sexy, satin-sheeted bed?" he drawled. Before she could respond, he released the crystal, leaned back in his chair, and said dispassionately, "You don't have to worry about that. I wouldn't make love with a mere mortal if you paid me."

Inexplicably, Ariel believed him. She was also disconcerted to realize that his words stung. It was as if he'd rejected her, which was ridiculous. To be rejected you had to want a man to desire you. There might be aspects of Lucien Morgret that appealed to her, but all she wanted from him was information about her brother's whereabouts.

Her common sense insisted that she throw him out of the house, but one look at his determined expression told her that such a battle would last all night. She was too fatigued to summon up the energy to fight him. If he was deranged enough to crawl into bed with her, he'd be in for a rude awakening. She'd be so sound asleep that she'd be about as much fun as a coma victim.

"Do whatever you want," she muttered as she climbed wearily to her feet. "I'm too tired to argue with you."

With that, she walked out without telling him good night or offering him a pillow and a blanket. Quite frankly, she didn't want him to have a good night. She wanted him to wake up with a crick in his neck and charley horses in his legs. And when she got her hands on Armand, he was going to regret making it necessary for her to become involved with Lucien Morgret in the first place.

Lucien glared down at his empty teacup after Ariel walked out. He'd lied to her about the spell being broken if he left, and he was feeling remorseful about it, which irritated the hell out of him. He had no reason to regret the lie, just as he had no reason to question the necessity of the spell he would cast on her once she was asleep. For her own safety, he had to make sure she was under his control.

Not that he planned to take her free will away from her, of course. She would function as she always did, making her own decisions and her own mistakes. However, they were going to have to venture onto coven ground to find Armand, and it was essential that he maintain a mind link with her. Since he would have to remain hidden, she'd be the one dealing directly with Galen. He had to be able to control her thoughts when she was with Galen, because the slightest misstep on her part would prove disastrous.

But regardless of the justification for his actions, he was still uneasy with what he was about to do. He didn't like tampering with other people's minds without their knowledge. Unfortunately, there was no way Ariel would knowingly cooperate with him. She distrusted him and was afraid of him, which was exactly the way he wanted it. Indeed, he had every intention of exploiting her fear, because a person who was afraid tended to be more cautious.

But there was an even more constraining reason for him to be reluctant. There was only one way to create the type of mental bond that would allow him to control her. He had to make love to her. Not physically, of course. One of the blessings of being a warlock was that he could visit Ariel in her dreams and make passionate love to her without ever touching her. He would establish an emotional hold over her. The problem was, in order for the spell to work, he would also have to let her establish an emotional hold over him.

He was playing with fire and he knew it. The only time a warlock let himself fall under a witch's control was when he was sure she was his lifetime mate. Only Ariel wasn't a witch. She was a mortal, and he had no intention of spending his life with a mortal. But the only way he could ever spend his life with a witch was to get himself reinstated in the coven. And the only way he could do that was to prove that Galen was corrupt. That was why he sent Armand into the coven. He hoped the mortal could get the proof for him.

But now it appeared that Galen had captured

Armand, and it was going to be up to Lucien to save them all. The worst that could happen was that Galen would kill him, and he'd rather be dead than to continue to live the life he was leading now.

He let his mind wander back to the plan that had begun to hatch the minute he looked down at the coin he tossed and saw that it was heads. His major obstacle was gaining entrance to the confines of the coven. Once he recognized the solution to the problem, he couldn't believe how simple it was. To get in, he needed an invitation from someone living there. All he had to do, then, was have Ariel establish residency. Once she had, she could invite him in and he would be able to come and go as he pleased. He wouldn't even have to worry about being detected, because Galen's spell had shut everyone off from him.

To put the plan in motion, however, Ariel would have to rent a house. The only house for rent within the coven boundary would be his family home, and since Armand had supposedly rented it, it shouldn't be available. If it was, then he'd know for sure that Galen had Armand, and he could put the plan into action.

He felt a flash of guilt when he found himself hoping that the house *would* be available. Even though it was an inadvertent wish of ill will toward Armand Dantes, it still went against everything he believed in. His conscience was also quick to remind him that by involving Ariel, he would be placing her in danger. But she'd be at much greater risk if she had to deal with Galen on her own. This way he could provide her with a measure of protection.

But before he could use her, he had to cast his spell over her. He touched the crystal to verify that she was asleep. She was, and he rose and walked into her living room, where he lay down on the sofa. He'd already sprinkled the potion on her pillow, so all he had to do was go to her in her dreams and make love to her. He closed his eyes and clutched the crystal. Then he let his mind mesh with Ariel's.

Chapter Three

Deep into that darkness peering, long I stood
　　there wondering, fearing,
Doubting, dreaming dreams no mortal ever
　　dared to dream before.
　　　　　—Edgar Allan Poe, *The Raven* (1845), st. 5

ARIEL shifted uneasily in her bed. She felt as if someone was calling her—summoning her—and she caught her breath in excitement when she rolled to her back, opened her eyes, and found herself gazing up at Lucien. He was standing beside her bed with lust in his eyes and his lips curved into a sexually provocative smile.

When he lifted the sheets and slowly lowered it to the foot of the bed, she shivered in anticipation. He was going to make love with her. She wanted him to make love with her, she realized with a sensual shiver of anticipation.

His hot gaze flowed down her, and she moaned as he traced the aureole of one breast through the silk of her nightgown with his fingertips. She moaned again as he touched her other breast.

She wanted him to stroke her nipples, but before she could make the demand, he slid his hand down her abdomen to the apex of her thighs. She groaned softly and moved her legs restlessly as he traced the inverted triangle of blond curls through the silk. Why was he tormenting her like this? Why didn't he just make love with her?

Because this is foreplay, Lucien answered without speaking.

It was then that she realized he was touching the crystal. It seemed to glow—to pulse—beneath his fingertips. Suddenly he stopped touching her, and he stared at her compellingly as he began to stroke the crystal slowly, deliberately. Her nipples grew taut. Heat arrowed its way down her inner thighs as she grew damp with wanton need. Her clitoris became swollen and sensitive. Her vaginal muscles began to contract and expand in the rhythm of lovemaking, and indeed, she felt as if he were inside her.

But he wasn't inside her, and the heated glow of his eyes told her that he was aware of every nuance of her body. That he was taking advantage of her involuntary reactions to sate his own lust. That he would make love to her without ever touching her and still achieve his satisfaction.

It wasn't anger so much as indignation that stirred inside her at the realization that he wanted his pleasure without participating. She wasn't going to let him get away with it. If he was going to make love with her, then he *would* be a participant.

She raised to her knees in the center of the bed, and with a boldness she hadn't even known she possessed, she slowly, alluringly pulled her nightgown over her head. She didn't hear his harsh gasp as much as sense it. It emboldened her, and she tossed the silk aside and slid her hands down her body, reveling in triumph as his gaze followed her every movement.

She heard his breathing grow more strident and watched his eyes grow opaque. The crystal began to glow more brightly—to pulse more quickly, and she held out her hand, silently beckoning him to her.

She could feel his reluctance even as he stepped closer to the edge of the bed. She slithered across the satin and slipped her hand into his open shirt front. His chest hair was crisp and thick, and his heart was racing beneath her palm. His muscles jerked as she caressed his nipple with her thumb. He started to pull away, but she caught the fabric of his shirt to hold him in place while she unbuttoned the remainder of it with her other hand.

She heard him catch his breath as she finished the chore, pulled the shirttail out of his denims, and then slid his shirt off his shoulders and down his arms. She caught her own breath as she stared at his naked torso. He was the most glorious man she'd ever seen.

Again she felt his need to withdraw. Before he could, she caught the waistband of his denims. As she lowered the zipper and pushed his pants down his hips, he began to breathe raggedly. He was barefoot, and when they hit the floor, he stepped out of them.

His erection was a prominent bulge in his shorts, and she again caught her breath as she caressed him. He groaned and clutched the crystal more tightly. Light arced from it, and it no longer pulsed. It throbbed.

She pushed his shorts off his hips and when they, too, hit the floor, she sat back on her heels to look at him. He was every woman's fantasy and more. She raised her eyes to his face and smiled in conquest. Then she lay back on her satin sheets and throatily murmured, "Make love to me, Lucien."

As he climbed onto the bed and positioned himself between her thighs, he shook his head, as though in denial of her request. She instinctively arched her hips toward him, and he again shook his head as he thrust into her.

Ariel's world exploded into sensation as he filled her. When he began to rock against her, she wrapped her legs around his hips, locking him in place. When he began to thrust more urgently, she met him eagerly.

Now! he yelled, though he again didn't speak.

One of his hands still clutched the crystal, and she instinctively wrapped a hand over it. She could feel everything he was experiencing, and she knew he could feel her own climax.

Ariel closed her eyes, holding on to the magic even as she felt Lucien leave her. His abandonment would have hurt if she hadn't recognized that he'd be back, and then the ecstasy would begin again.

Ariel's eyes flew open. It was morning, and she quickly ascertained that she still wore her nightgown. Then she scrambled out of bed and ran to the door. It was locked. She collapsed against it in relief. Making love with Lucien Morgret had been nothing more than a dream. But what a dream!

She groaned and buried her face in her hands. She couldn't believe that she'd had an erotic dream about him. For pity's sake, the man thought he was a warlock! He wore a charm bag at his waist and a crystal at his neck. He'd not only broken into her house, but he'd cast a spell on it. Even worse, she'd gone along with the entire game. Was she as crazy as he was?

It was a distinct possibility, she concluded as she headed for the bathroom. In defense of herself, however, she had to allow that she'd been under extreme pressure for the last couple of weeks. So what if she'd had a sexy dream about Lucien Morgret? She should be relieved that it hadn't been a nightmare.

She released a bitter laugh. In a way, it had been the worst of nightmares, because she'd managed to achieve in her dream what she'd never experienced in reality—a sexual relationship.

It wasn't that she didn't like men. Indeed, she adored them, and though she'd been infatuated innumerable times, she simply hadn't ever fallen in love enough to go to bed with anyone. Armand scoffingly claimed it was because she was looking for fairy-tale romance. That she was waiting for some knight in shining armor to come along, sweep her up into his arms, and carry her off to live happily ever after.

He was wrong. She wasn't looking for a knight in shining armor. What she was looking for was a man who would love her unconditionally, faults and all, and whom she could feel the same way about. She needed reassurance that he would remain steadfastly by her side through the good times and the bad, that nothing would ever tear them apart. Essentially, what she was looking for was a man with whom she could share the same type of absolute love as she shared with her twin, and in that regard she supposed Armand was right. She was looking for fairy-tale romance, and she was coming to the conclusion that there wasn't a man alive capable of loving her that completely, which meant she'd probably become the oldest living virgin. And that was damnably depressing.

But now was not the time to sit around feeling gloomy about her nonexistent sex life, she chided herself. Her brother was in trouble, and it was up to her to rescue him. She hoped Morgret would be more cooperative today about telling her Armand's whereabouts.

She blushed at the thought of facing Morgret after last night's X-rated fantasy. If he even suspected what she'd dreamed . . . She dismissed the thought abruptly. There was no way he could know. So why did she have this disturbing feeling that he did?

Lucien knew the instant that Ariel awakened, and he cursed. He couldn't believe that she'd somehow taken over his dream last night. It had been his fantasy, and he should have been in control. He was casting the spell, but he had a sinking feeling that she'd done some spell casting of her own. He had never experienced in a witch's arms what he experienced with Ariel last night. Even more worrisome was that he spent a sleepless night fighting the urge to return to her for a repeat performance. That, too, had never happened before, and he understood that what he feared most had happened. Ariel had her emotional hold on him, and it was going to be hard to break it.

Every survival instinct he possessed was clamoring for him to get as far away from Ariel as possible, but he had dangled his own carrot in front of his nose. He couldn't walk away from the chance of reclaiming his rightful place within his coven. And once he had, he would find a witch who had this effect on him.

He went to the kitchen and put on a pot of coffee. His attraction for Ariel was an irritating complication, but it *was* within his control, he reassured himself.

The coffee maker sputtered as it ended its cycle, and Lucien searched Ariel's cupboards for coffee mugs. By the time he located them, the coffee had finished brewing. He poured himself a cup and sat down at the table just as Ariel walked into the kitchen.

"Good morning," he stated formally as he studied her. She was wearing a long-sleeved beige silk shirt with ruffles at the neck and cuffs, and a pair of matching linen slacks. There was nothing particularly sexy about the outfit, but as his gaze swept down her body, he became aroused. Did she really have a small, star-shaped birthmark on her right hip or was that a figment of his imagination? He chose to believe it was imaginary, because it was too similar to a witch's mark. Witches who possessed such a mark were particularly alluring to a warlock. Ariel was too alluring as it was.

When Ariel didn't respond to his greeting, he sensed she was recalling their fantasy lovemaking. Suddenly, he was hit with an irresistible urge to goad her. "Did you have sweet dreams last night, Ariel?"

Ariel cursed the blush she could feel heating her cheeks at the question. She glanced away from him and strode purposefully toward the coffee maker. "I didn't know we were on a first-name basis. For your information, I didn't have any dreams last night. Thanks for making coffee."

"Everyone dreams, Ariel."

She glanced over her shoulder at him, her brows drawn together in a frown. "Not everyone remembers their dreams, Mr. Morgret."

"And you don't remember yours?"

"Never. When are you going to tell me where Armand is?"

"I always remember my dreams. Would you like to know what I dreamed about?"

"No!" Ariel answered sharply, her coffee mug shivering in her hand. He couldn't know about her dream. He *couldn't*! So why was he tormenting her like this? "I just want to know where Armand is."

"I never said I'd tell you were he is."

"You implied you would," she reminded him as she turned and carefully carried her mug to the table. She managed to get it there without mishap.

"I didn't imply anything. I said I'd help you if I felt he was in trouble."

She raised her eyes to his and found herself mesmerized by their silvery glow. He had come to her in her dreams. He touched her. He made love to her. He . . .

No! It had been nothing more than a dream!

"Tell me where Armand is, Mr. Morgret."

"I want you to call me Lucien," he commanded.

Ariel automatically bristled at the order. "I prefer to call you Mr. Morgret."

Something dark and dangerous flashed through his

eyes, and she experienced a shaft of fear as she watched his hand rise slowly to the crystal.

"Say it," he murmured.

His voice, deep and mellifluous, shimmered through her, setting off sparks. His piercing eyes were riveted on her, causing her heart to race and her pulse to pound. When he gently caressed the length of that damnable crystal, she felt as intimately connected to him as if they were in the throes of lovemaking. She was horrified by the sudden heat that spread down her inner thighs.

He placed his forearms on the table and leaned toward her. If she'd felt pierced by his eyes before, it was nothing compared to the invasion she now experienced. It was as if he joined with her mind as completely as he had with her body in her dream. She wanted to fight him, but she could feel herself giving in.

"Say it, Ariel," he coaxed as he lazily traced the curve of her bottom lip with one long, graceful finger.

"Lucien," she whispered breathlessly.

Triumph flared into his eyes, as though he had just proved something to himself, and his lips curved into a smile that could only be described as demonic.

Ariel was jolted back to reality by that smile, and she wanted to curse for falling under his spell. She refrained, however, because she was sure he'd meant to humiliate her. She wasn't about to give him the satisfaction of acknowledging that he had.

"Now, *Lucien*, let's get back to Armand," she said briskly. "Where is he?"

"He's at the coven."

"Where's the coven?"

"You'll know that when it's time."

"I think the time is now."

Lucien shook his head. "It will be when I say it is. I'm in charge, Ariel. You agreed to my terms."

Ariel wanted to argue with him, but he was right. She had agreed to his terms.

"What would you like for breakfast?" she asked.

"I'll have what you're having."

"I only have toast and juice for breakfast."

"Why?"

She was momentarily nonplussed by the question. "Why do I only have toast and juice?" When he nodded, she said, "Because I have to watch my weight."

His gaze flicked over her, but its swiftness didn't lessen its impact. When his eyes returned to her face, she could have sworn they had the same hot glow she'd seen in them in her dream. It was gone so quickly, however, that she determined she'd imagined it.

"Toast and juice will be just fine," he said in a bored tone that pricked at her ego. Moreover, she sensed that that was exactly what he meant to do.

She resisted the urge to stomp to the refrigerator. The man seemed to be making a career out of baiting her. She didn't like him. She didn't trust him. So why had she had that ridiculous dream about him?

They ate their breakfast in silence. Every time Ariel glanced up at him, it was to find his unsettling gaze upon her. She finally kept her head down, refusing to look at him. Refusing to talk to him. And most definitely refusing to think about last night's dream.

Nearly half an hour passed before she asked, "What about Armand?"

Lucien touched the crystal for the time. It was almost eight. Someone from the coven should be around to take her call. Once Ariel determined if his house was for rent—which it shouldn't be—he'd be able to give her an answer.

"Before we make any plans, you have to call a real estate agency," he told her. "Tell them that you're a rare book dealer, and you want to rent a house for a month so you can search the area for old books. If they have a house for rent, then I'll tell you my plans."

"And if they don't have a house for rent?"

"Just make the call, Ariel. And don't give them your real name. We don't want them connecting you with Armand."

Ariel wanted to press him for more information, particularly after his inference that if there wasn't a house for rent, they wouldn't look for Armand. But she decided to maintain her peace for now, and she walked to the telephone that hung on the wall. When she lifted the receiver, he gave her the number. She was tempted to write it down, but committed it to memory instead. If Lucien decided not to help her, she'd at least have this clue to follow up on.

Lucien touched the crystal, blocking the numbers Ariel was dialing and replacing them with the real numbers. If it appeared that Armand was safe, he couldn't have her showing up at the coven. When the phone was answered on the other end, he blocked the name of the real estate agency and inserted the name of a fictitious one into Ariel's mind. Then he hastily released the crystal. No one should be able to pick up on him, but he didn't want to take the risk.

He forced himself to sit back in his chair and relax as he listened to Ariel deliver her spiel. He immediately tensed, however, when she said, "It sounds like a wonderful house. Oh, dear, someone's at my door. Can you hold for just a moment?" and turned to face him.

She pressed the receiver against her stomach and said, "They have a house for rent. What now?"

"Ask them if it would be available immediately. If

so, tell them you'll be there sometime tomorrow," he answered. "You can leave that soon, can't you?"

"Of course."

As Lucien absently listened to her make plans to rent the house, he struggled with the jumble of emotions inside him. He was elated at the thought of finally going home, but he was also highly disturbed by the events that were allowing him to do so. Galen had Armand. That was now a certainty. It was also a certainty that Armand had taken the potion; otherwise, Galen would have found out that Lucien had sent him. And Galen surely would have come after him. He wished he knew when Armand had taken the potion and how long it would last. If Armand regained his memory while he and Ariel were within the coven's midst . . .

His troubled thoughts were interrupted when Ariel returned to the table and said, "Everything's set. Now tell me your plans."

"Before I do that, you have to invite me to accompany you."

Ariel gazed at him in confusion. "Why?"

"Because I can't set foot onto coven ground without an invitation from someone who resides there. Since you just rented a house, you're that someone."

"That's silly." When Lucien glared at her, she threw her hands up into the air and muttered, "Okay! Consider yourself invited."

He nodded. "Armand went to the coven specifically to investigate the high priest, Galen Morgan. The best way for us to locate Armand is to locate Galen. You're going to have to go into town and find Galen, but you can't ask about him directly. And for heaven's sake, *don't* let anyone know that you're Armand's sister or that you're involved with me. To do so could put us all in grave danger. Do you understand?"

His patronizing attitude pricked at Ariel's temper. If Armand was investigating the group, then of course the people were potentially dangerous. She didn't need Lucien to counsel her on her behavior!

"I know how to handle myself," she huffed, "so you can save your lectures for someone who needs them."

Lucien's temper erupted. Without even thinking about what he was doing, he touched the crystal and snapped his fingers. Ariel's nearly full coffee mug lifted off the table, flew around the room three times, then settled back down on the table without spilling a drop.

Ariel gaped at him, stunned. How had he done that? It had to be some kind of trick. There couldn't really be such a thing as a warlock! It was impossible!

But even as she denied the possibility, her mind was recalling every bizarre event that had taken place since she'd met him. There was the way he attacked those men without touching them. There was the way he bypassed her security alarm. There was the way he cured her headache and the way he knew about her visit to Armand's apartment. It was as if somewhere, deep within her, she'd known all along.

But most convincing of all was the unearthly silver glow of his piercing eyes as he watched her now, and the pulsing light that had begun to emanate from the crystal from the moment he snapped his fingers and sent her coffee cup flying. No matter how much she wanted to deny it, she knew instinctively that Lucien Morgret was indeed a warlock.

She shuddered at that knowledge, but oddly enough she wasn't afraid of Lucien. Some instinct assured her that even though he would scare the daylights out of her whenever possible, he would never harm her. He had been too gentle with her in her dream.

Lucien was furious as Ariel stared at him in amazement. He wasn't sure if he was angry with himself for showing off, or with her for not seeming to be frightened by what she'd seen. He knew that contemporary society didn't believe in the existence of true witches and warlocks. Their disbelief had been perpetuated by the covens around the world to ensure their survival. In this instance, he not only wanted Ariel to believe, he also wanted her to be afraid. He couldn't decide, however, if he wanted her to be more afraid of Galen or himself. He resolved that it would be best if she feared them both equally.

"Do you now understand that you won't be dealing with ordinary people, or do you need another example?" he asked ominously.

"I'm convinced!" Ariel quickly assured him. It was obvious that Lucien was livid, and she had a feeling that a second demonstration of his powers wouldn't be as mild as a coffee mug flying around the room.

"Good," he muttered.

"May I ask you a question?" Ariel ventured hesitantly. When he nodded she asked, "Since it's obvious that you know this Galen Morgan, why don't you go into town and look for him yourself?"

For a long moment he simply stared at her. Just when Ariel was convinced he wasn't going to answer, he said, "I can't go into town. I'm an outcast and shunned by my people, which is why it's imperative that no one know I'm involved with you."

Again Ariel gaped at him. She wanted to ask what he'd done to get into so much trouble, but she wasn't sure that she wanted to know what a warlock would have to do to become a shunned outcast.

"I have to go," Lucien announced abruptly as he stood. "I'll be back at midnight, and we'll leave early tomorrow morning. I suggest you stop by the bank and get as much cash as you can. Since you'll be using a fake name, you won't be able to use checks or credit cards. I'll rent a car so we can't be traced through the licence plate number."

"Wouldn't the police have to do that?" Ariel asked.

"Everyone in the coven is one of my people, Ariel, and that includes the police. I can provide you with a measure of protection, but Galen has cast a spell against me that limits my powers. In light of that, you may want to reconsider going after your brother."

It was his matter-of-fact tone that sent a frisson of fear racing through Ariel. Up to this point, all she'd been concerned about was finding Armand. She had, of course, recognized that there might be danger involved. Until this moment, however, it hadn't really registered, and suddenly her cowardly persona came rushing to the surface.

To appease it, she asked, "Just for the sake of argument, if I don't go after Armand, what is my recourse? Could the state police help me? Maybe the FBI?"

"Maybe, but probably not," Lucien hedged. Even if she could convince the authorities that she wasn't a nut, the last thing he could allow was for the police to start investigating the coven. Society was not ready to accept his race. Another witch-hunt could begin, and it was the witch hysteria of the past that had put his race on the brink of extinction.

"I'll take my chances with Galen Morgan," Ariel announced. If Armand had gotten himself into trouble, she couldn't walk away from him. He was her brother—her twin. She'd give her life for him.

Lucien nodded and left the room with a terse "I'll see you at midnight." The moment he disappeared, Ariel realized that her burglar alarm was still on.

"Lucien, wait! I have to turn off the burglar alarm," she yelled as she went after him.

But when she reached the hallway, he was already

gone. She ran to the door, confirming that the red light was still lit on the control box. Then she dashed to the front window and parted the curtains. Lucien was striding across her lawn.

How had he gotten out without setting off the alarm? And even though it was a silent alarm, she instinctively knew that he hadn't set it off.

He was a warlock who could go where he wished and take what he wanted, and nothing as mundane as a security system would stop him.

She shivered as last night's dream flickered through her mind. It *had* been a dream. If he had really made love with her, she'd know it. That certain knowledge didn't alleviate her unease. Her instincts for self-preservation were blaring, telling her that when Lucien returned, she should tell him she no longer wanted his help. After all, she now had a phone number and the name of a real estate agency. She could find Armand on her own.

On an inexplicable impulse, she crossed to the telephone and dialed the number he'd given her this morning. She wasn't surprised when she reached a recording that said her call couldn't be completed as dialed. She also knew in her heart that if she checked, the real estate agency wouldn't exist either. Lucien had tricked her, and without his help she'd never be able to find Armand.

"What have I gotten myself into?" she wondered aloud. But, as she invariably did, she already knew the answer. She had gotten herself into one heap of trouble.

Chapter Four

The worst is yet to come.
—Alfred, Lord Tennyson, *Sea Dreams* (1864) 1.301

ARIEL had been in business for five years, but she still experienced a thrill whenever she arrived at work. Even though her worries about Armand and her qualms about Morgret were uppermost in her mind, today was no exception.

When she pulled into the drive of the old Victorian mansion that housed her bookstore, she took a moment to absorb its Old World ambience. She couldn't help smiling as she recalled the day she'd first seen it and how it had changed her life.

The house was owned by her best friend and business associate, Jean Shelton. Jean had been Ariel's roommate in college. Six months before they graduated, Jean inherited the mansion, complete with a storehouse of antiques, from a spinster aunt. Jean's parents felt that the old estate was too costly to maintain and urged her to sell it.

Jean was on the verge of doing just that when she persuaded Ariel to visit the place with her. They spent the day exploring it, from the curio-cluttered attic to the antiques-jumbled basement. But it was the library that enchanted Ariel. It was filled with books, several of them more than a hundred years old. As a child, Ariel had developed a passion for books. They had been her best friends. They never deserted her, even as she moved from one part of the world to another.

On an impulse she asked Jean to let her buy the

books. Jean regarded her dubiously and asked what she would do with them. Ariel shrugged and said, "I don't know. Maybe I'll open up an antique-book store and sell them."

From that impetuous comment, Jean had come up with the idea of turning the entire mansion into an antique store. She confessed to Ariel that she'd always had an avid interest in antiques. She was sure she could make a go of it, but she lacked working capital.

Jean knew that Ariel had inherited a substantial sum of money from her mother's estate the year before. She told Ariel that if she would provide the initial working capital, she could have the books as her share of the business. Then Ariel could sell the books and Jean could handle the furniture. Ariel immediately fell in love with the idea, and they decided to go into business together as soon as they graduated.

Jean's parents declared them crazy. As they pointed out, Ariel and Jean were only twenty-two years old, and neither of them had a business background. Ariel's degree was in literature, Jean's in psychology. When the girls refused to listen to their arguments, they did, as they said, what any rational parent would under the circumstances. As a graduation present, they hired the girls a top-notch business consultant for a year. That was how Ye Olde Tomes and Ye Olde Junque came into being.

But even with the consultant's help, the first couple of years were rough. There was a glut of antique stores in the Philadelphia area, and the competition was fierce. However, Jean and Ariel eventually built a good reputation for selling quality goods for reasonable prices, and their business was now on solid footing.

Pulling herself away from the past, Ariel grabbed the stack of books on witchcraft that she'd picked up at the library and climbed out of the car. Recognizing that her knowledge on the subject was derived from a few old books, some horror novels, and the movies, she had decided it would behoove her to do a little further research. In just a short time, she was settled behind her desk with a cup of coffee and a book that claimed to tell the truth about modern witchcraft.

She scanned that book and was into one on Satanic cults when she was greeted with a high-pitched squeal and some garbled words that she chose to interpret as "Aunt Ariel," though they sounded more like "Gnats Rail." A moment later, Jean's eighteen-month-old son, Jamie, came racing toward her, sans clothes.

"How's my favorite godchild?" Ariel asked with a chuckle as she caught the giggling, naked toddler and swung him onto her lap.

"He's your *only* godchild, and I'm about to give him up for adoption!" Jean declared ominously as she stormed into the office with his clothes in her arms. "This back-to-nature phase of his is driving me crazy. Do you have any idea how many people he mooned on the way over here?"

"It's just a stage. He'll outgrow it," Ariel assured, grinning.

"The question is, will I live long enough to see it," Jean grumbled as she took him from Ariel, stood him on the desk, and began to dress him. He was docile while she performed the chore, but once she set him back on the floor he took off running toward the corner that contained his toys, already pulling his red-and-white-striped T-shirt over his head.

With an exasperated sigh, Jean raked her hand through her short auburn hair. "Am I going to have to glue his clothes on him?"

Ariel grinned again as she watched the T-shirt hit the floor and saw him begin to shed his pants. "Look at it this way, Jean. If nothing else, he adds a unique touch to this place. Not every antique store can claim to have a resident streaker. Maybe we can figure out a way to work him into our advertising."

Jean laughed wryly. "I can see it now. Get a free peep show with every item you buy."

Ariel grabbed her coffee mug, walked to the coffee maker, and refilled her cup. She filled another for Jean and carried it to her.

"Thanks," Jean said gratefully, balancing on the edge of Ariel's desk. As she sipped at the coffee, she picked up a book from the library pile and raised an eyebrow at the title. *"Witchcraft for the Nineties?* Since when have you gotten into witchcraft?"

"I'm just doing some research," Ariel mumbled as she slid into her chair.

"I'd say!" Jean declared as she picked up another book. *"The Black Magic Primer?"* She grabbed another book. *"Confessions of a Witch?"* Still another. *"Everything You've Ever Wanted to Know about Voodoo?* Ariel, what in hell is going on?"

Ariel hesitated at the question. Though she'd told Jean she thought Armand was in trouble, she hadn't given her the particulars. It was one thing to coerce her brother into telling her about his investigations. It was quite another to share the information, even if it was with her best friend, whom she trusted implicitly. Loyalty to Armand demanded that she maintain his confidence. Then again, she was getting ready to take off with Morgret, and she had better confide in someone. If she didn't, both she and Armand could disappear and no one would know what had happened to them.

Leaning back in her chair, she asked, "Jean, do you believe in witches and warlocks?"

"Hey, you've met my in-laws. What do you think?" Jean quipped as she crossed to her own desk and sat down.

Normally, Ariel would have laughed at the joke, but after the time she'd spent with Morgret, she wasn't in a laughing mood. "I'm serious. Do you believe in witchcraft?"

Jean shrugged as she, too, leaned back in her chair. Propping her feet on her desk, she said, "Sure. I took a course on contemporary witchcraft in school, and it's a well-recognized neo-pagan religion. Of course, most groups practicing witchcraft today focus on a return-to-earth religion and a reverence for nature, which is very different from Satanism. Unfortunately, it's the latter that most people tend to think of when they hear the terms 'witch' and 'warlock.' "

She paused to take a sip of coffee before continuing. "As I recall, most male witches don't like to be called warlocks. They consider it an insult, since 'warlock' is derived from an old Anglo-Saxon word, *waerloga*, which means 'traitor,' 'deceiver,' and 'liar.' Also the traditional warlock was a sorcerer or wizard with supernatural powers that he gained by making a pact with demons or the Devil. Since most practicing witches don't believe in the Devil, you can see that the title would be not only inappropriate but offensive. It's my understanding, though, that in Satanism, some men call themselves warlocks."

Ariel shook her head, amazed. "How did you remember all that stuff from school?"

"Damned if I know," Jean replied with a crooked grin. "My mind's usually a sieve. But seriously, Ariel, why this sudden interest in witchcraft?"

Running a hand through her hair, Ariel said, "I'm going to tell you an unbelievable story."

Over the next several minutes, she told Jean about Armand's investigation of a coven and about her encounters with Morgret, excluding her dream, of course. Jean might be her best friend, but she also had a bachelor's degree in psychology and was prone to indulging in amateur psychoanalysis. Ariel wasn't interested in Jean's Freudian opinion of her sex life.

By the time she was done, Jean was shaking her head in disbelief. "Wow! You really meet some wild people, don't you?"

"Armand meets wild people," Ariel corrected grimly. "And after putting together what I've just read with what you've said, I'm even more worried about him. If Morgret's calling himself a warlock, then I have to assume that the coven Armand's investigating is practicing Satanism. Not that I'm surprised. Armand wouldn't have started the investigation if he didn't think they were dangerous. I just hope I'm not too late to get him out of whatever mess he's gotten himself into."

Jean nodded solemnly. "Do you think you can trust Morgret?"

Ariel frowned in consternation. "My common sense says no. After all, he sent Armand to this coven in the first place, and I'm still trying to figure out why. I mean, if the man really has super ESP powers, why would he want to involve Armand? Why doesn't he just do something himself? The fact that he didn't tells me that he's involved in Armand's disappearance. On the other hand, he says he's a shunned outcast, so maybe sending Armand there was his way of seeking revenge."

"Can you imagine what it would be like to be shunned?" Jean reflected. "I can't think of anything more devastating than to be standing in front of people you care about and have them act as if you aren't there. It makes the poor man sound so . . . well, tragically romantic."

Tragically romantic? Strangely enough, Ariel found Jean's description of Lucien oddly suitable. Despite his sinister facade, there was a melancholic air about him. She'd heard it in his voice when he confessed to understanding her childhood feelings of homelessness. In that one brief moment, she sensed sadness and loneliness. Of course, that was probably just her overactive imagination, because the next moment he reverted to his threatening persona.

Still, she couldn't dismiss that she felt drawn to him in some inexplicable way, and that worried her because the feeling was totally irrational. After all, Lucien had gone out of his way to make it perfectly clear that he despised her.

"All I can say is I don't even want to think about what a warlock would have to do to become a shunned outcast," Ariel said with a shudder.

"Actually, his offense may not have been that bad," Jean offered contemplatively. "Societies, particularly closed ones like you're talking about, tend to have conventions that carry an absurd penalty if they're violated. Morgret may have done nothing more than seduce the wrong woman."

Jean's comment caused the memory of Ariel's erotic dream to come racing to the surface. Suddenly she had the worrisome feeling that Lucien had had a hand in her nighttime fantasy. But that was absurd. Lucien had also made it clear that he had no sexual interest in her, and even if he did, how could he have made her dream about him? It simply wasn't possible.

It would have been easier to believe her contention if she hadn't come to accept that he really was a warlock. But what possible reason would he have for making her dream about him?

Perplexed, she asked, "Why in the world would you choose seduction as an example?"

Jean shrugged. "Sex seems to be a universal taboo. Even in so-called enlightened societies, there are still sexual rituals that must be followed. Failure to do so usually results in some form of extreme punishment."

"Yeah, well, somehow I doubt that Morgret was cast out because of moral turpitude. He doesn't seem the type. He's too ..."

"Too what?" Jean encouraged when Ariel fell silent.

"Scary," Ariel answered firmly, though it was only a half-truth. Morgret was frightening, but he was also sexy in a macabre sort of way. He had the kind of repulsive charisma that she equated with a vampire.

"Ariel, I know you're worried about Armand, but are you sure that going with Morgret is a good idea?" Jean asked, her voice tinged with worry.

"I don't have a choice. When I told Armand's editor that I thought he was in trouble, he laughed at me. The police treated me like I was some kind of hysterical nut. Morgret is my only hope. He knows where Armand is, because he sent him there."

"You know, of course, that you could be walking into a trap."

"Yes, but what else can I do? If Armand is in trouble, I have to try and help him."

"Of course you do," Jean murmured, rising to her feet and crossing quickly to Ariel's side. She gave her a hug, and when they broke apart, she said, "You have to promise me that you'll call me every chance you get."

"Don't worry. Every time I get near a phone, I'll be checking in," Ariel reassured. "I just hope that what I tell you is accurate. As I just explained, Morgret has a way of distorting the facts."

"That's what he wants you to believe," Jean stated, frowning worriedly. "Your mind is your own, Ariel. No one can control it. As long as you remember that, you can fight against Morgret's psychic manipulations."

Before Ariel could respond, Jamie began to squall,

and Jean hurried to see what was the matter. As Ariel watched mother and son interact, she couldn't help feeling envious. She wanted what Jean had—a husband who adored her and a baby in her arms. Unfortunately she wasn't even dating anyone, and instead of looking for Mr. Right, she was going to be running around the countryside with a possible Satanist so she could rescue her foolish brother.

After the way Ariel had taken over his spell last night, Lucien had purposely refrained from having any mental contact with her during the day. A few more encounters like last night's and it might prove impossible to break his spell over her. Determined that that wasn't going to happen, he spent the day preparing himself for their next encounter. By the time he parked the rental car in her driveway, he was satisfied that she could greet him stark naked and it wouldn't have the slightest effect on him.

He stopped at the door and brushed a hand over the crystal to ascertain Ariel's whereabouts. She had fallen asleep on the sofa while waiting for him, intent on discovering how he was bypassing her security system. She was trying to convince herself that he wasn't a warlock but some kind of trickster.

He smiled in grim amusement. The convoluted workings of the mortals' minds never ceased to amaze him. If what they saw went against their beliefs, they refused to acknowledge it as authentic. No wonder it had been so easy for the coven to hide from them for more than three centuries.

Since he was already connected with her mind, he let himself delve deeper to learn how she'd spent her day. When he discovered that she'd told her friend about him, he frowned in displeasure. He wasn't worried about the breach. A simple incantation would take care of the problem. What irked him was that he should have anticipated such a move and taken precautions to keep it from happening.

And if he hadn't been so wrapped up in his lustful reaction to Ariel, he would have done so, he thought darkly. It emphasized how important it was for him to be in control of his libido. Once they entered the confines of the coven, he couldn't afford to make any mistakes.

Grumbling a curse, he clutched the crystal with one hand and opened her front door with the other. When he stepped into the living room a moment later, his mood grew darker. If Ariel had met him at the door naked he might have been able to ignore her, but she wasn't naked. She was wearing a baggy charcoal-colored running outfit so asexual it made him yearn to strip it from her.

As his gaze roamed the length of her body, desire swept through him. But when his eyes returned to her face, it was a more treacherous emotion that unfurled within him. She looked so small and vulnerable asleep, and her defenselessness filled him with an overpowering need to protect her. The alien feeling was so unexpected and so intense that it momentarily confused him. What in hell was happening to him?

The answer was obvious, and he cursed again. He'd been so focused on protecting himself from the sexual effects of the spell that he'd forgotten its fundamental premise. It didn't simply bond them together physically. It tied them together emotionally, and protectiveness was one of the most primal and binding emotions of all for a warlock.

Lucien's temper erupted as the import of that hit him. He *refused* to feel protective toward her. She was a loathsome mortal!

But the reminder of her imperfection didn't stop the

feeling. It made it more compelling, because it made her all the more vulnerable in his eyes. And that made his anger escalate to utter fury.

His first impulse was to hurl his rage into her mind, to punish her as he would a beguiling witch. But even as he reached for the crystal, he recognized that Ariel's mortal psyche might not survive such an onslaught of extreme emotion. He needed her help too badly to risk her sanity.

But his logic didn't quell his escalating temper, and he grasped the crystal, forcing his anger into it.

He must not have redirected his unruly emotions fast enough, because suddenly Ariel's eyes flew open. As her gaze shot from the crystal, which was growing hot in his hand, to his face, he not only saw her incipient terror, he could feel it mushrooming inside her.

Her fear seemed to feed his anger until he felt as if some violent beast had been unleashed inside him. He intuitively understood that if he didn't get it under control there would be dire consequences. The problem was, the outrage and anguish he'd been suppressing since he discovered his own mortal heritage at the age of seven had finally found an outlet. He suspected he was powerless to stop it.

Fear was not a new experience for Ariel. Indeed, Armand had often accused her of being afraid of her own shadow. But when she opened her eyes and found Lucien standing over her, she was inundated with pure terror.

The crystal in his hand was blood-red and pulsing, and his eyes were glowing so brightly that they had the incandescence of a high-wattage light bulb. His menace was apparent, and she had no doubt that it was directed toward her. The question was, Would he kill her or would she simply die of fright? The way her heart was pounding, she had a feeling it was going to be a toss-up.

Her survival instincts were urging her to run, but she quickly perceived that that was impossible. Even if Lucien hadn't been hovering over her now like some monstrous demon, she'd seen what he did to those men last night. He could kill her without even touching her.

Suddenly she was struck by the similarity of this situation with her erotic dream. In it he'd wanted his pleasure without participating. She hadn't let him get away with it then, and she wasn't going to let him get away with it now. If he was going to kill her, then, by damn, her blood was going to be on his hands.

Slowly she shifted to her knees on the sofa, never breaking eye contact with him. When she was kneeling in front of him, she defiantly lifted her chin. He didn't move a muscle, but she knew the silent dare had registered, because the crystal began to pulse more quickly, giving the entire scene a macabre strobe-light effect.

As she watched the flashes of red highlight his stark features, she had the inane impression that he was holding his heart in his hand. It was a strange thought, but one she couldn't shake, and suddenly a scene from her dream flashed through her mind. At the height of their passion she had wrapped her hand over his as it clutched the crystal and she'd been able to feel everything he was experiencing. But, more important, he'd known what she was feeling.

Did she dare try that now? And if she did, what did she want to project? Instinct told her that whatever it was, it had to be something so outrageous that it would break his concentration. On such short notice, she could think of only one outrageous thing. As she curled her hand over his, she concentrated on the erotic dream, reliving it in detail.

Lucien went rigid at Ariel's touch. As her thoughts meshed with his, he couldn't believe that she was assaulting him with the dream!

And an assault was the only way he could describe what she was doing, because she was taking him through the dream so slowly and with such intimate clarity that it was erotic torture.

He wasn't sure when illusion became reality. All he knew was that one moment he was reaching for the fantasy Ariel, and the next he was cradling the real woman against him.

Since their hands were still entwined around the crystal, he could feel the coursing of her blood, the pounding of her heart, and the restless desire stirring to life deep inside her. As he watched her eyes widen, he experienced her growing awareness of his own carnal reaction, and he pressed his erection firmly against her belly. Her breath caught in excitement at the movement, and though she didn't speak, her thoughts were as clear to him as if she had. She wanted him to kiss her, and she flicked her tongue across her lips in invitation.

Lucien ordered himself to leave her alone, but three years of celibacy and abject loneliness drew him to her. As he lowered his head to grant what she wanted, he reminded himself to be gentle. She was not a witch and would be unprepared for the sexual appetite of a warlock. That reason alone made him kiss her ruthlessly. The best way to extinguish his need for her was to make her fear him on a sexual level.

As his lips crushed hers and his tongue made a rapacious foray into her mouth, he expected her to recoil from him. Instead, she met his thrusting tongue eagerly, arching her body against him in an alluring entreaty.

But it was her mind that was proving to be the most

provocative temptation. She might be kissing him like an experienced seductress, but her thoughts were filled with the awe of an ingenuous virgin. Her seeming naiveté was positively bewitching.

As he felt the power of her passion enfolding him, drawing him into an inexorable vortex of need, an alarm began tolling in his head. It was one thing to make love to her in her dreams, but it was quite another to make it a physical reality. He had to get away from her, and he had to do it now. If he didn't . . . He didn't even want to consider the consequences. Calling upon every reserve he had, he thrust her away from him with such force that she tumbled to her back on the sofa.

Ariel felt as if she were surfacing from some sort of trance. As the haze cleared from her eyes and she found herself staring up at Lucien's glowering face, she tried to tell herself that despite the heavy, swollen feeling of her lips, she hadn't been wantonly kissing him.

But she was forced to accept that she had when Lucien contemptuously dragged the back of his hand across his lips and uttered disparagingly, "That was the most repulsive kiss I've ever had."

Humiliation coursed through her at his words, and she wanted to strike back to say something that would hurt him as badly as he'd just hurt her. But even as she opened her mouth, she changed her mind. By retaliating she would be admitting that he'd wounded her pride. Since she was sure that he had intended to do just that, she'd rot in hell before she'd give him the satisfaction.

Instead, she rose from the sofa with all the dignity she possessed and asked, "What time do you want to leave in the morning?"

He blinked, as though startled by her question. "We might as well wait until rush hour is over. Nine?"

"I'll set my alarm for eight," she said with a curt nod and marched out of the room.

Once she was in her bedroom she wanted to burst into tears for making such a fool of herself, but she gave an impatient shake of her head. To cry over Lucien's rejection was ludicrous. After all, the only reason she'd kissed him was that she feared for her life. If things had gotten a teeny bit out of hand, it was because her emotions had been running so high, not because of any feelings for him.

She might have been soothed by her conclusions if she hadn't been hit with a foreboding premonition that the worst was yet to come.

Lucien prowled Ariel's house. He told himself that he was restless because he would soon be confronting Galen, and then, one way or another, this nightmare would end.

Unfortunately, he was a warlock, which meant he'd been born with an innate honesty that wouldn't let him lie to himself. Though the upcoming journey had him on edge, it was Ariel that had him pacing. He hurt her when he rejected her, and he couldn't get her wounded expression out of his mind. It made him feel guilty, but worse, it made him want to comfort her. Another insidious effect of the spell.

Logic told him that the spell was too powerful for him to control and he should try to negate it immediately. But without it he would be unable to govern Ariel's thoughts. All Galen needed was a hint of his presence and they'd be doomed. Of course, if Armand regained his memory, Lucien's spell over Ariel would be worthless anyway. Not only would Galen discover Ariel's true identity, but through Armand, he'd be able to connect with Lucien. That was the trouble with spells. The spellbinder was inexorably linked to those whom he'd spellbound.

As he returned to the living room and collapsed on the sofa, he recognized that his only chance at survival was to get to Armand before the potion wore off. And as much as he hated it, the only way he could find Armand was to use Ariel. Suddenly he recalled a mortal saying that seemed morbidly apropos in this situation: He was damned if he did and damned if he didn't.

Leaning his head back against the cushions, he closed his eyes and fought the overpowering urge to touch the crystal and go to Ariel in her dreams. Eventually he won the battle, though he understood that he hadn't won the war. The longer it took to find Armand, the greater the temptation would become. As he drifted off to sleep, he couldn't help wondering if he was trading one nightmare for another.

Ariel awakened with a start and the certain knowledge that someone was in her bedroom. Panic fluttered in her stomach, but she forced herself to lie still and concentrate on her surroundings. The curtains were closed, so not even a glimmer of moonlight pierced the darkness. The only sounds she could hear were the familiar creaks and groans of the house. Yet the feeling of a malevolent presence was so strong that she knew she wasn't alone.

It had to be Lucien, she told herself. She'd locked her bedroom door, but if he could get through an elaborate security system in a matter of seconds, a simple lock would be child's play for him.

An image of how he had looked earlier, with the crystal glowing red and his eyes shining eerily, flashed through her mind. If she hadn't zapped him with her crazy dream, she was sure he'd have killed her. Was that why he was here now? Did he intend to finish what he'd started downstairs? Or, even more frightening, had he come to fulfill her erotic fantasy?

She was trying to decide whether she should switch on the lamp or make a dash for the door when something moved on the foot of her bed. It was small and heavy and released a low, fierce growl that sent a shudder of terror racing through her.

As it crept toward the head of the bed, its growl grew more ominous. Ariel's mind began to replay her childhood nightmares of monsters in the closet and under the bed. Only now it wasn't a nightmare. It was real. She had to get out of bed. She had to run for the door. She had to escape!

But, just like in her nightmares, she was paralyzed with fear. She couldn't move. She couldn't breathe. She could only lie waiting for it to attack her.

Suddenly its hot breath scorched her arm, which lay on top of the covers. Instinctively, Ariel screamed, and when she did, the paralytic spell broke. She scrambled out of bed and raced for the door. She was shaking so badly it took her a moment to get the lock turned. When she did, she threw open the door and collided with Lucien.

She knew she was only trading one demon for another, but at least Lucien was human. Clutching his shirt, she buried her face against his chest.

She heard him mutter a vile curse, followed by an angry "Omen! What in hell are you doing up here?"

There was an answering growl from her room, and Lucien cursed again. Prying Ariel's hands from his shirt, he muttered, "It's just Omen, Ariel. She's not going to hurt you. She just wanted to scare you. That's the problem with having a female familiar. They're possessive and jealous as hell, and I should have realized she would sneak up here. Come on. I'll introduce you."

Before Ariel could comprehend what he was saying, he guided her into the room and turned on the overhead light. Ariel stared incredulously at the large cat sitting in the center of her bed. It had the dark brown and burnished gold coloring of a tabby cat, but instead of stripes it had spots, like a leopard. Its eyes were huge and gleaming gold, and there was a feral look to its face. It was one of the most beautiful cats Ariel had ever seen, but though she adored cats, she made no effort to approach it. Despite Lucien's claim that the animal wouldn't hurt her, she sensed differently.

"What kind of cat is she?" she asked.

"A Bengal," Lucien answered, before curtly explaining, "That's a cross between a wild Asian Leopard and a domestic cat. In other words, she's a half-breed."

The grim emphasis he placed on the word "half-breed" made Ariel glance at him curiously. "You don't approve of crossbreeding?"

He didn't answer, but the disparaging look he gave her said it all. Switching his attention to the cat, he touched the crystal. Omen bared her teeth at him in vampiric fashion and hissed, but then she leaped off the bed and ran from the room.

Lucien gave a disgusted shake of his head. "She won't bother you again."

He left, closing the door behind him. Ariel sat down on the edge of the bed and raked a hand through her hair. In the past two days she'd been terrorized by a warlock and now his familiar was getting in on the act. Tomorrow she'd be going to a coven, and heaven only knew what was going to happen to her there. There was no doubt about it. She'd finally lost her mind, or, more accurately, Armand had lost it for her. It was almost enough to make her wish she'd been an only child.

Chapter Five

Enter these enchanted woods,
You who dare.
　　　—George Meredith,
　　　　The Woods of Westermain (1883), st. 1

MORNING didn't change Ariel's opinion of her mental health. While she ate breakfast, Lucien sat across from her, silent and intimidating. The cat sat on his lap and stared at her with overt enmity.

When Lucien carried her luggage out to the car, Ariel realized that this was her last chance to back out of the trip. She reminded herself that Lucien could be responsible for Armand's disappearance and was now going to get rid of her. Indeed, after last night's encounter in the living room, that scenario sounded more than plausible. The most rational thing she could do would be to go back to the police. There had to be a way to convince them that Armand was in danger.

She was still wavering in indecision when Lucien returned to the house. Eyeing her narrowly, he said, "The police won't believe you, Ariel. We are beyond the realm of their imaginations. Even you, after all you've seen, are still fighting against your belief. That's how we've managed to survive undetected among you for centuries."

Lucien had frightened her many times, but the fear that rippled through her now at his words was the worst yet. She was finally forced to admit that there was only one explanation for his remark. He had to have read her mind, and that, combined with everything else that happened, convinced her more than ever that he was indeed a warlock.

She took a step backwards and shook her head, though she wasn't sure what she was denying.

"Am I crazy to go with you? Can I trust you?" she asked hoarsely, impulsively.

"What do you think?"

"That wasn't an answer."

He shrugged indifferently. "You don't want an answer. You want reassurance. But even if I gave it to you, you wouldn't believe me, so there's no point in wasting my breath."

Oddly enough, his response inspired more confidence in her than reassurance would have. That didn't mean she trusted him, but she was more inclined to give him the benefit of the doubt.

"If I ask you a question, will you tell me the truth?"

"Yes."

"Is Armand alive?"

"In the context that you're referring to, yes."

"What does that mean?" she asked in alarm.

"It means that you wanted me to answer a question truthfully, and I did. Now it's time for you to decide whether or not you're going after your brother."

Ariel wanted to pursue his insinuation that there was something wrong with Armand, but his remote expression assured her that he was through with the conversation. It was time for a decision, and under the circumstances, she had only one choice.

"Let's go."

He nodded and walked out. By the time she joined him, he had started the car. She climbed in and fastened her seat belt, acknowledging that for better or worse, her journey had begun.

She waited until they'd left Philadelphia to venture

another question. "Now that we're on our way, will you tell me where we're going?"

"Lancaster County."

"Amish country?" Ariel stated incredulously. "I can't believe there'd be a coven there."

"Why do you think hex symbols are so prevalent in that area?"

He had her with that one, and she settled in for the three- or four-hour drive ahead of them.

Over the next hour the silence was broken only by an occasional growl from Omen. Whenever that happened, Lucien touched the crystal. As crazy as it seemed, Ariel had the distinct impression that he and the cat were communicating.

When the second hour rolled around, she decided that it was time she learned something about Lucien and the coven. She shifted in her seat so she could see him clearly and asked, "How long has the coven been in existence?"

He shot her a glowering look that would normally have intimidated her back into silence, but she refused to be cowed by him. Meeting his gaze head on, she demanded, "Well?"

As he returned his attention to the road, he said, "We can trace our roots back to the time of the Druids. Some believe that we're direct descendants from them, but others believe we're a race of people separate from all mortals."

Ariel was admittedly startled by his answer. She had imagined the coven to be a group of people who dabbled in Satanism and had somehow found each other. He was not only indicating an extensive historical background but suggesting the possibility of an entire race of people. It made her wish she'd had time to do some in-depth research on witchcraft. Were these common beliefs or unique to this coven?

"And what do you believe?" she asked.

"That you're a mortal who asks too many questions for her own good," he admonished.

Ariel was too curious to heed his warning. "When you refer to me as a mortal are you implying that you're immortal?"

He fixed her with a scowl so fierce that she immediately recoiled from it. But his expression wasn't nearly as frightening as the formidable rasp in his voice as he said, "If you're trying to determine whether you can destroy me, Ariel, forget it. You don't stand a chance, and believe me, if you tried, you wouldn't like my form of retribution."

"I'm not trying to figure out if I can destroy you," she quickly denied. "I'm merely trying to understand what you are. I am, after all, going to have to mingle with the coven. The more I know about them, the less chance I have of making a mistake."

"You don't need to worry about making mistakes. I've already taken care of that problem," he responded tersely.

Ariel stared at him warily. Just what did he mean, he'd taken care of the problem? She started to ask him, but he steered the car onto a freeway exit and pulled into a gas station.

As he switched off the ignition, he said, "If you need to refresh yourself, now's the time to do it. This will be the last opportunity you'll have before we reach the coven."

Ariel didn't need to use the bathroom, but there had to be a pay phone around here. This would be a good time to check in with Jean. She still didn't know their exact destination, but she could at least report where they were supposedly headed.

As she climbed out of the car, a middle-aged, grease-stained man exited the station and walked toward Lucien. Ariel hurried inside and was relieved to find a pay phone on the wall.

Lifting the phone receiver, she glanced furtively out the window. Lucien appeared to be in deep conversation with the station attendant. Having anticipated that she would have to make quick, clandestine calls, she had stored a dozen quarters in her pants pocket and memorized her calling card number. She dropped a quarter into the slot.

Before she could dial the first number, however, she heard a low, threatening growl behind her. She jumped and jerked her head around. Omen was sitting on the floor and staring at her malevolently. With a muffled curse, she glanced out the window in time to see Lucien's head snap toward the building. As he reached for the crystal, she hung up the phone.

"Tattletale," she accused the cat, who responded with a swish of her tail and raced back to the car.

Ariel considered going ahead and making the call. She doubted Lucien would do anything to her in front of a witness. The question was, What would he do once they were alone? The possibilities were too chilling to contemplate, and she quickly determined that there would be other chances to call Jean. There was no reason to provoke Lucien unnecessarily.

It annoyed Ariel to know she was wimping out. With a grumbled curse, she fed a couple of her quarters into a nearby soda machine. Then she went out to the car.

When she got in, Omen growled at her again, and she snapped, "Oh, just shut up, and stop being so smug. The next time we stop I'll make sure the windows are rolled up so you won't be able to get out of the car and spy on me."

When Lucien joined them, he looked at her intently for a long moment. She ignored him and sipped her soda. He frowned and opened his mouth as though to say something, but evidently decided against it, because he started the car without uttering a word.

Instead of returning to the highway, he turned onto the narrow two-lane road that ran west of the gas station. After they'd driven for several miles without seeing another car, let alone a house or any other sign of life, Ariel had the sinking feeling that she should have called Jean and risked Lucien's wrath. If he intended to kill her, this was the perfect place to do it. He could dump her in the thick woods they were traveling through and no one would ever find her.

Knowing that if she continued to think along those lines she'd soon be a nervous wreck, she decided to engage Lucien in conversation. "So, are you immortal?"

At first he looked as if he wasn't going to answer, but then he said, "Not in the traditional sense. However, it's not unusual for us to live far into our hundreds, and our biological processes are slightly different from yours. We age more slowly, and we aren't as susceptible to disease."

"Then, in the traditional sense, you are as mortal as I am."

He scowled at the windshield, as though he found the thought abhorrent. "In the traditional sense, I suppose I am."

Ariel experienced a perverse satisfaction at forcing the confession out of him. Her common sense told her to leave it alone, but she had a compelling urge to bait him.

"But because of your longevity and insusceptibility to disease, you feel superior to me. You express your disdain by calling me a mortal. Do you know what that makes you? A bigot. Shame on you, Lucien."

Her effrontery died beneath the blood-chilling glare

he sent her. Heckling Lucien was about as foolhardy as poking a pit bull with a sharp stick, and she had no doubt that it would have the same deadly result. Reason insisted that she apologize, but she meant what she'd said. She wasn't about to feign contrition.

She returned his stare with scoffing indifference. "What's the matter, Lucien? Did I hit a sore spot?"

With a curse, he turned his attention back to the road. "One day you'll push me too far, Ariel."

Again, her common sense told her to leave it alone, but again she felt compelled to taunt him. "And what will happen to me then? Will I become a ritual sacrifice?"

"There is a special harvest sabbat coming up," he intoned.

Ariel's blood ran to ice water at his response. When she had asked the question, she meant it sarcastically. He had, however, sounded perfectly serious, adding one more piece of evidence to her suspicion that she was dealing with a Satanic cult.

With a shiver, she leaned back in the seat and tried to relax, but her nerves were jumpy, at their rawest. Resting her head against the window, she watched the thick green forest flash by. There were no road signs to tell her where she was, nor did they pass through any towns.

Though she tried to concentrate on where they were going, her mind seemed to be muddled, unable to concentrate. She intuited that Lucien was causing her confusion, but she couldn't seem to fight it. After a while, she lost her sense of direction and her sense of time. They could have been driving for minutes or for hours when he suddenly turned the car onto a rutted path into the trees.

Her head shot up in alarm. He'd said they were headed for Lancaster County, which was farm country, and they were still in the mountains, so why was he stopping here?

It took her three tries before her voice rallied enough for her to ask, "What are you doing?"

"Stopping." He braked the car in a small clearing and pointed to the right. "Coven land begins at that stand of trees. It's too risky for me to enter until you're officially a resident. You have to go into town, get the house key and come back for me."

"You want me to go in there alone?" she gasped in horror.

Impatience slithered into his voice. "Ariel, I've already explained that I can't set foot on coven land until I'm invited by someone who resides there. Once you have the key, you'll be an official resident. Then we'll be safe, or at least as safe as we can be under the circumstances, and with any luck we'll find Armand. That is what you want, isn't it? To rescue your brother?"

That was what she wanted, but suddenly fear clutched at her stomach. If she could believe Lucien—and at that moment she had total faith in him—the group she'd be driving into the middle of was a collection of witches and warlocks. And these weren't ordinary people who tinkered with Black Magic. These were fanatics who had been practicing Satanism for years—no, for centuries! What would they do to her if they caught her? She could probably handle a quick, clean death, but if they decided to torture her . . .

Lucien frowned as he read the thoughts racing through Ariel's mind. He supposed he should reassure her, but if, as he suspected, Galen had broken coven law, her thoughts weren't that far off the mark.

He glanced toward the coven boundary in consternation. Perhaps he should keep her with him and figure out another way to rescue her brother. But, as his practical side was quick to remind him, even if he could find another way, it was imperative that he get to Armand before his memory returned—assuming, of course, that that hadn't already happened. And the easiest and fastest way to accomplish that mission was to stick to his plan.

But in order to do that, he had to calm Ariel. If Galen latched on to her panic, he would pursue it out of curiosity, because usually mortals entering coven land were immediately bewitched by its beauty and filled with an overwhelming sense of peace.

He considered casting another spell over her, but recognized that that was too dangerous. New spells were easily detected, and Galen would definitely be interested in a spellbound mortal.

Catching Ariel's chin, he turned her face toward him. When he was sure he had her attention, he said, "Ariel, all you have to do is drive down the road. In exactly seven miles, you'll enter the center of town. The business district is only three blocks long, and the real estate office is on the left in the second block. Go inside, pay them a month's rent in cash, and pick up the key. Then drive back here and pick me up. Don't go anywhere else, don't talk to anyone else, and don't mention my name or Armand's. If you'll just follow those simple rules, nothing bad will happen to you."

When she looked doubtful, he released his hold on her and said, "The only other choice we have is to leave, Ariel. I can't help you find Armand if I can't cross into the magic circle."

"The magic circle?" she repeated, her fearful expression changing to reflect her curiosity.

Though Lucien didn't want to take the time to give her a history lesson, he couldn't see any way around it. She had to go in alone to get the keys, and she had to follow his rules to the letter. Once they were separated by the circle, he would have limited contact with her. Only when she returned and they entered the circle together would the spell he had cast over her function properly. Maybe if she understood what was happening, she'd be emotionally equipped to pull this off.

"The coven originally came to this country with the Pilgrims. They were hoping to escape centuries of persecution. For more than seventy years they coexisted peacefully among their neighbors, but then the witch hysteria began here."

"You're talking about the Salem witch trials?" she asked.

"There were other trials, but those were the most famous," he confirmed. "By the time the hysteria ended, our coven was on the brink of extinction. They decided that the only way to ensure their survival was to move into the wilderness and create a sanctuary. To make a long story short, they ended up here. They combined their powers and formed a magic circle that is fifteen miles in diameter and stretches from ground to sky. It protects the coven, and within its confines they are omnipotent. That's why they rarely leave. I have been cast out of the circle, and if I enter it uninvited . . . Well, let's just say it isn't an event I'd care to experience."

Ariel glanced worriedly toward the trees. "Will they kill me or . . . torture me if they find out who I am?"

"I don't think so," he hedged, following her gaze. He knew that to the mortal eye the magic circle was invisible, but he could see the crystalline energy barrier perfectly well. He didn't want to believe that Galen would harm her, but he couldn't discount the possibility.

"I'm scared, Lucien," she whispered, a quaver in her voice. "What if I make a mistake? What if . . ."

"You aren't going to make a mistake!" Lucien interrupted, snapping his attention back to her. But as he took note of her pallor and the nervous way she was gnawing at her lower lip, he doubted the validity of his assertion. As frighted as she was, she was liable to make a mistake. Had he come this close to redeeming himself just to have the opportunity snatched away from him? Was Galen going to win after all?

Impulsively he removed the chain from around his neck and dropped it around hers. Tucking the crystal beneath her blouse, he said, "You don't need to be afraid. If something happens, all you have to do is touch the crystal and think of me, and I'll come to you. The crystal, however, is distinctive. You must not let anyone see it. Do you understand what I'm saying Ariel?"

Ariel nodded, her trepidation subsiding. The crystal still carried Lucien's body heat, and its warmth against her skin was oddly comforting. "I thought you said you can't enter the magic circle unless you're invited by someone who lives there. Will my paying a month's rent really make me a resident?"

He shook his head. "It's the house key that's important. According to our customs, the person in possession of the key is the resident of the house. So don't make any mistakes until you're in possession of the key, okay?" he stated gruffly.

She drew in a deep breath and let it out slowly. "Okay."

"Good." He climbed out of the car. Omen leaped across the seat and scampered out behind him. Ariel maneuvered herself behind the steering wheel and reached for the seat belt.

When she was buckled up, Lucien shut the door and bent to look at her through the open window. "Remember, Ariel. Get in and get out. The sooner you get back to me, the safer you'll be." He levered himself away from the door. "Hurry back."

With that, he turned and strode into the trees. Just before he disappeared, Ariel gripped the crystal. He stopped abruptly and swung toward her. He was several feet away and standing in shadow, but she could see the faint, eerie glow of his eyes.

"Just testing," she whispered.

He raised his hand in a parody of a salute and faded into the forest. Ariel reached for the ignition before she could lose her nerve.

Lucien watched Ariel turn the car around and head back to the road. When he could no longer see the automobile, he looked toward the coven's protective boundary. When it suddenly rippled, he knew that Ariel had penetrated it.

Involuntarily, he caught his breath and waited. If Armand's potion had worn off, Galen would know he was here and take immediate action. After nearly a minute ticked by and nothing happened, he exhaled in relief.

Beside him, Omen growled softly. Out of habit he reached for the crystal and was startled to find it missing. He felt vulnerable without it, and for good reason. His powers had been cut in half. But if the crystal served as a talisman for Ariel and got her through the next hour unscathed, it would be worth it.

He looked down at Omen. With his powers reduced, he'd have to concentrate on the cat to understand her. "What are you complaining about now?"

Fixing him with a feline glare, she gave a deprecating swish of her tail and repeated herself. Lucien nodded and returned his attention to the energy barrier. "I feel it, too. There is something wrong within the coven, but until the mortal returns with the crystal, I can't even try to figure out what it is."

That confession angered him. If he were a full-blooded warlock, he wouldn't need the crystal's powers to figure out what was going on. Of course, if he were a full-blooded warlock, he wouldn't be in this mess in the first place. As all the old resentment welled up inside him, he stalked deeper into the forest.

By the time he reached the familiar cliff that had been his childhood refuge, his frustration had eased, and he shook his head in wonder at the vista below him. There were farmhouses and barns scattered over a patchwork of green farmland that stretched as far as the eye could see. People, as small as toy soldiers, toiled in the fields. Some rode tractors, while others pushed hand plows or followed behind horse-drawn ones. An occasional car could be seen traveling a road, as well as the familiar horse and buggy of the Amish that drew so many tourists to Lancaster County.

Though Lucien had led Ariel to believe that the Amish feared the coven, the truth was, he doubted they even knew of its existence. They were gentle, peaceful people who lived simple lives and left others alone. Since the coven also practiced separatism and rarely left the circle, there had been few occasions for their paths to cross.

Lucien sat down on a nearby boulder. How many hours had he spent sitting on this cliff as a child? Too many to recall, but he would never forget the day he discovered this isolated haven. He was seven years old and had just been in a fight with Galen because Galen had called him a half-breed.

When he went home after the fight with two black eyes and a bloody nose, he expected his father to commend him for defending the family honor. Instead, his father told him that the horrible accusation was true—that Lucien's mother was a mortal. He then sat Lucien down and tried to explain that his union with the boy's mother had been necessary, but Lucien had been too devastated by the facts of his birth to listen to his father's explanations. He raced out of the house and kept on running until exhaustion forced him to stop at the edge of this cliff. His grandfather found him huddled here hours later and made him come home.

The subject was never brought up again, and three months later, his father was accidentally killed in a rockslide. His mother, who had never been comfortable in the coven, decided to leave. She begged Lucien to come with her, but he refused, remaining behind with his grandfather. With his father gone, he was the next designated leader of the coven. It was his duty to stay and be trained to take over.

Now, as he considered that painful part of his past, he couldn't help wondering why his father had felt it necessary to take a mortal as his mate. A warlock never did anything without a reason, particularly if it went against the coven's rituals. But the only people who might have known his father's motivations were his grandfather and his mother.

Now his grandfather was dead, and he had no idea if his mother was still alive. He had never really cared to know, because she was the reason he was different. It was because of her that he had become an outcast. She had also taught him a very important lesson, and that was that a mortal's love couldn't be trusted. No witch would have walked away from her child, no matter how miserable she was.

He couldn't help wondering, however, if his mother was still alive. It wouldn't be hard to find out. She was some kind of a medical physician, and he was sure she would be listed in some state or national register. A visit to a nearby library could probably give him the answer if he wanted it, which he didn't.

His musings were interrupted by a flash from the

crystal. He immediately leaped to his feet and faced the circle. Was Ariel in danger?

No matter how hard he concentrated, he couldn't pick up anything from her, not even a sense of her emotional state. Since she had barely had time to reach the coven, common sense told him that she had merely touched the crystal for reassurance. The logic didn't ease his disquiet, though, and to his further frustration, there was nothing he could do but wait and hope for the best.

As Ariel drove into Lucien's "enchanted" forest, she nervously eyed her surroundings. Everything he had told her had sounded too fantastic to be true. If she hadn't seen him perform some seemingly impossible feats, she would have written him off as certifiable. Now she was just praying that she could get to town and back without mishap.

It was probably her imagination, but there did seem to be something different about this section of the forest. The landscape looked healthier, and the colors seemed more vibrant. Even the air wafting in through her open window smelled fresher. Where before she'd seen an occasional clump of wildflowers, she now saw blankets of them.

After listening to Lucien, she'd expected this place to be ... well, hellish. Instead, she felt as if she had stumbled into the Garden of Eden. The farther she drove, the more she began to appreciate the wild beauty of the landscape.

As she rounded another curve that revealed a grassy meadow, she let out a gasp of delight. A herd of deer were grazing, and at the sound of the car a buck raised his head. He had the largest set of antlers she'd ever seen.

She was so captivated by the deer that she didn't realize she'd drifted to the road's dirt shoulder until someone yelled, "Hey! Watch out!"

Snapping her head toward the voice, she let out a frightened cry. There was a huge white horse galloping toward her at such speed that she had to jerk on the steering wheel to avoid colliding with him.

She lost control of the car, and as she watched a tree looming up in front of her she instinctively made a grab for Lucien's crystal. But even as she brushed her fingers across it, she recognized that summoning him was fruitless. He'd explained that until she had the house key, he couldn't help her. Not that that mattered now, she decided, closing her eyes only a second before she collided with the tree. In a moment, she'd be dead.

"Don't worry. You're all right. Your seat belt just squeezed the breath out of you."

Ariel opened her eyes at the reassuring words and found herself looking at one of the most beautiful women she'd ever seen. She was around Ariel's age, and her dark-brown hair was cropped to no more than an inch, but it enhanced the flawless features of her heart-shaped face. Her large brown eyes were framed with lashes so long and thick that Ariel would have hated her if her perfect cupid's-bow mouth hadn't curved into a genuinely friendly smile.

"I'm sorry I caused you to crash," she told Ariel. "Most of the tourists come up from the valley, so there's seldom anyone on this part of the road. That's why I give Portent his head through here."

"It was my fault," Ariel demurred, releasing her seat belt with shaking hands. "I wasn't watching where I was going."

"Well, I'll accept your apology if you'll accept mine."

"You've got a deal." The woman opened the door and helped Ariel out of the car. Other than feeling a little unsteady, she seemed to be okay, and she glanced toward the front of the car with a feeling of dread. "I guess I should check my car."

"I already have, and there's not a scratch on it."

"That's impossible."

The woman widened her eyes innocently. "If you don't believe me, check for yourself."

"Yes, well, nothing personal, but I think I will."

When she checked, she was dumbfounded. There were two or three inches between the car and the tree, and even upon close inspection, she couldn't find a scratch. She frowned in confusion. She knew she'd hit the tree, and with enough force to have the seat belt knock the breath out of her. How could the car have come through unscathed?

"I believe it's called a miracle," the woman murmured.

Her words sent a shiver slithering up Ariel's spine, and she slowly raised upright, regarding the woman warily. There was only one way a car could have come through the crash without a scratch. She was looking at a witch.

Studying her, Ariel realized that though her finely chiseled features and her graceful slenderness gave her an air of petite delicacy, the opposite was true. She was easily as tall as Ariel, and possibly taller. She'd also been riding that huge white horse, and to control him, she would have to be remarkably strong.

Instinctively Ariel raised her hand toward Lucien's crystal, but stopped herself with the reminder that until she had the house key, it wouldn't do her any good. Instead she said, "If I didn't know better, I'd think you just read my mind."

"Now that would be a great trick!" the woman said

with a tinkling laugh that didn't allay Ariel's unease in the least. "By the way, I'm Shana Morland."

"I'm Ariel Da- . . . Smith," Ariel corrected quickly.

"*You're* the woman who's going to rent the house in town?" Shana questioned in surprise. "They said you were an antique-books dealer, and I thought that you'd be . . . well, old."

"Many people tend to have that misconception," Ariel stated wryly. "Well, I guess I'd better get going. I want to get settled in."

"Why don't I meet you at the real estate office, and then I'll show you how to get to the house?"

"No!" Ariel realized she'd protested too vehemently when Shana arched a brow. "I'm sorry. I didn't mean to be rude. It's just that I want to do some exploring before the day's over, so I won't be going to the house until later. It was kind of you to offer, though."

A look of disappointment flickered across Shana's face. "Sure. Maybe we can have lunch while you're here?"

There was something wistful, almost lonely, in her tone that struck a familiar chord inside Ariel. "I'd like that."

"Great. I'll see you around."

Before Ariel could respond, Shana waved her hand in a circle above her head, and the horse came trotting up to them. Shana swung herself up into the saddle, and with another wave, they took off at a gallop.

Ariel sagged against the side of the car and buried her face in her hands. She hadn't even gotten to town and she'd broken Lucien's rules. If he found out, he'd probably strangle her—or more likely, sacrifice her. There was, after all, that special harvest sabbat coming up.

With a shudder, she climbed into the car and resumed her journey. This time she didn't indulge in an appreciation of the scenery. She did, however, contemplate her encounter with Shana Morland. Was the woman really a witch?

She'd been so friendly that it seemed preposterous, but there were too many odd aspects to their meeting to discount the possibility. And the first of those aspects had been the first words out of Shana's mouth. *Don't worry. You're all right. Your seat belt just squeezed the breath out of you.*

How had she known that? And what about the car? Why hadn't it been damaged? *I believe it's called a miracle*, Shana had said, and Ariel still had the feeling that she'd been reading her mind. There was also Shana's appearance. Like Lucien, she gave the impression that she was smaller and more delicate than she was. Not that Ariel had ever considered Lucien small or delicate. She just hadn't realized how big he really was.

But the point that really nagged at her was the name of Shana's horse. "Portent" was synonymous with "omen," the name of Lucien's sullen familiar. It was too much of a coincidence for comfort.

Ariel felt as if she had stumbled into a strange land, and she suspected it was only going to get stranger.

Chapter Six

The prince of darkness is a gentleman.
—William Shakespeare, *King Lear* 3.4.147

LESS than five minutes after Ariel left the accident site, she crested a hill and saw the small town below her. She felt as if she were looking down on some ancient European village. The buildings were designed in the Gothic architectural style that had been dominant during the Middle Ages, with slender towers, pointed arches, and flying buttresses. Lucien wasn't kidding when he said the business district was only three blocks long. What she found odd, however, was that that was all there was—three blocks of businesses backed by trees. There wasn't a single home in sight.

When she reached the town, a large sign proclaimed, Welcome to Sanctuary. She didn't know why the name startled her. After Lucien's story about the witch trials, it certainly made sense. But it seemed too mild a name for the home of a Satanic cult.

Locating the real estate office wasn't hard. It was exactly where Lucien had said it would be. Finding a parking space, however, was another matter. The town seemed to be crawling with tourists, which was another startling revelation. It made the place seem so normal.

On the other side of town, she decided to follow the tourists' example by parking along the highway and walking back. Not only would it give her a chance to get her still unsteady nerves under control, it would also give her an opportunity to look around.

She peered in the door of the first building she came to, shrugging aside the certainty that Lucien would disapprove of her actions. After all, she was just looking, and with all the sightseers around, she blended in with the crowd. Inside were two women. One was spinning wool on a spinning wheel, and the other was working on a hand loom. The next building was an old-fashioned apothecary. The one after that housed a tinsmith plying his trade, and the one after that a bakery, where the wares were baked in stone ovens heated by fires.

By the time she worked her way to the second block, Ariel came to the realization that Sanctuary's draw for the tourist trade was its enchanting replication of the past. Though she would have liked to do more exploring, she reminded herself that Lucien was waiting. Bypassing the next few shops, she entered the real estate office.

The receptionist's desk was vacant, and the place was eerily quiet. After waiting for several minutes, Ariel glanced at her watch. It was half past twelve. Was everyone at lunch? Stepping to an open doorway behind the desk, she called out, "Is anyone here?"

She was staring down a short hallway, with three closed doors. When no one responded to her call, she frowned. By now Lucien was probably steaming, but it wasn't her fault that the place was deserted.

She was trying to decide whether to stay or to go looking for a pay phone to call Jean when a matronly woman burst through the front door. She was pleasantly plump, with graying brown hair caught at her nape and an apple-cheeked complexion. She reminded Ariel of Mrs. Santa Claus.

"I'm so sorry," she wheezed, winded. "I had to run down to the post office. What can I do for you?"

"I'm Ariel . . ."

"Oh!" the woman interrupted with a gasp. "You're the antique-books dealer who wants to rent the house. Gracious, you're so young! I thought you'd be much older. I'm Corrine Morrow, but just call me Corrine." She bustled behind the desk and tugged open a drawer. "Ariel is such an unusual name, and a very beautiful one, I must say. No, where did I put the key? Ah, here it is."

She pulled a key ring out of the desk drawer and held it up with a triumphant smile. "Have you filled out the paperwork? But, of course, you haven't. I wasn't here to give it to you, was I? How long did you say you wanted the house?"

"A month," Ariel answered, feeling a bit dazed by the woman's rapid-fire monologue.

Corrine nodded and began digging through a stack of files on the desk. "You're very lucky, you know. We rarely have houses for rent. How did you come to choose our little hamlet for your headquarters, so to speak?"

The question had been delivered so smoothly that if Corrine hadn't used the antiquated word "hamlet," Ariel might have blurted out the truth. Instead, she examined the woman critically and realized her eyes had again deceived her.

Her first impression of Corrine had been that she was a small, round woman. Now she noticed that, like Shana, she was extraordinarily tall. Though she came across as a bit of a flake, there was a shrewd gleam in her eye that assured Ariel her flightiness was a facade.

Forcing a smile, Ariel invented, "A friend of mine came through here a few weeks ago. She was impressed with Sanctuary—said it was like taking a step back in time. Since she knew I was coming to this area to look for books, she thought I'd enjoy staying here."

"And I'm sure you will," Corrine announced,

handing over a piece of paper and a pen. "If you'll just fill out this rental agreement, we'll get you out of here."

Ariel swallowed in alarm as she stared down at the contract. She hadn't considered that she'd have to fill out something like this. Evidently Lucien hadn't either. What in the world was she supposed to do?

"Is something wrong, Ms. Smith?"

It took Ariel a moment to realize that she was *Ms. Smith*. Glancing up, she forced another smile. "Please, call me Ariel, and nothing's wrong. It's just that I, um, have an appointment in a couple of hours and had hoped to get settled in and freshen up first. I don't suppose you'd consider letting me pay you the rent now and fill out the form later?"

"Well, I don't know," Corrine murmured with a frown. "It's a bit unusual."

Ariel glanced down at the paperwork in consternation. She supposed she could lie, but if Corrine did any checking, she'd quickly figure out that she wasn't who she said she was. *Damn!* What should she do?

There was only one thing she could do, and that was go back to Lucien and see what he suggested. He knew these people, so he should know whether a lie would work.

"I'm afraid I don't have time to fill out the form before my appointment, so I'll come back later and . . ."

The phone rang, interrupting her. Corrine smiled apologetically as she reached for it. While she spoke quietly into the receiver, Ariel turned to look out the window.

When Corrine hung up, she announced, "I'm sorry, but I have an emergency to attend to, and I have to leave immediately. Since I'm alone today, I'll have to lock up. So let's just do as you suggested. You pay the rent up front, and then you can fill out the rental agreement later. Will you be paying by check or credit card?"

"Cash," Ariel said, dropping the pen and paper on the desk and opening her purse. She pulled out the bank envelope that held her money and began counting out bills. When she offered them to Corrine, the woman stared at her in disapproval.

"Is something wrong?"

"It's just that cash is a bit out of the ordinary."

Ariel realized she was going to have to do some quick thinking again. "Yes, well, I often find books in places like garage sales and flea markets, where people won't take checks or credit cards, so I've learned to travel with cash. It also keeps me from overextending myself on these buying trips."

Corrine still didn't look happy, but she accepted the money and handed over the key ring. As Ariel dropped it into her purse, she wanted to slump in relief. She had managed to bluff her way through this encounter. Now she just had to get back to Lucien.

She turned toward the door. "Thank you, Corrine. I'll stop by in a few days to fill out your paperwork."

"Haven't you forgotten something?"

Ariel pivoted, cautiously repeating, "Forgotten something?"

"The directions to the house."

"Of course! I don't know what's wrong with me today. I guess I'm worn out from the long drive."

Corrine studied her through narrowed eyes for a long, lingering moment, and Ariel had the foreboding sensation that she'd just made a major mistake. Instinctively she hugged her purse to her chest. At least she had the key, and Lucien had said that once she did he could come to her if she was in trouble.

She considered grabbing the crystal around her neck, but refrained. She wasn't sure what she was dealing

with here, and she didn't want to cry wolf. Her pru-
dence proved to be sound: Corrine sat down at the desk
and quickly drew a map.

"You shouldn't have any trouble finding it," she
said, handing over the sketch. "I would suggest, however, that you not go wandering around in the woods
while you're here. The house is isolated, and you could
easily get lost. We've also had a problem with rattle-
snakes this summer."

Ariel involuntarily shuddered. "Thanks for the warning. I hate snakes."

"I'm not too fond of them myself. I hope you enjoy
your stay here."

The phone rang again, and Ariel was saved from
having to respond. She hurried out the door. She
needed to get back to Lucien, but first she was going
to find a telephone and check in with Jean.

When she stepped out onto the sidewalk, however, she
suddenly felt disoriented. Nothing looked familiar, and
she couldn't remember where her car was parked.

She jumped when she felt a touch on her arm and a
deep male voice asked in concern, "Are you all right?"

Ariel looked up at the questioner, and her heart
skipped a beat. Everything about the man was golden,
from his hair to his eyes to the color of his skin. Never
before had she been tempted to call a man beautiful,
but that was the only description to apply to him. As
trite as it sounded, he was Adonis come to life.

"You're feeling ill," he murmured as he took her
arm solicitously and began leading her down the sidewalk. "It's the heat and humidity. Why don't you step
into my shop for a moment?"

Ariel wanted to refuse, but she again felt disoriented
and couldn't get her mind to focus long enough to
dredge up the words. A moment later she found herself
standing in a cluttered room of antiques.

As her eyes grew accustomed to the dim interior, she noticed a huge bookcase at the back of the room. "Oh! You have books."

"Yes. Some of them are very old. Do you like books?"

"I sell them."

"Ah. You must be the antique-books dealer who's renting the house."

"Good heavens, does everyone in town know who I am?" she asked in amused dismay.

His lips curved into a slow, devastating smile that left Ariel feeling a bit breathless. It had been a long time since she'd had a gorgeous man smile at her like this, and it did her ego good, particularly after the battering it had been taking from Lucien during the past couple of days.

"We're a small town, which means our biggest entertainment is gossip," he explained. "Since you've been the brunt of our idle talk, I suppose introductions are in order. You're Ariel Smith, right?" When she nodded, he said, "I'm Galen Morgan."

Ariel stared at him in disbelief. She couldn't have been more flabbergasted if he'd said he was the prince of darkness himself. Indeed, the way Lucien had talked about him, she'd expected him to be the Devil incarnate.

"It's nice to meet you, Mr. Morgan."

"Oh, believe me, Ms. Smith, the pleasure is all mine. And please, call me Galen."

"Only if you call me Ariel."

"I wouldn't have it any other way. Why don't you look at my books while I take care of some business in the back? It'll give you a chance to recover from the heat."

Ariel hesitated at the suggestion. Lucien had told her that she wasn't supposed to talk to anyone. She was only supposed to get the key and return to him. But the purpose for her coming here was to locate Galen, and now that she had, maybe she could learn something about Armand. "I'd love to look at your books."

Gesturing toward the bookcase, he said, "Then have at them."

He disappeared, and Ariel approached the books. All she had to do was look at the spines to confirm that Galen had been right. Many of them were old.

She pulled out a random sampling and sat down on the floor to look at them. Soon she felt as if she'd stumbled across a treasure chest. There were old self-help medical books, cookbooks, and school texts, all of which were great sellers, and they were priced ridiculously low. But it was the vast collection of children's books that enthralled her. There were dozens of them, and she kept pulling them down until they littered the floor around her. She couldn't believe it when she found what appeared to be an autographed first edition of Lewis Carroll's *Alice in Wonderland*. She flipped to the inside cover and was even more dumbfounded by the penciled-in price.

"You've found something you like?"

Ariel glanced up in surprise. She'd been so absorbed that she'd forgotten all about Galen. Now she wondered how that was possible. He was sitting on a stool, one foot hooked on a rung and the other stretched out in front of him.

Her gaze traveled the length of his long, denim-clad legs, over his slim hips and up to his broad chest. By the time she raised her eyes to his face, she'd reconfirmed that he was breathtakingly male. She had definitely found something she liked, and it had nothing to do with books.

"I've found a number of books I'm interested in, but are you sure of the prices?"

He frowned. "If they're too high . . ."

"They're not too high," she quickly assured him. "To be honest, many of them seem underpriced." She gestured toward the *Alice in Wonderland* edition in her lap. "For instance, this book may be a collector's item. If it is, you could get much more than what you're asking."

"Do you educate everyone on their mistakes, or am I special?" he drawled softly, intimately.

It was a loaded question, and Ariel had the good sense not to attempt to answer it. She was also realistic enough not to take his flirtation seriously. Galen Morgan was the type of man who would flirt with every woman he met. She hedged with "I don't believe in cheating people."

"That's an odd philosophy for a businesswoman."

She shrugged self-consciously. "Do unto others . . ."

He leaned forward, bracing his elbows on his knees. His face was so close to hers that she could feel his breath on her cheek as he murmured, "The prices in the books are the asking price, Ariel. I'm not out to make a killing, just a living, and my needs are very basic. So, whatever you want in this store is yours. All you have to do is make an offer."

Ariel had the distinct impression he wasn't talking about books. As she met his amber gaze, her suspicions were confirmed. He was staring at her with blatant sexual interest, which caused a yearning restlessness to stir inside her.

She quickly laid her hormones to rest by reminding herself that Lucien claimed Galen was the enemy. Right now, that was impossible to believe, but she couldn't make a judgment based on one meeting with the man. Appearances, as she'd so well learned during the last couple of days, could be deceiving.

Scooting backwards to put some distance between

them, she said, "If I gave you a deposit, would you be willing to hold the books for me?"

"I'll be glad to hold them for you under one condition," he answered, reaching out to catch a lock of her hair.

As he wrapped it in a curl around her finger and stroked it, Ariel gulped and asked hoarsely, "What condition is that?"

"It's almost closing time. Why don't you hang around for a few more minutes and let me take you to dinner?"

His request shocked Ariel, and she glanced down at her watch, horrified to discover it was almost five in the afternoon. She'd been so absorbed with the books that she'd lost track of time.

Instinctively she brought her hand up to her chest where the crystal rested beneath her blouse. The moment she touched it, it grew exceedingly hot. It didn't burn her, but it scared the heck out of her, because she sensed that its heat was the result of Lucien's temper. Facing an enraged Lucien Morgret was not a prospect she was looking forward to.

"Thank you, but I can't have dinner with you tonight," she said, rising hastily to her feet. "I'm, uh, supposed to meet someone and I'm already late. I'll try to come back tomorrow about the books."

Before Galen could object, she hurried out of the antique store. This time she didn't experience any disorientation, and she ran toward her car. By the time she reached it, the crystal was so hot she felt feverish.

"I'm coming, Lucien," she whispered anxiously as she jumped inside. "Just calm down. I'm coming!"

Lucien was frantic. Ariel's trip should have taken no more than an hour, and she'd been gone for nearly five hours. Except for that one flash from the crystal shortly after she left, he had received nothing from her. What in hell had happened to her?

He was pacing the edge of the clearing when he felt another flash from the crystal. Closing his eyes, he tried to focus on it, but if Ariel was trying to summon him, she'd been thwarted.

Opening his eyes, he stared at the energy barrier. His first impulse was to barge through it and go after her, but if Ariel hadn't gotten the house key, he'd be killed instantly. Even if she had gotten the key, he wouldn't be much help to her if Galen had taken her captive. Galen would find the crystal and destroy it, thus rendering Lucien virtually powerless, particularly within the circle. As the leader of the coven, Galen not only had his own powers but could instantly draw on the strength of the others.

Lucien's best bet was to lure Galen away from the aegis of the circle. Without the crystal, he'd still be at a disadvantage, but he might have a fighting chance in a one-on-one battle on unconsecrated ground.

Knowing he was making the right decision didn't ease his feelings of impotence, and that made him angry. As the minutes ticked by, his temper flared higher. He welcomed the anger, because it kept the fear at bay.

Suddenly Omen growled softly. Lucien didn't need to focus on what she was saying, because his own acute hearing picked up the sound of an approaching car. It had to be Ariel, because he could feel his powers growing by the second, which meant the crystal was getting closer. But then again, Galen could be using the crystal to throw him off guard.

Though it smacked of cowardice and grated like hell, he slipped back into the trees to wait. A direct confrontation with Galen might appease his ego, but he wasn't the only one at risk here. He had to consider

Ariel and Armand. Without him, they didn't have a chance.

Ariel pulled into the clearing a few minutes later. With the crystal so near, Lucien's powers were restored. After he quickly determined that she was alone and unharmed, his temper exploded. He recognized that his anger was caused by relief, but the realization only made its edge sharper.

As she climbed out of the car, he stalked toward her, demanding, "Just where in hell have you been?"

Ariel had been prepared for Lucien's fury, but nothing could have prepared her for the look of pure wrath on his face. *This* was the Devil incarnate! Every self-protective instinct she possessed was yelling at her to run for her life, but she was so scared she was rooted to the spot.

As he continued to advance on her, she swallowed around the fearful lump in her throat and said, "I know I'm late, Lucien, but I have a good reason."

"I'm listening," he stated in a low, sibilant rasp as he came to a stop in front of her.

He was standing so close that she had to lean her head back to see his face. His livid expression was even more terrifying up close, and she swallowed again. Then she launched into an account of her trip, beginning with the car accident and Shana and ending with her meeting with Galen.

With each word she spoke, the wind picked up speed until it was beating against her with gale force. It wasn't until she was finished that she realized that the wind was blowing only where she and Lucien were, nowhere else. She also became aware that the crystal was emanating a red glow through her white blouse.

Ariel didn't doubt for a minute that Lucien was causing both phenomena, and when his eyes began to glow she fearfully took a step back. He grabbed her arms and jerked her against him. Despite his steel grip, he wasn't hurting her, but she could sense he was on the verge of losing control.

"Lucien, please calm down," she urgently beseeched. "You're scaring me."

At first she thought he hadn't heard her, but then his eyes began to return to normal. A moment later he released her, and when he did, the wind stopped. Glancing down at her blouse, she was relieved to see that the crystal was no longer glowing red. While eyeing Lucien warily, she wrapped her arms around herself and took a deep breath in an effort to slow the rapid beating of her heart.

A few more encounters like this and Lucien wouldn't have to kill her. Her heart would simply give out from fright, she acknowledged, as she considered what had just happened. She'd already experienced his glowing eyes and the color change in the crystal, so she knew it was a reflection of his temper. That he was able to create a wind, however, was positively unnerving. It made her wonder what other abilities he had that he hadn't exhibited. That terrified her, because it emphasized just how much at his mercy she was. Conversely, it intrigued her, because she couldn't help wondering what would it be like to have such power.

As Lucien watched Ariel wrap her arms around herself protectively, he raked a hand through his hair. He'd always prided himself on his self-control. As his grandfather had often told him, the mark of an exceptional warlock was that he was always in command of his emotions. This characteristic was particularly critical for the warlock preordained to become the high priest, which had been Lucien's destiny until Galen had destroyed everything.

But since he'd met Ariel, he found himself losing control time and again, and that worried him. It could only mean that the spell he had cast over her was growing more powerful. It was critical that he find Armand quickly, because the longer it took, the harder it would be to break the spell.

"Did you see any sign of Armand?" he asked.

"No," Ariel answered.

"Tell me about your meeting with Galen."

"I already did."

"Tell me again, and don't leave out any detail, even if it seems inconsequential."

With a resigned sigh, Ariel repeated the story. When she was done, he said, "Tell it to me again."

She glanced at him impatiently. "Why?"

"Because you're leaving something out."

"Are you accusing me of lying?"

He arched his eyebrow. "Are you lying?"

"Of course not!"

"Then you won't mind telling me again."

"Lucien, there's no reason for me to repeat it. I've told you all the important details."

"You've told me all the *important* details? What have you left out?"

"It's nothing," she muttered, looking toward the woods.

"I'll make that determination," he declared in a tone that convinced Ariel he wouldn't drop the subject until she'd told him everything.

She shot him a withering glare, but he didn't even flinch. "All right, if you must know, Galen was flirting with me."

His brow shot higher. "He was *flirting* with you?"

"You don't have to sound so surprised," she muttered, miffed. "Believe it or not, *some* men happen to find me attractive."

Lucien walked over to the car, leaned a hip against

the front bumper, and fell into an introspective silence. Ariel watched him with growing apprehension.

When several minutes had passed, she couldn't stand the suspense any longer. "What's going on, Lucien?"

He blinked, as though surprised to see her standing there. "Galen knows who you are, or at least that you're somehow connected to Armand."

Ariel was so confounded by his statement that she could only gape at him. Finally, she regained enough composure to say, "That's ridiculous. Nothing he said or did indicated that he knows my identity."

"Believe me, Ariel, he knows. The first clue was when you were in the real estate office. Didn't you think it was damned convenient that Corrine suddenly had an emergency when you were hesitating about filling out the rental agreement?"

"I was too busy trying to find a way to get out of the situation to give it much thought," Ariel admitted. "But coincidences do happen, Lucien."

"It was no coincidence," he responded grimly. "The purpose of having you fill out the form was so they could verify who you were. When you said you'd leave and come back later, Corrine communicated that to Galen. He was probably afraid that you'd decided to stay outside the circle, and until he could figure out if you were a threat, it was imperative that he keep you within the sphere of his control. But it would have seemed strange for Corrine suddenly to tell you to forget the form. So he called to make it look legitimate."

Two days ago, Ariel would have scoffed at the idea that Corrine and Galen could have engaged in such complicated mental communication. But Lucien seemed to read her own mind on a regular basis. There was also that disturbing moment with Shana Morland when she was convinced that the woman was reading her mind.

Nervously shifting her weight from one foot to the other, she argued, "That still doesn't prove that he knows who I am. Maybe he was just checking me out because I'm a stranger."

Lucien shook his head. "He wouldn't bother himself with a stranger unless he felt you might be a threat. When you managed to avoid filling out the form and then insisted on paying cash, he was left with no other option than to approach you directly. He caused your disorientation, and then took you to the one place where you were sure to be distracted—the antique store with the books. He figured that if you were occupied with them, your defenses would be down and he could easily determine exactly who you were and why you're here.

"But my spell was in place, so everything he picked up was nonsensical. Recognizing you were spellbound, he decided flirt with you, hoping that by playing on your vanity he'd be able to trick you into telling him who the spellbinder was. That in itself is revealing, because if he suspected it was me, he would simply draw on the others to break my spell. Since he's being so cautious, it means he has reason to believe that he may be in danger from a warlock as powerful as he is. I just wish to hell I knew who it was and what it all means."

Ariel knew he didn't expect a response, and she didn't offer one. Instead she stewed over his insinuation that she was so shallow that a simple flirtation would get her to reveal all. Galen might be gorgeous enough to swoon over, but she had enough sense to keep his advances in perspective. She refrained, however, from voicing her sentiments. Lucien was too volatile, and she never knew what would set him off. One warlock temper tantrum a day was as much as her nerves could handle.

"Assuming that everything you've said is right, how did Galen learn my identity?"

Lucien shrugged. "He would have to have learned it from Armand."

Ariel's knees wobbled at his conclusion. Armand was always overprotective of her so she wouldn't be endangered by his work. The only way Galen could have learned her identify from him was if he had forced it out of him.

It was as if Lucien read her mind, because he suddenly said, "Ariel, I don't think Galen would physically hurt Armand."

She might have been able to accept his reassurance if he hadn't qualified it with "physically." Suddenly she recalled asking Lucien if Armand was alive. He'd replied, "In the context you mean, yes." It didn't take a genius to figure out that Galen had other ways of hurting her brother.

Why had she waited so long to come looking for Armand? Why had she let him go after this crazy story in the first place? From the moment he told her about it, she sensed that there was something wrong with it. If anything had happened to him, she would never forgive herself.

As the first sting of tears burned her eyes, she blinked against them, firmly telling herself that crying wasn't going to help. But the more she attempted to hold back the tears, the more determined they seemed to surface. Finally accepting that she was fighting a losing battle, she buried her face in her hands and began to weep.

When Ariel started to cry, Lucien stared at her, aghast. He didn't know how to deal with a crying woman. Witches never cried. They ranted and raved and sent things flying at a warlock's head. He did, however, vaguely recall that his mother had succumbed to this strange malady on a couple of occasions, and when she had, his father had hugged her.

Tentatively, Lucien approached Ariel and put his arms around her. When she pressed her face against his chest and began to sob inconsolably, he was convinced that he was doing something wrong. Since the hug didn't seem to be working, he decided to use the standard warlock solution for calming a witch. He caught her chin, raised her face, and kissed her.

Ariel's heart began to race when Lucien lowered his lips to hers. Last night his kiss had been ruthless, punishing. But this one was urgent, hungry, as if he couldn't get enough of her, and she was clinging to him before her mind could fully comprehend what was happening.

As she was overcome by the pleasurable ache of escalating desire, she inwardly wailed, *This is crazy! I don't even like this man!*

That didn't stop her from groaning in approval as he ground his hips against her, giving her ample proof of his own growing need. Her hand crept to the crystal on its own volition, and when her fingers touched it, her mind was flooded with erotic sensations. What was shocking was that they were all male, and so seductive that she was bewitched by them.

Physically, she felt Lucien's arms enfold her, but her mind was filled with how he felt with her taut nipples pressed against his chest and her pelvis crushed against his erection. When he slid his leg between her thighs and pressed into her heat, it was the throbbing heaviness in his groin that was so intense she thought she might die from it.

Eagerly he unbuttoned her blouse, but as he slipped his hand beneath the fabric to cup her breast, it brushed against the crystal. It was so hot Ariel felt it sear him, and she also felt his recognition that the heat was a reflection of her own arousal. That knowledge inflamed him, and that, in turn, inflamed her.

That was why she was so shocked when he suddenly thrust her away from him. As she gazed up at his face in bewilderment, she could have sworn she saw a flash of regret in his expression. She decided, however, that she'd imagined it, because he was now looking at her so coldly that she shivered from the chill.

Suddenly he turned his back on her and tersely ordered, "Pull yourself together, Ariel. We need to get to the house and start making plans to rescue your brother."

At first Ariel was stunned by his curtness, but then she experienced a flash of righteous indignation. Twice he'd kissed her and then treated her as if she were some sort of pariah.

The more she thought about it, the madder she got, and she mentally cursed him as she quickly buttoned her blouse. When she stalked past him a minute later, she vowed that if he ever laid a hand on her again, she'd punch him in his pompous, overbearing warlock nose.

Chapter Seven

What of soul was left, I wonder, when the kissing had to stop?
—Robert Browning *A Toccata of Galuppi's* (1855), st. 14

FOR three years Lucien had fantasized about coming home, but after he and Ariel got into the car and drove into the circle, the sense of wrongness within the coven was so strong he could almost touch it. Automatically he reached for the crystal to see if he could gain more insight, only to realize Ariel still wore it.

Damn! Why hadn't he gotten the crystal from her before they crossed over onto coven ground?

Because you were so caught up in kissing her that you forgot all about the crystal. It's mistakes like that that are going to get you both killed.

Shaking his head in self-disgust, he glanced toward Ariel to ask for the crystal. She was slumped against the door, fresh tears glittering in her eyes. Startled by her unexpected distress, he connected with her mind to see what was wrong. She was still worried about Armand, sure that something horrible had happened to him, and she was blaming herself.

Unfounded guilt was as alien to Lucien as tears, and he turned his attention back to the road, puzzling over her emotional self-flagellation. There was no logic to it, because she'd had nothing to do with Armand's decision to come here. For her to condemn herself for his predicament was thoroughly baffling and utterly ridiculous.

He considered expressing his opinion, but feared it might send her off into another crying jag. He would rather face a hundred furious witches than relive that experience. It was important, however, that he pull her out of her depression. His spell could control her thoughts, but it couldn't control her emotions. To deal successfully—not to mention safely—with Galen, she had to be calm and completely focused.

But how did one go about cheering up a mortal? he wondered, perplexed. Since they would soon reach the house, he decided to ponder the matter later. She wouldn't be meeting Galen tonight, and that left him plenty of time to come up with a solution. For now he had to worry about getting to the house unseen. As they neared the turnoff to his home, he pulled over to the side of the road.

Ariel looked at Lucien in confusion when he suddenly stopped the car. "Why are we stopping?"

"I'm sure Galen has someone watching the house. It's important that I find out who it is, so I'm going to walk the rest of the way," he explained. "All you have to do is drive around the bend, and you'll see a dirt road on your right. Drive down it for half a mile and you'll arrive at the house. When you get there, go directly inside and wait for me. If someone approaches you, *don't* invite them in. That's very important, Ariel. You must *never* invite *anyone* into the house. Do you understand?"

He was talking to her in a pedantic tone one might use with a child, and Ariel frowned in annoyance. "Of course I understand. I'm not a dimwit, Lucien. I can follow simple instructions."

Omen growled softly, as though in disagreement of Ariel's claim, and Ariel shot a glare her way. The cat bared her teeth and hissed in response. Lucien made a noise that sounded suspiciously like a chuckle, but since he was climbing out of the car, she couldn't verify it. If he was amused, the feeling was short-lived, because after she scooted over into the driver's seat, he shut the door and regarded her grimly through the window.

"Remember, Ariel. Go directly into the house, and . . ."

". . . don't let anyone in," she finished in exasperation. Just to make sure he didn't continue with the lecture, she said, "I'm leaving now. See you at the house."

Lucien nodded and walked into the trees, Omen at his heels. As Ariel watched them disappear, she was hit with a sudden twinge of panic at being left alone. She gave a deprecating shake of her head. All she had to do was drive to an empty house, for pity's sake. She was going to have to stop being such a chicken.

As Ariel drove off, Lucien cast a spell over himself and Omen that made them virtually invisible and deadened any sound they might make. And it was a good thing he did, because they came across a young warlock and his familiar at the entrance to the dirt road. When they saw a young witch a minute later, and then another young warlock, Lucien's stomach churned in apprehension. Galen was using the children to keep an eye on Ariel, and he couldn't have chosen a more diabolical ploy to breech her defenses. Lucien had told her not to let anyone into the house, but he was sure that she would let a child in, because mortals didn't consider children a threat.

Not that the coven children would—or could, for that matter—harm her. Their powers, even combined, weren't strong enough to perform more than minor spells. What they could do, however, was open the gateway Galen needed to begin to work his magic on Ariel.

Again, he cursed the fact that he hadn't retrieved the crystal from her. His spell would firmly connect their minds only when she was dealing with Galen. To connect with her otherwise, he had to be close to the crystal.

Damn! Why hadn't he anticipated something like this and made the spell stronger?

Because the stronger the spell was, the harder it would be to break. By trying to protect himself, he may have condemned them all.

When Ariel reached the house, she stared at it uneasily. It was an enormous three-story ivy-covered stone house with the same pointed arches and slender turrets as the businesses in town. Gigantic pine and oak trees grew on either side of it, creating a lush green canopy over the roof. The natural landscape had been maintained, so instead of a grass yard there was a profusion of ferns and wildflowers. Yet, despite the beauty surrounding it, something about the house seemed sinister, like a cursed castle in a fairy tale.

Reluctantly, she got out of the car and headed for the structure. She had just reached the front door when a small black-and-white dog came racing out of the woods. He stopped at the foot of the stoop and began barking at her.

Ariel immediately backed up to the door and eyed the dog warily. Though she liked dogs, she had been bitten by one when she was ten, and since then, she approached all dogs cautiously—particularly barking ones. She had learned the hard way that the old adage "His bark is worse than his bite" wasn't always true.

"Forecast won't hurt you. He's just saying hello," a small voice announced.

Ariel jerked her head toward the voice and saw a girl of about twelve standing at the corner of the house. She was at the gangling stage of adolescence—all arms and legs. With her wildly curly red hair and freckled face, she looked like Little Orphan Annie, but it was her eyes that held Ariel's attention. They were the same pale-blue color as Lucien's and just as eerily piercing. Was she a relative of his?

She smiled hesitantly and said, "Hi, I'm Ariel."

"I know," the girl responded, stuffing her hands into her pockets. She sauntered toward the dog, who had stopped barking. Standing beside him, she gazed curiously up at Ariel. "I'm Lily."

"I'm glad to meet you, Lily."

The girl nodded. "I'm thirsty. May I have a drink of water?"

"Sure," Ariel said, digging the key out of her purse and turning to unlock the door. "I'll just have to figure out where the kitchen is and find a glass."

She pushed the door open and turned back, intending to invite Lily in. However, Lucien's mandate suddenly skittered through her mind. *You must never invite anyone into the house.* Surely he hadn't meant a child!

But as Ariel met Lily's spooky gaze, she decided it was better to be overcautious than to provoke Lucien's temper. "I'll be right back with the water."

As she entered the house, she impulsively glanced back over her shoulder. Lily and the dog were gone.

She stepped outside and searched the area for some sign of them. There was nothing—no sound of movement or flash of color. How could they have disappeared so quickly and soundlessly? Had the girl and the dog been ghosts? But that was ridiculous. There was no such things as ghosts.

How do you know that? Until yesterday you didn't

*think there was such a thing as a warlock, but now you
know differently.*

Disconcerted and more than a little unnerved, she re-
entered the house, shut the door, and looked around her
uneasily. The way the trees shrouded the house, she
had expected the inside to be dark, but the large, un-
curtained windows let in adequate, if muted, light.

She was standing in what appeared to be a large living room with an inlaid hardwood floor and vaulted
ceiling. A stone fireplace filled one entire wall. The
stones had been laid so that there was a stone mantelpiece as well as dozens of narrow stone shelves running from floor to ceiling. The mantelpiece and shelves
were cluttered with old bottles filled with what looked
like dried plants. Sitting in front of the fireplace were
two obviously handmade wood-frame chairs with wide
armrests and faded cushions at the back and on the
seat. Except for a small handmade table positioned between the chairs, there wasn't any other furniture, not
even a lamp or a picture.

She walked farther into the room, her footsteps
echoing hollowly in the silence. Since her brother lived
like a Spartan, she wasn't as surprised by the austerity
as someone else might have been. Since Armand was
constantly gone, he had never bothered with furniture,
but Lucien had indicated that the members of the
coven rarely left the magic circle. If that was true,
logic would dictate that they make their homes as comfortable as possible.

She supposed that simplicity might be a part of their
lifestyle, but somehow that didn't mesh with her perception of the coven. If, as she suspected, they were
Satanists, wouldn't they be hedonistic? After all, what
would be the purpose of following the Devil if you
couldn't be materially rewarded for it?

Her curiosity aroused, she walked to the fireplace

and studied the bottles. They were definitely filled with dried plants, but there were no labels. Some of the bottles that were out of reach were covered with dust so thick she was sure they hadn't been touched in years.

"So, where is the eye of newt and pickled bat wings?" she mumbled, nervously turning back to face the room.

She wasn't sure what drew her attention to the floor. Perhaps it was simply that there was nothing else to focus on. But as her gaze traced the intricate inlaid pattern, she suddenly understood why there was no furniture in here. There was a huge pentagram built into the center of the floor, and it was surrounded by two circles. In between the two circles were strange-looking symbols that were as indecipherable and as disturbing as those she'd seen on the door at the Witches' Brew.

It was then that Ariel understood that this wasn't a living room, but a ... What did you call a Satanist's place of worship? Quite frankly, she didn't want to know. What she wanted was to get the heck out of here! She now knew where Armand was, and she could go to the nearest police station for help.

Except—she still had no proof that Armand was in Sanctuary. Without something to verify her story, she suspected she wouldn't get any more help from the police here than she had in Philadelphia. *Damn!* What should she do?

She jumped at a loud knock on the door, which was immediately followed with "Ariel, it's me. Open the door and ask me in!"

It was Lucien, and the sound of his voice brought all her misgivings racing to the surface. He kept saying he wanted to help her find Armand, but why had he sought Armand out and told him about the coven in the first place? The only reason she could think of was to get revenge for being an outcast, but if that was true, why hadn't he come with Armand, just as he'd come with her? Why had he sent him in here alone? Had Armand been a means to get him reinstated in the coven? Had he sent Armand here to be some sort of sacrifice? Had he brought her here for the same reason?

You're letting your imagination get the best of you, an inner voice chided.

But Ariel wasn't convinced she was being overimaginative. Indeed, the more she thought about it, the more her conclusions made sense.

So what should she do? she wondered, growing frantic when Lucien once again pounded on the door and yelled, "Dammit, Ariel, ask me in!"

Without even realizing what she was doing, she touched the crystal around her neck and whispered, "Armand, what should I do?"

There was a crackling noise and the air suddenly became charged with static electricity, raising every hair on her body. When light arced from the crystal, she let out a yelp and then stared at the scene in front of her in disbelief. Armand was sitting in the middle of the pentagram. His hair, which had always been unconventionally long, had grown past his shoulders and he had a full beard. But what horrified Ariel was that his hair and beard were completely white. Even worse, he was staring at her with vacant eyes.

"Armand!" she cried out in despair at his macabre image, but as she released the crystal to reach for him, he disappeared. When he did, the crackling noise became louder and the air even more charged, making it difficult to breathe.

"Dammit, Ariel, ask me in!" Lucien roared again, as he began to pound on the door. "Do you hear me, Ariel? You have to ask me in, and you have to do it *now*!"

Ariel glanced dazedly from the spot where Armand had been sitting to the door. Suddenly she felt weak and dizzy, and there was a shrill chanting going on around her. It was if the entire house was screeching at her, and the sound grew louder and louder until it felt as if her eardrums were going to explode.

When it reached a mind-rending level, she dropped to her knees, clamped her hands over her ears, and screamed, "Stop it!"

But her efforts to shut out the agonizing noise only seemed to amplify it. Recognizing that the only way to escape the din was to get out of the house, she tried to stand, but her muscles felt as if they had turned to mush. She fell to the floor in a quivering heap. She then tried to crawl, but her body simply wouldn't co-operate. She was trapped!

Oh, God, what am I going to do?

Touch the crystal and think of me so I can come to you! The words shocked Ariel, because she could have sworn that it was Lucien saying them. But that was impossible. Lucien wasn't here.

But he was here, she vaguely realized. Above the ca-cophony she could hear him still pounding on the door and yelling her name. So why hadn't he come to her rescue? Was he putting her through this torture? That had to be it. He'd done something ghastly to Armand, and now he was doing it to her.

Dammit, Ariel! Touch the crystal, and think of me!

The fury behind Lucien's mental order jarred Ariel into reflexive obedience, though reaching for the crys-tal wasn't easy. Her arm seemed to ignore her brain's demand that it move. Closing her eyes, she forced her-self to shut out the crippling noise as much as possible and concentrate on performing the task.

It seemed to take forever before her hand finally lifted, and she barely made it to the crystal. But she did make it, and she no more than touched it before the door burst open.

Lucien flew into the room with such speed that he was no more than a blur. Standing over her, he threw what looked like gold dust into the air and yelled some garbled words. A moment later the noise stopped.

Ariel gazed up at Lucien weakly, unable to decide if she should be relieved or terrified to see him. He was still standing above her, his legs spread apart and his arms akimbo. His stance alone communicated his fury, but as he stared down at her, his expression was so livid she wouldn't have been surprised to see him transform into a slavering demon.

She licked nervously at her lips and tried to sit up. She'd no more than pushed up on her elbows when Lucien scooped her into his arms with about as much effort as it would take to lift a toddler.

As he cradled her against his chest, she found herself eye to eye with his glowering countenance. That was unnerving enough, but combined with the sudden realization of just how strong he was, it was downright scary. He could probably do her in with one good squeeze.

But if he meant to harm her, he wouldn't have just saved her life, she rationalized. And she had no doubt that if she'd been exposed to that horrible noise much longer it would have meant her demise.

As he carried her down a gloomy hallway, she rested her head against his shoulder and closed her eyes. Her muscles still felt like mush, and she couldn't remember ever feeling so exhausted.

She must have dozed off, because the next thing she knew, Lucien was putting her down on a bed. She gazed up at him in confusion. There was something she had to tell him, but for the life of her she couldn't remember what it was.

She started to speak, but before her mind could figure out what she wanted to say, Lucien lifted a small vial to her lips and poured the contents into her mouth.

As Ariel's eyelids dropped heavily, she suddenly remembered that she had to tell Lucien about Armand! She tried to fight her way back to consciousness, but Lucien pressed his hand against her forehead and intoned, "I'm in charge now, Ariel, and it's important that you obey me. Don't think. Just sleep."

His voice had a strange, melodic cadence that lulled her despite her mind's insistence that she stay awake. When she felt herself drifting away, she kept hearing him say, *"Obey me, Ariel. Obey me."*

The command made her shiver, because she finally understood that she didn't have a choice. Somehow Lucien had managed to gain control of her soul, and she recognized that she couldn't fight him if she wanted to.

As Lucien stared down at Ariel's pale, sleeping face, his emotions were in such turmoil that he didn't even try to sort through them. Instead, he cursed himself for being a fool. He should never have sent Armand here, or compounded that mistake by bringing Ariel here. If she had spent one more minute in that dissonance, she would have lost her mind. Even now there was a chance that there had been irreparable damage. That was why he gave her the sleeping potion. It was important that she sleep so her psyche would have a chance to recover from the trauma.

He raked a hand through his hair, still stunned by what had happened. Through Omen he had learned about Lily's approaching Ariel. The cat had gleaned the information from Lily's familiar. She also learned that Ariel had refused Lily entrance into the house. That was why he was been so surprised when, after he arrived at the house and knocked on the door, spell-casting lightning had suddenly started crackling around it.

But how had Galen invoked the spell? he wondered, mystified. Once Ariel took possession of the house, the only way Galen could have obtained that kind of power was if he or someone under his command had entered at her invitation, and she had turned Lily away. Lucien supposed that Galen could have cast a spell over the house before Ariel's arrival, but he still shouldn't have been able to execute it without some form of invitation. So how *had* he done it?

There was only one way to find out, he grimly realized. He was going to have to use the crystal to delve into Ariel's mind and make her relive the minutes before Galen's spell went into effect. But was she strong enough to survive such an invasion? If she wasn't, he might end up accomplishing what Galen had set out to do—destroying her sanity.

His initial impulse was to give her time to heal, but he understood that it was too dangerous to wait. Until he knew what had set the spell in motion, he couldn't counter it. If he waited until she regained consciousness, she might inadvertently set it off again, and the next time he might not be able to save her.

Before he could change his mind, he undid the first few buttons on her blouse and reached for the crystal, which was nestled between her breasts. As his flesh touched hers, his own spell was immediately invoked, sending ripples of pleasure through both their bodies.

Ignoring the growing tightness in his groin and the desire he could feel stirring in her womb, he gently probed her mind. After reassuring himself that she was resting peacefully—or at least as peacefully as awakening desire would allow—he led her mind back to where he and Omen had left her on the road.

Over the next few minutes, he relived her drive to the house and her encounter with Lily and Forecast. When he experienced her agitation at Lily's disappearance, he began to insert reassurances into her mind. Only when he was sure that she was calm did he lead her further into the memory.

He relived her perusal of the bottles on the shelves, and when she recognized the pentagram on the floor, he was astonished. Because of the general spell that fell over any mortal entering the coven, she should have never seen it, let along figured out what it was! So why had she seen it—and recognized it?

Because Galen wanted her to see it, to recognize it.

But why would Galen want that? he wondered in bewilderment. The answer had to lie ahead. He led Ariel into the memory cautiously, knowing that he'd reached the dangerous stage. Her fear was tangible as she tried to decide whether or not to go to the police, and then he knocked on the door, sending her into a real panic.

He cursed himself as violently now as he had then. He had been so intent on ensuring that she didn't invite anyone else into the house that he'd forgotten to have her issue him an invitation. Without it, he simply couldn't enter, which was why he hadn't been able to come to her rescue until she touched the crystal and summoned him.

He again began to lead her through the memory. When she touched the crystal and asked her brother what she should do, he was just as shocked by Armand's appearance—both figuratively and literally—as she had been.

Quickly he released his hold on the crystal, knowing it was too dangerous to take the memory any further. Besides, he didn't need to go on. He had his answer, and for the first time in his life he experienced true fear. Galen hadn't cast a spell over the house. He'd cast a spell over Armand. Anyone speaking his name within the coven's boundaries and then responding to his image would immediately be subjected to the punishment Ariel had just endured. What made it so frightening was that the only way Galen could accomplish such a dangerous, sweeping spell was if he was practicing the Old Ways.

Even as he reached his conclusion, Lucien gave a disbelieving shake of his head. Galen couldn't be practicing the Old Ways. They had been banned more than two centuries ago! Even Lucien's grandfather, who had been the coven's high priest, hadn't known the spells that went along with them. They involved the use of the dark forces and, if not controlled properly, were not only dangerous but inherently evil.

As he stared again down into Ariel's pale face, however, he knew that was how Galen had defeated him so he could take over the coven. It also explained the strange dreams he'd been having about the coven, which had caused him to seek Armand's assistance, as well as his feelings that there was something wrong here. The evil he'd dreamed about had been real.

Any hope Lucien had of defeating Galen died with that knowledge. Even the mightiest of warlocks would be hard-pressed to overcome such power. He was an outcast half-breed who needed a crystal to bring him to the level of a full-bred warlock. As soon as Ariel woke up, he'd put her in the car and get her the hell away from here.

And what about Armand? his conscience nagged. *You sent him here, so it's up to you to save him.*

But is he salvageable? Lucien countered grimly, as he surged to his feet and began to pace. If the image he'd seen had been a true reflection of Armand's condition and not some macabre vision created by Galen, he doubted it. Not only had Armand slipped into old age, but the vacancy in his eyes said that his mind was gone.

Unmitigated anger flooded through Lucien, and he knew it was directed as much at himself as at Galen. It was true that he didn't have any great love for mortals, but he also didn't have any right to throw them into the middle of his war without their full knowledge and consent. By violating those ethics he had apparently destroyed Armand, and by bringing Ariel here he had all but destroyed her, too.

Now that Galen knew what she looked like, he'd be able to locate her by simply conjuring up a spell. Her only chance for survival was if he could persuade the high priest of another coven to protect her. But only Galen, as high priest, knew the exact locations of the other covens, and they were all in Europe. Lucien recognized that it would be next to impossible for him to find one in time to save her. Galen would be not only tracking Ariel but trying to learn who her spellbinder was. Eventually he would discover that it was Lucien, and when he did, he'd destroy them both. They were in a hopeless situation.

But then again, that might not be true, Lucien realized, a sudden thought occurring to him. When Ariel had gone into town, Galen had known who she was or, more accurately, he had known that she was somehow connected with Armand. Lucien had assumed he'd gotten that information from Armand, but if he had, why hadn't he come looking for her in Philadelphia? And why, when he discovered she was spellbound, hadn't he made an effort to break the spell?

Again, the only conclusion that made sense was that Galen was being cautious because he feared he was in danger from another warlock. But if, as Lucien suspected, he was practicing the Old Ways, what warlock would be powerful enough to make him fearful?

Lucien raked a hand through his hair, feeling as if he were trying to put together a jigsaw puzzle that had half its pieces missing. The only person who could provide the answers was Galen, and that wasn't going to happen. Instead of trying to solve the unsolvable, he should be concentrating on how to get Ariel and Armand out of this mess alive, assuming, of course, that Armand was still alive. Unfortunately, he could see only one possible way to save them, and it was slim at best, because it meant he'd have to put Ariel at even greater risk.

He stopped his pacing and walked to the foot of the bed. As his gaze roamed Ariel's face, the protectiveness he'd experienced toward her last night stirred restlessly within him. She was so very vulnerable, so ill-equipped to fight Galen, that even to consider using her was insane. Yet he knew in his heart that she alone possessed the only power that could possibly defeat Galen—love for her brother.

But was her love strong enough—pure enough? In another mortal, he would have had serious doubts, but Ariel and Armand were twins. If he could believe the information he'd read about twins, they had a bond as strong as a mated witch and warlock. Did he dare take a chance that what he'd read was right?

Again Lucien was faced with too many unanswerable questions. He was also confronted with a very personal decision. If he decided to use Ariel, he was going to have to make the spell he'd cast over her stronger—make himself completely susceptible to her. In other words, he was going to have to risk falling in love with a mortal.

But he had until dawn to make that decision. In the meantime, he would try to ascertain if his conjecturing about Galen was true. There was a chance, albeit a slim one, that he was off base—that Galen wasn't practicing the Old Ways.

After making sure that Ariel was asleep, he went in search of Omen, cursing when he didn't find her in any of her usual haunts. He considered summoning her, but he knew she would ignore him. She'd been in a jealous snit ever since he'd become involved with Ariel. That was why she had purposely terrified Ariel last night and continued to provoke her at every opportunity. If she'd been misbehaving with a witch, he would have asserted his dominion over her, but he saw no reason to cause dissension between them over a mortal.

Now he was thankful he hadn't interfered, because he needed Omen's help. Since they hadn't united until after his expulsion from the coven, she wasn't included in the spell that kept him incommunicado. That meant she could roam through the coven and surreptitiously glean information shared between the coven's familiars and their masters, just as she had with Lily and Forecast earlier. With any luck she might get him some answers.

But before she could do that, he had to find her and ask for her help. Since familiars were not compelled to do their masters' bidding, it made them damn contrary. Considering Omen's mood, he'd probably have to beg her and he had never begged for anything in his life, not even clemency from Galen after his victory over Lucien in the bid for the high priesthood.

Lucien knew that when he had refused to ask for clemency, the majority of the coven thought he was being too prideful. He was willing to admit that on some levels they were right. However, he had chosen banishment mainly because, in order to stay, he would have had to swear his undying allegiance to Galen. He suspected at the time that Galen was unscrupulous, but he was unable to prove it. And once he took the vow to accept and follow him, his hands would be tied. After that vow, even if he found evidence that Galen was breaking coven law, to expose him would mean instant death.

And coming here now doesn't carry the same penalty? an inner voice scoffed.

This is war. That would have been unqualified surrender!

And he wasn't about to surrender, because he understood the dire consequences if the council of high priests caught Galen practicing the Old Ways. There was no greater crime, and under high coven law, the entire coven would be annihilated. Lucien's family had guarded the coven for more than three hundred years, and he'd be damned before he'd let Galen destroy it.

Purposefully, he headed for the second floor, which, until his grandfather's death, had been his own quarters. When he didn't find Omen there either, he was disconcerted. Since he could sense her presence, he knew she was in the house, but where?

He paced the second floor hallway three times before he remembered the third floor. The only time he had been to that part of the house was when he was nine. His grandfather had taken him there to impress upon him the fragility of the coven, and the empty third floor was symbolic of that fact.

As with any race, the coven had genetic weaknesses that were inherent. In this case, it was procreation. A witch could only bear only one child during her lifetime, and a warlock could sire only one child during his. At their zenith, the covens had flourished, and it had been commonplace to have four generations living in one household—the great-grandparents, the grandparents, the parents, and the child. But then the persecutions began with the Romans in the first century A.D.

and continued through the seventeenth century. Eighteen hundred years of slaughter had been devastating to the covens' numbers.

All thirteen houses within this coven had been built with the traditional three stories in the hope that eventually their numbers would increase, bringing them back to their millennium. But after more than three hundred years, only two families had managed to fill their homes to capacity, and rumor had it that the other covens were just as desperate. Some even predicted that within a few centuries their entire race would cease to exist—another reason why he had to stop Galen if he was using the Old Ways. If this coven was destroyed, it would make the risk of extinction even greater.

He went to the staircase leading to the third floor and climbed it. The door at the top should have been locked, but he wasn't surprised to find it open, and he stepped inside. The room was empty except for an old trunk at the far end. Omen sat on top of it in a classic Bast pose.

He eyed the trunk curiously. Where had it come from, and whom did it belong to? When he walked to it, Omen jumped down with a triumphant swish of her tail. As Lucien popped open the latch and lifted the lid, he was startled by the contents. A gold pen, engraved with the initials A.D., was nestled on top of a pile of clothing, confirming that he was looking at Armand Dantes's possessions.

The ramifications of his find had Lucien's mind racing. Someone had entered the house, packed Armand's belongings into the trunk, and stored them up here. It couldn't have been Galen. He would have destroyed the evidence. So who had done this, and why? It didn't make sense.

"What in hell is going on?" Lucien mumbled, disconcerted. Unfortunately neither the trunk nor its contents could talk.

Well, that wasn't exactly true, Lucien corrected himself thoughtfully. The pen was Armand's, and Lucien had watched him toy with it during every one of their meetings. Psychometry wasn't one of Lucien's best-developed skills, but he was sure that if he meditated on the pen, he could get some idea of what had happened to Armand.

Before he did that, though, he had to deal with Omen. She was sitting on the floor, staring up at him guardedly.

"You know what I want," he said. "Will you go out into the coven and see if you can get me information?"

She emitted a low growled as she glared at him accusingly.

Lucien nodded solemnly. "You're right. You warned me that getting involved with the mortals was going to get me into trouble. I also appreciate the fact that you found the trunk for me. But you haven't answered my question. Will you go out into the coven?"

Her tail bristled, and she bared her teeth and hissed at him. Then she raced out of the room before Lucien could respond.

Lucien shook his head and sighed heavily. Omen was going to help, and she was furious with him for even doubting that she would. Of course, if he had assumed she would help, she'd have been furious and accused him of taking her for granted.

Accepting that he would never understand the female gender, Lucien fished a handkerchief out of his back pocket and carefully lifted the pen. He didn't want to risk touching it until he was properly prepared.

Downstairs, he placed the pen in the center of the pentagram, along with half a dozen jars from the shelves. Then he retrieved the sacred candles and the censer from behind the secret stone in the fireplace.

It was only after he had gathered everything he needed that he remembered he hadn't gotten his crystal back. *Damn!* For the type of magic he wanted to perform he needed the crystal. Unfortunately, he had *given* it to Ariel, so he couldn't just take it back. He had to ask for it, and while she was under the influence of the sleeping potion, he couldn't do that.

Lucien couldn't recall ever having been so frustrated. All his life he'd lived by coven rules, but in the last few days he'd learned how restrictive they could be. It seemed as if every time he turned around he was having to ask for something; as a warlock, he was used to demanding.

The obvious solution was to wait until Ariel woke up, but he knew that was too dangerous. She had gone to sleep thinking of Armand, and he would fill the first thoughts she'd have when she woke up. If she said his name before Lucien could stop her, Galen's spell would go into effect. Even a momentary exposure to it might be a fatal shock to her system. Before she awakened, he had to cast a spell prohibiting either of them from speaking Armand's name. Such a spell, however, would require powerful magic, and the only way he could achieve such power was through the crystal.

There was only one thing he could do, he realized with chagrin. He would have to use Ariel as a channel between him and the crystal.

Lucien immediately balked at the idea, because if he used her as a channel he wouldn't be able to keep them as separate entities. Though Ariel wouldn't physically move, she would see everything he saw, do everything he did. In her mind's eye, this would be her experience, and he had to be able to control her emotions. If she panicked and released the crystal in the middle of a spell, it could have serious repercussions. The only way he could be sure that wouldn't happen was to be so intimately connected with Ariel that he felt what she felt at the very moment she felt it. The trouble with such emotional intimacy was that it would bind them together so thoroughly that he might be joined to Ariel for the rest of his life. If that happened, he would never be able to mate with a witch, and since he would never choose to mate with a mortal, he wouldn't be able to father a child. For all intents and purposes, his life would be over.

Could he take such a gamble? Did he *want* to take such a gamble?

He knew he didn't really have a choice. He was morally compelled to protect the coven, even at the risk of condemning himself to a life alone.

With a resolved sigh, he went to the room where Ariel slept. Sitting beside her on the bed, he placed her hand over the crystal and covered it with his hand. Then he meshed with her mind. When they were fused, he made the crystal the center of their focus, inserting the command that she couldn't release it until he told her she could. Then he left her side to go to the penta-gram, knowing that in Ariel's mind, she was the one making this journey.

Chapter Eight

Was it a vision, or a waking dream?
Fled is that music:—Do I wake or sleep?
                    —John Keats, *Ode to a Nightingale*, st. 8

ARIEL felt weightless, as incorporeal as a ghost.
Even her mind had that hazy mist of unreality as
she walked down a long, dark hallway. When she entered a large room with a huge stone fireplace, panic
began to chatter at the back of her brain. She had to get
away from this place!

*It's all right. There's nothing here that can harm
you.*

The inner voice was so calm, so reassuring, that she
walked farther into the room, inexplicably drawn to the
curious collection of paraphernalia lying on the floor.
Without knowing why she did it, she picked up a fat,
squat candle and blew on the wick, which immediately
burst into flame.

Again she became uneasy, but again that inner voice
whispered, *It's all right. You're safe here. Nothing can
harm you. You're safe.*

Over the next several minutes, she performed strange
ritual motions, as if she'd done them all her life. First she
placed the candle at the top of a five-pointed star, and
then she lit four more candles and placed them on the remaining points. When that was done, she sat cross-legged
in the middle of the star and opened half a dozen jars, re-
moving a pinch of dried plant matter from each and dropping it into a blackened metal bowl.

After putting the lids back on the jars, she blew into

the bowl. A small puff of black smoke rose from it, and a moment later a slim column of fire shot toward the ceiling.

Ariel shrieked in surprise and fear, but even as she considered running from the fire, the voice whispered, *It won't hurt you. See?*

Before she realized what she was doing, she extended her hand into the flame. It curled around her flesh and danced through her fingers, but it didn't burn. Indeed, it wasn't even warm. Pulling her hand out, she stared at the flame in mesmerized fascination and began to intone words she didn't understand.

She had no idea how long she chanted, but suddenly she felt constrained to pick up a gold pen lying at her feet. The moment she lifted it a tiny shock of recognition raced through her, and she gasped when Armand's image appeared in the flame.

Bewildered, she watched Armand walking through Sanctuary. She saw him stop and speak congenially with several people, and she became uneasy when Galen approached him. But Armand didn't seem upset. He was smiling jovially.

Suddenly the image shimmered, and Armand was no longer in the town. Now he was skulking through the woods. He kept bending and making marks at the base of tree trunks until he came to a small clearing. Crouching behind some bushes, he watched a group of children, his expression one of frustration.

Again the image shimmered, and Armand was standing inside this very room, engaged in passionate conversation with a man so visually striking that Ariel couldn't stop staring at him. He wasn't by any means handsome. He had shoulder-length dark-brown hair, a hooked nose, and fanatically glittering dark eyes. Armand's expression was serious, and he was frowning, as though he was worried.

The image shimmered still again. Now Armand was dressed in black and slipping a flashlight into his pocket. Suddenly he removed his pen and laid it on the table between the two chairs. Then he slipped out into the night, a look of avid excitement on his face.

"No!" Ariel cried out frantically when the flame suddenly died. "Come back! Come back!"

It's okay, the voice crooned, but Ariel shook her head in frenzied denial. It wasn't okay. She'd felt the evil waiting for Armand, and he had blithely walked into its clutches.

Calm down! the voice urgently commanded. *You must calm down!*

But she wouldn't—*couldn't*—listen to the voice. She had to find Armand. He was in terrible danger! She had to get to him before it was too late! She had to save him! She had to . . .

Suddenly, the sound that had assaulted her earlier was again screeching in her ears. It was so excruciating she wanted to tear at her hair, but she couldn't make her arms move. Terror tangled with the pain. What was wrong with her? Why couldn't she move?

The pain that hit Ariel was so sudden, so crippling, that it momentarily incapacitated Lucien. As soon as he fought his way out of it he severed the link between them. Her extreme emotional distress had reactivated her memory of Galen's spell.

Jumping to his feet, he ran down the hallway to her room. *Damn!* he should have known better than to use her as a channel, but he'd been so sure that as long as he was fused with her, he could control her emotions. Now he realized he had underestimated her spiritual link with Armand. She had sensed evil waiting for him as he stepped into the night, and her love for him was so powerful that she managed to break Lucien's hold over her.

What he saw when he burst into the room was worse than he had imagined. Her eyes were closed tightly and her face was marble-white. Her body was rigid and she was breathing stridently. As he rushed to the bed, he allowed his mind to brush against hers. She was on the verge of a seizure, and he didn't know what in hell he was going to do. He could stop a spell, but he couldn't stop a memory.

He muttered a violent curse. Why hadn't he thought to cast a spell that would make her forget Galen's?

Because he'd been in such a hurry to find out what he could from the pen that he hadn't considered a mortal's propensity for reverting to the past. They seemed to have an almost morbid fascination with memories, sometimes using them to make themselves feel better and other times exploiting them in order to torture themselves.

Lucien recognized that here. Ariel, realizing her twin was walking into danger, had panicked. Unable to help him, she'd chosen to punish herself by regressing to the horror that she herself had faced here.

She was still clutching the crystal, and Lucien sat on the bed, wrapped his hand over hers, and ordered, "Open your eyes, Ariel. You *must* obey me. Open your eyes, and open them now!"

Her eyelids fluttered and then slowly raised. He'd hoped that by getting her to focus on him, she would come out of the memory. But the dazed, empty look in her eyes told him she hadn't. He'd never felt so powerless. There had to be a way to reach her, but, dammit, how?

On pure instinct he kissed her while projecting the memory of their dream lovemaking into her mind. For a moment, nothing happened. Then, with a groan, she wrapped her arms around his neck and arched up against him. Lucien again let his mind brush hers. She had finally released the memory of Galen's spell, and as she fixated on their dream lovemaking, he was stunned by the intense passion gathering inside her. It was as if all her emotions had gone rampant and were coalescing into one—unadulterated lust.

When she started tugging frantically at his shirt, he caught her hands and pinned them above her head. There was no way he was going to make love to her, and since she was in charge of the crystal, he wasn't about to indulge in a lovemaking fantasy either. If he ever let her control him with the crystal, he would no longer be able to avoid her questions or hedge his answers. If she asked him something, he would be compelled to tell her the truth. He could never place that kind of trust in a mortal, because for every truth he gave her, he would be surrendering a piece of his soul to her. The only person to whom a warlock surrendered his soul was his mate, and regardless of what happened between him and Ariel, he would never mate with her. *Never!*

His resolve began to crumble, however, when she gazed up at him in tearful appeal and plaintively whispered, "Lucien, please help me. You have to make it go away."

Lucien didn't need to ask what "it" was, because he could feel the intensity of the passion coursing through her, and he felt torn. If there hadn't been tears in her eyes, he might have been able to walk away from her. But there *were* tears in her eyes, and that made her all too vulnerable. Overwhelming protectiveness surged through him, and he knew he couldn't let her suffer like this.

But you can't give her that kind of power over you! Even as he argued with himself, he was lowering his

lips to hers. The moment their mouths joined, he
thought, *Hold the crystal, Ariel, and show me what you
want.*

Ariel had been kissed many times, but never before
had a kiss thrilled her the way Lucien's did. As he
came over her, sank against her, his tongue flicked
across her lips, seeking entrance into her mouth. She
eagerly granted it, and he sought her tongue and engaged it in a sensual duel that had her clinging to him
with a consuming need that was as frightening as it
was exciting.

"Oh, God, Lucien!" she gasped, pulling away from
the kiss and again reaching frantically for his shirt. She
wanted him so badly that she'd rip his clothes off if
she had to.

He caught her hands and wrapped them around the
crystal. Resting his own hand over hers, he resumed
kissing her, plunging his tongue into her mouth. Now
she was no longer experiencing her passion, but his.
She felt the softness of her mouth as he explored it—
the excitement of her tongue thrusting and parrying
with his. When he rocked his hips against hers, she felt
her heat send a rush of hot pleasure into his loins until
he was so hard she groaned with his need.

"Lucien, please!" she gasped, jerking her hands
from the crystal and pushing at his shoulders.

What do you want, Ariel?

"You!" she cried. "You! You!!!"

His eyes glowing, he straddled her hips and raised to
his knees, stripping off his shirt. Ariel flicked her
tongue across her lips as she reached up to caress his
chest, reveling in the feel of the crisp, dark hair and the
sensual tightening of his pectoral muscles at her touch.
Slowly, tauntingly, she trailed a finger down the narrow ridge of hair that disappeared into the waistband

of his jeans, and he sucked in a harsh breath as she teasingly played with the snap.

"Do you really want me, Lucien?" she asked throatily, as she popped open the snap and then trailed her hand over the denim covering the hard bulge of his erection.

He didn't answer, but the hot glitter in his eyes told her everything she needed to know. Boldly, she unzipped his pants and slid her hand inside, touching him through the fabric of his shorts. His penis quivered at her touch and, though it seemed impossible, grew even harder.

She glanced up at him and ordered, "Undress for me, Lucien. I want to see how much you want me."

One corner of his lips lifted sardonically as he climbed off the bed. Ariel watched him as he hooked his thumbs beneath both his jeans and shorts and stripped them off in one smooth motion.

"God, you're beautiful," she murmured, shifting to a kneeling position on the edge of the bed. She ran her hands over his shoulders and down his chest, delighting in the different textures of him.

As her hands moved lower, caressing his hard, flat stomach, he sucked in another breath. When she caressed the silken length of his penis, his entire body stiffened and then began to tremble.

Desire arced through Ariel, and as she continued to stroke him, she stared at his face in fascination. The incandescence of his eyes was so brilliant it was almost blinding, and she felt as if she were being sucked into their depths.

She forcefully pulled herself away from his spellbinding gaze and lay back on the bed, commanding, "Now, Lucien, undress me."

He immediately climbed onto the bed. Straddling her hips again, he unbuttoned her blouse, popped open the front clasp of her bra, and brushed the sexy red lace away from her breasts.

This time it was Ariel who sucked in a harsh breath as he gently scored his nails across her nipples, bringing them to aching peaks.

"Oh, Lucien!" she gasped, burying her hands in his long hair when he lowered his head and drew one nipple into his mouth while teasing at the other with his fingers.

Over the next several minutes, he disrobed her slowly, exploring each inch of flesh he exposed with his mouth and his fingers, until she was writhing beneath him.

When he finally had her as naked as he was, he kissed the top of her foot and began trailing kisses up her leg. As he reached her inner thigh, she again tangled her hands in his hair, and she cried out in pleasure when he settled his mouth against her heat.

His tongue flicked against and circled her clitoris. Ariel had never known such sweet torment, and she exulted in the deluge of passion that swept her toward climax.

Just before she reached the peak, he suddenly pulled away. She cried out in dismay and then sighed in relief when he settled between her thighs and surged into her. The pace he set was frantic and sent her careening toward climax. When it hit, it was so powerful that she felt as if she'd shattered into a million pieces, and she clung to Lucien weakly as he shuddered with his own release.

Exhaustion overcame her, and as she closed her eyes, she heard Lucien whisper, "Sleep now, Ariel, so you can heal. Sleep and heal."

When Lucien rose off the bed and stared down at Ariel's sleeping face, urgent desire surged through him at the memory of the fantasy they'd just shared. He wanted to awaken her and repeat every moment of that dream in reality.

That shook him to the core, because he had never before wanted to trade fantasy for reality. That he did now forced him to acknowledge that by giving her control of the crystal and letting her dictate what happened between them, he had allowed their relationship to change. It was no longer just warlock and mortal. And he wasn't ready to define exactly what it was. So he ignored it and set about undressing her, knowing she'd sleep better without the encumbrance of her clothes.

After he'd stripped her down to her sexy red lingerie, he covered her with the sheet and retreated hastily. The farther away he was from her, the better the chance that he would be able to avoid temptation.

He headed back to the pentagram. The magic candles were still burning, and he settled down to meditate on what he'd learned from Armand's pen.

Three of the scenes were easy to interpret. The first, where Armand had been meeting with people, had simply been one of his explorations of Sanctuary. The second had obviously been his success in locating the crystal cave. Lucien had understood Armand's need for something tangible that would verify Lucien's claims of witchcraft, so he'd purposely told him about the cave, knowing Armand would seek it out. The fourth and final scene was rather vague, but he figured it was most likely the last time Armand had been in the house.

It was the third scene that Lucien focused on, because it was the one that had him worried. He hadn't recognized the warlock who had been talking to Armand, and the only way the warlock could have entered the house was by invitation. Since Lucien had impressed upon Armand how dangerous such an invitation would be, he could think of only three reasons that Armand would have violated the rule.

The first was that Armand had felt he could trust the warlock. Lucien didn't put much faith in that theory. Armand was an investigative journalist, and as such, he was naturally distrustful. It was one of the reasons Lucien had chosen him to infiltrate the coven. Distrust spawned caution, and caution had been essential to his plan.

The second option was that the warlock had tricked Armand. That didn't sit any better with Lucien. Again, because he was distrustful, Armand would not have been easily tricked.

The third reason was the one that, quite frankly, frightened Lucien. And that was that the warlock had cast a spell over Armand. Since Armand had already been spellbound by Lucien, it would have taken great power to invoke another spell over him. Galen might have been able to do it. He did, after all, have the entire coven to draw upon for help. But if he had evoked that much power, he would have come to Armand himself, rather than sending another in his place.

No, if a spell had been used, then the warlock would have had to cast it, and there were only two ways he could have that much power. He would have to be an emissary from the council of high priests, or he would have to be practicing the Old Ways. Both options meant unmitigated disaster for the coven.

Lucien raked a hand through his hair in frustration. Who was the unknown warlock, and why had he been with Armand? Was he the warlock Galen feared? And if he was, was he a council representative seeking proof that Galen was involved with the Old Ways, or was he another rogue warlock? Finally, was he,

Lucien, too late to save the coven or, more important, was he *strong* enough to save it if he wasn't too late?

Recognizing that only time would give him the answers, he forced his frustration to the back of his mind and conjured up a spell that would make Ariel's memory of Galen's cacophony spell, as well as her participation in the psychometry of Armand's pen, vague. He would have preferred to wipe out both memories altogether, but to do that he'd have to use Ariel as a channel again. After what had happened to her the last time he simply couldn't take the risk.

When he was through, he cleared the pentagram. After he put everything away, he returned Armand's pen to the trunk. Then he unloaded the car. He put Ariel's luggage in her room, carried the groceries to the kitchen, and decided to wait there for Omen. Maybe she would come up with something that would give him some answers.

It was nearly dawn when Omen returned, and she did not bring good news. Indeed, she didn't bring any news, because the entire coven—including familiars— seemed averse to even thinking about Galen. She also hadn't picked up anything about the unknown warlock.

As Lucien stood at the back door and watched the sunrise, he again cursed the fact that he hadn't retrieved his crystal from Ariel. Though it was doubtful that it would help him learn anything specific, it might give him a good sense of the emotional state of the coven. And if he could get a grasp on that, he might have an idea of what he was facing.

As soon as light filled the sky, he headed for the stove. He sensed Ariel's moving toward wakefulness, and he knew that when she awakened, she'd be disoriented from the sleeping potion. She'd also probably have some minor physical side effects from Galen's spell. He would brew her some tea that would help her reorient herself as well as ease any discomfort that might be plaguing her. Then as soon as she was alert enough to understand what he was saying, he'd ask her for the crystal.

Ariel opened her eyes to mottled sunlight splashed across an unfamiliar stone and wood-beamed ceiling. Blinking groggily, she tried to figure out where she was, but her brain was too muddled to give her an answer. She tried to sit up, but her head began to pound and spin and she was hit by a wave of nausea.

Collapsing back against the pillows, she closed her eyes and massaged her temples. The last time she'd felt like this was when she and Jean had had too much champagne while celebrating the opening of their business.

"Drink this and you'll feel better."

Her eyes flew open, and as she stared up into Lucien's perpetually scowling face, a memory rushed back like a flood tide. It was a very vivid recollection of them making love.

Heedless of her aching head, she bolted upright, heat burning her cheeks. *Dear God, they hadn't really made love, had they?*

As he regarded her, something dark, almost sexual, flared in Lucien's eyes, causing an apprehensive shiver to crawl up her spine. Then his gaze flicked down her body disparagingly as he drawled, "If I were you, Ariel, I'd cover myself."

She glanced down, mortified to see that she was wearing nothing but her lacy red underwear. With a gasp, she jerked the sheet up to her neck and regarded him in horror. *Had they made love?*

No. It *had* to have been a dream, she quickly reassured herself. After all, she was wearing her underwear. If they'd really made love, she would be naked.

What makes you so sure about that? an inner voice nagged. *He could have simply put your underwear back on so you'd think it was all a dream.*

It was a possibility too disturbing to consider, so she pushed it aside and glared at him accusingly. "You undressed me!"

He arched a brow. "You weren't in any condition to undress yourself. And don't worry. I'm not interested in what you've got." Extending the mug, he reiterated, "Drink this."

Suddenly she recalled his pouring something into her mouth last night, and she eyed the mug distrustfully. "What is it?"

"It's an herbal tea." When she didn't accept the mug, he released an impatient sigh. "What's the matter, Ariel? Do you think I'm trying to poison you?"

"The possibility has crossed my mind," she replied baldly.

He muttered something that sounded suspiciously rude and took a healthy swallow of the liquid. "See? It's safe."

"Unless you already took an antidote," she pointed out.

A muscle twitched angrily in his jaw, and he plopped the mug down on the bedside table. "Fine. If you want to suffer that's your prerogative." Crossing his arms over his chest, he announced, "I'd like my crystal back."

His request sent Ariel's still befuddled mind reeling back in time. She was standing in the room with the pentagram, and when she touched the crystal, Armand appeared in front of her.

"My brother!" she gasped.

Maintaining her hold on the sheet with one hand, she grasped the crystal with the other. She frowned in dismay when Armand didn't reappear in front of her.

"It wasn't the crystal that summoned his image," Lucien said. "It was his name."

Ariel glanced up at him and shook her head. "No. It happened when I touched the crystal."

"No. It happened when you said his name. It was just coincidence that you touched the crystal at the same time."

"You're trying to trick me," she charged, scooting away from him and clutching the crystal more tightly. "You know it was the crystal, and now you want it back so you can keep me away from my brother."

Irritation flickered across his face. "Ariel, it was not the crystal that summoned his image. It was his name. That's why I cast a spell that won't allow us to speak it." When she regarded him doubtfully, he challenged, "You can think his name whenever you want, but it's impossible for you to say it. Go ahead and try to say his name, Ariel."

"My brother," she said, her brow contracting in confusion. She'd meant to say "Armand." She tried again. "My brother."

"See?" Lucien declared smugly.

"That doesn't prove anything," she argued. "Just because I can't say his name doesn't mean the crystal won't summon him."

"Dammit, Ariel! The crystal doesn't have a blessed thing to do with your brother!"

"Well, if that's true, then why do you want it back so badly?" The ferocious look he gave her would normally have had her cowering, but she refused to be intimidated by Lucien. Regardless of what he said, she was sure the crystal was a link to Armand. Glaring right back at him, she said, "I'm waiting for your answer."

He clenched and unclenched his hands at his sides, and the crystal began to grow warm in her hand. Ariel had had enough experience with the phenomenon to know it meant he was losing his temper.

"Ariel, I want the crystal," he said in a voice so impassive it was deadly.

"Why do you want it?" He didn't answer, but the crystal began to grow hotter, and his eyes began to glow. When she felt a breeze begin to swirl around her, she gulped but held her ground, insisting, "Why, Lucien?"

"Because I can't function at full capacity without it," he bit out furiously. "Now give me the crystal!"

His response was so unexpected that she frowned at him, perplexed. "What do you mean you can't function at full capacity without it?"

His eyes became incandescent, the crystal took on a rosy hue, and the breeze became stronger. His voice held a razor edge as he said, "Ariel, I want the crystal, and I want it now."

"And I want an answer," she replied, knowing that pushing him was about as sane as playing Russian roulette. However, instinct told her it was important that she pursue this conversation. "Why do you need the crystal to function at full capacity?"

"Because I'm a half-breed!" he roared as the crystal flared to a brilliant crimson and the breeze turned into a howling wind.

"A half-breed?" she echoed, nonplussed. "What does that mean?"

His expression was livid, and his mouth opened and closed three times before he finally spat out, "My mother was a mortal."

Ariel's jaw dropped in shock, and Lucien spun on his heel and stormed out of the room, slamming the door behind him. The moment he left, the wind stopped, but the crystal was still crimson.

"A mortal?" Ariel murmured with a dumbfounded shake of her head. "I don't believe it."

But it had to be true. Why else would he be so angry? Oddly enough, his revelation struck a sympathetic chord inside her. Considering his antipathy toward mortals, she suspected that Lucien had been an outcast in the coven long before he was officially declared one.

She considered going after him and apologizing, but the crystal's enduring red sheen made her reconsider. He was too angry, and she understood that even when his ire had cooled, it would be a subject best left alone.

But she didn't know if she'd be able to leave it alone. Despite Lucien's disclaimer, she still felt the crystal was a connection to Armand. Until she was convinced otherwise, she was not about to give it back to him, and she knew that that was going to make Lucien mad as hell.

As she climbed out of bed and went to her suitcase, she couldn't help wondering why Lucien hadn't taken the crystal from her while she was asleep. For that matter, why hadn't he taken it just now?

It was a puzzling question, but her mind was still too foggy to even attempt to figure it out. Instead, she pulled her robe out of the suitcase and pulled it on. Then she gathered a clean set of clothing and went in search of a bathroom, hoping that a hot bath would clear her mind enough that she could face Lucien's wrath.

Chapter Nine

By the pricking of my thumbs,
Something wicked this way comes.
Open, locks,
Whoever knocks!
　　　—William Shakespeare, *Macbeth* 4.1.44

LUCIEN was furious when he slammed Ariel's bedroom door behind him, but as he picked up on her thoughts, he became so livid that a wind swirled violently around him, rattling the nearby doors and windows. She—a mortal—was feeling sorry for him! He immediately broke off his connection with her mind before he lost all control.

It's your own fault, his conscience chided as he stalked toward the kitchen. *You should have never given her the crystal, but once you did you should never have let her control you with it. You knew how dangerous it was, that you'd have to truthfully answer any questions she asked once you let her control you.*

Yes, he had understood the repercussions. But who would have believed that one of the first questions out of her mouth would make him reveal the circumstances of his birth!

By the time he reached the kitchen he managed to regain enough self-control that the wind died, but he was still mad enough to want to tear the room apart. That, however, would be wanton destruction and unbecoming to a warlock, and despite the mortal blood running through his veins, he was first and foremost a warlock.

So instead of wreaking havoc in the kitchen, he poured himself a mug of coffee and sat at the table to analyze the situation. It was true that without the crystal he was handicapped, but he was far from powerless. The real problem was Ariel, he admitted. The longer she was in control of the crystal, the more questions she'd ask. Considering that in less than ten minutes she managed to learn the facts of his birth, it stood to reason that it wouldn't take long before she knew him as intimately as he knew himself. Once that happened, she would be in full possession of his soul and it would be the end for him.

His musing was interrupted by the scent of a delicate perfume, and he glanced up to see Ariel standing in the archway.

Automatically, his gaze flicked over her. She was wearing a simple cotton blouse and a pair of loose-fitting slacks. The outfit gave her a straitlaced look, but he'd become acquainted with both her risqué bedroom and her sexy underwear and he knew there was nothing straitlaced about her. Why did she hide her passion, deny it? He knew instinctively that that was what she was doing. He also knew it was a question that he was better off not even thinking about.

He returned his attention to her face. She was staring at him with acute anxiety, but when he connected with her mind he learned that she'd vowed to fight him tooth and nail to maintain her link with Armand. That frustrated him, but he also couldn't help admiring her determination. She was proving to be an intriguing paradox of fear and courage.

Lifting his coffee mug, he took a sip before drawling, "There's coffee on the stove and juice in the refrigerator. Feel free to help yourself, but don't forget, I may have poisoned them—after taking an antidote, of course."

Ariel felt heat flare into her cheeks at Lucien's gibe, and that irritated her. She was willing to concede she may have overreacted about the tea, but she did remember his giving her something last night. After that, everything was a blur of strange images that she couldn't pull into focus, let alone any cohesive order.

Not everything is a blur, an inner voice taunted as she crossed to the stove.

They had not made love! she told herself firmly. Not even Lucien would be so despicable as to make love to her and then try to make it look as if it hadn't happened. It was just a dream, and she refused to believe otherwise.

Half a dozen coffee mugs were stacked on the counter. She filled one and, turning toward Lucien, took a sip of coffee. When she did, an expression flickered across his face that she couldn't really define, but it looked suspiciously like relief. It suddenly occurred to her that when she accused him of trying to poison her, she might have hurt his feelings.

She found the concept that Lucien had tender feelings hard to swallow. He seemed to have only one persona—menacing. Indeed, the only time she wasn't afraid of him was in her dreams. In fact, perhaps that was why she was having them. Maybe the only way she could deal with the reality of him was to humanize him on a subconscious level.

Good heavens, I'm doing the same type of amateur psychoanalyzing that Jean would do! she thought in disgust.

Walking to the table, she sat across from Lucien. He was staring at her through hooded eyes, and she barely managed to refrain from squirming beneath his scrutiny. She knew he was trying to intimidate her, and to her chagrin, he was doing a damn good job of it.

Deciding that her best defense would be a direct offense, she asked, "Is something on your mind, Lucien?"

"You know what's on my mind," he answered impassively.

"I'm not giving you the crystal."

"It doesn't connect you with your brother."

She shrugged. "Maybe not. All I know is that when I touched it, I saw him."

"You saw him because you said his name."

"I only have your word on that, and until I can verify it, I'm not giving up the crystal," she declared with a determined lift of her chin.

He raised an eyebrow. "And how do you intend to verify it? Ask Galen if he cast a spell that goes into effect when you say your brother's name?"

"Of course not," she said impatiently.

"Well, at least you have some sense," he muttered derisively.

Ariel took the taunt in the spirit it was given. He was frustrated and angry, and in his place, she'd have felt the same way, particularly if what he said about the crystal was true.

"Will it, um, hurt you not to have the crystal?" she asked.

"If you're asking if it will cause me physical distress, no."

"But it does . . . limit you not to have it?"

"Yes."

"If the crystal is so important to you, why didn't you just take it from me while I was asleep?"

A muscle jerked in his jaw, and she sensed he didn't want to answer, but then he said, "I gave it to you, so you must give it back."

Ariel was admittedly surprised by his response. "And what would happen if you just took it?"

"It would lose its power."

"Oh." Not knowing what else to say, she took another sip of coffee. Several tension-filled seconds passed before she finally found the nerve to ask, "What happened last night?"

He leaned back in his chair and hooked one arm over the back. "If you want me to answer that, you'll have to be more specific."

"I can't be more specific," she confessed, raking a hand through her hair. "I remember arriving at the house. I remember meeting a girl and her dog outside. I remember touching the crystal and seeing that horrible image of my brother, and then my mind was muddled until . . . morning," she lied, not about to confess her erotic dream. "I want to know what happened after I saw my brother."

A corner of Lucien's lips lifted sardonically, as though he knew she was lying. "When you said his name, his image appeared and Galen's spell went into effect. It would have destroyed your mind if . . ."

"If?" Ariel encouraged when he abruptly stopped speaking.

His brows drew together in a dark frown, but his voice was flat when he said, "If you hadn't touched the crystal and summoned me."

Instinctively Ariel lifted her hand to where the crystal rested beneath her shirt. As she touched it, images solidified in her mind. She was lying on the floor, and she had to struggle to touch the crystal. But the moment she did, Lucien burst into the house and . . .

"Dammit, Ariel, leave the memory alone!" Lucien ordered harshly.

She jerked her head up to look at him, and as their gazes clashed, she gulped at the feral gleam in his eyes and the angry set of his jaw.

But as frightening as his expression was, she regarded him in bemusement. "You saved me."

"Of course I saved you," he muttered. "I sure as hell didn't want a mortal dying in my house."

Ariel blinked at him in surprise. "This is your house?"

"It is—or was—my family home," he conceded grudgingly. "But that doesn't have anything to do with last night."

It was obvious that he didn't want to talk about the house, which aroused Ariel's curiosity. She wanted to pursue the subject, but decided that now was not the time.

"Okay, you saved me, and then what happened?"

"I put you to bed and gave you a sleeping potion so you could sleep and heal."

At his words, another memory flashed through Ariel's mind, and she felt the color draining from her face. It was at the end of the dream where she and Lucien had made love, and she heard him whisper, "Sleep now, Ariel, so you can heal. Sleep and heal."

Heaven help her, they had made love!

No! It was a dream!

But what if it wasn't a dream? What if . . .

She gave a sharp shake of her head, refusing to let her mind go down that path. He had just said he gave her a sleeping potion, which meant she'd been drugged. He'd probably said the words when he gave her the potion, and she'd just gotten them mixed up with her fantasy.

Sitting back in her chair, she stared at Lucien. There was a question she had to ask him about Armand, but she had been avoiding it, because she feared the answer. She knew, however, that she couldn't evade it any longer. She had to know the truth.

Drawing in a fortifying breath, she asked, "The image of my brother, was it real?"

"I don't know," Lucien answered, lifting his arm

from the back of the chair and shifting so he could prop his forearms on the table. He cradled his coffee mug between his hands before elaborating. "My instincts say it was not a true reflection of his physical condition, but an image that Galen conjured up so you'd be frightened."

"But the image could be true?"

Lucien looked at her, his expression grave, "Let's pray it isn't."

Ariel was severely rattled by his response. "Do warlocks pray?" she asked, struggling to maintain control over her emotions. Falling apart wouldn't help Armand. She had to be strong.

"Daily."

Ariel wished she could find solace in that, but she couldn't, because she recalled to *whom* they prayed. "So what do we do now?"

"Galen is focused on you. Wherever you are, that's where he'll be until he can figure out if you're a threat," Lucien stated. "That's why I want you to go into town and play tourist. It will keep Galen occupied while I search for your brother. He has to be somewhere inside the circle. Once we know his location, we'll come up with a plan to rescue him."

"You make it sound easy," Ariel said.

"Believe me, there is nothing easy about this," he replied grimly. "Eventually Galen will become so infuriated because he can't figure out who you are and why you're here that he'll draw on the power of the coven to see if he can break my spell over you. When that happens, we'll be in terrible danger, because he'll realize that I'm your spellbinder. That's why we have to find your brother and get out of the circle as soon as possible. On unconsecrated ground we might have a chance of defeating him, but here . . ."

Ariel shuddered as his voice trailed off. He didn't

have to finish the sentence, because her imagination was doing a great job of finishing it for him. Her cowardice rushed to the surface, telling her that if she had even an iota of common sense, she'd get the hell out of here and find another way to rescue Armand.

"It's too late to run, Ariel," Lucien stated forebodingly. "Now that Galen has met you, he's locked onto your aura and you can't escape him. He'll find you wherever you go, and eventually he'll destroy you. Your only chance for survival is to stay and fight him."

She opened her mouth to ask how she was supposed to fight him, but before she could speak, an eerie, hollow sound echoed through the house.

"What is that?" she gasped, as Omen raced into the room, leaped onto Lucien's lap, and let out a yowl that made every hair on Ariel's body stand on end. Lucien was staring toward the front of the house, his face so empty of expression that he looked lifeless.

His voice was equally devoid of emotion when he announced, "According to Omen, Galen's at the front door."

"Oh, God!" Ariel whispered in horror. "What's he doing here?"

Lucien slowly pivoted his head toward her. "I'd say he's looking for you."

"What am I supposed to do?"

"Answer the door," he suggested.

"And then what?" she asked, baffled by his relaxed manner.

He had just spent the past few days telling her how evil Galen was, and now, when the man—no, *the warlock from Hell*—was knocking at the door, he was acting as if nothing was wrong.

He shrugged. "As long as you don't invite him in, it doesn't matter what you do."

"And if he insists on coming in?"

"He won't."

"What makes you so sure of that?"

"Because I'm a warlock and I know the rules of the game," he answered. "Now, go answer the door. Just turn left in the hallway and it will lead you right to it."

As Ariel entered the gloomy hallway, that hollow sound echoed through the house again, causing her to shiver. She took in the barren stone walls and the dim lighting and decided that her first impression of the house hadn't been wrong. This place was nothing less than creepy.

When she entered the room with the pentagram, she was hit with a blur of images that were as confusing as they were disquieting. If there hadn't been a third knock on the door at that very moment, she'd have hightailed it out of there.

Instead, she hurried to the door and cracked it open. Peering out, she noted that Lucien's grumpy cat had been right. Galen Morgan was standing on the stoop, looking even more handsome than he had yesterday. He was also holding a huge bouquet of red roses wrapped in green tissue paper.

"Good morning," he said, smiling. "I hope I'm not interrupting anything."

"No, I was, uh, just getting ready to leave."

"Well, I'm glad I caught you." He extended the roses.

"These are for you."

Reluctantly, Ariel opened the door wider. "They're very beautiful, Mr. Morgan, but I'm afraid I can't accept them."

"Ariel, you're suppose to call me Galen, and of course you can accept them. They're just my way of saying welcome to the neighborhood, and if you refuse them, I'll be heartbroken. You don't want to break my heart, do you?"

He gave her such a charming and patently false look of despair that an involuntary smile tugged at Ariel's lips. "Well, if it means that much to you, I suppose I could accept the roses."

No! Lucien's voice roared inside her head with such force that she took a step back. She shook her head, feeling dazed. She'd come to accept that Lucien frequently read her mind, but to have him suddenly talking inside her head was damned unnerving.

"Ariel, are you all right?" Galen asked in concern.

"Uh, yeah," she mumbled, raking a hand through her hair.

"You're sure?"

"Positive," she reassured, forcing a smile to her lips.

"Okay," he said, but he didn't look convinced. He was staring at her so intently that when he extended the roses again, she automatically took them so they could serve as a screen to cover her confusion.

"They really are beautiful. Thank you."

"You're welcome. I'm sorry they're not in a vase, but it seems we have an unexpected shortage of vases in town."

"That's okay. I'm sure there's a vase around here somewhere."

He nodded as he searched her face, his brow creased in a worried frown. "You look tired. Didn't you sleep well?"

Ariel shrugged uncomfortably. "You know how it is. It's hard to get used to a strange bed. It'll take me a few days to get adjusted."

He nodded again, but didn't say anything. Ariel realized he was waiting for her to invite him in and tried to think of a way to dismiss him without insulting him. After all, Lucien had said he wanted her to keep Galen occupied while he searched for Armand. That would be hard to do if Galen was mad at her.

"Look, Galen . . ."

"Ariel, I . . ." he said at the same time.

They both stopped, and he smiled apologetically. "I'm sorry. You go first."

"I was just going to say that I have an appointment to keep, so I'm going to have to leave right away."

"I understand, and I'll get out of your hair. I just wanted to say that I really enjoyed visiting with you yesterday, and I wondered if you'd have dinner with me tonight."

Ariel blinked when another emphatic *No!* flashed through her mind. This time it wasn't quite so startling, and she recovered more quickly. "Dinner? Gosh, Galen, I don't know what my schedule is going to be like and . . ."

"Well, if dinner is bad for you," he broke in quickly, "maybe we could have lunch together."

"Lunch?" she repeated hesitantly, waiting to see what Lucien had to say about that. When she received nothing from him, she said, "I think I can swing lunch. What time's best for you?"

"Whenever you're free. Just come to the shop. I'll be waiting."

"Okay," she agreed as he went down the steps. When he stopped at the bottom and glanced back at her, she said, "Thanks again for the roses."

"You're welcome. I'll see you later."

Ariel waited until he was driving away before she closed the door, and she let out a startled cry when Lucien harshly ordered behind her, "Drop the flowers, Ariel, and drop them now!"

"Don't you ever sneak up on me like that again! You scared the daylights out of me!" she yelled, clapping her hand over her heart as she spun around to see him striding purposefully toward her.

"Drop the flowers!" he repeated ominously, ignoring her complaint.

His eyes were beginning to glow, so she threw the roses to the floor, snapping, "There. Are you satisfied?"

He grunted something, but she didn't hear what it was and suspected it was just as well she hadn't. When he reached her side, he grabbed her arm and began hauling her down the hallway at such a swift pace that she had to run to keep up with him.

A moment later he propelled her into the minuscule bathroom where she'd bathed earlier and shoved her up against the sink. He banged her hip in transit, but she realized he wasn't purposely being rough with her. It was just that the bathroom was too small to accommodate two people.

After flipping the overhead light on, he grabbed her hands and began examining them front and back as he ground out, "Did they prick you?"

"What are you talking about?"

"The roses," he snarled. "Did they prick you?"

"No."

"Are you sure?"

"Of course I'm sure."

"Wash your hands."

"What?"

"Dammit, Ariel, you are *not* deaf!" he bellowed. "Now do as I say!"

It was obvious that Lucien felt there was something wrong with the roses, and a shiver of fear rippled down her spine as she turned to the sink. While washing her hands, a wave of panic began to build inside her. If she couldn't trust something as ordinary as a bouquet of roses, how was she supposed to deal with these people?

She drew in a deep breath. Panicking wasn't going to solve anything, and she could deal with these people. She had to believe that, because the alternative was untenable.

When she finally managed to regain control, she grabbed a hand towel off the rack and turned to face Lucien. "Would you mind telling me what that was all about?"

Instead of answering, he demanded, "Why did you ignore me?"

"I don't know what you're talking about."

"The hell you don't. I *ordered* you not to take the roses, so why did you take them?"

It was the condescending way in which he said the word "ordered" that lit Ariel's temper. She knew she was being foolish. He was already angry with her. Arguing with him would only make matters worse, but after recalling how he'd suddenly been speaking in her head, she couldn't help herself. It was bad enough that he could read her mind, but when he started taking it over, it was downright scary. It left her feeling helpless and out of control, and if he took her self-control away from her, she'd have nothing left.

Straightening her spine, she said, "I hate to break this to you, Lucien, but I happen to be a grown woman. I don't take *orders* from anyone, and I particularly don't take them from pompous, overbearing warlocks who invade my privacy by invading my mind!"

She tried to shove past him, but he grabbed her upper arms and jerked her against him. His voice was as soft and sibilant as a whiplash as he rasped, "You came to me and asked me to help you find your brother. Against my better judgment, I agreed to help you. But if you think I'm going to stand by and let you get me killed because you're too damn obstinate to obey me, you'd better think again. This is my game, and you'll play by my rules. If you don't, Galen won't have to worry about you, because I'll take care of you myself. Is that clear?"

Ariel's defiance drained out of her, and she nodded, too frightened to speak. She'd known Lucien was angry, but this was more than anger. It was a rage so deep that it had turned the crystal to ice, chilling her to the bone.

Thankfully, he seemed to accept her nod as agreement, because he released his hold on her arms and said dispassionately, "Wash your hands again and then join me in the kitchen."

With that, he turned and strode away without a backward glance.

Ariel rubbed at the spots on her arms where he had held her, absently acknowledging that though his grip had been like steel, he hadn't hurt her. Ordinarily that would have eased her fear, but in this instance it heightened it. If he could be that profoundly enraged and still maintain enough control not to hurt her, she had no doubt that he could—and would—carry out his threat to harm her if she didn't obey him.

Knowing that if she dwelled on that realization she would fall apart, she forced her mind to go blank, turned back to the sink, and began to wash her hands.

As Lucien knelt on the floor and carefully tossed the thorny roses into a trash can, he recalled a fairy tale his mother had once told him about a princess named Sleeping Beauty, who had been cursed by a jealous fairy. If his memory served him right, on her sixteenth birthday the princess had pricked her thumb on a spin-

dle and fallen into a deep sleep. She finally awoke
when a prince kissed her.

Even as a small child, Lucien had recognized the
foolishness of the tale. In the first place, everyone
knew there were no such things as fairies. They also
knew that no curse could be lifted by a kiss. However,
his mother had seemed so enchanted by the story that
he hadn't had the heart to tell her the facts of life.

"And what curse did you have in store for Ariel
when she pricked her thumb, Galen?" he murmured as
he lifted the final rose and eyed it thoughtfully.

Whatever it was, he knew it wouldn't have been
something as simple as having Ariel fall into a deep
sleep. More likely, it would have been an eternal nightmare.

Tossing the last rose into the container, he sat back
on his heels and let his mind connect with Ariel's. It
was oddly blank, and as he delved deeper, he learned
that he'd frightened her so badly she was refusing to
let herself think.

Sighing heavily, he massaged the bridge of his nose
with his thumb and forefinger. He shouldn't have
scared her like that, but when she defied him, something inside him snapped.

*Admit it. You were scared out of your wits, and that's
why you lost control.*

As much as he wanted to deny it, he had been scared
witless. Galen surely knew that Ariel had activated his
spell last night. He also would have to know that
someone had stopped it. When Lucien had realized
Galen was at the door, the only reason he could think
of to explain such daring was that Galen had figured
out that Lucien was Ariel's spellbinder and had come
to confront him.

Obviously that hadn't been the case, and that made
Lucien even more uneasy. Galen was too smart to take

unnecessary risks, and for him to walk boldly up to the front door meant he was running scared. But from whom? The unknown warlock? That had to be it, because nothing else made sense.

It also placed Ariel at greater risk, because Lucien suspected that Galen thought she was connected to the mystery warlock. If that was true, it was even more critical that she instantly obey any command he gave her.

Unfortunately she was now more afraid of him than she was of Galen, and Lucien recognized the danger in that. Considering both Galen's innate charm and the peculiar workings of the mortal mind, Ariel was liable to persuade herself that Lucien was the real enemy and turn to Galen for protection. To make sure that didn't happen, he was going to have to find a way to undo the damage he'd done when he lost his temper with her.

With another sigh, he stood and carried the trash can to the fireplace. Not knowing what kind of spell Galen had placed on the roses, he decided to wait until after Ariel was gone to burn them.

He put the container on the hearth and headed for the kitchen. Somehow, he had to make Ariel understand the rules of the game. He also had to make sure she understood that she had to be wary of warlocks bearing gifts.

Chapter Ten

Submit to the present evil, lest a greater one befall you.
— Phaedrus, *Fables* bk. 1. fable 2.31

ARIEL felt as crazed as Lady Macbeth. She couldn't stop washing her hands. Recognizing that she was on the edge of hysteria, she forced herself to turn off the water. Then she looked in the mirror, barely recognizing the woman who stared back at her. She was so pallid she looked ghostly, and her eyes had a hunted—or maybe that was a haunted—look. Both words were accurate descriptions of how she felt.

"You have to pull yourself together," she mumbled to the mirror.

Unfortunately that was easier said than done. She could still see Lucien's enraged face and feel the crystal turning ice-cold against her skin. Recalling his threat, she felt gooseflesh spring up on her arms.

This is my game, and you'll play by my rules. If you don't, Galen won't have to worry about you, because I'll take care of you myself. Is that clear?

Ariel didn't think anything had been clearer in her life. She also recognized that to stay here with Lucien was absolute insanity. As soon as she could get her legs to stop shaking she'd get the hell out of here.

But what about Armand?

She closed her eyes, only to see the horrible image of Armand, aged and vacant-eyed, reflected against the backs of her lids. Was it a true image? Lucien didn't seem to think so, but why should she believe him? It was possible that he, not Galen, was the one who had created the image. He had said this was his house. He sent her here alone, and he drugged her after . . .

Damn! she thought in frustration as she opened her eyes. Why couldn't she remember what had happened after she'd seen Armand? Why was everything so hazy? Just what had been in that "sleeping potion" Lucien had given her?

There were too many questions, and only one person had the answers—Lucien Morgret. In the next few minutes she had to decide whether she was going to stay and confront him or run as fast as she could.

"As if I really have a choice, right? There's no way I'm leaving here without my twin, even if it means fighting a horde of warlocks and the Devil himself," she muttered, as she again eyed her reflection. Thankfully, the color was back in her cheeks, and her eyes had returned to normal.

Reaching for the hand towel, she drew in a deep breath and released it slowly. By the time she finished drying her hands, she was ready to face Lucien. She had several questions that needed answering, and the first one was why he had sent Armand to Sanctuary in the first place.

Heading for the kitchen, she decided that this might be Lucien's game, but as far as she was concerned, when he put Armand into the middle of it, he left the rules up for grabs. He might be physically stronger than she was, and he might have super psychic powers, but David had felled the mighty Goliath with a sling-shot and she would find a way to beat Lucien Morgret.

When she reached the kitchen, Lucien was sitting in the same chair he'd been in when Galen had arrived. In front of the place where she'd been sitting was her normal breakfast—a tall glass of orange juice and two pieces of buttered toast. She met his gaze warily. Was this supposed to be the proverbial last meal for the condemned woman?

When he gave her what she assumed was his version of a pleasant smile, she became downright suspicious. In the first place, his features were simply too stark for anything, even a smile, to make him look other than what he was—dangerous and menacing. Second, he'd been too angry with her to have done a complete about-face in such a short time. He was up to something. She just wished she knew what the heck it was.

"Sit down and eat, Ariel, and then we'll talk," he encouraged. "And I promise I haven't done anything to your food. It's as safe as if it had come out of your own refrigerator."

Ariel suddenly recognized that the meal was, in effect, a peace offering, and she felt the residual terror of their encounter fade away. That didn't mean she wasn't still scared of him, and she certainly didn't trust him, but she instinctively knew that at this moment she wasn't in imminent danger from him.

She walked to the table, sat down and forced herself to eat. She wasn't hungry, but since she was getting ready to declare war on a warlock she needed to keep up her strength. Besides, the normalcy of the routine helped to steady her nerves.

After she popped the last bite of toast into her mouth, she washed it down with the remainder of the orange juice. Then she leaned back in her chair and looked at Lucien. His expression and posture were relaxed, but she sensed his underlying tension.

When several seconds passed, it became evident that he wasn't going to be the first to break the silence, so she took the plunge and asked, "Why did you send my brother to Sanctuary?"

He mimicked her by leaning back in his chair. Folding his hands across his stomach, he said, "That isn't the question uppermost in your mind, Ariel. Why don't you ask me what you really want to know?"

"And what is that?"

"If I can truly read your mind."

Ariel frowned, because that was the question, or at least a variation of it, that had been deviling her the most. She'd already accepted that Lucien did read her mind, but did he know *all* her thoughts? The possibility that he might was highly distressing. It made her feel . . . well, violated. It also meant that fighting him would be impossible.

No! she upbraided herself. *Nothing is impossible.*

To Lucien, she parried, "If that was what I was thinking, then you've already answered my question, haven't you?"

"Have I?" he countered.

She regarded him speculatively, and on an inexplicable impulse she raised her hand toward the crystal.

"What in hell are you doing?" he snapped, his eyes fixed on her hand as it hovered above the spot where the crystal lay beneath her blouse.

"Since you're so adept at reading my mind, I shouldn't have to tell you."

His brows drew together in a fierce frown as his gaze shot from her hand to her face. "You can't read my mind by touching the crystal, Ariel."

"And why should I believe that?"

"Because it's the truth."

"Well, I'm sure you won't mind if I prove that to myself."

Before he could object, she dropped her hand to her blouse. Even through the fabric, she could feel a surge of power ripple through the crystal, and then she was hit with a tangle of emotions—anger, frustration, and something similar to fear, though it didn't have a sharp enough edge to be true fear.

She jerked her hand away from the crystal almost as soon as she touched it. The emotions had been so potent that they almost overwhelmed her, and she eyed Lucien warily. She might not be able to read his mind, but she could definitely pick up on his feelings. Right now they were highly volatile.

"Are you satisfied?' he asked in a dangerously low voice.

"For now," she answered. "How often do you read my mind?"

"When it's necessary."

"And how often is it necessary?"

He heaved an impatient sigh. "I'm not reading your thoughts twenty-four hours a day, Ariel. Believe me, I have better things to do than wallow in the convoluted meanderings of a mortal mind. I connect with you when I need to know how you're responding to any given situation, and when you're dealing with Galen our minds automatically connect."

"Are you saying that when I'm with Galen, you know everything we're saying and doing?" When he nodded, she gave a disbelieving shake of her head. "What are you? Some sort of telepathic peeping Tom?"

"What I am is your protector!" he declared irritably.

He was her protector? Personally, she'd rather have a Doberman pinscher. At least you could put a muzzle on it.

Shifting in her chair, she asked, "Why do our minds automatically connect when I'm with Galen?"

He put a hand on the table and drummed his fingers against the wood. "Don't you think we've exhausted this subject?"

"You're evading my question. That tells me we haven't. Why do we automatically connect?"

"It's the only way I can protect you."

"That wasn't what I was asking, and you know it."

"What in hell do you want from me?" he growled as he shot up out of the chair and began to prowl the room with the same agitated manner as a caged tiger.

The crystal began to warm against her skin, and Ariel's survival instincts went on red alert. Though she still wanted to pursue the subject she decided to drop it for now. Instead, she asked again, "Why did you send my brother to Sanctuary?"

Lucien froze at the question. He had managed to deflect it earlier, but now he would not only have to answer it, he'd have to answer it truthfully. Once he did, she would come up with more questions, and by the time her interrogation was over, she'd probably know everything.

Damn, damn, and damn, again! Why had he given her the crystal? If he could just go back to that moment . . .

He stopped himself. There was no sense in indulging in self-recrimination. He couldn't go back to that moment, and even if he could, he wouldn't change what he'd done. Ariel had needed the crystal for emotional support, and without her he wouldn't be back on coven land. In the long run that was what mattered. If they got out of this mess alive, he could simply cast a spell over her that would wipe out her memory.

Except that for every truth you give her, you lose a piece of your soul to her, and the bond is growing stronger by the hour. What will happen to you if you do wipe out her memory? Will it be the same as losing a mate? Will you, in effect, become a widower, destined to spend the remainder of your life suffering from the grief and despair that come with such a loss?

It wasn't a question Lucien could afford to think about, so he sat down at the table and said, "Maybe it's time I told you everything."

That was exactly what Ariel wanted—to know everything. But as she met Lucien's piercing gaze, something told her that the last thing she wanted to hear was the confessions of a warlock who was a shunned outcast.

"Damn. Where should I begin?" Lucien muttered.

"The beginning?" Ariel suggested.

"That's a hell of a long story, because the beginning started more than three hundred years ago."

"I think we have time, Lucien. The only pressing engagement I have is lunch with Galen, and the more I know before I meet him the better off I'll be."

"Knowledge isn't a weapon you can use against Galen. At least, not the type of knowledge I'm going to give you," he stated grimly.

"Any knowledge is better than no knowledge," she pointed out.

He shrugged. "You may be right."

"So let's go back three hundred years. What happened?"

He propped his forearms on the table and rolled his empty coffee mug between his hands. "Actually, we need to go back much farther than that. As I told you yesterday, we can trace our roots to the time of the Druids. We consisted of thirteen covens, and each coven had thirteen family units. Like the Druids, we were the seers and the healers, and the mortals revered us. Then the Romans came and set out to destroy us. That was the beginning of what was to become centuries of persecution. The witch hysteria reached its highest point during the Inquisition, and by the time it was over we were decimated and had gone into permanent hiding.

"At the beginning of the seventeenth century, the council of high priests met," he continued. "Most of them felt that if our race was to survive, we had to stay in hiding. But one of the high priests claimed to have had a vision of the settling of a new land, which would be called the Americas. In this new land there would eventually be thirteen colonies, and freedom of religion would dominate. The mystical meaning of this was obvious—we were thirteen covens, with thirteen family units. Emigrating to a country that would evolve into thirteen colonies could only be a good omen."

He paused to glance up at Ariel. She was staring at him, enthralled. "Go on."

He nodded. "There were, of course, some high priests who were leery of the vision. If this was the answer to our problems, then why had only one of them had it? Literally years of arguments ensued, but then it was learned that the Pilgrims were preparing to set sail for the Americas. It was finally agreed that one family from each coven would emigrate with them. It was determined that if these families could coexist with the Pilgrims for one hundred years, then the remainder of the covens would emigrate to the new land.

"For more than seventy years we resided harmoniously with the settlers, and it looked as if we had finally found a place where we could live in peace and safety. But then the witch hysteria began in Massachusetts. It happened so quickly and unexpectedly that we weren't able to get passage back to Europe where we could rejoin our covens, so we fled to this place and founded Sanctuary."

Ariel gave an amazed shake of her head. "And you've been here ever since?" When he nodded, she asked, "How could you remain in hiding for so long and not be discovered?"

"We're protected by the magic circle. When a mortal enters it, he or she sees and remembers only what we want. For many years, we didn't let mortals remember anything. But at the turn of this century the high priests met and agreed that it was time for us to start integrating with the rest of the world. Mortals no longer believed in us, a fact that we encourage whenever possible, and science was making strides that even our magic couldn't emulate."

"What kinds of strides?" Ariel asked, curious.

"Electricity, running water, and indoor plumbing are the first things to come to mind," Lucien answered. "Even we appreciate such modern wonders. Anyway, the covens around the world opened their doors, so to speak, to tourism. It allows us to earn money so that we can purchase the material things we want or need. It also allows us to intermingle with mortals so we can glean the necessary information we need from their minds in order to conform to their world."

Ariel considered what he'd just told her. It seemed too fantastic to believe, yet, inexplicably, she did believe every word of his story. "So what does all this have to do with my brother?"

Lucien scowled down at his coffee mug. "Again, we need to go back three hundred years. As I said, one family from each coven was selected to emigrate to this country, which, in effect, meant a fourteenth coven was being formed. This new coven needed a high priest, so after the families were selected there was a challenge—a kind of contest—to see which warlock was the most powerful. It turned out that two warlocks, my great-great-grandfather and Galen's great-great-grandfather, were evenly matched.

"Normally, this would have resulted in several more challenges until one was defeated," he explained, "because once a high priest is selected, the position stays within the family as long as there's a son to fill it. But this was supposed to be a temporary coven that would exist only until either the remainder of the covens came to the Americas or we returned to Europe. In either case, the families would return to their original covens. The council decided that since the high priesthood would also be temporary, the emigrating families would be allowed to choose which warlock they wanted to follow rather than waste time on several challenges. The families chose to follow my great-great-grandfather. Needless to say, Galen's great-great-grandfather was not pleased, but since it was only a temporary position, he conceded defeat and vowed his fealty to my family."

Ariel, understanding where the story was headed, said, "Only it didn't turn out to be a temporary position because of the witch-hunts in Massachusetts, which separated you from the rest of the covens, and Galen's family ended up resenting yours."

"You're very astute," Lucien said. "In any case, my father was killed in a rock slide when I was seven, and when my grandfather died three years ago, the high priesthood should have passed on to me. But Galen disputed my right to the position because my mother was a mortal. Since I'm the first and only half-breed in existence, the council of high priests decided that Galen and I should engage in a challenge to determine who was the most powerful."

"And Galen won," Ariel guessed when Lucien, glaring at some unseen spot above her head, fell into silence.

"No. He cheated," Lucien stated tightly as he switched his glare to her. "But I couldn't prove it, so I was faced with the choice of vowing my allegiance to him or becoming a shunned outcast."

"I see," Ariel murmured, mulling over the information. In all honesty, it sounded as if Lucien was suffering from a bad case of sour grapes, but she knew better than to tell him that. "I think I can figure it out from here. You couldn't prove Galen cheated, so you sent my brother here to get the proof for you."

Lucien brushed his hand across his eyes before replying, "No. I had accepted my fate and was willing to live with it. Then, about six months ago I started having a strange dream. Galen was surrounded by a black aura, and I could sense that the coven was in danger. At first I dismissed it as . . . well, as a dream. But it kept recurring, and the sense of danger to the coven kept escalating. We believe in dreams, particularly persisting ones. I finally decided that someone in the coven must be alerting me to the fact that Galen had put the coven in danger, and that someone was asking me for help.

"There was only one way to find out if my premise was right, and that was to send in a spy," he continued. "But the spy had to be someone who knew how to avoid detection. I happened to run across your brother's series on how he'd infiltrated a survivalist group, and I realized he had the type of investigative talents I needed. I approached him and told him about the coven, and that's how he ended up here."

Ariel regarded him in disbelief. "You sent him here because of a *nightmare*?"

"In essence, yes," Lucien agreed.

Ariel continued to stare at him, torn between skepticism and outrage. She knew Armand would never have taken on this investigation if he'd known it was based on nothing more than a dream. That meant that to get him involved, Lucien would have had to lie to him. Even as she reached that conclusion, however, she didn't want to accept it. It would mean that she had placed her trust in a man who couldn't be trusted.

"Did you tell my brother about this dream?"

He glanced guiltily away from her. "No. I only told him about the coven. But believe me, Ariel, I never intended for any harm to come to him. All I wanted was for him to gather enough evidence for me to bring Galen down and give me a chance to come home."

"Oh, come on, Lucien! I'm not stupid," she declared derisively. "You can try to justify your actions from now until doomsday, but the truth is, when you approached my brother, it was with one thought in mind—getting your revenge against Galen for defeating you."

"Ariel, that's not true."

"Isn't it?" she seethed as she surged to her feet, placed her hands on the table and leaned toward him. "I might believe that if you'd told my brother what you just told me. But you led him to believe that he was going to be investigating a Satanic cult that posed a threat to society, not chasing after something that was no more than a figment of your imagination. If he had known that, he'd never have come here in the first place. You *lied* to him!"

"Ariel, you're upset, and . . ."

"You're damn right I'm upset!" she interrupted harshly, slapping a hand on the table for emphasis. "You couldn't gracefully accept that Galen Morgan was more powerful than you. You wanted to get back at him, and you used my twin to do it. So what if it costs him his life? He's just a *mortal*, which makes him dispensable in your eyes, right?"

"That's enough!" Lucien declared in a voice so low it sounded like a shout. He, too, rose to his feet, planted his hands on the table and leaned forward, almost nose to nose with Ariel.

Ariel recognized that she was treading on dangerous ground, but she didn't care. "What's the matter, Lucien? Did I hit too close to home?"

"*Ariel!*"

Never before had Ariel heard her name issued as a

threat, but that was exactly how she perceived his utterance of it.

She raised her chin a notch and stared at him defiantly as she drawled, "What are you going to do, Lucien? Kill me?"

Before he could respond, she said, "I don't think so, because if you do, I'll no longer be in residence, which means you'll no longer have an invitation to be here. Tell me, what would happen to a half-mortal warlock if that protection was taken away?"

Rage leaped into his eyes. "You're pushing me, Ariel."

"Oh, believe me, Lucien, I haven't even begun to push," she retorted with a furious toss of her head. "I also think it's only fair to warn you that if anything happens to my twin, you'll wish to God you were dealing with Galen rather than me."

He muttered a violent curse and spun away from the table. With his back to her, he propped his hands on his hips and drew in several deep breaths.

To her surprise, when he turned back to face her, the fire in his eyes had died, though the warmth of the crystal against her skin confirmed that he was still angry.

His lips suddenly twisted into a parody of a smile as he asked, "Is that a promise? If anything happens to your brother, will I really wish I were dealing with Galen rather than you?"

"You can take it to the bank," she declared adamantly.

"Good." He sat back down and gestured toward her chair. "Please, sit down. I need to tell you the rules when it comes to dealing with Galen."

Ariel regarded him suspiciously. He'd gone from furious to almost amiable in a matter of seconds. She was tempted to touch the crystal to see what his true emotions were. But, recalling the impact they'd had on her the last time, she decided to take him at face value for the moment.

Sitting down, she crossed her arms over her chest and said, "I'm listening."

He nodded. "The first rule is never accept a gift from Galen, no matter how insignificant it seems. He'll have cast a spell over whatever it is, and I can guarantee that when the spell goes into effect, it won't be pleasant. I can't emphasize this enough, Ariel."

"Fine, Lucien. You don't need to beat the point to death," she muttered.

He arched a brow at her retort, but evidently decided to let it go, because next he said, "The second rule is that you must never meet with him at night. We are most powerful at night, and that's when you'll be at greatest risk. At the first touch of night, you must be in this house, and you must stay here until the sun rises."

Ariel regarded him dubiously. "Should I also start wearing a necklace of garlic and carrying around an oak stake and a bottle of holy water?"

"This is not a joke!" he warned, anger again flaring in his eyes. "If you aren't going to take me seriously, then forget about your brother, because I'll pack my bags and get the hell out of here."

One look at his resolute expression told Ariel he was serious. "I'm sorry, Lucien. I'll follow your rules. It's just that all this sounds like something out of a bad horror movie."

"You should be so lucky," he rejoined ominously. Evidently, he felt she was sufficiently apologetic, because he continued, "The third rule is that you must never invite Galen to do anything with you. Don't invite him into the house. Don't invite him to lunch. Don't invite him to walk down the sidewalk with you. In other words, don't *invite* him, period. Whenever you extend an invitation to a warlock, you give him a small amount of control over you. Galen is a high priest, which means he has tremendous powers. Letting him have even the slightest amount of control over you could destroy any chance we have of rescuing Armand."

He paused, as though giving her time to let his words sink in. Then he went on, "The last rule is that all of the above rules apply to everyone you meet in Sanctuary. You can't trust anyone, Ariel, not even the children. Everyone in the coven is bound by loyalty to Galen, and if he can't get to you himself, he will try to use others to open a gateway for him. Do you have any questions?"

"No," Ariel replied.

"Are you sure?"

"Of course I'm sure," she said with a sigh. "I may be a mortal, Lucien, but I'm not dense. Your message came across loud and clear. All I have to do is say no to everything and everyone, and I'll be fine."

"Right."

Ariel rose to her feet. "Well, now that we've gotten the lecture out of the way, I'd better get going."

He also stood. "Yeah."

Though she knew it was ridiculous, Ariel suddenly felt reluctant to leave. "I guess I'll see you later."

He shoved his hands into his pants pockets. "Yeah."

"Should I pick up anything in town? Like maybe some groceries?"

"We're fine for the next few days."

"Okay. Later, then."

She'd almost reached the door when he said, "Ariel?"

"Yes?" she replied, turning to face him.

"If you need me, you have the crystal. But remember, it isn't enough for you just to touch it. In order for me to come to you, you must summon me. Don't forget that."

"I won't forget." Though she knew she should leave it at that, she couldn't resist adding, "I guess it's a good thing that I held on to the crystal."

Something flashed in his eyes, but it came and went so swiftly she couldn't even begin to guess what the emotion was.

There was a strange gruffness in his voice when he replied, "I guess it is. Be careful, and make sure you follow the rules."

With that, he pivoted on his heel and walked out the back door. As Ariel watched him disappear, she gave a troubled shake of her head. The more she was around Lucien, the less she trusted him, and yet there was something about him that made her feel . . . well, she didn't know what she felt.

What she did know, however, was that she and Armand had become pawns in a three-hundred-year-old family feud between two warlocks. Unfortunately, she didn't know if she was on the right side, and there was only one way to determine if she was: Hear Galen's side of the story.

Heaving another sigh, she headed for her bedroom to get her purse, deciding that for now she'd be better off dealing with Lucien, the devil she knew, than to risk everything by approaching Galen.

Chapter Eleven

All is not well;
I doubt some foul play.
    —William Shakespeare, *Hamlet* 1.2.254

LUCIEN knew he had to stay away from the house until Ariel was gone. She had his emotions in a tailspin, and he recognized that only by distancing himself from her would he be able to regain control.

Sitting beneath an ancient oak tree, he absently stroked Omen, who had joined him. After only ten minutes he felt the crystal's power begin to weaken, and he knew that Ariel was driving away from the house. He also knew that the farther away she was, the less power he'd have. A twinge of anxiety assaulted him. Again he was going to be handicapped, and he hated the feeling.

But even as the uneasiness hit him, Ariel's earlier words skittered through his mind. *I guess it's a good thing that I held on to the crystal.*

Only after she made the statement had he realized that it *was* a good thing that she had the crystal. As long as she had it, she could summon him the instant she needed him. Of course, he wasn't sure what he could do to help her if she did summon him. Challenging Galen without the crystal would be as useless as storming a nest of machine guns with a baseball bat.

That's why it was imperative that he find Armand Dantes as soon as possible, but he had no idea where to look. Even more perplexing was the question of why Galen had imprisoned Dantes in the first place. All

Galen would have had to do was cast a spell over him that would make him forget everything he'd seen and done in Sanctuary. So why had Galen taken him prisoner instead? What could he possibly want from Armand? Lucien knew Galen had to want something. It was the only explanation for his actions.

His troubled thoughts were interrupted by a nervous yowl from Omen, which was immediately followed by the unmistakable crackle of spell-casting lightning.

Lucien jerked his head toward the house and watched the lightning encircle it. Dread filled him at the realization of what was happening. Galen's roses must have had a time-delayed spell. *Damn!* Why hadn't he burned them when he had the chance?

Because you wanted to protect Ariel.

Now he truly understood just how dangerous his protective instincts toward her were. He was placing her safety above sound witchcraft practices, and he was witnessing firsthand the formidable consequences of such a choice.

As soon as the lightning disappeared, he hurried into the house. He suspected what he'd find, and when he reached the trash can that had contained the roses, he discovered he was right. All that was left of them was a handful of ashes. He muttered a vile curse. Now there was a spell loose in the house, and without the crystal he had no way of tracking it down. That meant he would have to delay his search for Armand, because he didn't dare leave the house until Ariel returned. The moment she walked across the threshold she would be in danger, and he had to be here to protect her.

Raking a hand through his hair, Lucien vowed that when Ariel returned, he would recover the crystal, even if he had to seduce her into giving it to him.

* * *

Ariel gave an amazed shake of her head when she drove into Sanctuary. It was shortly before ten on a Thursday morning, and the streets were already packed with tourists. After hearing Lucien's story, she couldn't help wondering if the coven used some form of "magic" to create such a booming business.

Again, she ended up parking on the roadside at the other side of town. Walking along the tree-lined road, she was glad to see that the town hadn't chosen to handle the overflow of traffic by sacrificing the ancient trees for a parking lot. She loved trees, particularly old, towering ones. As far as she was concerned, to destroy them for progress was sinful.

When she reached the town proper, she decided that before she did anything else, she'd find a telephone and call Jean. She was halfway down the first block when she heard a woman call out behind her, "Ariel! Wait up!"

With a feeling of dread, Ariel stopped. Her first thought was that it was Corrine Morrow from the real estate office beckoning her. What was she going to do if Corrine insisted that she come to the office and fill out the rental form?

Damn! She should have thought of that possibility and asked Lucien what to do if it happened.

When she turned she discovered it wasn't Corrine hailing her; she stared disbelievingly as Shana Morland hurried up the sidewalk. Shana was dressed in sandals, a full, rainbow-hued skirt that hit her at midcalf, and a matching scarf, which was tied around her head. A brilliant red peasant blouse bared her slender shoulders. She was also wearing at least a dozen necklaces, and both arms were filled from elbow to wrist with jangling bracelets.

Ariel couldn't help feeling envious. If she tried to wear an outfit like that she'd look like she was dressed for Halloween. Shana looked like a beautiful, exotic gypsy.

"That's quite an outfit," she remarked when Shana reached her.

Shana chuckled. "That's very tactful, Ariel, but you don't have to spare my feelings. I know I look foolish, but today's my day to tell fortunes, and the tourists seem to like this look."

"You *don't* look foolish," Ariel reassured, then asked, "You tell fortunes?"

Shana made a wry face. "Only when I can't get out of it. But I'm glad I ran into you. Would you like to have lunch today?"

Ariel shook her head regretfully. "I'm sorry, but I'm having lunch with Galen Morgan."

"Galen?" Shana gasped.

"Is something wrong with that?"

"Of course not," Shana replied quickly. "It's just that Galen doesn't, um, date much."

Ariel regarded her thoughtfully. Even if Shana was a witch, she seemed friendly. It was possible she could be a good source of information. Ariel would just have to pump her carefully.

"I'm surprised to hear that. I'd have thought that a man as handsome as Galen would date all the time," she said.

"You think Galen is handsome?"

"You *don't* think he's handsome?"

"Let's just say I don't consider him to be my idea of the perfect dream lover."

Ariel was startled by Shana's choice of words. "Dream lover" was too close to her own fantasies about Lucien.

Telling herself that Shana's use of that particular phrase was just a coincidence, she asked, "Do you know where I can find a public telephone?"

"Well, there's one at the restaurant, but it's located near the video games. I'm afraid it's so noisy you can't hear yourself think, let alone talk. If you like, you can use the telephone at the fortune teller's shop."

Ariel hesitated at the offer. Lucien had made it clear that she was not to trust anyone. It could be that Shana was working with Galen; if so, she'd be better off using the public telephone. Then again, the restaurant would probably be filled with coven eavesdroppers who would hear everything she said anyway, particularly if she had to shout to be heard. If she kept her conversation with Jean neutral, it would surely be all right to use Shana's phone.

"Well, if you're sure it wouldn't be any trouble, I would appreciate using the phone," she said. "It's a long distance call, but I'll be putting it on my calling card."

"It's no trouble at all." As they walked down the street, Shana said, "I hear you're from Philadelphia."

"Yes, I am."

"It must be wonderful to live in a big city."

"It has its advantages, but to tell you the truth, I'd rather live in a small town like this."

Shana stared at her as if she'd just lost her mind. "You've got to be kidding. I mean, look at this place. You see the same places and the same people every day, and as far as entertainment goes, forget it."

"But you've got constancy in your life, a sense of belonging, and there's a lot to say for that," Ariel pointed out.

"Personally, I'd rather have some excitement," Shana muttered, stopping in front of a building. "Here's the shop."

They entered a hallway. On the right was a door with a sign overhead reading Candlemaker. Shana opened the door on the left, where the overhead sign declared Forture Teller.

Shana turned on the lights, and Ariel let out a gasp of delight. The lights filtered through a drop ceiling that had been painted midnight blue and was filled with twinkling stars and a crescent moon. The walls had been painted with detailed depictions of a deck of tarot cards. The floor was covered with a plush midnight blue carpet. There was a small, round glass-topped table in the center of the room, and its wooden base was a delicately carved and undeniably erotic rendition of entwined lovers. On top of the table sat a deck of tarot cards and a large crystal ball, which was cradled on the back of a pewter Pegasus. The winged horse looked so real that he appeared ready to take flight.

"This room is fantastic!" Ariel declared.

Shana grinned. "It's a bit overdone for my taste, but the tourists love it. The phone's in the office."

She walked to the tarot card on the wall labeled "The World" and opened a door that had been incorporated into the painting so well it was invisible.

Switching on a light, she said, "The phone's on the desk. If a customer happens to come in before you're done, I'll ring the buzzer so you'll know. I'd appreciate it if you'd wait to come out until I'm finished. My readings rarely last longer than fifteen minutes. There are some magazines in the bottom desk drawer if you have to wait."

"No problem," Ariel said, stepping into the office. It was a small, windowless room with a modern desk and chair and a file cabinet. The top of the desk was empty except for the telephone. "I really appreciate this."

"Hey, it's no big deal. I'll be out here if you need anything."

When Shana closed the door Ariel was struck with a

pang of unease, coupled with a touch of claustrophobia. What if Shana locked her in here? She'd be trapped with no way out!

She immediately surveyed the door and discovered that the locking mechanism was inside the room. It relieved her tension somewhat, but she was still uncomfortable enough to want to get out of here as soon as possible.

Sitting behind the desk, she pulled the telephone in front of her and dialed her work number. As she listened to the phone ring at the other end, she reminded herself that she had to keep her conversation with Jean cryptic. Just because Shana had shut the door didn't guarantee privacy. She might be able to hear everything Ariel said, or she might even be listening in on an extension.

The phone was picked up on the fourth ring. Ariel opened her mouth to speak, only to have her jaw drop in shock when she heard the voice on the other end. It wasn't Jean speaking, but herself. She hadn't reached the office; she'd reached her own answering machine at home!

As she hung up, she tried to tell herself that she had dialed her home number by mistake. But even as she lifted the receiver and carefully redialed, she knew she hadn't made a mistake. When she again reached her answering machine, fear rushed through her. Someone was stopping her from contacting the outside world. The question was, who?

Her first thought was that it was Shana. It was, after all, Shana's phone. But even as her suspicion of Shana surfaced, she angrily whispered, *"Lucien!"*

The moment his name left her lips, she clapped her hand over her mouth. Time and again he'd warned her how dangerous it would be if anyone knew she was

with him. How could she have just blurted out his
name that way?

*Because of nerves, frustration, and outright anger,
that's how,* she muttered to herself as she heard her answering machine beep, indicating it was time to leave
a message.

Since she couldn't reach Jean, she decided she'd
better leave a message, and so she said, "Hi, this is
Ariel. I got to Sanctuary safe and sound. Lancaster
County is proving to be everything I thought it would
be. I'll check in again soon."

Hanging up, she reassured herself that by leaving the
message, she at least had made it clear where she and
Armand were. She just hoped that it wouldn't be too
late by the time someone discovered the message. She
also decided to try again later from the public telephone. It was possible that Shana, not Lucien, had mis-
directed her call, and until she tried again, from
another location, she wouldn't know for sure.

Since Shana hadn't buzzed her, she left the office.
Shana was sitting at the table, a frown contracting her
brow as she laid out tarot cards in front of her.

"Bad news?" Ariel asked, as she closed the door behind her.

Shana's head shot up in startlement, and she smiled
ruefully. "Let's just say the cards aren't showing me
what I want to see."

"And what do you want to see?" Ariel asked, curious despite her wariness.

Shana shrugged. "I don't know. Escape. Excitement.
Something—*anything*—beyond the ordinary, but the
cards say that my life is going to be as boring as ever.
Would you like me to read the cards for you?"

"You don't really believe ... that, do you?" Ariel
said, gesturing toward the tarot deck and the crystal
ball.

"Ah, I have a disbeliever at my disposal." Shana grinned and waved dramatically toward the chair across from her, causing her bracelets to jangle. "Sit down, Ariel, and let me fill you in on your future."

Ariel wasn't sure why she decided to go along with Shana. Perhaps it was curiosity, or perhaps there was a part of her that wanted to believe Shana could tell her what the future held. After all, being forewarned meant you could be forearmed. Of course, she wasn't sure how she could arm herself against a town full of witches and warlocks.

"What now?" she asked as she sat down.

Shana handed her the tarot deck. "Shuffle the cards until you feel comfortable with them, and then split them into three piles in front of me."

Ariel shuffled the cards a good dozen times before dividing them. Shana lifted the top card on the first pile and placed it face up on the table.

"Ah, the Empress," she announced melodramatically. "You're dissatisfied with your personal life, but you aren't sure what you should, or can, do to fix it."

"Is that bad?" Ariel asked, amused by the ambiguity of Shana's statement. She doubted there was a person alive who wasn't somewhat dissatisfied with their personal life and wasn't sure how to fix it.

Shana grinned. "No. Most of us are confused, Ariel, particularly when it comes to our personal life."

She flipped over the second card and studied it for a long time before murmuring, "The Knight of Wands. You'll go through a period of extreme stress that will be fraught with difficulties and disappointments, but then someone will enter your life and change things for the better."

"I'm not sure what that means," Ariel said.

"It's pretty simple. You're going to be faced with a

lot of problems, but someone will help you solve them."

"And who is that someone?"

Shana shrugged. "The tarot only predicts, Ariel. It doesn't give the particulars. Do you want me to go on?"

"Sure."

Shana flipped the third card over and arched a brow. "Strength. This indicates that your best course of action is to change the way you react to the world around you. Only when you let go of your fears and doubts will you achieve your desired goal and be happy."

Before Ariel could think that through, Shana flipped over a fourth card. "Judgment. A new partnership or relationship is about to begin, and you shouldn't turn away from it, though you'll be tempted to do just that."

She lifted one more card, but she didn't put this one on the table. Instead, she regarded the card with a solemnity that, despite Ariel's disbelief, sent a shiver of apprehension racing down her spine.

"What is it, Shana?"

Shana put the card back on the pile she'd taken it from and gathered the others together as she said portentously, "Very soon you'll have to choose between dark and light."

"And what does that mean?" Ariel prompted, disquieted by the way Shana was refusing to look at her.

Shana glanced up with a smile that didn't quite reach her eyes. "I have no idea, Ariel. As I said, the cards predict, they don't give particulars."

Ariel had the distinct feeling that Shana was lying to her, that she knew something she was averse to revealing. "It sounds pretty ominous."

"Anything can sound ominous," Shana said as she shuffled the deck and put it on the table. Propping her elbows on the glass top, she cradled her chin in her hands. "But regardless of what your future holds, the cards gave you the best possible advice, and that is that if you want to be happy, you must change the way you view the world and let go of your fears and doubts."

"That's easier said than done."

"Amen to that," Shana said, rolling her eyes. "If I'd done that, I'd have left this town years ago."

"So why haven't you left?"

"I could give you a million reasons, but what it really boils down to is fear of being alone in a world I don't understand."

"Well, you could try it for a while, and if it didn't work out you could always come home."

Shana shook her head sadly. "It wouldn't be that simple."

Before Ariel could ask why it wouldn't be that simple, the door opened. Two middle-aged women entered, and Shana immediately stood up, her sadness instantly replaced by a welcoming smile.

As she greeted the customers, Ariel left, deciding that she would go to the restaurant and try again to call Jean. If she still reached her answering machine, she would know for sure that Shana wasn't causing the problem. And if that was the case, she and Lucien were going to have a long, heart-to-heart talk.

While she walked toward the restaurant, she mulled over her conversation with Shana. On the surface, there was nothing to indicate that she was anything more than a normal young woman bored with life in a sleepy town. It wasn't even abnormal that she was afraid to venture out on her own. The only disturbing part of the conversation had been Shana's intimation that if she left she wouldn't be able to return. If she left Sanctuary, would she become a shunned outcast like Lucien? If so, Ariel could certainly understand why she was reluctant to leave. That meant that she might

get out into the world, find out she hated it and then be
stuck.

When Ariel entered the restaurant, she discovered
that it was just as noisy as Shana had said it was. She
stepped around the long line of people waiting for a table and headed for the video games in the back. There
were four of them, all in operation. Between their
high-pitched electronic whines and the crush of boisterous kids waiting to use them, Ariel figured she'd be
lucky if she got out of here with her hearing intact.

It took her a minute to find the telephone, which was
located around a corner from the games. Unfortunately,
it was still so near them that even if she did manage to
reach Jean, she'd never be able to carry on a conversation. Then again, that might be for the best. The less
she said, the less anyone could overhear. And despite
the noise, Ariel suspected that if a member of the
coven wanted to hear what she was saying, he or she
would hear it.

Digging a quarter out of her pocket, she lifted it to
the slot. Before she could drop it in, however, someone
bumped against her, knocking the coin from her hand.

With a muffled curse, she turned toward her "assailant," figuring it was one of the kids. But it wasn't a
kid. She gulped when she found herself staring at a
chambray-covered chest as broad as Lucien's.

When she lifted her gaze to the man's face, a feeling
of déjà vu swept over her. He had shoulder-length
dark-brown hair, a hooked nose, and fanatically glittering eyes, so dark she couldn't decide if they were
brown or black.

She frowned in confusion, because she knew she'd
seen him before, but she couldn't remember where. All
she knew was that she was afraid of him, and she instinctively raised her hand toward Lucien's crystal. Before she could touch it, the man spun away from her

and charged into the crowd. Ariel watched his retreat and then, on an impulse, went ahead and touched the crystal, though she didn't summon Lucien. She wasn't feeling threatened. She just had an inexplicable feeling that the crystal and the man were somehow connected.

The moment her hand came to rest on the crystal, the man jerked to a stop. He glanced back at her with a malevolent look that was ten times worse than any Lucien had given her. Then he barged through the crowd, ruthlessly elbowing people out of the way.

Ariel was barely aware of his headlong escape. Her mind was filled with a hazy image of Armand engaged in passionate conversation with the man.

By the time the image disappeared, the man was leaving the restaurant. Ariel charged after him, yelling, "Wait!"

The crowd didn't part as easily for her, and when she finally burst out the door, he was gone.

She stood on the sidewalk and glanced up and down the crowded street in frustration. Where had he gone? Who was he? What was his connection with Armand? And why had he run from her?

She decided to grab hold of the crystal and summon Lucien. Surely he would know who the man was and where they could find him. But before she could reach for it, Galen appeared at her side.

His voice was filled with concern as he asked, "Ariel, are you all right?"

"I'm fine," she muttered, barely managing to bite back a curse. Galen might be handsome, but he definitely needed to work on his timing.

"Are you sure?"

She started to tell him to stop hovering but reminded herself that she was supposed to be befriending him. She'd just have to wait until she got back to the house to talk to Lucien.

"I'm fine," she repeated with a forced smile. "I thought I saw someone I knew, but he got away before I could catch up with him. Are you ready to have lunch?"

"Sure," Galen said, grasping her arm and hurrying her down the sidewalk.

"Galen, the restaurant is back there," she reminded him, trying to free her arm from his hold. He only tightened his grip.

"I know that, Ariel, but there's something I want to show you before we eat. Don't worry. I'm not kidnapping you. I'm taking you somewhere special. You'll love it. Honest."

Ariel started to protest, but Lucien's voice suddenly echoed through her mind. *Relax, Ariel. Galen's not going to hurt you.*

The sound of Lucien's voice chased away all thoughts of Galen. *Lucien, there was a man at the restaurant, and he knows Ar . . .*

I know, Ariel. We'll talk about it later. Just relax. Relax.

It was like being under the influence of a hypnotist, and Ariel felt the fight drain out of her. As she let Galen lead her to God knew where, she remembered Shana's prediction.

Soon you'll have to choose between dark and light.

Had she meant Lucien, who was dark, and Galen, who was fair?

Lucien cursed the fact that when he had formed the bond between Ariel and him, he'd made it connect their minds only when she was with Galen. Now he realized he should have also made it possible to see what was happening. Ariel's emotions were too erratic, which kept him from getting a clear perception of what was going on.

As he continued to reassure her, he retrieved the magic candles and the censer. Then he gathered the jars he needed for the scrying fire. Since Ariel was wearing the crystal, he should be able to create a strong enough link with her mind to get a visual image in the fire's flame.

While he lit the candles and set them around the pentagram, he reassured himself that Galen wouldn't try to harm Ariel. It was nearly noon, which meant the coven's energy was at its lowest, making them nearly as weak as mortals. Besides, with the time-delayed spell in the house, it would be a senseless move. Galen didn't know Lucien was here to protect Ariel, so as far as he was concerned, all he had to do was wait for her to come home and let the spell take over. Then he'd be able to do with her what he wanted.

Nonetheless, Lucien felt uneasy when he settled cross-legged in the center of the pentagram and began to go through the motions to conjure up the fire. He'd been startled when Ariel touched the crystal earlier and instead of summoning him relived the scene between Armand and the unknown warlock. His surprise had turned to incredulity when he realized that what had brought her memory into focus was an encounter with the warlock.

But then the warlock had run out of the restaurant and disappeared, and Galen had immediately arrived at Ariel's side. Had he been luring Ariel out of the restaurant for Galen? Were the two of them working together? Lucien found it hard to believe. Galen was too egocentric to conspire with anyone, but Lucien couldn't come up with any other reason for the warlock to have made himself known to Ariel. And Lucien knew that he'd purposely made himself known to her. Warlocks simply didn't have chance encounters.

He blew into the censer and watched the flame shoot

toward the ceiling. Then he began to chant, relaxing somewhat as the flame first shimmered and then gave him a clear vision of Galen and Ariel.

A moment later he stiffened as he watched Galen lead Ariel into the forest. Galen had told her he was taking her somewhere special, and the only "special" place in the woods was the crystal cave. Surely he wasn't taking her to the coven's place of worship!

Lucien soon realized that that was exactly where Galen was taking her. If it hadn't been the time of day when the coven's power was weak, he would have been worried that Galen intended to try to find out who was Ariel's spellbinder. But that was impossible. So what in hell was he up to?

Chapter Twelve

Lord, what fools these mortals be!
—William Shakespeare,
A Midsummer-Night's Dream 3.2.115

DESPITE Lucien's insistence that she relax, Ariel became anxious when Galen led her into the woods. She tried to keep track of where they were going, but they kept hitting forks that branched off in at least two and sometimes as many as five different directions. When they reached what had to have been at least the dozenth fork, Ariel accepted that she was lost. What if Galen abandoned her? She'd never find her way back!

Don't worry. Galen isn't going to abandon you, but if he does, I'll lead you back, Lucien reassured her.

Unless you're conniving with Galen, she proposed darkly.

She would have never believed that a long-suffering sigh could be mentally communicated, but that was exactly what she sensed as Lucien said—thought?—*Ariel, stop being melodramatic.*

Before she could respond, Galen led her into a clearing, and she saw the entrance to a cave. She hated caves—or, more accurately, their inhabitants. When he began guiding her toward it, she came to an abrupt halt and again tried to tug her arm out of his hand.

This time he released her and eyed her in puzzlement.

"What's wrong, Ariel?"

"I don't go into caves," she answered. " I don't like bats or any other creatures that live in them."

He grinned. "There aren't any cave creatures in there, Ariel. I can also guarantee that once you see the inside, you'll be happy you went in."

Go in, Ariel. Galen's right. There are no creatures in there.

I'm not going into a cave!

I thought you wanted to rescue your brother.

Are you saying Armand is in there?

No, but Galen is up to something. In order for me to figure out what it is you have to do what he asks.

"Ariel, if you're really afraid of caves, we don't have to go in," Galen said, interrupting her mental dispute with Lucien. "It's just that it's such a fantastic natural phenomenon, I wanted to show it to you."

She still hesitated, and then cursed inwardly when Lucien taunted, *Are you going in, Ariel, or are you going to let your fears take priority over your brother's rescue?*

"Ariel," Galen broke in, "do you want to go back to town?"

That was exactly what Ariel wanted to do, but Lucien's taunt had hit its mark. Armand was what was important, even if it meant braving bats and other disgusting cave dwellers.

"I think I would like to see the cave," she said, walking to the entrance before she could lose her nerve.

She had to crouch to enter, and she followed a small circular passage to the right. Within moments she was in the cave itself. Straightening, she gasped as she took in the magnificent crystalline interior. Was this where Lucien's crystal had come from?

"I told you there were no creatures in here," Galen

announced as he came in behind her. "It's beautiful, isn't it?"

"I've never seen anything like this," Ariel murmured in awe. "Where is the light coming from?"

"It's some type of organic phosphorescence. Don't ask me for the particulars. I was never any good at science."

"What's the wood for?" Ariel asked, studying the huge waist-high block of gleaming wood in the center of the luminescent floor. It should have looked out of place, yet somehow it seemed to belong here.

"It serves as a table," he answered. "The cave is a kind of community center for Sanctuary. We have parties and meetings and even an occasional wedding in here."

Ariel could imagine getting married in the cave. It was a perfect setting for exchanging vows. There was something so . . . mystical, almost holy, about it.

"I'm surprised you haven't opened the cave to tourists," she remarked. "I'm sure people would be more than willing to pay to see this."

"We considered it," Galen replied. "But then we decided that the cave was too special to have people traipsing in and out of it. Would you like to have lunch here? It would only take me a few minutes to run back to town and pick up something."

No! Lucien roared.

Ariel blinked, startled. Lucien had been quiet for so long that she'd forgotten he was hanging around inside her head. "I, um, don't think so, Galen. As beautiful as this place is, I'm afraid I have a touch of claustrophobia. I need to get out of here."

"I understand. How about a picnic in the clearing outside?"

No! Lucien roared again.

She glanced at her watch. "I'm sorry, Galen, but I

only have a limited time for lunch. I'm afraid that as enjoyable as this little side trip has been, it has used up most of it. Maybe another day."

"Of course," Galen murmured pleasantly, though Ariel could have sworn she saw a flash of frustration in his eyes. "We'd better go so you can eat something before you have to rush off."

After they left the cave and started back toward town, Galen said, "You know, Ariel, I would be happy to call some of the antique shops in the area and see who has old books on hand. I could even drive you around. It might save you some time."

Don't accept his offer!

"That's very kind, Galen, but if the shop owners know I'm a dealer, they won't be so eager to bargain with me. For now, I'd rather keep a low profile."

"If you're sure."

"I'm sure."

They were quiet for several minutes before Galen suddenly asked, "Are you married or involved with someone, Ariel?"

Ariel was so surprised by the unexpected question that she automatically said, "No. Why?"

"You just seem . . . tense around me. I thought maybe it was because there's someone special in your life." He stuffed his hands into his pants pockets and smiled sheepishly. "Sorry. That sounds egotistical, doesn't it? I didn't mean it that way. I also realize that I've been coming on a bit strong, and if I've offended you, I apologize. I hope you won't hold it against me, because I really would like to get to know you."

Ariel regarded him warily. He looked and sounded sincere, but she sensed an underlying emotion that she couldn't quite identify. It wasn't anger, but it had the same kind of keen edge, and that made her nervous.

"There's no need to apologize, Galen. You haven't

offended me, and I'd like to get to know you, too. If I seem tense, it's because I'm here on a buying trip, not a vacation. I have to put business first and pleasure second."

"I understand completely," he assured her, as they arrived back at town.

They'd almost reached the restaurant when Galen suddenly came to an abrupt halt and frowned at something across the street. Ariel followed his gaze, but she didn't see anything except the normal crowd of tourists.

"Excuse me for a moment, Ariel," he said, leaving her on the sidewalk and crossing the street. He disappeared into a building that she hadn't explored yet, and she couldn't see any sign that identified what it was.

Nearly five minutes passed before he came back. He looked worried when he said, "I'm sorry, Ariel, but something's come up. Can I have a rain check on lunch?"

"Sure. I hope it's nothing serious."

He smiled, but she could tell it was forced. "It's not serious, but it is important. I need to take care of it immediately. Maybe I'll see you tomorrow?"

"I should be around."

"Great. Stop by the shop when you get a chance."

As he hurried back across the street, Ariel frowned thoughtfully. Something was definitely going on, and she had a feeling it was more serious than he'd let on. She considered following him but decided against it. Until she found out if he was involved in Armand's disappearance, she couldn't afford to alienate him, and that was exactly what would happen if he caught her spying on him. With a resigned sigh, she headed for the restaurant. She needed to try to call Jean again.

The line at the restaurant had diminished somewhat, but the horde of kids around the video games seemed to have gotten larger. Before she headed for the phone, she surveyed the crowd, looking for the man she had seen earlier. He wasn't there, and she shook her head in frustration. Who was he, and why had he run away from her?

She made her way to the phone. A few minutes later she carefully dialed her work number and reached her home answering machine. Mumbling a curse, she hung up. Then she had a sudden inspiration. Was she cut off just from Jean or from everyone?

Recovering her quarter from the coin box, she dialed "0" and waited for the operator to come on the line. She could ask the operator to dial the number for her. She couldn't believe it when her own answering machine picked up again. She slammed down the receiver. She was sure this was Lucien's doing. How dare he cut her off from the outside world! Just who did he think he was?

A warlock, that's who, an inner voice answered.

"Oh, shut up," she grumbled as she headed for the door, deciding that when she got back to the house, she was going to give Lucien holy hell.

Lucien stood in the shelter of the woods, waiting for Ariel's return. He could feel the crystal's power growing, so he knew it wouldn't be long.

Omen, who'd searched the area and proclaimed it safe before Lucien came outside, suddenly appeared at his feet. She growled, informing him that she'd searched the area again and there was still no one watching the house.

He supposed he should be grateful that the house wasn't under surveillance. It would make it easier to stop Ariel from going inside. But, the fact that Galen hadn't posted lookouts confirmed that the spell waiting for her was a powerful one. Worse, Lucien had a sinking feeling that he knew what type of spell it was, and if he was correct, he had to get the crystal back from Ariel.

When she finally arrived, he hurried to the car, pulling open the passenger door. Ariel let out a startled yelp as he climbed inside, and then she glared at him.

"Dammit, Lucien! If you sneak up on me one more time, I'm going to punch you in the nose!" she railed.

"Sorry," he said unremorsefully. "We need to talk."

"You bet we need to talk," she stated angrily as she released her seat belt and turned to face him. "How dare you cut me off from the outside world!"

He arched a brow. "Cut you off from the outside world?"

"Don't play innocent with me, you . . . you . . . *warlock*!" she charged. "I tried to call my business partner today, and guess what happened?"

He didn't even blink. "You got your answering machine at home."

"So you don't deny it? You admit that you cut me off from the outside world?" she gasped in disbelief.

"I admit that I cast a spell that limits you to calling your home telephone number, but you're hardly cut off from the outside world, Ariel. All you have to do is drive out of the circle, and you can go anywhere you want."

"I just can't call home, right?"

"On the contrary. You can call home. You just can't call anywhere else."

He was sitting there looking so smugly self-possessed that Ariel wanted to scream. She drew in a furious breath and announced, "I want you to undo the spell, and I want you to undo it now."

"I can't do that."

"You mean you *won't* do it."

"You really do have a preoccupation with semantics, don't you?"

"Lucien, I swear if you don't undo that spell, I'm going to . . ."

"You're going to what?" he prodded softly, tauntingly, when she fell silent.

"I don't know, but I *will* think of something," she threatened.

He gave an unconcerned shrug. "Fine. While you're plotting your revenge, I need my crystal."

Her hand flew to the crystal. "No way."

"Ariel, I don't have time to debate this issue," he said with an irritable sigh. "The roses Galen gave you this morning had a time-delayed spell on them. It went into effect while you were gone, and now there's a spell loose in the house just waiting for you to walk in the door. The only way I can track it down and negate it is with the crystal. So, please, give it to me, and give it to me now."

She leaned back against the door and eyed him skeptically. "There's a spell loose in the house, and it's waiting for me?"

"That's right."

"I see. Is a loose spell sort of like a mouse? It just kind of scurries here and there, jumping out when you least expect it? I bet it even hides under the stove and raids the refrigerator at night, right?"

"Ariel, this is not a game!" he snapped.

"Oh, come on, Lucien," she drawled contemptuously. "You can't believe I'm so stupid that I'm going to fall for something as ridiculous as a spell loose in the house."

Ariel was unprepared for his reaction. One moment she was leaning against her door, and the next moment Lucien had grabbed her arms and jerked her toward him so that she was practically sitting in his lap. All the unmistakable signs of his anger were there—the glowing eyes, the heating of the crystal, the beginning gust of wind.

"You may think this is a joke," he said with soft menace, "but you won't think it's so funny if Galen's love spell goes into effect. I don't like mortals, but he considers them an abomination, and I'm speaking from personal experience. He'll use you and abuse you, and when he's through with you, he'll destroy you—if you're lucky. He may just keep you around to torture you for sport."

"Love spell?" Ariel echoed tremulously, too frightened to even contemplate the rest of his words. "I thought you said it was a loose spell."

"It's both," he growled, releasing her. "That's why he took you to the cave and tried to get you to eat there. The cave is our place of worship, but it's also an integral part of our mating ritual. It has a mystical power that lowers inhibitions and reinforces the need for personal as well as race survival. Food is the most essential ingredient for personal survival; procreation is the essence of race survival. If you had eaten there, your inhibitions would have fallen away and you'd have found Galen extraordinarily attractive. Then, when you returned to the house and his spell went into effect . . . Well, let's just say that you'd have been dangerously enamored of Galen."

Ariel rubbed her arms against a sudden chill. She didn't want to believe what he was suggesting, but she couldn't quite dismiss it either, because she recalled the frustration in Galen's eyes when she refused to eat at the cave.

"If Galen hates mortals as much as you say he does, why would he perform a . . . mating ritual with me?" she countered, latching on to the one weak point of his argument.

"He wouldn't have participated in the ritual," Lucien answered. "He'd have plied you with food, but he wouldn't have eaten a crumb himself, because he doesn't want to mate with you. He just wants you under his control."

"I see," Ariel murmured weakly. She turned her head and stared at the house through the windshield, shuddering at the fate that awaited her beyond its front door.

She jerked her head back toward Lucien when he murmured, "Good. You finally believe me."

Recognizing that he had again read her mind, she said, "Yes, I believe you, but I'm still not going to give you the crystal."

She expected him to fly into a rage at her announcement, but instead he regarded her with a baffled expression. "Why?"

Ariel shook her head, not sure how to explain it so he would understand. The fact that she didn't know how to express herself brought unexpected tears to her eyes. She knew that she couldn't cry. It would only reinforce Lucien's opinion that she was weak, and it wasn't weakness that was making her feel weepy. It was that the last few days had just been too stressful. She was tired and scared and so worried about Armand that she felt positively ill. On top of that, she was caught between two feuding warlocks with powers she couldn't even comprehend, let alone fight.

She blinked, trying to hold back the tears, but without success. As they began to roll down her cheeks, she wiped impatiently at them and said, "I won't give you the crystal because it's my only link to my twin. I know that probably doesn't make sense to you, but he's always been there for me. He loves me unconditionally, faults and all, and I feel the same way about him. If I have to become some sort of . . . love slave of

Galen's to hold on to this small piece of my brother, then I'll gladly sacrifice myself. Some contact with him is better than no contact, because without him I feel this horrible, aching loneliness inside. No torture that Galen or anyone else can dream up could be worse than that."

Her tears rattled Lucien, but it was her words that pierced him to the depths of his soul. He knew exactly what she was talking about, because he had felt that same horrible, aching loneliness ever since he'd become an outcast. And, like her, he would have gladly sacrificed himself for any kind of contact with his own kind, no matter how small.

The problem was, the crystal was nothing more than a placebo for her, whereas he needed it to be complete. No matter how much empathy he felt for her, he had to get it back.

But when he opened his mouth to explain all that to her, the words simply wouldn't come. She looked so defeated and fragile with her misty green eyes and tearstained cheeks that a fierce feeling of protectiveness assailed him. He wanted to sweep her into his arms, cradle her against his chest, and vow to do whatever it took to reunite her with her twin, even if cost him his own life.

If her words had pierced him to his soul, the realization that he was willing to give his life for her shook the very foundations of his existence. The only people a warlock ever felt that strongly about were his mate and his child. If he didn't know better, he'd think he had fallen in love with Ariel!

It's just the bonding spell, the voice of reason reassured him. *It has created the impression of love, but it isn't real.*

He clung to the explanation with the same urgency as a drowning man would cling to a life ring. Unfortunately, that didn't solve his problem with the crystal. Since she refused to part with it, the only thing he could do was weave some kind of spell that would, hopefully, protect her.

"If you aren't going to give me the crystal, then I need something of yours that I can cast a protective spell over," he told her. "Something that you can wear at all times. Maybe a piece of jewelry? Earrings?"

Ariel caught her breath when he suddenly reached over to lift the hair away from her face. She knew it was an impersonal gesture. He was merely checking for earrings. That didn't stop a bolt of electric excitement from shooting through her at his touch.

She knew her reaction to him was crazy. She'd seen how deadly he could become in the blink of an eye, and she wasn't foolish enough to think it was an act. So why were her insides quivering at his touch? Why did she yearn to throw herself into his arms?

She swallowed around the nervous lump in her throat and said hoarsely, "I was in such a hurry this morning that I didn't put on earrings. I probably have some in my purse, though."

"Fine. Get them," he said, releasing her hair and leaning forward to pick up her purse, which sat on the floor at his feet.

After he handed it to her, Ariel opened the voluminous bag and started digging through it. It seemed she'd barely gotten started when Lucien muttered a curse, snatched her purse away from her, and dumped its contents into his lap.

"What do you think you're doing?" she gasped in horror as she grabbed the empty purse away from him.

"I thought I was saving some time," he replied, staring at the clutter in amazement. "I always wondered what mortal women lugged around in these monstrosities. I think I should have remained ignorant."

"Everything I have in my purse is a necessity," Ariel declared indignantly, as she watched him gather a handful of lipstick tubes and examine them.

He eyed her dubiously. "You have six lipsticks, and three of them are the same color. That's a necessity?"

"It's my favorite color, and I don't want to chance running out of it," she defended, scooping the tubes out of his hand and dumping them back into her purse.

While she was doing that, he gathered a handful of foil. Holding it out to her, he said, "Empty gum wrappers are a necessity?"

"I don't believe in littering," she snapped, taking the wrappers and squeezing them into a tight ball that she tossed back into the purse.

"I guess that explains all these old movie stubs," he drawled, handling her a good dozen of them.

"So I haven't cleaned my purse out for a while," she grumbled. "You don't have to make a federal case out of it. Let's just dump everything back in."

She leaned forward to grab some of her possessions, but he raised his arm, holding her back. "I haven't done anything this fascinating in years, Ariel. I'm not going to let you deprive me of my fun."

"You're just doing this because I won't let you have the crystal," she accused.

"In a roundabout way that's true," he agreed. "If you'd given me the crystal, I wouldn't have had to resort to this."

She glared at him. "And if I give you the crystal, you'll let me dump everything back into my purse, right?"

"Wrong. As I said, I haven't done anything this fascinating in years."

"In case no one's ever told you, it's rude to go through someone's personal possessions."

He ignored her and handed over her wallet and her

checkbook. Then he zipped open her bulging cosmetics bag, tentatively prodding at the contents with his index finger.

"Amazing," he mumbled, as he zipped it closed and passed it to her.

When he lifted a small plastic pouch, she yanked it away from him. He eyed her questioningly, and she cursed the blush she could feel crawling up her neck and into her cheeks. "This is none of your business. It's for, um, personal hygiene."

"Ah," he murmured sagely as he went back to the mess in his lap.

Deciding that the best way to handle this humiliation was to ignore him, Ariel leaned back in her seat and closed her eyes. Several minutes passed before he said, "This is perfect for our needs."

Ariel's eyes flew open, and she glanced over at him. He'd unwrapped a handkerchief to reveal a slender gold and silver braided bracelet.

She sat up and exclaimed, "I've been looking for that for months!"

"Well, now you know where it is," he said, placing it on the dash beside half a dozen pairs of earrings.

Gathering the earrings, he put them in the center of the handkerchief and knotted the ends. After dropping the bundle into her purse, he closed it and put it back on the floor.

"Did you enjoy yourself?" Ariel questioned sarcastically.

"Immensely," he answered, flashing her one of his evil smiles. "I've learned a lot about you."

Ariel suspected that he was issuing that announcement as a threat, and she took it as one. It almost made her wish she'd given him his blasted crystal.

"So, what do we do now?" she asked.

"Well, the first thing you need to do is take out the

crystal. Since you won't give it to me, you're going to have to help with the spell."

Intrigued despite her wariness, she reached beneath the collar of her blouse, grasped the chain, and pulled the crystal out.

He handed her the bracelet. "Put the bracelet on and then take hold of the crystal." After she'd done as he instructed, he said, "In a minute I'll ask you to close your eyes and focus your attention on the bracelet. You need to form a clear image in your mind of what it looks like, how heavy it is on your wrist, and what its surface feels like against your skin. Try to distinguish the warmth of the gold from the coolness of the silver. Shut everything out of your mind but the image of the bracelet and the sound of my voice, and don't, under any circumstances, release the crystal until I tell you to release it. That's very important, Ariel, because if you release it before it's time, the spell might backfire and cause us more problems than Galen ever could. Do you have any questions?"

"No."

"Okay. On the count of three, I want you to close your eyes and do everything I said. When you're focused, I'll touch the crystal and the bracelet. You'll experience a sudden surge of power, but it's nothing to be afraid of. Are you ready?" When she nodded, he said, "One. Two. Three."

Ariel closed her eyes and focused on the bracelet. When she had the image of it in her mind, she tested its weight. Then she concentrated on the feel of it against her skin, surprised that there really was a difference in the temperature of the two metals.

She was so centered on the bracelet that she flinched when Lucien twined one hand with hers over the crystal and placed his other hand around her wrist. A definite surge went through her, but it wasn't one of power. It was a frightening bolt of desire.

Easy, he whispered in her mind. *You're safe, Ariel. Nothing I do will harm you. Trust me. Trust me.*

There was a nagging voice in the back of Ariel's mind that insisted that trust was the last thing she could give Lucien. But even as it railed at her, she felt herself giving in to his bewitching urging. Her will was further stripped away as he began to chant in a melodic, mesmerizing cadence that was as strangely familiar as it was totally alien.

She had no idea how much time had passed when Lucien said, "You can open your eyes and release the crystal, Ariel."

She opened her eyes and stared at him. She felt giddy, as if she'd had too much to drink, and for no discernible reason she giggled.

Lucien arched a brow. "What's so funny?"

"I don't know," she said, giggling again.

He frowned. "It must be some type of feedback from the crystal."

That struck her as absurdly funny, and she burst into uproarious laughter.

"Ariel, try to calm down," he ordered.

"Try to calm down?" she repeated on a howl. "I'm running around with a warlock, who threatens me on a regular basis, and I'm spying on another warlock, who's turned a spell loose in the house and wants to turn me into a love slave. I've been terrorized by your ill-tempered familiar, whom I suspect is just waiting for the right moment to rip out my throat. You've put a spell on me that won't let me call anywhere but home, and you spend more time hanging around inside my head than I do. My brother is missing and may be a mental vegetable, and you want me to calm down? You really are funny, Lucien. Absolutely hysterical!"

By this time, she was laughing so hard that she was clutching her sides. Lucien shook his head as he watched her. Hilarity was a mortal idiosyncrasy that he found both fascinating and baffling. It had no rhyme or reason to it and was often brought on by circumstances that were not amusing.

"You really don't get the joke, do you?" Ariel choked out between guffaws.

"No, I don't."

She wiped tears of laughter from her eyes. "I guess you had to be there."

He frowned in puzzlement. "I was there."

That sent her into new gales of jollity. When she'd finally laughed herself out, she said, "God, that felt good. Whoever said laughter was the best medicine knew what they were talking about. So what are we going to do now?"

"If you're feeling up to it, we should go into the house and see if our spell works."

"You mean it might not work?" she gasped in alarm.

He shrugged. "Since I can't track the spell down, I don't know for sure what it's meant to do. Your bracelet is braided, so I was able to weave several protective spells into it. It should work, but there's always a chance that it won't."

"And if it doesn't work?"

"You'll be in great need of some more of that medicinal laughter," he answered grimly.

She gulped as she looked toward the house. If Lucien was right, in a few minutes she could be in a hell of a lot of trouble.

"You know, Ariel, you don't have to put yourself at risk," he pointed out. "All you have to do is give me the crystal, and I can take care of Galen's spell."

She pivoted her head toward him. "Let's just suppose that I did give you the crystal. When you were through tracking down the spell, would you give it back to me?"

He regarded her for a long, unnerving moment before countering, "Would you believe me if I said yes?"

That was a hard question, and Ariel frowned as she contemplated the answer. On one level she distrusted him completely. He had used Armand as a pawn in his game of revenge, and, as he was so quick to point out, he had no love of mortals. She had no doubt that everything he was doing was motivated by self-interest, and that alone made him suspect.

Yet, oddly enough, she also had total faith in him. He'd saved her at the Witches' Brew when those two men had tried to assault her. He'd saved her yesterday when she saw Armand's image, though she still couldn't recall exactly what had happened. He was trying to save her now. And to his credit, he had seemed to answer all her questions truthfully, even though his explanations were unpalatable.

Did she trust him? No, but she did believe that if he gave her his word, he would uphold it.

"Yes, I would believe you," she said. "So, if I give you the crystal, will you give it back to me after you've taken care of Galen's spell?"

Myriad emotions raced through his eyes, and she sensed he was at war with himself. Finally, he gave a curt nod. "Yes, I'll give it back."

She pulled the chain over her head. "Then here's the crystal."

He quickly slipped the chain over his head, and as the crystal came to rest against his chest, he drew in a deep, fortifying breath. Ariel told herself it was her imagination, but she could have sworn she could see him growing stronger.

He opened his mouth as though to say something, but then he closed it and quickly climbed out of the car. As Ariel watched him stride purposefully toward the house, she hoped she wasn't making a fool of herself.

Chapter Thirteen

The ancient folk with evil spells, dashed to earth, plowed under!
—Navaho war chant

A S Lucien entered the house, he experienced a flashback to his youth. While mortal children played hide-and-seek, young warlocks conjured up minor spells. Then other young warlocks tried to track them down and negate them.

He had been the champion conjurer and spell tracker in his age group, and Galen had been infuriated that a "half-breed" was better at the game than he was. So he had started sneaking after the other young warlocks, surreptitiously learning what spells they were casting. With that knowledge, he had, of course, been able to best Lucien.

His chicanery had gone on for nearly a month before Lucien's grandfather had caught him cheating. To practice deceit against any member of the coven was one of the most dishonorable acts a warlock could commit, and the punishment was harsh. An adult warlock would have been cast out of the coven forever. A child's punishment was almost as severe. Galen had been stripped of his powers for a year. He had also been shunned during that time, even by his own family.

"But you didn't learn your lesson, did you, Galen? You're still a cheater," Lucien murmured as he moved slowly through the house, the crystal clutched in his hand. Spells were not only elusive, they were almost invisible. If you concentrated hard enough, however, you could pick up the faint outline of their aura. "Now, if I were a love spell, where would I hide?"

The answer came to him in a flash. Loose spells didn't have awareness, but they did have predatory instinct. When Ariel held the roses, the spell would have picked up on her scent. It would then seek out the area where her scent was the strongest. Since she'd only been in the house overnight, that place would be her bedroom. Not only had she slept there but also it contained all of her personal possessions.

He hurried to her room. When he stepped inside, he closed the door and cast a sealing incantation over both it and the window. If the spell was in here, it was now trapped.

Catching a slight movement out of the corner of his eye, he spun toward it. The spell was skittering along the floorboard, and then it dived under the bed. It was so small and so faint he couldn't tell what it looked like, but he had found it and that was what mattered.

Lucien clutched the crystal tighter and smiled in triumph. A loose spell was kinetic and could never stay still for more than a few moments. Its energy kept it in perpetual motion.

He began the chant that would negate it the minute it sprang back into sight, and he gasped in disbelief when it suddenly charged from beneath the bed, heading straight for him. What in hell was happening? The spell was meant for Ariel, wasn't it?

Just before the spell reached him, he leaped aside, and it raced headlong toward the wall, hitting it with a force that reverberated in Lucien's ears. Then it exploded into a fiery burst of light.

Lucien stumbled backward as he watched an ancient, teeth-gnashing demon take form out of the scattered molecules. It was no bigger than a mouse, but it was so evil that it filled the room with its rotting stench.

At that moment Lucien knew without a doubt that Galen was practicing the Old Ways. Only that kind of witchcraft dealt with the dark side of nature, which was the primary reason the high council had banned the practice. Though Lucien's race believed that for nature to be in balance there had to be both light and dark forces, it was difficult to control the dark forces, and in the wrong hands they were inherently dangerous.

That was why mortals referred to it as Black Magic. It was also what had precipitated the witch hysteria.

As he tried to decide what to do, he recognized that the spells he had woven into Ariel's bracelet wouldn't have protected her from this atrocity. Indeed, he'd be lucky if he got out of here alive, because none of the standard witchcraft practices he knew applied to dealing with a demon.

Suddenly his grandfather's voice echoed in his ears. "Evil is an insidious state of mind, and the only way it can gain reality is if someone acknowledges its existence. If you're ever faced with evil in spell form, concentrate on the purest form of good you know and refuse to believe that the evil exists. If it can't persuade you to give it reality, it will have to go back to where it came from."

Lucien clutched his crystal in both hands and sent his mind racing in search of the purest form of good he knew. He was startled to see an image of Ariel form in his mind's eye, but then he realized that her unconditional love for her brother was the purest good he'd ever known.

He focused on her image and refused to listen to the demon as it bewitchingly cajoled him with promises of untold wealth, power, and pleasures of the flesh if he would only acknowledge it. When its coaxing didn't work, it resorted to threats of torture and death so hideous that they made the hair on Lucien's body stand on end and caused him to break out in a sweat. But he kept his attention centered on Ariel and the pure love she had for her brother.

After what seemed like an eternity, the demon suddenly roared in rage and agony. Lucien's eyes flew open and he watched it begin to dissintegrate. He'd beaten it! But the thought no more than entered his mind than the demon began to take form again.

It's still alive! he realized in horror as it sprang toward him.

He jumped aside, barely managing to elude it, but it twisted in midair, never touching the ground, and came at him again. As it lunged for his throat, Lucien balled up his fist and swung at it with all his might. The blow sent the demon flying across the room, and as it slammed against the wall, it faded to almost nothing before it again began to take form.

It was then that Lucien understood that the demon wasn't yet alive. When he had opened his eyes before it was gone, he gave it physical recognition. However, he hadn't give it spiritual recognition, so there was still a chance that he could defeat it.

Without waiting to see what the demon would do next, he closed his eyes and clutched the crystal. As he focused on Ariel and her love for her brother, he began to chant, "You are not real! You are not real!"

It was the only way he could keep from opening his eyes as he felt it leap onto his leg and begin to scuttle up his body. By the time it reached his shoulder, he was shuddering with revulsion and outright terror. But he kept his mind focused on Ariel, even when he felt its sharp claws on his neck and its rankness became so strong that he couldn't breathe.

It seemed that another eternity passed before the demon again screamed in rage and agony, nearly deafening Lucien from its spot so close to his ear. He kept his eyes closed until long after the scream had died.

When he finally opened them, there was no sign that the demon had ever been there. Even its stench was gone, and he knew that he really had beaten it this time.

No, he corrected himself, as he raked a shaking hand through his hair. Ariel had beaten it, and he knew that her love for her twin was a force to be reckoned with.

Ariel was worried sick about Lucien. He'd been in the house for nearly an hour. Just how long did it take to track down a spell?

Climbing out of the car, she began to pace along its length, trying to decide if she should go inside to help. Not that she knew a blessed thing about spells, let alone how to track them down or get rid of them. If she went charging in now, she might screw everything up. She could just imagine Lucien's response to that.

She leaned against the car and told herself that she was worrying for nothing. It wasn't as if Lucien was doing something dangerous. He was tracking down a love spell, for pity's sake, not some demon from hell. She just wished he would use some of that mental telepathy of his to let her know that he was okay. It was as if her wish conjured him up, because he suddenly opened the door of the house.

"Did you get the spell?" she asked, hurrying toward him.

"Yes," he answered, stepping aside to let her in.

"It took you so long—I was starting to get worried," she told him as he closed the door. When he turned to face her, he removed the crystal from around his neck, holding it out to her.

Ariel was momentarily startled. Though he had told

her he would give the crystal back to her, she hadn't anticipated that it would be this easy. She had honestly thought she'd have to ask him for it.

Taking it from him, she smiled and slipped the chain over her head. "Thank you, Lucien."

"There's no need to thank me," he said stiffly. "I told you I'd give it back to you, and I always keep my word, even if it means giving up something that is rightfully mine."

Realizing he was still irritated about her refusal to give him the crystal, she decided to change the subject. "So, tell me about the spell. Where did you find it?"

"In your bedroom," he answered.

She supposed that made sense. After all, what better place for a love spell to hang out than the bedroom?

"Did you have trouble getting rid of it?"

"Neither of us has had lunch. Why don't we go into the kitchen and get something to eat?" he suggested.

He was avoiding her question, and Ariel regarded him suspiciously. "What are you trying to hide from me, Lucien?"

"I'm not trying to *hide* anything from you," he denied, scowling at her.

She saw right through his evasion. "Let me rephrase the question. What aren't you telling me about the spell?"

His scowl deepened to a dangerous glower. "Leave it alone, Ariel."

"No," she declared firmly. "That spell was meant for me, and I have a right to know about it. Now, please, tell me what happened."

He pushed away from the door and strode purposefully toward the hallway leading to the kitchen, ignoring her request. She rushed after him. He was halfway across the room before she caught up with him, and she grabbed his arm, tugging on it until he stopped.

When he turned to glare at her, she sighed. It was obvious he was looking for a fight, but she decided not to give him one.

"Please, tell me about the spell, Lucien."

"I said to leave it alone," he repeated.

Ariel shook her head. "I'm sorry, but I can't do that. The only way I can protect myself is if I know what's going on."

"Fine!" he exploded, causing Ariel to start. "If you want all the gory details, I'll give them to you. Galen didn't just conjure up a spell to make you infatuated with him. He conjured up a vicious little demon. In other words, he doesn't want you to adore him. He wants possession of your soul!"

At first she stared at him in bewilderment. What was he talking about? But then his words began to sink in, and when they did, the image of Armand, old and vacant-eyed, flashed into her mind.

"Oh, God, is that what he's done to my brother? Has he stolen his soul?" Clutching Lucien's shirt front, she gazed up at him in frenzied appeal. "We have to save him, Lucien!"

Lucien stared at her in open-mouthed shock. He had just told her that her own soul—the very essence of her being—was in grave danger, and all she was concerned about was her brother? Didn't she have *any* instincts for self-preservation?

Of course she did, but they were being overridden by love, he realized, when she pleaded, "Please, Lucien! We have to save him!"

"If Galen is in possession of your brother's soul, there's nothing I can do about it," he said regretfully. "Galen's practicing the Old Ways, and I'm not trained to fight against them. I was barely able to destroy the demon."

"But you did destroy it," she pointed out, refusing to

believe that he was powerless to help Armand. He was a warlock. He could do anything! "What do you need to fight Galen? The crystal? That's it, isn't it? You need the crystal."

She released her hold on his shirt and jerked the chain over her head. Holding the crystal out to him, she said, "Here. It's yours. I'm sorry I wouldn't give it back to you, and you have every right to be angry about that. But you can't turn your back on my brother because you're mad at me. He needs you. *Please!*"

Though Lucien knew he should take the crystal, he couldn't. She was giving it to him out of desperation, and if he accepted it she'd be convinced that it gave him the power to fight Galen.

With a heavy sigh, he took the crystal from her hand and put it back around her neck, reiterating, "Ariel, I just explained that I'm not trained to fight against the witchcraft that Galen's using. The crystal won't make any difference."

"Of course it will!" she said, her voice edging toward hysteria. "It helped you destroy the demon."

He shook his head. "I didn't destroy the demon. You, or more accurately, your love for your brother destroyed it."

When she peered at him in confusion, he explained, "For evil to exist it must receive affirmation of its reality from the first person who sees it. If you don't acknowledge its existence, it has to go back where it came from. So when I saw that demon, I focused on the purest form of good I could think of, which was your love for your twin. That allowed me to disbelieve in the demon, and that's how I defeated it."

"You can do that again," she said eagerly. "It worked once, so it will work again."

He shook his head. "No, Ariel. The demon was still in spell form, so I had to acknowledge it before it

could exist. Galen isn't stupid. He'll figure out how the
demon was defeated. Any other demons he throws our
way will be real, because he'll affirm their existence
when he summons them. The only chance I might have
at fighting him would be if you let me . . ."

"If I let you what?" Ariel pressed when he abruptly
stopped speaking.

"Believe me, Ariel, it is not a suggestion either of us
wants to consider. Besides, there would be no guarantee that it would work."

"But you said it was our only chance, so we have to
take it!" she argued as she again clutched his shirt
front. "Please, Lucien. I will do anything to save my
brother, and I mean *anything*. Just tell me what I have
to do!"

As Lucien stared down into her imploring green
eyes, he knew she wasn't lying. She *would* do anything
to save her brother, even risk her soul, and for some
reason that infuriated him.

"You might be willing to do anything, but I'm not!"
he stated harshly as he pried her hands away from his
shirt and pushed her back.

"Damn you, Lucien! You sent him here, so this is all
your fault!" she yelled, tears welling up in her eyes.
"You have to do whatever you can to help him!"

Lucien's temper erupted into full-blown rage at her
accusation. "Your brother is a grown man, Ariel. I did
not force him into coming here. He came of his own
free will!"

"But you didn't tell him the truth!" she retaliated furiously. "You lied to him, and because you did, you
owe him. I will not let you turn away from him. Now
tell me what I have to do so you can fight Galen!"

"All right," he rasped as he grasped her chin roughly
between his thumb and forefinger and glared down at her.
"The only chance I have of fighting Galen is to draw on

the power of your love for your brother. In order to do that, I will have to cast a love spell over you. You will have to grant me full access to your thoughts and your feelings—the very essence of what you are. In other words, you will have to surrender your soul to me. You'll also have to mate with me, and I can assure you I have a very voracious and inventive sexual appetite."

A hot blush flew into her cheeks, and she tried to turn her face away from him, but he held her ruthlessly in place. "You should also know that once the spell goes into effect, it can't be undone. You'll never be able to love anyone but me, but your love will never be returned, because I would *never* take a mortal as my mate. So, if you're willing to become my love slave instead of Galen's, fine. I'll be back by the witching hour. You be standing in the middle of the pentagram—naked and willing!"

With that he stormed out of the house, slamming the door behind him. Ariel stumbled toward the fireplace and collapsed into one of the chairs.

He was just trying to frighten me, she told herself. She had made him mad when she blamed him for this mess, and this was his way of punishing her. But even as she tried to deny his ultimatum, she knew he meant every word he'd said.

"Oh, God," she whispered in despair. "What am I going to do?"

After spending an unfruitful afternoon and evening looking for Armand, Lucien took up a vigil in the trees edging the crystal cave. It was nearly eleven at night, and the coven was gathering for the nightly ceremony. He wasn't sure what he was looking for. Maybe some sign as to whether or not the coven knew that Galen was practicing the Old Ways. Not that it mattered one way or the other. They were bound to him, so they couldn't stop him even if they did know.

As Lucien counted their number he discovered that four adult members were missing. Unfortunately, everyone in the clearing was wearing the hood of their ceremonial robe, so he wasn't able to ascertain exactly who was gone.

He frowned. It wouldn't be unusual for one or two members to be absent. Though the coven enjoyed excellent health, there was an occasional bout with minor illness. It was one of the prices they paid by letting mortals, who seemed to be rife with germs, come onto coven land. But illness was the only reason they would ever miss a ceremony, and for four of them to be ill at one time was so unusual that it was reason for serious concern. Yet no one in the group seemed worried in the least, and that unsettled him.

As they started to file into the cave, he raked a hand through his hair. The ceremony would begin in a few minutes and peak at the witching hour. He had to get back to Ariel, and it wasn't a prospect he was looking forward to. Indeed, this afternoon, within minutes of leaving the house he had regretted his outburst.

Everything he'd told her was true. His only real chance at defeating Galen was to be able to draw upon the power of her love, and the only way he could do that was to cast the traditional mating love spell over her.

But what would he do if she agreed to go through with it? When he took over her soul, he would have to give her his. Though he'd told her he would never take a mortal as his mate, he wasn't sure it was a vow he could keep. A warlock could never be at peace with himself unless he fulfilled the life cycle of procreation. It was not a choice but an instinctual drive that he couldn't control. If he went through with the spell and then managed to defeat Galen, would he be able to walk away from Ariel? Or would the primal need for race survival keep him with her? Would he be condemned to repeat his father's mistake?

No, I'll never make the same mistake! he told himself firmly as he headed back to the house. He would never condemn his own child to the misery he himself had suffered. Besides, he was probably worrying over a moot issue. He was sure Ariel wouldn't even think of going through with the spell. As much as she loved her brother, she had to have enough survival instinct to keep from sacrificing herself, didn't she?

When he neared the house a short time later, the full power of the crystal washed over him. He stopped at the edge of the trees. All he had to do was connect with Ariel's mind and he'd know her decision, but he held back, understanding that the time for his own soul-searching had arrived.

If she had chosen the love spell, would he—*could* he—go through with it?

He had to, he realized. He might condemn himself to a lifetime of loneliness and misery, but that was inconsequential when compared to the fate of the coven. Since the coven hadn't been annihilated, he had to assume that the council of high priests didn't know Galen was practicing the Old Ways. If he could stop him before they found out, there would never be a need for them to know. There was also the fact that he was the only one who could fight Galen, because he was the only one who hadn't sworn allegiance to him.

"So what's your decision, Ariel?" he whispered, closing his eyes and connecting with her mind.

Ariel glanced at her watch as she paced the room with the pentagram. In half an hour midnight—the witching hour—would be here, and she still didn't know what she was going to do.

Ever since Lucien had stormed out of the house, she'd been debating with herself. One minute she told herself she had to let Lucien cast his love spell over her, because it was the only way to save Armand. The next, she told herself that she was a fool even to consider it. Lucien first claimed that Galen had been trying to get possession of her soul by using some kind of demonic love spell. Then he turned around and said the only way he could fight Galen was to cast his own love spell over her and claim her soul.

To use the same spell for two such diametrically opposed purposes seemed very suspicious to her. Indeed, she didn't even know for sure that there had been a loose spell or a demon in the house. It could have been a scam Lucien dreamed up to get her to go along with him. He might not even be planning to cast a love spell, but some other type of horrible spell that would leave her as lifeless as the image of Armand she'd seen. There was no way she could take that risk.

But what if he was on the level? If he was, she couldn't turn him down, she bemoaned, as her argument came full circle for at least the thousandth time.

"Time is running out," she mumbled, coming to a stop in front of the fireplace and staring at the collection of jars. "So what's it going to be? Do you let him cast the spell over you, or do you tell him what he can do with his spells?"

"So many questions and so few answers," Lucien drawled behind her.

She let out a startled scream and spun around to face him. He was leaning against the front door, his arms crossed over his chest and his eyes hooded.

"You sneaked up on me again!" she accused, too rattled at the realization that her time had run out to think of anything else to say.

He shrugged dismissively. "Warlocks walk softly."

"Well, it's not good manners to sneak up on people," she snapped.

"I'll try to remember that." Before she could come up with a retort, he said, "The witching hour will be upon us in exactly thirty minutes. I'll be back in twenty to find out what you've finally decided."

Oh, God, tell me what to do! Ariel thought frantically as she watched him stride across the room and disappear into the hall. *Is he telling me the truth? Can I trust him?*

Unfortunately, no advice came to her from on high, which meant she was going to have to rely on her own instincts. As they continued to war, she resumed her pacing.

It seemed to take forever for Lucien to reappear, but when he did come back into the room, he was carrying what looked like a small picnic basket. He also had a large bundle thrown over his shoulder, but it was rolled, so she couldn't tell what it was. After placing the items in the center of the pentagram, he walked to the fireplace. She waited for him to say something, but he didn't speak as he began to gather jars off the shelves and carry them to the pentagram. Finally, he moved one of the stones in the fireplace and retrieved candles and a bowl-shaped object that looked like an antique incense burner.

"What are you doing?" she asked nervously.

He carried the candles and the bowl to the center of the pentagram and placed them on the floor before facing her. "Preparing for the witching hour. It's now or never, Ariel. What's your decision?"

Ariel searched his face, looking for something that would tell her whether or not she could trust him, but his expression was as neutral as white on white. Rubbing her hands against her thighs, she asked, "Can't my decision wait until tomorrow night?"

"No."

"Why not?"

"Because Galen was suspicious of you before I destroyed his demon. Now his suspicions about you have been confirmed, and that makes him twice as dangerous. Even as we speak his power is peaking, and he'll come up with a new plan to either spellbind you or destroy you come morning."

If he had stated his argument passionately, Ariel might have been able to discount it. However, he delivered it with a cool indifference that made her shiver. But was he telling her the truth?

Touch the crystal! an inner voice suddenly urged. *If nothing else, you'll know what he's feeling.*

Slowly, deliberately, she raised her hand toward the crystal, leaving him no doubt of her intention. Though his gaze followed her hand, he made no objection.

When she finally touched it, the feelings that enveloped her were so strong that the breath rushed out of her at their impact, but she didn't release the crystal. She forced herself to face his emotions, which seemed to be a raging tempest of anger and frustration, but there were also overwhelming feelings of love and devotion. As she latched on to them, she felt him mentally flinch, but he didn't try to withdraw from her.

Finally, she released the crystal. Regarding him speculatively, she asked, "Who is it you care so much about?"

"The coven," he replied. "They mean almost as much to me as your brother does to you, and they are in just as much danger. If the council of high priests learns that Galen is practicing the Old Ways, every member of the coven will die, even the children."

"Even the children?" Ariel gasped in disbelief. When he nodded, she said, "But that's cruel and unfair!"

He shrugged. "To you it seems cruel and unfair, but to us it makes perfect sense. It was our original practice of the Old Ways that turned society against us. If we hope to survive, then we can't do anything that might alert the public to our existence. There are too many aspects of the Old Ways that involve dark forces, and mortals consider those forces evil. Because they fear them, they are quick to pick up on them. All it would take is one mortal accusing us of witchcraft, and the witch hysteria could begin again.

"That's why the council made the punishment so harsh," he continued. "A warlock might be willing to risk his own life by breaking coven law and practicing the Old Ways, but he would never risk the lives of his family, particularly his child, who is his immortality. Since Galen doesn't have a mate or a child, he has nothing to bind him to the rules. Add to that the fact that he's now the high priest and all-powerful within the coven, and you come up with a very dangerous warlock."

Ariel shook her head as she tried to absorb the information. It sounded so fantastic, like something out of a science fiction novel. She didn't want to believe it, but she'd seen too many instances in the past few days when the unbelievable had been true.

"What happens to my brother if the coven is destroyed?" she asked.

"As far as I know, a coven has never been destroyed, so I have no idea," he answered. "If he is under Galen's control, it might free him. Then again, it might destroy him, too."

"And what about you?" she questioned next. "If the coven is destroyed, will you also die?"

"I'm a shunned outcast, so again, I don't know, but in all honesty, I hope so."

"You can't mean that!" she objected.

"Oh, but I do," he replied simply. "If the coven is gone, I'll have lost my roots, the fundamental basis of my existence. I don't think I could survive without the dream that someday I might be able to come home, even if that dream never came to fruition."

Ariel was shaken by his words. Having spent the first eighteen years of her life moving from one part of the globe to another, she knew what it felt like to be rootless. That's why her home was so important to her. But she also understood that he was speaking of more than a home. His claim that he would rather die with the coven than live without it convinced her that they did mean almost as much to him as her brother meant to her.

"Why have you told me all this?" she asked curiously. "I could walk out of here, drive to the nearest town, and tell the world all about you and the coven."

"You could, but you won't," he said.

"And how do you know that?" she challenged.

"Because you'll never do anything to jeopardize your twin." His gaze lowered to her breasts and then wandered even lower in a suggestive manner that sent a tremor of both fear and desire shooting through her. His voice was husky and impatient when he returned his gaze to her face. "So what's your answer, Ariel? If you're going to become my love slave, we have three minutes to get started."

She turned away from him and stared at the fireplace. If he was telling her the truth, then she had to go through with the spell. So why was she still torn? What was keeping her from committing herself?

He'd said she would be in love with him forever and he would never reciprocate her love, and she knew she could deal with that. She could even deal with never marrying and having a family. Armand was her twin, and she couldn't trade his life for a fantasy. And that's

all a husband and family were at this time—merely a
dream that might never come true.

What she was having trouble dealing with, she suddenly recognized, was the thought of actually making
love with Lucien. What would he do when he found
out that she was a virgin? What if it turned out that she
was miserable in bed? And if she was, would that
cause a problem with the spell?

"You have one minute, Ariel," Lucien warned softly.

Still looking at the fireplace, she said, "If I don't go
through with this, you won't fight Galen, will you?"

"Regardless of your decision, I will fight him to the
best of my ability, but it will probably be a losing battle," he answered.

She turned to face him and was surprised to see that
he'd lit the candles and placed all but one on the points
of the star. The last candle he held in his hand as he
stood at the point where it belonged.

Frowning, she searched his face for some sign that
would tell her that she could trust him, but his expression was still neutral.

*He told you he'd give you the crystal back, and he
kept his word. Wasn't that an act of trust?*

"It's time," Lucien said, extending his free hand.

Ariel stared at it uncertainly. She either took his
hand or she walked away, but she had to make the decision now.

Praying that she wasn't making the biggest mistake
of her life, she reached out to him and stepped into the
pentagram.

Chapter Fourteen

A few strong instincts, and a few plain rules.
—William Wordsworth,
Alas! What Boots the Long Laborious Quest? (1815) 1.2

"SO, what do we do now?" Ariel asked uneasily, as she watched Lucien bend to place the last candle on the floor, sealing them into the pentagram.

"The first thing you do is relax," he replied, rising and turning to face her. "There's no reason for you to be nervous, Ariel. In order for the spell to work you must enter into it willingly. Right up to the moment of consummation you can change your mind."

Ariel felt a hot blush fly into her cheeks, and she glanced down at her feet. "There's something I should tell you, Lucien. I'm not sure I'm good at sex. I just thought you should know in case it would cause a problem with the spell."

Lucien stared at her bent head, perplexed. What did she mean, she wasn't sure she was good at sex? He'd visited her in her dreams, and he knew she was not only good, she was spectacular!

Yet when he connected with her mind, he learned she was completely serious. When he delved deeper to find out why, he exclaimed in shock, "You're a *virgin*?"

Her head shot up and she frowned at him irritably. "You don't have to make it sound like I have some horrible disease."

As far as Lucien was concerned, it did sound like a horrible disease. Virginity, or at least virginity as mortals defined it, was not a part of his culture. Despite their limited procreation abilities, his race had highly active libidos. From the moment witches and warlocks hit puberty, they were encouraged to explore their sexuality through dream lovemaking. As adults, it was perfectly acceptable, even expected, for them to have an affair every now and again. Once they found their lifetime mate, they were devoted, monogamous spouses, but for them to stifle their natural biological urges in the meantime would have been considered positively unnatural.

That was why he found it impossible to believe that Ariel could have kept her passion bottled up all this time. And, virgin or not, she did have a profoundly passionate nature. Her dreams alone had proven that to him.

Suddenly it occurred to him that she didn't keep her passion bottled up—that that was what her bordello bedroom and her sexy lingerie were all about. It even explained how she'd taken over their dream lovemaking so easily. He'd bet she did a lot of fantasizing in that bedroom.

"I know my virginity might be a hindrance," Ariel said, interrupting his thoughts. "But as long as you know about it ahead of time, you can compensate for my inadequacies, can't you?"

"Might be a hindrance? Compensate for your inadequacies?" he repeated incredulously. "You sound as if this is some kind of business venture! I also can't believe we're having this conversation. Why in hell are you a virgin at your age, anyway? Are you afraid of sex?"

"No, I am *not* afraid of sex," she said indignantly. "I just happen to be one of those old-fashioned people who believes that when you make love, there should be love involved. Since I've never been *in* love, I've never *made* love."

"Though I find this conversation utterly fascinating, I'm afraid we don't have time for it. At this very moment Galen is enhancing his power and dreaming up some new plan of attack. I need to figure out a way to fight him."

"We've already figured out a way," she reminded. "You're going to cast a love spell over me."

He shook his head. "That was before I found out you're a virgin."

"What does that have to do with it?" she demanded impatiently.

"It has everything to do with it," he said with a scowl. "In the first place, I don't know if it will work on a virgin. We don't revere chasteness the way mortals do. By the time we use the spell, we're experienced lovers. Second, once the spell goes into effect you will never be able to make love with anyone else, and I mean *never,* Ariel. If you'd had some experience, I would at least feel that you knew what you were doing here. Without that experience, you can't possibly understand what you're giving up. Therefore, I can't, in all good conscience, let you make such an uninformed decision."

"And since when have you developed a conscience?" she shot back angrily. "Furthermore, how dare you presume to make my decisions! We're talking about *my* life, and I'm the one who decides what I'm going to do with it!"

"Dammit, Ariel, you've just told me that you've never made love because you've never been in love!" he returned just as angrily. "It's a principle you've upheld for all these years. How can you turn your back on it now?"

"I'm not turning my back on my principles," she rebutted. "You're going to cast a love spell over me, so when we make love, I'll be in love, right?"

"Wrong!" he rasped, as he began to pace from one end of the pentagram to the other. "The spell won't go into effect until we achieve a simultaneous climax, which is another reason this causes a problem. From what I've heard, it's nearly impossible for a mortal woman to achieve a climax her first time. That means we'll have to make love until we get it right."

He stopped and spun around to face her, ruthlessly demanding, "Are you up to that, Ariel? Can you have continuous, uninhibited sex—and I mean totally uninhibited, no-holds-barred sex—with me? Because that's what it's going to take, and there won't be *one ounce* of love involved."

Acutely embarrassed, Ariel glanced down at her feet again. When he had talked about the love spell, she'd been so sure it would be in effect right from the beginning. Could she do what he was proposing? Could she make love with no love involved?

He suddenly appeared in front of her and said, "There's no reason to torment yourself, Ariel. Just give me the crystal, and I'll figure out another way to fight Galen."

She jerked her head up at his words and accused, "That's what this is all about! You just want the crystal back, and you're trying to frighten me into giving it to you so you won't have to go through with the love spell. Why don't you want to go through with it, Lucien? Are you afraid?"

"I am *not* trying to frighten you into giving me back the crystal!" he ground out between clenched teeth, as he shoved his hands into his pants pockets. It was the only way he could keep from grabbing her and shaking some sense into her. He was offering her an out, dammit! Why wasn't she leaping at it?

"I am telling you the unadulterated truth," he went on, "and you're damn right I'm afraid. Any warlock in his right mind would be afraid of what we're up against, but I have more reason to worry than most. I'm a half-breed, and I don't know if I'm powerful enough to fight Galen. Unfortunately, I'm the only one who can fight him, because I'm the only one who didn't swear allegiance to him. That's why I can't afford to take risks, and trying the love spell on you right now is one hell of a risk. For all I know, your virginity might cause it to backfire and make me weaker than I already am."

Propping her hands on her hips, she glared at him. "That's the most ridiculous thing I've ever heard! What's more, I thought the purpose of the spell was so you could draw on my love for my brother to fight Galen. If that's true, then I don't see what my virginity has to do with it. It doesn't change my love for him."

"And what about your principles?" he challenged. "What about your decision not to make love unless love was involved?"

"Love will be involved," she stated adamantly. "I love my brother enough to do anything to save him, even if it means having . . . What was it you called it? Continuous, uninhibited, no-holds-barred sex with you? That doesn't mean it won't embarrass me, because I'm sure it will. But if the spell works, and we all get out of this mess alive, it will be worth it."

"But if the spell works, and we do get out of this mess alive, you'll be condemned to live an empty, lonely life," he reminded grimly. "I wasn't kidding when I said I'll never take a mortal as my mate. I'll walk away from you, *abandon* you, Ariel. You will never know intimacy again."

She gave a fatalistic shrug. "You're missing the point, Lucien. I don't care what you do to me. *I* won't abandon my brother. As for the intimacy, well, for the past twenty-seven years I've survived just fine without sex. I don't think living the rest of my life without it will be that hard, particularly if the alternative is death. And the way I see it, if we don't go through with the spell and I die, then I'll never know what it was like to make love. At least this way, I'll have had the experience, and if you're half the warlock I think you are, you'll make sure this is a night I'll remember for the rest of my life."

"Half the warlock you think I am?" he repeated, his eyes narrowing dangerously. "What in hell is that supposed to mean?"

She winced. "Sorry. That was a bad choice of words. I just meant that I have faith in you. I know that I can trust you to do the right thing."

"You're wrong, Ariel. You can't trust me," he stated, provoked. He'd just told her that he would abandon her, and she trusted him to do the right thing? She had to be crazy! "And if you're doing this because you think you can, then you'd better get out of this pentagram right now. I don't give a damn about you or your brother. All I care about is me and the coven."

She frowned, as though perturbed by his words. "Fine, Lucien. I can accept that, too, because if you use me to save the coven, you'll also be saving my twin. So how about if we stop arguing and get this show on the road?"

As Lucien stared into her determined eyes, he came to the conclusion that he also was crazy, because he knew he was going to go through with the spell. She was right. Its purpose was to draw on her love for her brother, and her virginity wasn't going to change that love. If anything, it probably made it stronger, purer, because if she'd never been in love with another man, then the bond with her twin had never been breached. Her loyalty had always lain with him. Lucien couldn't help wondering what it would be like to be the object of that kind of devotion. After the spell was cast, he'd be able to demand that from her and more.

But that was a dangerous path to follow. He closed his mind to it and said, "All right. I'll take a chance on the spell."

Her voice was no more than a whisper when she said ruefully, "See, I knew you'd do the right thing."

Lucien wasn't sure he was doing the right thing, but he did understand that he had to put this in perspective. This wasn't just about Ariel and Armand and him. It was also about the coven. He had to do everything in his power to save them, even if it meant sacrificing a mortal virgin on their behalf.

Guilt swamped him as the significance of that hit him. Ariel deserved more than a one-night stand with a half-breed warlock. If he hadn't involved her brother in his scheme to catch Galen in the first place, she wouldn't be facing an empty future.

With a weary sigh, he decided she had been right about one thing. He would make this a night she'd remember for the rest of her life. It shouldn't be that hard to accomplish. They already had the bonding spell between them, and the crystal could draw on the mystical powers of the cave to lower her inhibitions. Before the night was over, he would make sure that all her fantasies came true. Since he was using her, his conscience insisted that he owed her that much.

Ariel watched Lucien unroll the large bundle he'd brought into the pentagram. It was a plush, white fur pelt that was large enough to cover a bed. She knew intuitively what the fur was for. They would be making love on it.

So why wasn't she the least bit nervous, she won-

dered as she watched him kick off his shoes and then
carry the basket, the jars, and the bowl onto the fur.
She was going to be giving her virginity to this
man—no, this *warlock*. If she could believe him, when
it was over, he would be in possession of her soul.
That alone should scare the daylights out of her, because if Lucien practiced Satanism wouldn't she, in effect, be giving her soul to the Devil and condemning
herself to an immortal Hell?

Even as the question arose, she couldn't believe that
that would be her fate. Lucien's powers were beyond
her range of understanding, and there was no doubt in
her mind that he was dangerous. But she knew instinctively that he wasn't evil. She also knew in her heart
that if it was within his power, he would never allow
harm to come to her.

Could I be falling in love with him? she wondered,
as her gaze roamed over him.

She quickly concluded that that question was so ridiculous it bordered on the absurd. He'd just told her
he didn't give a damn about her or her brother. He also
despised her because she was a mortal, and he'd done
nothing but argue with her and terrorize her. Those
were hardly qualities to inspire love. But she did have
a strong physical attraction for him, and she'd had it
from the first night they'd met. Why else would she
have had erotic dreams about him?

That attraction escalated when he walked to the edge
of the fur, held out his hand, and bade her softly, seductively, "Come to me, Ariel."

She couldn't have ignored his summons if she had
wanted to. She went to him, stopping only long enough
to kick off her sandals. Stepping onto the fur, which
was thick and plush beneath her feet, she took his
hand.

As their fingers entwined, he tucked his other hand

beneath her chin and raised her head, so that she was gazing into the depths of his silvery eyes.

"You have nothing to fear," he reassured. "The spell does not hinge upon your performance, but upon your willingness to commit to me. If at any point you're uncomfortable, just say so. We have all night to do this, and I won't get angry with you, nor will I force you to do anything you don't want to do. So just relax."

Oddly enough she did relax. When he led her to the center of the fur and urged her to sit down in front of the jars and the bowl, she did so willingly. After she was seated, he sat cross-legged beside her. Opening the jars, he removed a pinch of dried plant from each and dropped it into the bowl. She frowned as she watched him, because there was something so familiar about what he was doing.

It was as if he sensed her unease, because he glanced up and said, "It's okay, Ariel. There's nothing here that can harm you."

Her frown deepened at his words, which seemed as familiar as what he was doing. "I feel as if I've done this before."

"In a way you have, but it's nothing for you to worry about," he said, reaching over to cup her chin. "For now you have to concentrate on us. That's very important. At this point in time, you can't think about anything but us, or the spell won't work. Just relax, and let me take care of everything."

As he finished speaking, he skimmed his thumb over her lips, sending a shiver of pleasure racing through her. He must have felt her reaction, because he did it again, and then he leaned forward, drawing her mouth to his.

His kiss was no more than a brush of his lips against hers, but it sent a sweet ache of desire coursing through her.

"That's it," he encouraged, lifting his head so that he was staring deeply into her eyes. "Think about us, Ariel. Think about all the things you want me to do to you, of all the things you want to do to me. Tonight is your night, and we're going to make all your fantasies come true."

His gaze was so intense that Ariel couldn't look away from him, and she was barely aware that he was unfastening the top few buttons of her blouse. She gasped in pleasure when he slipped his hand beneath the fabric and ran it from the base of her throat to the center of her breasts where the crystal lay.

With his finger, he traced the slender length of the crystal, making it heat against her skin and sending an electrifying ripple of desire through her.

"Lucien!" she whispered hoarsely.

"I know," he murmured huskily as he eased her to her back and lay down beside her. Propping himself up on his forearm, he traced the crystal again, causing an even stronger ripple of desire to shoot through her.

When she groaned softly, he crooned, "It's sweet torment, isn't it? But it's going to be even better, Ariel. So much better. Just close your eyes for now and let yourself go with the feelings. *Close your eyes and feel.*"

I'm bewitched! Ariel thought, as her eyelids drooped heavily of their own accord, but she didn't care. Lucien was now stroking the crystal, causing wave after wave of ecstasy to wash over her until she could think of nothing but the exquisite pleasure engulfing her body. Never had she felt so alive, so vibrant, so *womanly!*

Ah, you are so much more than a woman, Lucien's voice whispered provocatively in her mind. *You're an enchantress, a seductress, a temptress. Tempt me, Ariel. Enchant me. Seduce me.*

I don't know how!

Of course you do. Just live out your fantasies. Make them all come true.

Those thoughts were still echoing in her mind when Lucien's mouth closed over hers. His kiss was both soft and hard, tentative and urgent. It was as if he felt all the confusion of feelings swirling inside her and was leading her through their different textures. And the entire time he never touched her body, but continued to stroke the crystal.

She groaned when he pulled away from her lips and trailed kisses from her cheek to her ear. He traced its shell with his tongue before murmuring, "Are you hungry?"

Until that moment hunger, or at least hunger for food, had been the last thing on her mind, but suddenly she was ravenous.

"Starving," she replied on a breathless sigh as he caught her earlobe between his teeth and gave it a gentle nip.

"Then let's eat."

He left her so abruptly that her eyes flew open in surprise. She sat up and saw Lucien sitting in front of the bowl with the dried plants. He leaned forward and gently blew into the bowl. When a flame suddenly shot out of it and toward the ceiling, she had a dizzying sense of déjà vu. She knew she'd seen that flame before, but when she tried to pull the memory into focus it eluded her.

"Don't think about it, Ariel," Lucien urged compellingly as he shifted to face her. "Just hold on to the crystal, stare into the flame and think of the crystal cave. Do it, Ariel. *Do it now.*"

I really am bewitched! she thought as her hand automatically went to the crystal at his bidding and her gaze fixed on the flame. The image of the crystal cave immediately flooded into her mind with such detailed

clarity that she knew this wasn't just her memory.
Lucien was enhancing it with his own memory. He was
inside her head, controlling her thoughts!

She attempted to fight the hold he had over her. But
no matter how hard she tried, she couldn't wipe out the
vision of the cave, nor could she release the crystal.
She could only peer into the flame and remember what
Lucien wanted her to remember, see what Lucien
wanted her to see.

She let out a startled gasp when the flame suddenly
shimmered and then flared so brightly that she had to
close her eyes. When she opened them a moment later,
they were no longer in the pentagram. They were sitting in the crystal cave!

That was impossible! It had to be an illusion, she
told herself as she rubbed her hands across her eyes.
When she pulled them away, however, the cave was
still there.

"Eat, Ariel," Lucien commanded huskily, pushing
the basket in front of her and opening the lid.

It was then that Ariel realized what he was doing.
He had said that Galen had wanted her to eat at the
cave so she'd lose her inhibitions. Evidently Lucien
had decided to use the same ploy. She understood his
reasoning. If she was to make uninhibited love with
him, then she had to be, well, uninhibited. But regardless of her grasp of the situation, she resented that he
was using tricks.

Her resentment didn't appease her appetite, however.
She was still ravenous, and she peered into the basket.
There was a bottle of white wine, a large bag of
chocolate-covered cookies, a jar of honey, two ripe
peaches, and two bananas. It wasn't exactly the type of
menu she would have chosen, but at that moment any
food would have been better than no food.

Chocolate was her passion, and she grabbed the

cookies. After ripping open the bag, she devoured three while studying Lucien's face. By the time she swallowed the third cookie, she decided she liked the way he looked. It was true that his features were too stark to make him classically handsome, but there was a rugged appeal to them.

Unexpectedly, she had an overwhelming urge to touch his face, to trace every plane and hollow. She held back though, because she sensed it wasn't a natural impulse but an effect caused by the cave.

Again resentment stirred, and when it did, Lucien's expression became wary. It was then that she realized he was reading her mind, and that made her mad. If he was going to seduce her with his cave, the least he could do was give her some emotional privacy.

She grabbed another cookie and took a bite before drawling, "What's the matter, Lucien? Aren't things going the way you planned?"

Lucien arched a brow at her taunt. He was admittedly surprised by her sudden ire, but as he watched her finish the cookie, he realized he should have expected it. From the first bite she'd taken, her inhibitions had started fading. It was logical that anger and fear would be the first emotions bared. She was going along with the spell to save her brother, not out of a desire to mate with Lucien. Only when her feelings of resentment were out of the way would she be able to move on to lust.

"Let's just say you aren't exactly reacting the way I expected," he answered.

"Well, you know how we mortals are," she said with an eloquent shrug, as she finished off the cookie and reached for another one. "You can always count on us to do the unexpected."

"So I'm learning."

"I know what you're doing," she announced. "You're trying to get rid of my inhibitions."

He regarded her thoughtfully. "Does that frighten you?"

"You're a warlock, not Sigmund Freud, so stop trying to analyze me," she said. "Besides, I don't have to answer your questions. You can read my mind, remember?"

"You don't have to be afraid, Ariel."

"That's easy for you to say. You aren't the one who's going to lose control," she shot back defensively.

Lucien realized that her statement was not only revealing but made perfect sense. Her love life had consisted of fantasy, so she had always been in command of what happened. But now she was faced with real lovemaking, which involved the needs and desires of two people. He could see where she would find that unnerving.

"Would it be easier if I let you take control?" he asked.

She regarded him suspiciously. "You're trying to trick me."

He shook his head. "No. As I told you, for the spell to work you have to enter into it willingly. That means I can't use tricks."

"If that's true, then why did you conjure up the cave?" she demanded.

"I've already explained about the cave," he replied. "It's an integral part of our mating ritual. Under normal circumstances, I would take you to it. Since I can't do that, I have to rely upon the crystal to bring its mystical powers to us."

"Then I was right. The crystal's from the cave," she said, raising her hand to it.

"Yes, it's from the cave," he managed to get out before she touched it. Only then did he realize that since she had already consumed half a dozen cookies, her inhibitions were almost nonexistent, and her anger and fear were unrestrained.

Her emotional turmoil assailed his mind with an explosive force. It was as if a thousand of Galen's vicious little demons had been turned loose inside his head and were screaming in his ears. As he tried to fight his way out of the intense flood of feelings, he closed his eyes tightly and pressed his hands to his temples. Without warning, the attack suddenly stopped.

When he opened his eyes, Ariel was kneeling in front of him. She was staring at him worriedly, and there was panic in her voice as she asked, "What's wrong, Lucien? Please answer me! Are you okay?"

He couldn't answer, but it wasn't because of the emotional assault he had undergone. It was because he realized she was genuinely worried about him.

Of course she's worried about you. If anything happens to you, she won't be able to save her brother.

But even as he offered himself that explanation, he knew it wasn't true. There wasn't a thought in her mind about Armand. Her entire attention was focused on *him*. She was anxious about *him*. She *cared* about him, and so much so that her concern for him had overridden her own exposed emotions, which was why the attack had stopped so abruptly.

It had been so long since anyone had really cared about him, that he could only stare at her, stunned. He finally managed to recover his voice when she frantically said, "Lucien, please answer me! Are you all right?"

"I'm fine," he assured gruffly.

She sat back on her heels, worry still etched on her face. "Are you sure?"

"I'm positive," he reaffirmed. "Now, where were we

in our conversation? Ah, yes. We were talking about control, and whether it would be easier if you were in control. Would it, Ariel? Would you like to be in control tonight?"

Ariel frowned in frustration. He was evading her again, and she didn't know whether to yell at him or punch him. He had just scared the daylights out of her, and it was obvious he had no intention of telling her what had happened. All she knew was that one minute he'd been sitting there looking perfectly normal—or at least as normal as he was capable of looking, considering that he was a sullen warlock—and the next he'd been pressing his hands against his temples as if his head was ready to explode.

She wanted to ask—no, *insist*—that he tell her what was going on, but she sensed that it would only cause another fight. Besides, he did seem to be okay now. So okay, in fact, that she began to suspect that he hadn't been in distress at all. Had this just been another one of his tricks to get her to do what he wanted?

After scooting back until a good three feet separated them, she sat down, drew her knees up to her chest, and linked her arms around her shins. "Considering my inexperience, don't you think giving me control would be a bit like handing over your car keys to a blind man?"

He partially mimicked her by drawing one leg up and draping his arm across his knee. "It's true that at the time of actual intercourse I will have to assume a certain amount of control, but I'm willing to let you dictate events up to that point."

Eyeing him distrustfully, she said, "I'm not sure what that means."

"It means I'll give you control over what happens between us until the very end. I'll do whatever you want, whenever you want me to do it."

She pondered that for a long moment before finally saying, "So, if I establish a set of rules, you'll follow them?"

He arched a brow. "Rules?"

"Yes, rules. You know, a list of things you can or cannot do."

"I know what rules are, Ariel," he said impatiently. "That wasn't, however, exactly what I had in mind."

"But that's what control is all about, Lucien," she rejoined. "Someone establishes rules and you obey them. So is it a deal?"

"I suppose that depends upon what your rules are," he stated warily.

"No, Lucien. I want a simple yes or no."

Cautiously he said, "Let's compromise. You tell me your rules, and I'll tell you which ones I'm willing to follow."

She gave an adamant shake of her head. "I didn't ask for that type of concession on your part when I agreed to the spell, so it isn't fair for you to ask it of me now. All I want from you is a simple yes or no."

Every instinct Lucien possessed told him to say no. His common sense, however, told him he was being overly suspicious. After all, she was a virgin, so any rules she established couldn't be that hard to swallow.

"All right," he agreed, albeit reluctantly. "I'll follow your rules."

She sighed in relief and said, "Okay, here they are. The first rule is that you have to eat with me. Here. In this illusionary cave."

"Fine," Lucien agreed, not bothering to tell her that he had to eat anyway, or the spell wouldn't work. Besides, he understood where her demand was coming from, and he had to admit that, for a mortal, she was damn smart. He'd told her that Galen wouldn't eat at the cave with her, and she was trying to make sure he wasn't using her in the same way Galen would have.

"The second rule is that at no time, and I mean at *no time,* even at the end when you take control, will you invade my privacy by reading my mind. I want you completely out of my head unless I invite you in."

Lucien frowned at that one. "Ariel, by reading your mind, I can figure out what you want, what is best for you. It will help me enhance your pleasure."

She gave another adamant shake of her head. "I'm serious about this, Lucien. I don't want you inside my head unless I give you permission to be there."

He wasn't happy about it, but he said, "All right. I'll stay out of your head unless you invite me in."

She nodded as she drew her knees closer to her chest and wrapped her arms tighter around her legs. Lucien frowned again. She was closing in on herself, and that wasn't auspicious body language.

"The third rule is that I don't want you to use the crystal either before or during our lovemaking," she announced.

"I can't agree to that," he said instantly. "The crystal is an enhancement of my power. It's what makes me a warlock. I have to use it."

"Are you saying that if you don't use it, the spell won't work?"

He scowled. "Ariel, I just told you that the crystal is an enhancement of my power."

"That's not an answer to my question," she said doggedly. "Do you need the crystal to complete the spell?"

"Dammit, Ariel!" he yelled.

"Yes or no?" she yelled right back.

"Why are you doing this?" he roared, as he leaped to his feet.

She stared up at him, her lips set into an obstinate

line. "Do you need it to complete the spell? Yes or no, Lucien."

He had to answer her truthfully, and he had never resented it more than he did at this moment.

"No!" he rasped harshly.

She nodded. "Then I don't want you to touch the crystal at any time, not even at the end."

"Why?" he demanded, both furious and frustrated.

"Because I'm a woman, not a witch," she answered. "I don't want to make love with a warlock who manipulates me. I want to make love with a *man*. So, will you follow the rule? Will you leave the crystal alone?"

He raked his hand through his hair. "I don't know if I can do it, Ariel. I've never made love without the crystal."

"Well, I guess that makes us even, because I've never made love at all," she responded.

He glared down at her. "Is that the last of your rules?"

"Other than that I accept your offer to let me be in control of what happens until the end, that's it," she responded, so cheerfully that he would gladly have strangled her.

He turned his back on her, his gaze focusing on the flame of one of the candles. Could he make love to her without the enhancement of the crystal? Well, "could" was probably the wrong word to use. She was damned attractive. She had turned him on from the first night he'd seen her. It wasn't so much a question of *could* he do it as *would* he do it.

He gave an amazed shake of his head when he realized he was arguing semantics, just as she was prone to do. If he was thinking like her, then he'd spent too damn much time among mortals.

"I'm waiting for your answer, Lucien," she said.

He turned back around to face her. As his gaze

roamed over her beautiful face, he knew he couldn't walk away from her, and he knew that his decision didn't have a damned thing to do with her brother or the coven. The truth was, all his life he'd struggled to make his mark, to be accepted for who and what he was. This was one instance where he didn't have to struggle and he didn't need to worry about failure, because he'd be making love to a mortal as a mortal. There was even an inexplicable, totally alien part of him that reveled in the knowledge that he would be the first and only man who would ever touch her as he would tonight. She would forever and always be his.

With a nod, he said, "I agree."

She didn't respond. Instead, she held her hand out to him. He took it and sat down in front of her, suspecting that he was about to make a mistake he would regret for the rest of his life. Oddly enough, he had a feeling it would be worth it.

Chapter Fifteen

The kiss you take is better than you give.
—William Shakespeare, *Troilus and Cressida* 4.5.38

ARIEL decided that being in control wasn't as easy as it sounded. Lucien was watching her expectantly, and she didn't have the faintest idea what to do.

"Why don't we have some wine and talk for a while?" he suggested. "It might help us relax."

"*Us* relax?" she repeated skeptically.

"Yes, us. You aren't the only one feeling nervous, Ariel."

"Why are you nervous?" she asked, intrigued.

"I don't think I've ever met anyone who asks so damn many questions," he complained mildly. "And before I answer another one, you have to answer mine. Shall I pour us some wine?"

"Sure."

When he withdrew the wine bottle, a corkscrew, and two glasses out of the basket, something elusive began to nag at the back of Ariel's mind. It was only when he'd filled the glasses and handed her one that she figured out what was bothering her.

"You tricked me!" she accused.

"What are you talking about?" he asked, looking bewildered.

"*This* is what I'm talking about," she said, holding up her glass. "There are two glasses. *Two,* Lucien."

"So?"

"So, there's enough food for two. When you agreed

to my rule, you weren't agreeing at all, because you planned to eat with me all along!"

He arched a brow. "Forgive me for being dense, but as I recall, you asked me to eat with you and I said I would. In my book, that's agreement."

"Not when you'd already planned to do it," she insisted stubbornly.

He took a sip of wine before saying, "You're arguing semantics again, Ariel, and I don't think you really care whether or not I planned to eat with you. I think you're looking for an excuse to be angry with me."

"That's ridiculous!"

"Is it?"

"Has anyone ever told you that you have an irritating habit of talking like a psychologist?"

"No."

"Well, you do," she grumbled, as she took a sip of wine. "And there's nothing more annoying than an amateur psychologist. No, I take that back. An amateur *warlock* psychologist is definitely worse."

"You know, Ariel, this is going to be a first for me too," he said. Lifting his glass toward her in a parody of a toast, he expounded, "I'm going to be having three first-time experiences tonight. It will be the first time I've made love with a mortal, the first time I've made love with a virgin, and the first time I've made love *without* my crystal. So how about if you stop being so nervous and defensive and sit back and enjoy your wine?"

Ariel stared at him in amazement. "You've never made love with a virgin?"

He groaned and leaned his head back. Staring at the ceiling, he said, "I can't believe it. You're *still* badgering me with questions."

"I'm sorry, Lucien, but this is very important to me. Are you telling me the truth?"

"Yes, I'm telling you the truth," he answered, returning his attention to her with a resigned sigh. "As I've already told you, we don't revere chasteness the way that you do. We have highly active libidos, and though we aren't promiscuous, we do have an occasional affair. The witches I've been with had already lost their physical virginity to someone else."

"What do you mean by *physical* virginity?"

He frowned as he finished off his wine. Setting his glass aside, he said, "Ariel, I don't think this is the time for us to discuss that. Let's talk about something else."

She shook her head. "I want an answer, Lucien. Why did you qualify it as physical virginity?"

Raking a hand through his hair, he muttered what sounded like a curse. Then he said, "We also engage in dream lovemaking. It isn't quite as satisfying sexually as actual lovemaking, but it's close enough to make it worth our while."

Ariel felt the color draining from her face. He engaged in dream lovemaking. That's why she had felt as if he'd had a hand in her erotic dreams. They hadn't been *her* private fantasies. They'd been his!

"Damn you, Lucien Morgret!" she yelled, as her temper exploded. "You've been assaulting me in my dreams!"

"*Assaulting* you?" One moment he was sitting three feet away from her, and the next he was kneeling in front of her. Before she could fully absorb what was happening, he grabbed her arms and jerked her toward him until they were nose to nose.

His eyes were glittering so brightly that they nearly blinded her, as he stated in a deadly rasp, "It's true that I visited you in your dreams, but you took them over. I only did what *you* made me do. I'm not a damn mortal, and I don't have to assault women to get my kicks!"

He was so furious that Ariel knew she should be frightened, but instead she was feeling strangely aroused by his display of temper. It took her a second to realize that there was a rational explanation for her untoward reaction. She found everything about Lucien daunting, from his extraordinary psychic abilities to his superior physical strength. The only time he didn't make her feel wretchedly "mortal" and inferior to him was when she made him lose his temper. Whenever that happened he was out of control, and that allowed her to feel as if she had a semblance of control over her own life.

Tonight, more than ever, she needed to have that sense of control, which was why her rules had been so important. If she was going to make love with him, then she needed to feel as if they were on equal footing, or at least as equal as her inexperience would allow.

But even when Lucien had agreed to follow her rules, she had still felt overwhelmed by him, and that had made her feel inadequate. Only now did she understand that if she could make him lose his temper, she could also make him lose control during lovemaking. Just the thought of having that kind of power over him was highly erotic.

She wanted to throw her arms around his neck and kiss him for all she was worth, but she recognized the folly in that. He was too angry, and she instinctively understood that to kiss him now would only result in transforming his anger into an uncontrollable passion that would overwhelm them both. Instead she wanted to do exactly what he had urged earlier, and that was tempt him, enchant him, and seduce him. She wanted

to drive him out of his mind with desire and desire
alone.

With that resolve in mind, she said, "I'm sorry if I
offended you, Lucien, but try to put yourself in my
place. In the last few days everything I've ever believed in has been challenged. It's hard enough to accept that people like you exist, but then I learn that
even my dreams aren't safe from you. Can't you see
what that means? I have no place to run and hide. I
have no *sanctuary,* and you, of all people, should know
how scary that is."

As she spoke, he slowly released his grip on her
arms, and his eyes began to return to normal. By the
time she was finished, he was sitting on his heels with
his hands resting on his thighs.

Several moments passed before he said, "I never
thought about it that way."

"Of course you didn't. You're a warlock, and I'm a
mortal. You don't understand me any better than I understand you. But we have to reach some sort of understanding tonight, because like it or not, we're in this
mess together, and we're the only ones who can get
ourselves out of it."

"So you're still willing to go along with the love
spell?"

She smiled ruefully. "Wild horses, or maybe I
should say wild demons, couldn't drag me out of this
pentagram. So how about if you pour us some more
wine? I'm afraid that when you grabbed me I ended up
wearing the contents of my last glass."

His gaze dropped to her soaked shirt front. When
she realized he was staring at her breasts, her nipples
began to harden. When he returned his gaze to her
face, his eyes were aglow again, but this time she
knew it wasn't from anger, and an aching yearning
stirred inside her in response.

"I think you'd better get out of that wet blouse. You can wear my shirt for now," he stated gruffly and began to unbutton it.

Ariel didn't bother answering. She was too busy watching him reveal his chest. When he shrugged out of the shirt, she caught her breath. He looked *exactly* as he'd looked in her dreams, from the breadth of his shoulders and the thick thatch of dark hair across his chest, right down to the small mole slightly above and to the right of his navel!

On their own accord, her eyes traced the narrow line of hair that disappeared into the waistband of his denims, which hung low on his narrow hips. As they skimmed lower, she wondered if the rest of him was exactly as he'd been in her dreams, and she felt heat flare into her cheeks at the provocative possibility.

"There's no need to be embarrassed, Ariel."

"I'm not embarrassed," she denied, lifting her gaze to his face, and oddly enough, it was the truth. "I'm just . . . thinking."

He dropped his shirt into her lap and retrieved her empty glass from the fur. "Well, while you're thinking, you can change into this. I'll get us some more wine."

Ariel decided she had to give him credit for sensitivity. He turned his back and kept it turned while he refilled their glasses. She shed her blouse, and as she pulled on his shirt, two sensations struck her simultaneously. One was amazement at how large it was on her. He'd had the cuffs rolled halfway up his forearms, but the sleeves still fell to her hands. It made her feel dainty, and at five foot ten, she never felt dainty. The second sensation was the manly scent that enveloped her. It wasn't strong, nor was it perfumed in any way. It was just a good, wholesome smell that teased at her senses and caused that yearning to stir again.

Drawing in a deep breath, she quickly rolled the

cuffs higher and buttoned the shirt. When she was done, she said, "You can turn around now."

He turned and handed her wine to her. As he took a sip of his own, his gaze roamed over her, and he frowned.

"Is something wrong?" she asked nervously.

"No. It's just that no female has ever worn my clothes before."

"Does it bother you?"

"Not in the way you mean," he said gruffly.

There was nothing subtle about his innuendo, and Ariel barely managed to resist dropping her gaze to the front of his trousers to see just how "bothered" he was.

Heat again flared into her cheeks, and this time it was from embarrassment. To cover her self-consciousness, she grabbed the bag of cookies. She took one and then held the package out to him. He took it, his lips curved in sardonic amusement, leaving no doubt that he was aware of her discomfort, or rather that he knew she was aware of his discomfort.

"So, why don't you tell me something about yourself," she said as he took a cookie out of the bag and began to munch on it.

"What would you like to know?"

She shrugged. "I don't know. Tell me about your family."

"There isn't anything to tell. My father died when I was seven, my grandmother when I was twenty-eight, and I lost my grandfather three years ago."

"And your mother? Is she still alive?"

"I have no idea. She left a few weeks after my father died, and I haven't heard from her since."

"She *abandoned* you?" Ariel gasped in disbelief.

He arched a brow. "Why is that so hard to believe? Don't you read the newspapers or watch television? Mortal mothers abandon their children all the time.

Then again, I suppose I'm being a bit unfair. My mother did ask me to go with her, but I refused. I belonged here, not in the mortal world. She preferred the mortal world to being with me."

"So she just walked away and that was it?"

"That was it," he agreed easily, fishing another cookie out of the bag.

He sounded so blasé, but Ariel could sense the bitterness beneath the surface. No wonder he had such a chip on his shoulder when it came to mortals. Her desertion had to have devastated him.

If it had been anyone but Lucien, she would have offered her sympathy. Instinct, however, told her that he would construe it as pity. She'd spent enough time with him to recognize that he would consider that a direct attack on his pride and that would infuriate him.

Instead, she decided to offer her understanding in the one area they shared. She said, "I know how hard it is to grow up without a father. My father was a Pulitzer prize–winning war correspondent. He was killed in Vietnam when my brother and I were infants, so I have no memories of him. My mother used to tell us wonderful stories about him, but they always made me sad. I didn't want stories. I wanted him. I used to make up fantasies where my father would come home. He'd tell us that he really hadn't died, that it was all a mistake, and that now we'd be a family. You know, I still have that dream every now and then. I guess we never really get over the traumas of our childhood."

"Maybe not," he agreed, staring at her as he ate another cookie.

Tension suddenly curled between them, and Ariel was hit with an overwhelming need to kiss him. Nervously, she flicked her tongue across her bottom lip. Lucien's gaze immediately focused on the action with such intense concentration that she felt it all the way down to the pit of her stomach and beyond.

"Lucien?"

He dragged his gaze upward until he met her eyes. "Yes."

"I think it's time," she said breathlessly.

His brow shot upward at a rakish angle. "Time for what?"

"Everything."

"We haven't finished eating."

"I'm sure I'll be hungry . . . afterwards. So, are you going to come here and kiss me?"

She barely managed to get the last word of her question out before his lips were over hers. His kiss was hot and urgent as he eased her down to the fur and came over her. When his tongue demanded entrance into her mouth, she granted it with a pleasurable sigh, running her hands over his bare shoulder and up his neck, tangling her fingers in his hair.

"*Ariel!*" he rasped, her name sounding like both a blessing and a curse as he pulled away from the kiss and stared down at her. Then he tangled his fingers in her hair and sealed his mouth over hers again before she could respond.

When his tongue engaged hers in a feverish duel that simulated a far more intimate act, she groaned and arched her hips into his. The proof of his need made her lower body ignite. She trailed a hand down his bare back, sliding her fingers beneath the waistband of his jeans and urging him even closer.

He took her cue and rocked his hips against hers until she felt as if her entire body was nothing but one raw nerve of escalating desire.

"Lucien, touch me!" she gasped as she dragged her mouth away from his and pushed against his shoulders.

He immediately sat up. Straddling her hips, he unbuttoned his shirt and pushed the fabric aside to expose the lacy black satin covering her breasts. At the sight, he drew in a harsh breath. Then he snapped open the front of her bra, swept the fabric away, and lowered his head, drawing a taut nipple into his mouth.

From that moment on, Ariel lost all ability to think. All she could do was feel as he paid homage to one breast and then the other. She was so absorbed in the passion building inside her that she was barely aware of him stripping off the remainder of their clothes. All she knew was that one minute they were constrained by fabric, and the next they were tangled together in exquisite nakedness.

His hands moved over her like quicksilver, learning where and how to touch her to bring her the most pleasure. She was doing her own sensual, if more tentative, exploration, delighting at his approving sighs and mumbled words of encouragement.

When he parted her legs with his hand and began to trail kisses down her abdomen, she tangled her hand in his hair in anticipation. She gasped when his lips settled against her intimately, and his tongue began to tease her clitoris, proving that her dreams hadn't been wrong about his expertise. Her climax hit so swiftly that she let out a cry of surprise and relief.

She was still riding the waves when he settled between her legs and came over her. Resting his weight on his forearms, he tangled his hands in her hair again and said, "Ariel, look at me."

Slowly, dazedly, she opened her eyes. His were brilliantly luminous, and she raised a hand and caressed his cheek.

"You're beautiful, Lucien."

Surprise flickered across his face, and then his expression settled into a troubled frown. "It's time for me to make you mine, Ariel. This is your last chance to back out. Are you sure you want to go through with it?"

"I've never been more sure of anything in my life," she answered throatily as she wrapped her legs around his hips and arched up against his erection. Just the feel of him, silken and hard and vibrating with life, was enough to send her senses flying again. "Make love to me, Lucien."

His frown deepened. "It's going to hurt, Ariel. Let me hold the crystal and take away the pain."

"No," she said with an adamant shake of her head. "If you take away the pain, it won't be real. It has to be real, Lucien. It *has* to be."

He tenderly brushed her hair back from her forehead. "Then let me hold the crystal and experience the pain with you. Let me help you through it."

Ariel stared at him in confused anguish. He'd already told her that after tonight there would be nothing between them. He was going to walk away from her. *Abandon* her. That was why it was so important that she feel everything to its fullest. It was the only way she'd know it hadn't been a dream. So why did he want to experience this with her?

"Why?" she asked hoarsely.

Why, indeed? Lucien wondered as he stared down at her face. She'd said he was beautiful, and he knew her words were nothing more than a combination of passion and the influence of the cave. But she was truly beautiful, with her skin flushed to a tantalizing peach hue, her hair in tangled disarray, her eyes gleaming like emeralds, and her lips swollen from his kisses.

But her outer beauty was nothing compared to the inward beauty he had come to know over the last few days. He had thrust her into an alien world that she couldn't even begin to comprehend, that frightened her. But she'd pushed her fears aside and charged full speed ahead without so much as a blink of her eyes. She might be a mortal, but he didn't think there was a witch alive who could beat her when it came to courage and devotion.

"Because if you won't let me experience it with you, it won't be real for me," he told her. "Let me hold the crystal and share it with you. *Please,* Ariel."

It was his last entreaty that snatched away Ariel's reservations. She was sure that he couldn't count on one hand the times he'd said "please" to anyone. He wasn't the kind of man—no, warlock—who would plead. He'd take whatever life dished out with stoicism and suffer in silence. Just the fact that he would break that code while making love with her—a mortal— brought tears to her eyes.

"All right," she whispered. "You can share it with me."

He didn't respond, but he didn't need to, because he lowered his lips to hers and the gentleness of his kiss said it all.

When he lifted his head, he took her hand and placed it over the crystal. Then he twined his hand over hers. Ariel knew that the moment of realizing her full womanhood was upon her.

Their eyes met and held as he probed her with the tip of his penis. She stiffened when she felt him begin to slide inside her.

Relax, Ariel, his voice whispered in her mind. *I'll warn you when it's time. Right now, I'm just testing. I won't hurt you. I promise.*

She forced herself to relax. If Lucien said he wouldn't hurt her, then he wouldn't hurt her. She felt him come up against the barrier of her virginity and then withdraw.

Lucien?

It's okay, he reassured her, as he slowly slid into her

until he reached the barrier again, and again he withdrew. *One more time, okay?*

Lucien!

One more time, and then we'll do it, he reassured as he again slid into her and withdrew. She felt him flex his hips before he mentally exclaimed, *Now, Ariel!*

His warning barely registered before she felt a quick, sharp pain that caused her to gasp. But before she could fully absorb it, she felt Lucien pulling it away from her.

No! her mind cried out. But her objection was extinguished by a wave of pleasure that swept through her with such intensity that she thought she might die from it. She knew it wasn't just her pleasure overwhelming her. It was also Lucien's. She was receiving his feelings through the crystal.

That's it, Ariel. Ride through it with me, Lucien urged as he began to move inside her urgently.

You're cheating! she accused, but it was only a half-hearted complaint. Her body, indeed her entire soul, was spiraling toward climax.

Oh, yes! Lucien mentally shouted as they reached the edge of the plateau and toppled over it together.

As they shuddered in each other's arms, Ariel opened her eyes and watched the crystal cave shimmer and then disappear. Tears welled into her eyes because she knew that now it was over. The spell was cast, and all she could do was wait for Lucien to break her heart.

"Damn you, Lucien," she whispered hoarsely, as her tears began to roll down her cheeks. "You promised to fulfill all my fantasies, and now you've taken that away from me."

"You're wrong, Ariel," he murmured, brushing away her tears with his fingertips. "I promised you we'd fulfill them, and we have until dawn to make them all come true."

"But the spell is cast, isn't it?" she asked, staring up at him.

"It's cast," he agreed solemnly, stroking her hair back from her forehead. "But that's good, Ariel, because it means that all we have to do is concentrate on each other for the remainder of the night."

Ariel was torn by his announcement. One part of her was exultant that their lovemaking wasn't over, but the other part warned that it was too risky to share any further intimacy with him. Already she could feel the effects of the spell taking hold. There was a tenderness toward Lucien welling up inside her that was so strong it was almost painful. She also had a tremendous need to touch him, to hold him, to whisper "I love you" into his ear. Even worse, she wanted him to give her the words back, and she knew that wasn't going to happen. He'd made it clear that he had no intention of getting involved with a mortal. Come morning, he would walk away from her forever. For her own self-protection, she had to make the break from him right now, before the bond could get any stronger. The longer she waited, the more it was going to hurt.

But even as her instincts were prodding at her to get up and run from him, her arms were entwining themselves around his neck and her lips were lifting to his. He'd promised her he would fulfill all her fantasies, and she was going to make him live up to that promise. She might regret it in the morning, but she knew that if she didn't give herself this night, she would end up regretting that for the rest of her life.

Chapter Sixteen

It is always darkest just before the day dawneth.
—Thomas Fuller, *Pisqah Sight* (1650), bk. 2, ch. 2

AS Ariel's lips moved provocatively beneath Lucien's, he was shocked to realize his body was already beginning to harden with renewed need for her. Thankfully, he still had enough presence of mind to realize he might be capable of another round of lovemaking, but this had been Ariel's first time. Her body needed some time to recover.

Reluctantly, he eased away from her kiss and stared down into her face. As she looked up at him, she gave him a soft smile, and her eyes took on a dreamy glow. All his life Lucien had heard about the magic of the mating love spell, but he always figured it was an exaggeration. After all, the people going through it were in love in the first place, so the real magic had to come from them.

Now, as he gently traced her beautiful smile with his fingertips, he knew he'd been wrong. The emotions he was experiencing toward her—tenderness, protectiveness, and an overwhelming possessiveness—were so primeval that they had to be feelings of love, and he had to attribute that to the spell. The only other explanation was that he had been in love with her beforehand, and he knew that wasn't possible. Over the past few days he had developed a grudging admiration for her, and the bonding spell had made him feel protective toward her. He'd even desired her, but they hadn't been together long enough for him to have fallen in love with her.

He was drawn away from his thoughts when Ariel ran her hand along his jaw and murmured, "Kiss me, Lucien."

"In time," he said, with an indulgent smile as he rose to his feet and then bent down to scoop her up into his arms.

"What are you doing?" she gasped, linking her arms around his neck.

"Giving you some tender loving care."

"But, Lucien—"

He silenced her objection with a swift, hard kiss. "Trust me, Ariel. You're going to enjoy this."

As he carried Ariel out of the pentagram and down the hallway, she was feeling too mellow to argue with him. They bypassed her bedroom and entered a door at the other end of the hall. She regarded the room in amazement. They were in what she assumed was the master bedroom. It was easily three, maybe even four, times larger than the room she'd been using. Whereas the remainder of the house was decorated sparsely, this room was decadently opulent.

Dominating the room was the largest antique tester bed she'd ever seen, and it stood so high off the floor it required four steps to get into it. Lining one wall were four antique armoires and a dark-blue-velvet chaise lounge large enough to accommodate two people occupied a corner, along with an equally oversized matching velvet wing-backed chair. The floor was covered with oriental rugs, and the mahogany-paneled walls were covered with tapestries whose scenes of naked lovers were so erotic they made her blush.

She was still trying to take it all in when Lucien carried her through a door at the other end of the room, and she gasped in disbelief. They were in a huge marble bathroom that rivaled the bathhouses of ancient Greece, complete with an enormous sunken tub. But what shocked her the most was that the same erotic scenes she'd seen in the tapestries were etched into the marble walls.

"May I assume that that sexy little gasp of yours means this room meets with your approval?" Lucien asked, amusement coloring his voice as he lowered her to her feet.

Ariel blushed again. "It's . . ."

". . . rife with indecent fantasy," he finished huskily, lowering his lips to hers.

Ariel's embarrassment fled with his kiss, and she murmured in protest when he pulled away before she could wrap her arms around his neck.

He smiled wryly as he stepped away from her and turned on the water taps for the tub. As he lifted an old-fashioned bottle from a small shelf above the tub and poured what looked like bath oil into the water, he said, "You're too enticing for your own good, Ariel."

"Are you complaining?" she asked.

"I'm not complaining, but you will be if you don't give yourself some time to recover," he answered, chucking her under the chin. "You start soaking. I'll be back in a minute."

Before Ariel could respond, he left the room. She glanced into the mirror above the sink and curiously studied her reflection. She'd always wondered if making love would make her look different, and now she had the answer. Her long hair was in wild disarray, her lips were seductively swollen, and her entire complexion had a warm flush of color. She looked exactly like she felt—a woman who'd been well loved and was ready for more.

"Wanton," she mumbled to herself as she grabbed a brush lying on the vanity and went to work on her hair.

When she'd removed all the tangles, she opened a cupboard drawer beneath the sink in search of something to clip up her hair. There was a box of old-style embroidered hairpins buried at the back of the drawer, and she pulled them out. She was sure they were Lucien's grandmother's, and she hoped he wouldn't mind her using them.

After securing her hair in a twist at the back of her head, she removed the crystal and the braided bracelet and laid them on the vanity. She had let Lucien use the crystal once tonight, and he had taken control. From here on out, the night was going to be hers, and the best way to ensure that was to remove temptation.

After turning off the water, she stepped into the sunken tub and sat down with a pleasurable sigh. Leaning back against the edge, she studied the erotic scenes carved into the surrounding marble, deciding that Lucien had described them perfectly. They weren't detailed enough to be explicit, but they were rife with suggestive fantasy. Desire stirred inside her as she considered what it would be like to re-create those fantasies with Lucien.

"Mm, you look delicious," Lucien murmured from the doorway.

Ariel turned her head toward him. He had retrieved the wine and the basket from the pentagram. As he set them at the edge of the tub and stepped into the water, her gaze automatically climbed his body. Her pulse picked up speed, and there was a strange catch in her breathing by the time she reached his face.

"Like what you see?" he asked raggedly.

"Oh, yes," she whispered on a sigh.

"Me, too," he rasped as he sat down in front of her, his penetrating gaze fixed on the water lapping at her breasts.

Suddenly he shook his head, as though trying to

clear his mind. Then he reached for the wine bottle, filled their glasses, and handed her one.

Ariel took a sip as she watched him lean back against the edge and take a sip of his own. They sat quietly for several minutes before she asked, "Who designed this bathroom?"

"My grandmother," he answered. "My grandfather was appalled by both it and the bedroom. He said it didn't reflect proper decorum for a high priest. My grandmother said that was the entire point. She hadn't married a high priest; she'd married a warlock, and that's who she wanted in her bed. Whenever she felt he was getting too 'priestly' she'd drag him in here. When she'd finally let him come out, he'd tell me that when I mated for good I needed to make sure I settled down with a malleable, obedient witch who knew her place. There was always a big smile on his face when he was giving me that lecture."

"It sounds as if they were very much in love," she noted.

"They were," he agreed solemnly. "He once said she was the *fun* in his life. After she died, he was never the same."

Ariel wasn't sure what it was that tugged at her heart strings—the story of his grandparents or the emphasis he placed on the word "fun." It suddenly occurred to her that she had never seen Lucien smile in simple enjoyment, nor had she ever heard him laugh.

Upon contemplation of everything he had told her about himself, she realized he really didn't have anything to smile or laugh about. He was a shunned outcast, which was grim enough. On top of that, he was apparently alone in the world. Since Armand's disappearance, she had felt that way herself. She wanted to slide into his arms, hold him close, and tell him he was no longer alone, that she'd always be there for him.

Only it wasn't true, she reminded herself. They had tonight, and tomorrow they'd go back to the status quo. After they rescued Armand—and they would rescue him, because she refused to believe otherwise—Lucien would walk away from her and she'd never see him again.

The thought caused a sharp little pain close to her heart, which she ascribed to hunger. To attribute it to anything else would have been depressing, and she refused to let anything ruin tonight.

Setting her wine on the edge of the tub, she opened the basket and extracted a peach. It was firm and ripe, and when she bit into it, juice ran down her chin.

She raised her hand to wipe it away, but Lucien caught her wrist and said huskily, "Let me."

There was a lambent light in his eyes that caused a shiver of excitement to race through her as she whispered, "Okay."

He leaned forward and pressed his lips to her chin. Then he began to slowly lick the juice away. By the time he was done, desire was coiled so tightly inside her that she felt like an overwound spring. When he sat back, she held the peach out to him. He took a bite, and as the juice ran down his chin, she returned the favor.

She didn't have his restraint, however, because she couldn't pull away from him. Instead, she rose to her knees, slid her arms around his neck, and pressed her lips to his. He groaned softly and settled his hands at her waist, pulling her toward him until she was kneeling astride his lap. With a groan of her own, she rocked herself against his erection.

"Ariel, don't," he said, jerking away from her kiss. "You need some time to recuperate."

"I'll have my whole life to recuperate," she countered, as she gently nipped at the soft underside of his jaw, and then trailed her lips down his neck and to his chest. He gasped when she flicked her tongue against a hard nipple peeking out from a whorl of dark hair. As she trailed kisses to his other nipple, she murmured, "I want to make love again, Lucien. Right here. Right now. It's a favorite fantasy of mine, and when we're done with this one, I have another one that we can fulfill with that jar of honey in the basket."

Between the suggestive timbre of Ariel's voice and the gentle onslaught of her mouth on his body, all of Lucien's gallant resolve to give her recuperative time dissolved. He caught her chin in his hand and raised her mouth to his at the same time that he slipped his other hand beneath her buttocks, lifting her over his erection. As she sank slowly onto him, drawing him into her silken heat, it took every ounce of his control to keep from surging up to meet her. By the time she'd enveloped all of him, his entire body was trembling with need. He put his hands on her hips, intent on establishing the rhythm of their lovemaking, but she grabbed his wrists and pulled his hands away.

"You took control last time," she said throatily, as she threaded her fingers through his and pushed his hands to the bottom of the tub. "The rest of the night is mine."

Lucien couldn't respond, because she'd begun to undulate her hips in a manner that wiped out all coherent thought. All he could do was let her lead him into a night of what promised to be replete with sexual fantasy.

He watched her smile in satisfaction when, a short time later, she brought them both to climax. Collapsing against his chest, she pressed a kiss to his shoulder and murmured, "One fantasy down. Only ninety-nine to go."

"I can't believe it," he grumbled good-naturedly. "I've hooked up with an insatiable mortal."

"Are you complaining?" she asked, as she propped her arms on his chest and stared at him.

He shook his head as he ran his hands up her slender back. "I'm a warlock, remember? You can't keep me down for long."

"I'm glad to hear that." She pressed a kiss to the cleft in his chin before provocatively drawling, "As I said, I have this wonderful fantasy that has to do with honey."

He took a deep breath and released it slowly. "I can't wait."

She flicked her tongue suggestively across her bottom lip, slipped her hand between their bodies and slid it down to stroke him boldly. "Neither can I."

Ariel knew that time had run out. She could see the sky beginning to lighten outside the window. Lucien had fallen asleep a short time before, and he had an arm around her waist and a leg tossed over hers. She wanted to shake him awake and demand that he cast a spell that would stop time and leave them in this limbo. Instead, she closed her eyes and let herself relive the night they'd shared.

After she had taken over their lovemaking in the bath, they'd smeared honey all over each other and licked it off. That had ended in a sticky bout of wild lovemaking on the bathroom floor, followed by another bath. From there they'd retired to bed, where they'd alternately made love slow and easy, and then fast and hard. And then they'd returned to the bathroom and started all over again.

It had truly been a night Ariel would remember for the rest of her life, but it wasn't just the lovemaking that made it memorable. It was that she had opened her heart and soul to Lucien, and she knew he had opened his heart and soul to her. Sadly, because he had let her come so close to him, she recognized that their emotional connection didn't make a difference between them. She was a mortal, and right or wrong, he simply couldn't accept her. No matter how much it hurt, she had to accept that.

She shifted on her pillow to look at his face. With a morning beard darkening his jaw he looked fiercer than ever, and she decided that fierceness suited him. He was, after all, a warlock.

Her fingers itched to trace the sharp planes and angles of his features, to feel the coarseness of his beard. She resisted the urge, sure that if she touched him he'd awaken, and then she'd be tempted to beg him for more time. If she hoped to survive through this scene with her pride intact, then she had to leave him before he told her to go. But before she left him, there was one thing she had to do.

Slowly, so as not to disturb him, she untangled herself from his arm and leg, slipped out of bed and padded into the bathroom. She put on the bracelet that Lucien had cast a protective spell over, and then she lifted the crystal off the vanity and carried it back to the bedroom.

Stepping to the side of the bed, she noted that he'd kicked away the sheets. She let her gaze roam over his glorious body, memorizing every tiny detail from the top of his head to the tip of his toes. Then she placed the crystal on the pillow where she'd lain. It was hard letting go of it, because it was the only link she had with her twin. But Lucien had said he needed the crystal to function at full capacity, and if he was to defeat Galen and save Armand, he had to be whole.

With that mission accomplished, she slipped out into the hallway and headed for her bedroom. Tears were hovering at the back of her eyes, but she refused to cry over a night of wonderful lovemaking. Instead, she climbed into bed and fell into an exhausted slumber.

Hair teased at Lucien's nose. He mumbled sleepily as he shifted away from it, and then he stretched his arm out to grab Ariel and bring her delicious body up against his. When all he encountered was a small ball of fur, his eyes flew open and he found himself peering into Omen's accusing golden eyes. Before he could fully comprehend what was going on, she hissed at him and fled, leaving him staring across the empty expanse of the bed.

Lucien frowned when he realized that Ariel was gone. *Damn!* Had Omen done something to run her off? If so, he and the cat were going to have a hell of a long discussion about the familiar's role in a warlock's life.

He sat up, glancing toward the windows. He squinted against the sunlight streaming through the glass. It was strong enough to hurt his eyes, and he instinctively turned his head away from the glare. When he did, his gaze settled on the pillow beside him. The crystal winked refracted light up at him.

He blinked in disbelief. Ariel would never willingly part with the crystal. *Never!* He reached out to it, sure he was imagining it. But when he touched it, he felt the familiar surge of power.

The first thought that entered his mind was that somehow Galen had gotten into the house and stolen Ariel out of his bed. Even as panic surged through him, however, he knew that wasn't true. He could feel Ariel's presence, and as he lifted the crystal, he immediately tuned in on her. She was in her own room, dreamlessly asleep.

Anger surged through him. He'd made love to her

all night, fulfilled her every demand, and she'd abandoned him in his sleep! He shot out of bed, the crystal clutched in his hand and fury pulsing through his veins. Muttering a string of curses, he stalked across the room, threw open the door, and headed down the hallway.

When he reached Ariel's room, he threw open her door with such force that it slammed against the wall. As far as he could tell, she didn't even flinch at the sound, and that made him even more infuriated. How could she sleep so blissfully after the night they'd shared? Even for a warlock, he had performed far above the norm. She shouldn't be sleeping. She should be sobbing her eyes out that their magical night was over! What in hell was the matter with her?

As he stomped to her bed, some rational part of his brain was telling him to leave well enough alone. She had evidently accepted her fate, which meant he wasn't going to have to deal with mortal hysterics. As an added bonus, she had returned his crystal. So everything was back to normal.

But the irrational part of him wasn't in the mood to be reasonable. He'd cast the mating spell over her, and now he was irrevocably in love with her. He wanted her to . . . He didn't know what he wanted her to do, but it wasn't this!

He grabbed the covers and stripped them off her. When she still didn't move, he grabbed her shoulder and gave her a hard shake. Even then, it was several seconds before she rolled onto her back.

She yawned widely and then sleepily blinked at him as she drawled groggily, "Lucien? What's wrong?"

"*This* is what's wrong!" he snapped, dangling the crystal in front of her face. "What in hell do you think you're doing?"

She wiped at her eyes with the heels of her hands

before she said around another yawn, "I'm giving you back your crystal."

"Why?" he demanded.

"Because you said you need it to function at full capacity, and if you want to save my brother, you have to be functioning at full capacity, right?"

He stared at her in disbelief. "That's all you're concerned about this morning? Your brother?"

"Of course," she said, eyeing him warily as she sat up and reached for the sheet. She pulled it up to her chin in a belated show of modesty.

"And what about us?" he demanded tautly.

"What about us?" she repeated, looking bewildered.

"Dammit, Ariel, I cast the mating spell over you! Doesn't that mean anything to you?"

"It means that you can draw on the power of my love to save my brother," she answered.

"And that's *all* it means to you?"

"Is it supposed to mean more to me?" she asked, looking even more bewildered.

Lucien stared at her, stunned. He couldn't believe it. The spell must not have worked on her! That was the only explanation for her bizarre behavior! He didn't know why he was so shocked. He should have realized it would take more than a one-night stand to mate permanently with a mortal. As his own mother had taught him, they weren't reliable when it came to love. Even worse, he should have recognized the problem earlier. Not once during the night had she said she loved him or made any other verbal commitment to him.

"You're damn right it's supposed to mean more," he growled as he tossed the crystal to the foot of the bed, caught her face between his hands, and levered it up until he was glaring into her eyes. "I cast a love spell over you, and that makes you mine!"

She raised her chin a notch and glared back at him

in defiance. "It's true that you cast a spell over me and made love to me, but you don't have any claim on me, Lucien. You gave up that right when you declared that there would never be a future between us."

"So as far as you're concerned, what we shared last night meant *nothing*?" he questioned, growing even more furious.

"No," she answered with feeling. "What we shared last night was wonderful, but it's over. Now it's time for us to get down to business and save my brother. So I'd appreciate it if you'd leave. I'll get dressed, and we'll meet in the kitchen and start working on our plan."

It was her dismissal that wiped out the last vestige of Lucien's self-control. Without even thinking about what he was doing, he lowered his lips to hers in a bruising kiss. He was the warlock, and if anyone was going to do any dismissing around here, it would be him. He was also going to make love to her until he knew for a fact that she was as spellbound as he was.

"Lucien, no!" she protested, jerking away from his kiss as he tumbled her onto the bed. He yanked the sheet out of her hand and straddled her hips as she said, "It's over between us!"

"It's not over until *I* say it's over," he rasped angrily, putting a hand on either side of her head and scowling down at her.

As Ariel stared up into Lucien's livid face, she was amazed that she wasn't afraid, but she knew in her heart that he would never harm her. She was, however, completely mystified by his behavior. If she was correctly interpreting the situation, he was furious with her for leaving him the crystal, and that didn't make any sense. Ever since he'd given it to her, he'd been trying to get it back. She would have thought he'd be pleased, not acting like some madman.

Obviously there was something going on beneath the surface that she didn't understand. It made her wish she was still in possession of the crystal so she could touch it and get a fix on his emotions. Since she couldn't do that, however, she was going to have to rely on her instincts to calm him down.

She raised her hands to his shoulders and lightly massaged them as she asked, "What is it you want from me, Lucien? Just tell me what it is and it's yours."

A series of emotions flashed across his face, but they were so elusive she couldn't put a name to any of them. All she knew was that she could feel the anger draining out of him and a new tension taking its place. It was a tension she'd become all too familiar with last night, and as he again lowered his lips to hers, she knew she should fight him. Walking away from him this morning had been hard enough. She wasn't sure she could do it again and still maintain her dignity. But as his mouth closed over hers, she welcomed him with an inward sigh of defeat.

"Love me, Lucien," she whispered plaintively, as he trailed kisses from her chin to her breast.

"Better than ever," he whispered back darting his tongue across a taut nipple.

That wasn't the reassurance she was asking for, but she'd take whatever he was willing to give, she decided, arching beneath his mouth as he began to trail kisses down her abdomen. She tangled her hands in his hair when he finally settled against her in an intimate kiss, bringing her to a climax.

"You're mine!" he gasped, as he slid up her body and entered her with swift urgency, sending her flying toward a second climax while she was still trembling from the first one. "Say it!"

"Yes, Lucien, I'm yours!" she gasped as she

wrapped her legs around his hips and met him stroke
for stroke. As they climaxed together in a shuddering
release, she knew he was right. She was his and would
be until the end of time.

I love you, she thought morosely.

It's about time you realized it, he replied, making
Ariel wonder how a thought could sound so smug.

The moment Lucien collapsed against Ariel, he
rolled to his side, bringing her with him. As he posses-
sively cradled her against him, he knew he was behaving like a barbarian staking a claim. But quite frankly,
he was feeling damn barbaric toward her, and he'd
meant what he said. It wasn't over between them until
he said it was, and he wasn't ready for it to end.

You're playing with fire, his conscience admonished,
but he ignored the warning. All his life he'd faithfully
followed the rules, and all it had gotten him was expulsion from the coven. Besides, within forty-eight hours
they would have either defeated Galen or they would
be dead. One way or the other, Ariel would be gone, so
what harm could come from sharing the few hours they
had left?

"Are you all right?" he asked, as he ran his hand
down her satiny back and over an equally satiny hip.

She moved languidly against him. "Mmmm."

"I'm sorry if I frightened you."

She leaned her head back and gave him a perplexed
look. "You didn't frighten me. I know you'd never purposely hurt me."

Guilt stirred inside him at her words, and he felt
obliged to challenge them. "You're wrong, Ariel. If
you'll recall, I've just cast a spell over you that has
basically ruined the rest of your life. That alone should
prove that I would not only purposely hurt you, but I'd
do it without a qualm."

She startled him by bolting upright. Glaring down at him, she angrily declared, "If you think I'm going to let you take credit for the love spell, you're crazy, Lucien Morgret. I *chose* to let you cast the spell over me, and I practically had to force you into doing it. So don't you dare lie there and pompously suggest that you used me!"

He stared at her, dumbfounded. He'd just confessed that he'd done her a terrible disservice, and she was mad at him for suggesting that he'd used her? He wasn't the one who was crazy here!

Scowling at her, he sat up. "You know, Ariel, you have an innate talent for testing my patience, and one of these days, you really are going to push me too far."

"Well, until that day arrives, I suggest you concentrate on fulfilling your duty," she retorted as she scrambled to the bottom of the bed, grabbed his crystal, and tossed it at him. "Put on your crystal, Lucien, and get out there and save the day!"

Her mandate made his temper erupt. Snatching up the crystal, he lunged across the bed and tumbled her to the mattress.

After tossing a leg over her so that she was pinioned beneath him, he slipped the chain over her head as he furiously rasped, "When I want the crystal, I'll ask for it, Ariel. In the meantime, I expect you to wear it. I also expect you to remember that I do *not* take orders from you. *I'm* the warlock. *You're* the mortal. It's time you got that straight!"

She raised her chin a rebellious notch. "And what are you going to do to me if I don't get it straight?"

Her insolence made him so angry he considered showing her exactly what he could do, but instinct told him that to prove his mastery over her would only make matters worse.

Deciding that they both needed some time to calm

down, he climbed off the bed and said, "Get dressed and meet me in the kitchen. If you aren't there in ten minutes, I'll come looking for you and we'll begin to explore my alternatives at proving to you who's boss around here."

With that, he strode out of the room, slamming the door behind him.

Chapter Seventeen

[Of the Battle of Borodino, 1812] It is the beginning of
the end.
—Charles Maurice de Talleyrand-Périgord,
  from *Edouard Fournier, L'Esprit dans l'histoire* (1857)

A S Ariel watched Lucien's melodramatic exit, she
gave her head a frustrated shake, concluding that
trying to figure him out was a hopeless endeavor. She
knew he needed the crystal to enhance his power, and
he'd been hassling her for it almost since he'd given it
to her. So why was he refusing to take it back? It didn't
make sense, but what else was new? Nothing about
Lucien made sense!

Unable to solve that riddle, she climbed out of bed
and headed for the armoire, turning her attention to another irksome matter—Lucien's maddening chauvinistic attitude. Though she was willing to allow that he
was the expert in dealing with Galen, they still had to
function as a team. If he thought she was going to sit
quietly by and let him boss her around, he was definitely in for a surprise. He had cast a love spell over
her, for pity's sake, not given her a lobotomy! She was
going to make sure he understood that, even if she had
to hit him over the head with something to get it across
to him.

When she entered the kitchen a short time later,
however, she forgot all about confronting Lucien. The
room looked as if a tornado had gone through it. The
chairs had been knocked over. All the cupboard doors
were open, and broken dishes and pots and pans were

scattered across the floor. Fear rushed through her. Had there been another demonic spell in the house?

"Lucien?" she called out in panic when she realized he wasn't in the room.

"I'm right here," he said behind her.

She let out a startled yelp and spun around. He came in, carrying a broom and dustpan. She quickly scanned his body for any sign of injury. He was dressed in his familiar black denims and shirt and seemed to be okay. She wanted to throw her arms around him in relief. However, the ominous scowl on his face stopped her from carrying through with the impulse.

"What happened?" she asked instead.

"Omen," he muttered grimly.

"Your *cat* did this?" she gasped in disbelief. "Why?"

"Because she's possessive and jealous as hell."

"Are you saying that she did this because we . . . ?"

"Mated," he supplied. "Would you take out the crystal for a moment? I need to touch it."

Ariel automatically grabbed the chain and tugged the crystal from beneath her blouse as she asked, "Are all familiars this jealous?"

"Only those belonging to warlocks," he answered in a disgruntled tone.

As he spoke, he touched the crystal and then snapped his fingers. Ariel watched in amazement as all the broken glass came together in a pile. It was a trick that she was sure nearly every woman alive would sell her soul to possess.

"Does the crystal also do windows?" she jested.

The contemptuous look he gave her assured her he wasn't in the mood for her joke. Of course, from what she'd seen, he was never in the mood for a joke.

While he retrieved the wastebasket, which had also been a victim of Omen's jealous rampage, and carried it to the pile of glass, she asked, "Why do only warlocks' familiars behave like this?"

"Because for a true master-familiar relationship to work, the familiar has to be of the opposite sex," he explained as he began to sweep glass into the dustpan. "For a witch, the alliance works well, because a male familiar serves mainly as her protector. A female familiar, however, is primarily a warlock's companion and resents anyone who captures his attention. That's why warlocks rarely take on a familiar."

"So why did you take on one?" she asked, fascinated.

He shot her an annoyed look. "Do you ever stop asking questions?"

"If you stop asking questions, you stop learning, Lucien. So why did you take on Omen?"

He gave a resigned shake of his head and returned his attention to sweeping up the glass. "When I ran across Omen, I was a shunned outcast. I couldn't abide the company of mortals, and I felt she'd make an intelligent companion. Besides . . ."

"Besides what?" Ariel prodded when he abruptly fell silent.

He stiffened, and for a moment she didn't think he'd answer, but then he said, "Besides, she was a half-breed."

Of all the things he'd told her, she found that simple statement the most enlightening, because it said everything there was to say about him. He was a half-breed, and because he was, he hadn't fit into the coven. But when he'd been cast out, he hadn't fit into the mortal world either. Alone and lonely, he'd chosen a companion who shared his curse.

Her heart went out to him, but she knew better than to say anything. A warlock would never accept compassion from a mortal, and in his mind he was a warlock. She wondered if he'd ever be able to come to grips with his mortal side. She hoped so, because she instinctively knew that he would never be at peace with himself until he did.

"Well, I'm sure that once you explain our situation to Omen, she'll forgive you for your . . . indiscretion," she told him.

He swept the last of the glass into the dustpan and emptied it into the wastebasket. "She isn't interested in explanations. She ran away, and as far as I'm concerned, good riddance."

Despite his words, Ariel knew Omen's desertion had to hurt, but again she refrained from saying anything. They had enough matters to argue about without getting into an altercation over his feelings for his pet. Moreover, she was sure that eventually the cat would return. If she felt so strongly about Lucien that she would cause this much damage, she wouldn't be able to abandon him forever. Indeed, Ariel suspected that the minute she was gone from his life, the cat would be back.

Noting that all but one of the coffee mugs had survived, she walked across the room, picked up the coffeepot from the floor and set about making coffee. Somehow the toaster had missed being victimized, so while the coffee brewed she made some toast. By the time she was done, Lucien had salvaged the few remaining dishes, put the pots and pans away, and righted the chairs.

After they were seated at the table, she tried to figure out a diplomatic way to bring up the subject of his refusal to take the crystal back.

Before she could, Lucien said, "If you want to know why I refused the crystal, just ask, Ariel."

It was obvious he was reading her mind, and she

frowned at him. "You know, Lucien, mind reading really is a rude invasion of privacy."

"So is asking personal questions, but that doesn't stop you from pestering me with them," he parried as he leaned back in his chair and crossed his arms over his chest.

"Well, there's a big difference between what you do and what I do," she defended. "I have no way of keeping you out of my mind. You, however, don't have to answer my questions."

"What makes you so sure about that?"

"So sure about what?" she asked, puzzled.

"I think I'll let you figure it out, and to save some time, I'll answer your question before you ask it. I didn't take the crystal back for two reasons. The first is that as long as you have it, you can instantly summon me if you need me. Second, before you go into town today, I want to cast a spell over you that will allow the crystal to act as a kind of video camera and record everything you see."

"You want to cast *another* spell over me?" she questioned warily.

He smiled ruefully. "Don't worry, Ariel. There aren't any lasting effects from this one. It will just be a simple incantation that will disappear when you return to the house."

"Why do you want to record everything in town? Do you think that's where my brother's being held?"

He shook his head. "It would be too dangerous to keep him that close to people, but Galen has to have someone guarding him. By noting which coven members aren't in town, I may be able to figure out who the guard is. That's why I want you to look at every person in every shop and on the street, even if they appear to be an obvious tourist. The more you record, the better chance I'll have of narrowing down the search."

"I may already be able to narrow down your search," she told him excitedly. "Yesterday, I ran into a man at the restaurant. I had the strangest feeling that I knew him. For some reason, I felt an overwhelming urge to touch the crystal. When I did, I saw this hazy image of him talking with my brother. He ran away before I could talk to him, but he must be guarding my brother."

Lucien shook his head. "You're talking about the unknown warlock, Ariel, and I'm sure he doesn't have your brother."

"The unknown warlock?" she repeated in bewilderment. "What's an unknown warlock?"

"I just call him that because he's not from this coven, and I don't know who he is," he explained. "If you see him again, I want you to stay away from him. I'm convinced Galen's afraid of him. I also think that Galen believes he's your spellbinder, and if he sees you with him, he might feel more threatened."

"But this unkown warlock was talking to my brother, Lucien. He might be able to tell us what happened to him," she objected. "Don't you think I should at least approach him?"

Without warning, Lucien shot forward in his chair and slammed his hand down on the table with such vehemence that their coffee cups jumped as he yelled, "Dammit, Ariel, haven't you heard a word I've said? Galen is afraid of this warlock. If he's afraid of him, then we sure as hell had better be terrified of him. So if you see him, you get away from him and stay away from him. Have you got that, or do I need to repeat myself until you finally get it right?"

"You know, Lucien, I am sick and tired of playing imbecilic mortal to your tyrannical warlock," she said in a voice low with fury. "I'll concede that you are the expert in this situation, but even with your superior mental abilities, you are *not* infallible. If you were, neither of us would be in this predicament in the first place. Since you aren't perfect, that gives me the right to make suggestions. If you disagree with them, then I expect you to discuss your objections with me in a reasonable and civilized manner instead of behaving like a rabid maniac. Have *you* got that, or do *I* need to repeat myself until you finally get it right?"

He glared at her, and she glared right back. Several seconds passed before he grudgingly snapped, "Fine. In the future I'll *try* to be reasonable."

"And I'll *try* to stay away from your unknown warlock," she yielded just as grudgingly.

His dour look said he wasn't satisfied with her response, but he said, "Now that that issue's settled, let's move on to Galen. I'm sure that by now he has come up with a plan to either spellbind you or destroy you, which means you have to exercise extreme caution around him. His powers are weakest from noon until dark, so I don't expect him to take any blatant action against you while you're in town. However, don't go anywhere alone with him, don't take anything from him, and don't issue him any form of an invitation. Also, make sure you're back here before sunset. If you aren't in the house by the first touch of night, you'll be in serious danger. Do you have any questions?"

"No," she replied.

He rose and walked around the table to where she sat. Opening the charm bag at his waist, he removed a small, cloudy vial and handed it to her, instructing, "Hold the crystal and drink this so I can cast the spell over you."

As she stared at the vial, she recalled his giving her the sleeping potion. She remembered how that had left her confused and disoriented, and she still couldn't recall what had happened after he'd given it to her.

Doubt suddenly stirred inside her. Somewhere along the line she'd started trusting Lucien, but now she realized that he had really done nothing to gain her trust. Indeed, last night he'd told her himself that she couldn't trust him, and his mood swings this morning had been positively schizophrenic. He claimed the potion was benign, but what if he was trying to drug her again?

But why would he try to drug you now? What could he hope to gain from it? You are cooperating with him.

It was a valid argument. There was no apparent reason for the potion to be anything other than what he said it was, but that didn't alleviate her misgivings. As he had also told her last night, he didn't give a damn about her and Armand. That meant that she had to be on guard around him. If she wasn't, she might never rescue her twin.

Slowly she raised her gaze to his face, searching for something—anything—that would prove that he was her ally not her foe. His eyes had taken on that familiar luminosity and his expression was so neutral his face could have been carved in stone. She knew he was reading her mind, so why didn't he offer her some reason to trust him? she wondered in frustration.

Since he refused to help her out, she reached for the crystal in search of his feelings. When she touched it, she blinked in startlement, because there was nothing there but a cold, dark void. It was as if he'd emotionally shut down, and a fearful shiver crawled down her spine.

"So what's it going to be, Ariel?" he drawled in a voice as devoid of feeling as his expression was. "Are you or are you not going to let me cast this spell over you?"

Logic said that she couldn't possibly let him cast another spell over her. But the spellbound part of her that was in love with him argued that because he was a half-breed he had spent his entire life having to prove himself worthy of trust. It was time someone gave it to him based on nothing more than simple faith. Since she was the one in love with him, she had to be the one to take the first step.

Praying that she wasn't making a mistake, she reached for the vial and drank it before she could change her mind. There couldn't have been more than a quarter teaspoon of liquid in it, but it was so foul-tasting she both grimaced and shuddered while Lucien mumbled some words. Then he handed her her coffee mug and said, "The spell is cast."

Ariel quickly drank the lukewarm coffee to wash the awful taste out of her mouth. After setting the mug on the table, she stood and said, "Well, I guess I'd better get to town."

He nodded. "Remember, be careful around Galen, don't go near the unknown warlock, and be home by the first touch of night."

He looked and sounded as dispassionate now as he had before she'd gone against her instincts and submitted to his spell. That hurt, because she wanted him to give her some kind of acknowledgment that she had placed her trust in him. The fact that he didn't made her wonder if she'd made a terrible blunder.

But it was too late to worry about that now, she determined with chagrin. The spell was already cast.

"I'll see you later," she said, heading for the door.

He didn't respond, but she could feel his eyes boring into her back. She resisted the urge to look at him. He had her totally bewildered, and she had a sinking feeling that it was a state of mind she'd be in for the rest of her life.

* * *

Lucien waited until Ariel had driven away from the
house before he allowed his emotions to surface. When
she had suddenly begun to doubt and distrust him over
the spell, it had hurt him so badly that he'd had to lock
his feelings away or explode.

Now, as his emotions ran the gamut from anger to
wounded pride, he gave a disgusted shake of his head.
He tried to tell himself that this was only an effect of
the love spell, but he knew it wasn't true. From the
moment he'd met Ariel, she'd had him on an emotional roller coaster. It was maddening, but in a bizarre
kind of way it was also enjoyable. If Ariel was nothing
else, she was challenging. Even when he was reading
her mind she had a way of surprising him and keeping
him off balance. He was going to miss her when she
was gone.

Now, *that* had to be an effect of the spell! he immediately concluded. She was a stubborn, unpredictable,
infuriating mortal, and the sooner she was out of his
life the better. And the fastest way to make that happen
was to find her twin, he decided, heading for the back
door. Since he couldn't do anything else until she returned with the crystal, he might as well continue with
his search. With any luck he might find Armand before
she got back from town.

He had just entered the woods when he heard a cat's
plaintive yowl, and he stopped instantly at the sound.
He knew it was Omen, but he'd been preoccupied so
he hadn't understood what she was saying.

Forget the stupid cat! an inner voice urged. *She tore
up your kitchen and ran away. If that's all the loyalty
she has for you, you're better off without her.*

He might have persuaded himself to walk away if
she hadn't yowled again. He still couldn't understand
what she was saying, but her tone implied she was in
trouble. He knew it was crazy, but he headed in the di-

rection of her cry. For three years she'd been his only
friend and companion. He simply couldn't desert her if
she needed him, even if she had arbitrarily abandoned
him because he mated with Ariel.

As he moved cautiously through the woods, he projected his mind, trying to connect with the cat. But
other than her letting out another yowl he didn't receive anything from her.

He hadn't gone far when the air in front of him suddenly shimmered. Before he could fully register what
was happening, the unknown warlock was standing in
front of him.

"Is this who you're looking for?" the warlock asked,
as he stroked a frantically squirming and spitting
Omen, whom he held firmly in his arms.

That was why he hadn't been able to connect with
her, Lucien realized. The unknown warlock had cast an
invisible spell over them.

"Who are you and what do you want?" Lucien demanded, instinctively taking a step backward as he
sized up his opponent. They were equally matched in
height and weight, but he could sense the tremendous
power radiating from the warlock. Even if he had had
his crystal, he knew he wouldn't have stood a chance
against him. It also explained why Galen was afraid of
him. Lucien suspected that even by drawing on the
powers of the coven, Galen would be hard-pressed to
match this warlock in magical strength.

"My name's Sebastian Moran," the warlock said, releasing Omen. She rushed to Lucien's side and then
growled viciously at Moran. He shook his head in
amusement as he glanced from the cat to Lucien. "If I
were you, I'd cast a servility spell over her. She is the
most ill-tempered familiar I've ever met."

Lucien shrugged with feigned nonchalance. "I enjoy
her disposition."

Moran arched a brow. "Somehow, I don't find that surprising. It's in keeping with your profile."

"What profile?" Lucien asked warily, though he was afraid he knew the answer. Moran had to be an emissary from the high council. *Damn!* He was too late. The coven was going to be annihilated, and there was nothing he could do to stop it. But if Moran knew what Galen was up to, wouldn't the council have done something by now? Maybe it wasn't too late; maybe if he played it cool during this meeting, he might still have a chance to save them.

"The one I was given to help project your actions," Moran replied. "I have to admit, though, that you've far surpassed my expectations. Using a mortal female to get back on coven land was pure genius. When I tracked your crystal yesterday and found her instead of you, even I was caught off guard. It wasn't until this morning that I realized that if the crystal was on coven land, you had to be here too. Then I realized that the best place for you to hide out would be in your own house. Even Galen wouldn't expect you to be that bold."

Lucien eyed him suspiciously. The way Moran was talking, he was the pawn in some kind of game that Moran was overseeing. But that was ridiculous. Or was it? "What do you want with me, Moran?"

"Please, call me Sebastian, and let's just say I'm a friend who has come to give you some vital information. Armand Dantes is on the brink of recovering his memory. By my calculations, you have until nightfall to rescue him."

"I don't know what you're talking about," Lucien bluffed, startled to realize that Moran had spoken Armand's name and nothing had happened to him. Did that mean Galen's spell had had a limited life span? Or was it simply that Moran had too much power for any of Galen's spells to work on him? Instinct told him it was the latter, which only added more weight to his suspicions that Moran was an emissary.

Sebastian released a harsh laugh. "Don't play games with me, Lucien. I know what you're up to, which is why I've decided to give you some information. Four other members of the coven have become outcasts since your departure. They are living in a cabin a mile beyond the coven's eastern boundary. One of them can tell you how to rescue Dantes. I suggest you locate this outcast immediately and ask for his help, because once Dantes recovers his memory, Galen will destroy you."

It was Sebastian's claim of four outcasts that captured Lucien's full attention. That was the exact number of people who had been missing at the nightly ritual. If they'd become outcasts, that would explain why no one seemed upset about their absence.

"Assuming that I did know what you were talking about, why don't you just tell me where this Dantes is?" Lucien asked. "Why do I need to seek the help of an outcast?"

"Because those are the rules."

"Whose rules?" Lucien asked, becoming even more convinced that Moran was from the high council.

"I can't tell you more until this is over. Just look for the outcasts. Time is of the essence."

If, as he suspected, he was the pawn in some kind of game, Lucien knew he'd be crazy to do as Moran suggested. Furthermore, if he left coven land, he would lose his connection with Ariel. If she needed him, he wouldn't be able to go to her.

"If you don't get to Dantes before his memory returns, Galen will destroy you, and she will be in far greater danger than she is at the moment," Sebastian noted.

Lucien stared at him in shocked surprise. It had been

so long since someone had read his mind that he felt positively violated. Suddenly, he understood why Ariel found it so irritating. She was right. It was a rude invasion of privacy. That feeling was compounded when he tried to read Sebastian's mind in return and couldn't. Evidently the warlock was powerful enough to block him. It gave him a feeling of helpless impotence, and that angered him.

"Who the hell are you, and what do you want with me?" he demanded.

"I can't tell you anything now, Lucien. Just trust me."

"Give me one good reason why I should," Lucien shot back.

"Because you don't have any other choice," Sebastian answered. "If you get to Dantes before he regains his memory, Galen won't know you're here until you're ready to reveal yourself. If you don't act on my information, however, you'll lose the element of surprise. He'll destroy you, and then he'll turn his wrath on the mortals for helping you. You've known him longer than I have, Lucien. What do you think he'll do to the mortal woman when he finds out she mated with the half-breed he's hated all his life?"

Lucien was stunned. How had Moran known that he and Ariel had mated?

One corner of Moran's lips lifted in wry amusement. "There's a look to a newly mated warlock that can't be missed, Lucien. I'm sure you've seen it yourself. But we don't have time to discuss that now. You must go to the outcasts, and you must go now. You have to do it for your mate. Remember how much Galen hates you."

Lucien shuddered to think what Galen would do to Ariel if he learned she was his mate. Still, he was reluctant to trust Moran. "Why are you helping me?"

Sebastian gave a regretful shake of his head. "I'm sorry, Lucien. I can't tell you anything until this is over."

Lucien decided to use a page out of Ariel's book and asked, "You *can't* tell me, or you *won't* tell me?"

Sebastian looked baffled by the question, but said, "I can't tell you. It's forbidden."

Lucien was torn as he carefully weighed everything Sebastian had said. If it was true that Armand was about to regain his memory and the other outcasts could help him, then he had to go in search of them. Then again, he'd be leaving Ariel alone. With the crystal so far out of range, he couldn't connect with her unless she was with Galen, and then it would happen automatically. He supposed he could wait until she ran into him, but that might be hours. If he hoped to get to the outcasts and get back in time to rescue Armand before nightfall, he needed to act now.

Damn! When Ariel and he had mated, why hadn't he thought to increase their mental link so he could directly connect with her whenever he wanted? At least he would then be able to tell her what was going on.

But he hadn't increased the link, and now he had to make a decision. The only logical one was to do what Moran said—go look for the outcasts. He soothed his worried conscience by reminding himself that Ariel shouldn't be in any danger. It was past noon, so Galen was at his weakest, and as long as she was in the house before the first touch of night, she would be safe.

"I need more specific directions to the cabin. You said it's a mile beyond the eastern boundary, but the circle is fifteen miles in diameter, so the eastern boundary encompasses three or four miles."

"I'm sorry, Lucien, but I can't be any more specific than that. It's against . . ."

"The rules," Lucien interrupted disgruntedly. "When this is over, I expect you to explain it all to me."

"When it's over, you'll probably hear more than you want to know," Sebastian answered. "Now go. Your time is running out."

"I hope I'm doing the right thing," Lucien mumbled as he began to jog toward the coven's eastern boundary, instinctively knowing that, right or wrong, this was the beginning of the end. Soon the nightmare would be over.

Chapter Eighteen

But with unhurrying chase,
And unperturbed pace,
Deliberate speed, majestic instancy,
They beat—and a Voice beat,
More instant than the Feet—
"All things betray thee, who betrayest Me."
—Francis Thompson, *The Hound of Heaven* 1.10

ARIEL would never have believed that looking at people could be so exhausting or time-consuming. She'd already been in Sanctuary for more than an hour, and she hadn't even managed to cover one entire side of the street. Of course, her job would have been easier if Lucien hadn't ordered her to look at everyone, even the obvious tourist.

From the first day she arrived she'd been amazed by the crowds that visited the town, but today was Friday and there seemed to be twice as many visitors. She didn't even want to imagine what it would be like over the weekend. The town would probably be so crowded you wouldn't even be able to walk through it.

When she came to the building Galen had disappeared into the day before, the sign on the door said, "Private. Haven, Inc. Headquarters." Even if Lucien hadn't instructed her to go into every shop, she would have wanted to go in here out of simple curiosity. However, the word "private" was so prominent that she recognized she couldn't just go barging in. She needed an excuse to be inside. She hadn't seen Galen around, so she supposed she could say she was looking for him. But what if he was in there? If Lucien was

right about Galen, she didn't want to encourage his at-
tentions. Indeed, she'd just as soon not see him at all.

She jumped when someone suddenly clutched her
arm and said, "If you tell me we can't have lunch today, I'm going to do something drastic."

It was Shana, and Ariel sagged in relief. Because she
had been thinking about Galen, she had thought for a
moment that it was he who grabbed her arm.

"Hi, Shana," she said, taking in the woman's outfit.
Today she was dressed in fringed denim cutoffs, a
patchwork halter top, and a wide-brimmed straw hat.
Ariel gave a wry shake of her head. Even dressed like
Daisy Mae, Shana was gorgeous. "I'd love to have
lunch with you today."

"Great!" Shana said enthusiastically. "I need to run
in here and pick up my work schedule for next week,
but then I'm free. Also, unless you'd prefer to have a
hot lunch at the restaurant, we can eat at the bakery.
They have a room in the back where they serve cold
sandwiches to local residents. The place isn't fancy,
but at least we'll be able to hear each other talk, and no
one will be trying to run us off so they can have our table."

"The bakery sounds wonderful," Ariel quickly replied, unable to believe her luck. Not only would
Shana get her into Haven, Inc., but eating at a place re-
served for local residents should be ideal for "recording" faces for Lucien.

When they entered Haven, Inc.'s headquarters, Ariel
expected some large, modern office. Instead, she was
disconcerted to see that it was as old-fashioned as the
rest of the town. There were two women and a man
working at antique desks in a large open space. One
wall was filled with antique filing cabinets, and both
women were typing on manual typewriters so old that
if they weren't antiques yet, they would be soon. The

only modern office equipment Ariel could see was a copy machine. Just what *was* this place supposed to be?

All three employees looked up when they entered, but Shana was the only one who spoke, saying, "I'm just here to get my work schedule, and she's with me."

They went back to their tasks without so much as a nod.

Outside, Ariel asked, "What kind of a business is Haven, Inc.?"

"It manages all the businesses in town, and it also handles mail orders for our crafts," Shana answered.

"Considering the size of your tourist trade, you must make quite a bit of money."

"I have no idea, Ariel. I'm afraid I'm not the business-oriented type. In fact, I'm so disorganized that I have trouble keeping up with my work schedule."

A disorganized witch? Somehow that sounded like an oxymoron to Ariel. "Do you work exclusively in the fortune teller's shop?"

"Unfortunately, yes."

"You don't like working there?"

"It's not that I don't like it. It's just that people expect you to tell them something wondrous and exciting. Sadly, most of them have lives as predictably boring as mine, but I can't say, 'Hey, the future is going to be the same old grind.' So I have to make up something reasonable that will make them feel they got their money's worth without giving them false expectations."

"Is that what you did with me? Make something up?" Ariel asked teasingly.

"No," Shana answered so seriously that it startled Ariel. "I'd never lie about a friend's future, and from the moment I met you, I had the feeling that you and I could be friends."

They had just reached the bakery, so Ariel didn't respond. But oddly enough she, too, felt that they could be friends. She also knew it would never happen. If she got out of Sanctuary alive, she'd never be back.

She followed Shana to an unmarked door in the back of the bakery, and they entered a large, windowless room. Shana hadn't been kidding when she said the place wasn't fancy. The walls had been painted white and were devoid of any decoration. Instead of tables and chairs, there were two long picnic tables sitting on a nondescript beige tile floor. Half a dozen people were sitting at the table closest to the door. When they glanced up, Ariel was disappointed to recognize all but one of them. She consoled herself with the fact that it was just shortly after noon. More people should be coming in while she was here.

When Shana introduced her to the people, Ariel became perplexed. There was an older couple whose last name was Morcombe, and a young couple whose last name was Moroney. Two middle-aged women completed the group, and their last names were Moresby and Morley. As she added the four additional people she knew to the list—Lucien Morgret, Galen Morgan, Shana Morland, and Corrine Morrow—it dawned on her that all their last names began with the letters "M-o-r." She wanted to ask Shana about the phenomenon, but decided it was a question she should save for Lucien. She would, however, go down to the restaurant and check the local phone book.

The middle-aged women Ariel hadn't recognized took their order. Ariel decided on a chicken sandwich, Shana on roast beef, and they both ordered iced tea. After they got their food, Shana led her to the far end of the second table, saying, "We'll have some privacy down here."

Ariel would have preferred sitting closer to the door, but she selected the side that would give her the best view of it. After they were seated, Shana began to ask her questions about life in Philadelphia. Ariel dutifully answered all of them, glancing up whenever someone new entered.

When Shana learned that Ariel had lived all over the world, she was ecstatic and began to question her about the places she'd lived. Ariel had just finished telling her about the three years she'd spent in Japan when Lucien's unknown warlock entered the room.

"Shana, who's that man?" she asked.

Shana glanced over her shoulder. "Sebastian Moran. Why?"

"He looks familiar. Is he from around here?"

"No. He's from England."

"England?" Ariel repeated in surprise. "How did he end up in Sanctuary?"

"He's a distant cousin to a family who used to live here. In fact, you're renting their house."

Ariel blinked, sure she had misunderstood her. "I'm renting his cousin's house?"

When Shana nodded, uneasiness swept through Ariel. Lucien had said he didn't know who the warlock was, and now Shana was saying that he was Lucien's cousin. How could Lucien not know his own cousin?

"If he's a cousin of the family, why isn't he staying at the house?" she asked.

"Well, when he first arrived someone else was renting it, so he set up a camp in the woods. After that tenant left, Sebastian was offered use of the house, but he said he preferred to stay where he was. Actually, that's lucky for you. If he had moved in, you wouldn't have been able to rent it."

Yes, my luck really is amazing, Ariel thought darkly, as she pondered Shana's information. She was coming to some conclusions that she didn't like at all. None of them had to do with luck and all of them had to do with Lucien. She now understood why Lucien had made such a big deal about her staying away from Moran. He was afraid she would learn he was his cousin.

She also began to suspect who had been the tenant before her—Armand. Why hadn't she realized it before? It wasn't as if Sanctuary was overflowing with rental properties. Indeed, when Lucien had had her call about renting the house in the first place, he had indicated that if there wasn't one for rent, they wouldn't be coming to Sanctuary. She now suspected that the purpose of the call had been to make sure that his cousin had done whatever he was supposed to do with Armand.

She decided to try a bluff to verify her hunch. "You know, Corrine Morrow mentioned that the man who rented the house before me . . . Gosh, I can't remember his name."

"Adam Douglas," Shana supplied.

Since Ariel was expecting to hear Armand's name, she was momentarily thrown off balance. But then she recalled that he went by another name during his investigations, though he always kept the same initials. Hearing his pseudonym now added one more piece of evidence to her growing suspicions about Lucien.

"Yes, I think that was the name. Corrine said he left unexpectedly?"

"Yeah, it was rather surprising," Shana said. "He'd rented the house through the end of September, and then one night he up and cleared out without so much as leaving a note."

Ariel wanted to ask Shana some more questions, but

she was afraid of making her suspicious. Besides, she wanted some time alone to think about what she'd learned.

Glancing at her watch, she said, "Gosh, Shana, I hate to end our visit, but I have some business to take care of."

"Hey, that's okay. I'm just glad we finally got together. I'll walk you out."

"No, don't bother," Ariel replied, as she stood. "You stay and finish your sandwich. I'll see you later."

Outside, Ariel headed for the restaurant to check the phone book. It was as noisy and crowded as ever, and she was frustrated to find a man using the phone. Leaning against the wall, she scanned the crowd. When the door opened, she glanced toward it and felt a frisson of fear at what she saw. Lucien's cousin, Sebastian Moran, had just entered. Since he had just eaten at the bakery, she could think of only one reason for him to be here. He was following her. When he looked over to where she was and their eyes met, he turned around and left abruptly, confirming her suspicion.

Had he been following her all along? she wondered. And if so, why? The answer was obvious. He was probably making sure that she wasn't doing anything that would jeopardize his and Lucien's plans.

The man on the phone finally hung up, and Ariel immediately went to it. Lifting the phone book, which dangled by a chain, she noted that it contained listings for several small towns in the area. She flipped through it until she came to Sanctuary. It didn't even fill a page, and she was quickly able to determine that her premise was right. There were twelve residential numbers listed, and all of them started with the letters M-o-r. If she added Lucien's last name to the list, she

Carin Rafferty

came up with thirteen families. If she'd had any doubt that there really was a coven, it was now alleviated.

Leaving the restaurant, she decided that the best place to do some private contemplating was her car, which was again parked along the road outside town. She headed in that direction, her mind reeling with everything she'd learned.

She was now sure that Lucien and his cousin had kidnapped Armand, but she didn't know what to do about it. Her first instinct was to confront Lucien with her proof. However, even if he did confirm her conclusions, it wouldn't get her brother back. What she should do was go to the police, but she still didn't have any evidence to prove that Armand had even been here, let alone that he was missing. And even if she could persuade them to help her, it probably wouldn't do her any good. Lucien would most likely just cast some spell over them to convince them she was crazy.

She'd just passed the last business when she heard Galen call her name. She stopped and turned around. He was jogging down the sidewalk toward her, and at the sight of him all the frustration she was feeling coalesced into anger. The last thing she wanted to do right now was to deal with another warlock.

"What is it, Galen? I'm in a hurry," she said with asperity when he reached her.

He gave her a rueful smile. "I'm sorry. I seem to have bad timing with you. Look, I'll just back off, and if you decide you want to see me, you can let me know."

For a man who supposedly had evil intentions toward her, he sure was behaving civilly. Of course, if she was right about Lucien, Galen wasn't the bad guy. She also realized that he might be the only person who could help her. Until she figured out what to do, she couldn't afford to alienate him.

"I'm sorry if I was rude," she told him. "I just have a lot on my mind right now."

"Anything I can help with?" he asked.

She opened her mouth to answer, but stopped when she caught a furtive movement out of the corner of her eye. Turning her head in that direction, she saw Sebastian Moran duck into a nearby doorway. He *was* following her!

She felt another frisson of fear. Returning her attention to Galen, she realized he was regarding her in concern. She gave him a weak smile as she said, "No, you can't help, but if you like, you can walk me to my car."

"I'd love to walk you to your car," he said.

The moment the words left his mouth, she realized she had broken one of Lucien's cardinal rules. She'd issued Galen an invitation. When panic began to flutter in her stomach, she got angry. She was tired of being afraid. Besides, the road was filled with people, so Galen couldn't do anything devious to her if he wanted to.

"Are you sure I can't help with whatever's bothering you?" Galen asked as they strolled toward the car.

Ariel shook her head. "It's a personal matter."

"Would you like to talk about it? I'm a good listener."

"I'm sure you are, Galen, but I'm not ready to talk right now."

"I'm pushing again, aren't I?"

Ariel glanced up at him, and he gave her such an engaging grin that she couldn't help smiling. "Yes, you are."

"Well, at least I got you to smile," he said, looking pleased. "So, what have you been doing today?"

"I wandered around town for a while, and then I had lunch with Shana Morland."

"No wonder you're looking so grim," he drawled. "Lunch with Shana can be pretty taxing."

"Now, why would you say that?" Ariel asked, feeling irritated on Shana's behalf.

He eyed her askance. "Come on, Ariel. Shana's a nice girl, but you must admit she's a bit immature. I bet she spent the entire time getting you to tell her about every town you've ever been in in your entire life."

There was a condescending note in his voice that pricked at Ariel's temper. "In the first place, Shana is not a girl, Galen. She's a woman, and I don't find her immature. I think she's intelligent and beautiful and funny. I also think she's lived in the protected environment of a small town all her life and she's naive. She thinks big cities are full of adventure and excitement, but I'm sure that if she spent some time in one, she'd quickly change her mind. So instead of criticizing her, you should be encouraging her to get out into the world for a while so she can find out the truth."

He gave her a placating smile. "It's obvious that you like Shana, Ariel, and I'll agree that she's everything you said she is. But I've known her longer than you have, so I also know that she's willful and impulsive, and trouble seems to follow her around like a shadow. Believe me when I say that the last thing the world needs is Shana running around loose in it. What she needs is a husband who can control her and teach her her place in life."

It had been so long since Ariel had heard such chauvinistic drivel that she couldn't believe what she was hearing. "Tell me, Galen, just what do you consider Shana's *place* in life?"

Evidently he didn't hear the sarcasm in her voice, because he shrugged and said, "The same as any woman's. She should find herself a husband and devote herself to being a good wife and mother."

"And what if Shana doesn't want to be a wife and a mother? What if she'd rather explore the world?" Ariel asked, her temper escalating.

"Don't be ridiculous, Ariel," he scoffed. "All women want to be wives and mothers. Unfortunately, some of them are like Shana. They get these preposterous notions that they need more out of life. But one of these days Shana will find a man who can control her, and he'll teach her what her proper role is."

Ariel's temper erupted at his statement. She came to a stop, propped her hands on her hips, and glared at him as she said, "That is the most insulting, patronizing, and *stupid* statement I've heard in years! You think that if a woman is a little different from what you consider proper, then just give her to a man who can crush her spirit and kick her back into line, right? Well, Galen, believe me when I say that the last thing the world needs is insufferable, egotistical, testosterone fools like *you* running around in it! Now, if you will excuse me, I have business to attend to."

She turned and strode away from him before he could respond. She suspected that if he uttered one word, she'd probably kick him. What really irked her was that she shouldn't have been surprised by his philosophy. Lucien also had a control fetish, which she'd experienced firsthand on several occasions. Evidently the coven was an archaic patriarchal society. She suspected that Lucien's grouchy cat had more freedom than the witches did.

By the time she reached her car, she had come to the conclusion that if Lucien and Galen were examples of the average warlock, she was glad she was a mortal and not a witch. If she had to put up with their overinflated machismo day in and day out, they'd probably end up burning her at the stake, because she would incite a witches' revolt. Indeed, it looked to her as if the coven could use a good, old-fashioned liberation movement!

With her adrenaline still running high, she decided she was going to go directly to Lucien and confront him with everything she'd figured out. Then she would demand that he take her to Armand.

Starting the ignition, she pulled out onto the road and started ticking off her conclusions in her mind.

First, Lucien's "unknown" warlock was really his cousin. Since Lucien was seeking revenge against Galen, she had to presume that his cousin was here to help him. She was also convinced that it was the cousin who had taken Armand. After all, she'd seen that image of him talking with her brother. She figured he'd kidnapped him so Lucien could frame Galen for the crime. If he was found guilty for something like that, he'd probably be cast out of the coven, which meant Lucien could come back. What really infuriated her was that Lucien had led her to believe he was alone in the world. He had drawn on her compassion, and it had all been a lie!

Furthermore, there was the matter of Armand's name. Lucien had told her that Galen had put some kind of horrible spell over her brother that went into effect when anyone said his name. But if Armand had been known in Sanctuary as Adam Douglas, the only way Galen could have known his real name was if he could read his mind. Lucien had said that he cast a spell over her that wouldn't let Galen read her mind, so it made sense that he would have done the same thing to Armand. That meant that when she spoke Armand's name, the spell that had gone into effect had to have been cast by either Lucien or his cousin. Her money was on Lucien. He sent her to the house alone, and then he gave her a sleeping potion that scrambled her memory so he could get away with it.

The way she had it figured, Lucien and his cousin had had a tidy little plan, and then she came charging in looking for Armand. Lucien had probably been afraid that she would screw everything up by searching for her brother, so he brought her to Sanctuary with him. Then he set about convincing her that Galen was the bad guy. Worse, she fell for every one of his tricks, right down to his absurd loose spell in the house, which had conveniently turned into a demon and which, of course, she hadn't seen. Then he made the biggest coup of all by talking her into letting him cast a love spell over her. God, she couldn't believe she'd been such a fool!

"Well, Lucien Morgret, you can make a fool out of me once, but you'll never make a fool out of me twice," she muttered angrily. "I may be a mortal, but I have just begun to fight!"

Lucien stood in the middle of the woods and glared around in frustration. When Sebastian Moran had told him that the outcasts were in a cabin a mile beyond the coven's eastern boundary he'd known it wasn't going to be easy to find them. What he didn't consider, however, was that he couldn't walk in a straight line but had to follow the curvature of the boundary. Without his crystal, he couldn't gauge the distance exactly, so he had to zigzag to make sure he wasn't missing the cabin. He went south first, and found no sign of the cabin. Now he had just finished backtracking to where he'd begun. As soon as he caught his breath he would start searching to the north.

He looked up at the position of the sun. It was past two in the afternoon. Even with the longer summer days, time was becoming critical. For all he knew,

Armand was being held at the farthest point from where he stood. That meant he would have to walk a mile to the boundary, and then another fifteen to get to him. Assuming he could rescue him immediately, which was unlikely, he didn't think he could get him off coven land and get back to Ariel before the first touch of night. And instinct told him he had to get back to her by then. Something was going on with her. He could feel it, and that was making him even more frustrated. If anything happened to her . . . He wouldn't let himself finish the thought.

He began to jog ahead, comforted to see Omen running along beside him. She hadn't spoken to him since Moran had released her, but she was by his side. He knew that it would be only a matter of time before she forgave him for mating with Ariel. The real irony was that if he had waited another day, Omen would have had nothing to forgive. He would have met Moran and rescued Armand. Then Ariel would have gone home and gotten on with her life, and he would have gotten on with his. But he hadn't waited, and now they were irrevocably bound together forever.

He was so lost in his thoughts that if Omen hadn't suddenly growled at him, he would have missed the thatched roof peeking through the trees off to his right.

"Good job!" he praised, pausing long enough to scoop her into his arms before heading in the direction of the roof. She allowed him to hold her for only half a dozen steps, then leaped out of his arms and disappeared into the thick underbrush.

Soon he heard the sound of someone chopping wood, and he moved quietly to the edge of the trees that overlooked the cabin. He needed to make sure it was the place he was looking for, and if so, he didn't want to startle whoever was there. If he had learned nothing else as a shunned outcast, it was that without the circle to protect you, you became overly defensive. If four of his kind turned on him at once, he'd be in a hell of a lot of trouble.

When he finally had a clear view, he was truly shocked at what he saw. Boyd and Myrna Morpeth were working in a small garden plot, and Roan Morrell was beyond them, chopping wood. Lucien could have understood Roan's expulsion from the coven. He was a few years younger than Lucien and known for his hot temper. Even Lucien's grandfather had frequently lost patience with him. But Boyd and Myrna were both well into their hundreds and so quiet you had a tendency to forget they were even around. What could they possibly have done that would make Galen treat them like this? He searched the rest of the clearing for the fourth person, but whoever it was was either inside the cabin or away from it.

He was trying to figure out how to make his entrance without startling them when someone said behind him, "I wondered how long it would take for the mortal's spawn to show up."

Lucien spun around to confront the voice, and his jaw dropped. If he had been shocked before, he was now dumbfounded. The warlock standing in front of him was none other than Griffith Morgan, *Galen's own father.*

"Well, don't just stand there gaping," Griffith muttered irritably. "Give me a hand with this wood."

It was then that Lucien realized that Griffith was carrying a sling over his back that was filled with freshly chopped lengths of a log. He leaped forward to take the sling from the older man, still too stunned to speak.

As he followed Griffith into the clearing, he had a

worrisome feeling that he knew which of the outcasts could help him find Armand Dantes. The question was, would Galen's father betray his son the way his son had evidently betrayed him?

Chapter Nineteen

Nobody's enemy but his own.
—Charles Dickens, *David Copperfield*, ch. 25

BY the time Ariel arrived at Lucien's, she had worked herself into a fury. Climbing out of the car, she headed toward the house, deciding that when she was done with him he'd wish to God—or whoever the hell he worshiped!—that he'd been dealing with a demon instead of her.

When she entered the house, she slammed the door behind her and yelled, "Lucien Morgret, I want to talk to you, and I want to talk to you *now!*"

There wasn't a response, but she hadn't really expected one. His warlock egotism wouldn't deign to respond to the demand of a mere mortal.

She stormed down the hallway, tossing open doors as she went. By the time she reached the kitchen, it was obvious that he wasn't on the ground floor, so she backtracked and climbed the stairs leading to the second floor. All she found up there was rooms filled with furniture draped in dustcovers.

"Damn you, Lucien! Where the hell are you?" she said as she stood in the gloomy hallway, her hands perched on her hips.

She was ready to head back the way she'd come when she spied a staircase just a few feet from where she stood. It hugged the back wall and stood in such deep shadow that it was almost invisible. She rushed to it and hurriedly climbed the steps. At the top she opened the door and stepped into a large room that was empty except for an old trunk.

Recognizing that Lucien wasn't anywhere in the house made her so frustrated that she wanted to scream. Instead, she crossed the room to the window. If he was outside, maybe she could see him from up here.

When she looked out the window, however, all she could see was the clearing surrounding the house and dense woods. With a curse, she walked to the trunk and sat on it. She wanted to confront Lucien, and she wanted to confront him before her temper had time to cool. Without her anger she was afraid he'd persuade her to believe some other lie.

Muttering another curse, she glanced down at her feet. When she did, she frowned. In the dust on the floor were several paw prints and some footprints too large to be hers. Obviously Omen and Lucien had been up here, and it was apparent that their visit had to do with the trunk.

She stood and opened the trunk's latch. When she lifted the lid, all her suspicions about Lucien were confirmed. The pen she'd given Armand when he was first hired at the newspaper was lying on top of the shirt she'd given him on their last birthday. As she quickly dug through the remainder of the trunk, she verified that it was filled with Armand's clothes.

"Damn you, Lucien!" she declared furiously. "What have you done with my twin?"

Tears burned her eyes, but she blinked them back impatiently and began to gather Armand's clothes up out of the trunk. She would pack them with hers and put the suitcase into the car. Then, when Lucien returned, she'd demand he take her to Armand. If he refused she'd drive into town and find Galen. She was

sure that once she told him her story he would help her
rescue her brother.

Lucien sat in the cabin and listened to his friends'
stories about how they had ended up here. His assump-
tion of Roan's circumstances turned out to be accurate.
He'd lost his temper over something Galen had told
him to do. Boyd, however, had been expelled because
he protested Galen's decision to cast his own father out
of the coven. Myrna had refused to live without her
mate of more than ninety years and chose to go with
him.

When he turned to Griffith to learn his story, the
middle-aged warlock glared at him in belligerent silence. Lucien understood his animosity. With the centuries of rivalry between their families, it had to be
galling to face Lucien after his own son had turned on
him. Thankfully, Lucien already suspected what had
caused his expulsion. He was sure that, if he was right,
Griffith would tell him where Armand was. He would
have to handle their conversation carefully, however,
because pride might keep Griffith silent until it was too
late.

To Boyd, Myrna, and Roan, he said, "I know this is
your home, and I would never do anything to offend
you in it. However, I need to ask Griffith for some advice on a very serious matter. Do you think we could
be alone for a while? If, of course, Griffith agrees to
meet with me privately," he quickly added, glancing
toward him.

For a moment Griffith did nothing but glare at him,
but finally he nodded.

After the others were gone, Lucien leaned forward
in his chair and rested his forearms on his knees. Linking his fingers together, he said, "Griffith, I know this
is hard for you, but as you're aware, Galen has taken

a mortal hostage. I need you to tell me where he's holding him so I can rescue him."

"What makes you think I know anything?" Griffith asked harshly.

"Because I remember a lecture you once gave to our class when I was a young warlock," Lucien replied. "You said that as far as you were concerned, the greatest sin a warlock could commit was to use his powers against a mortal. You stated that because they are weaker than we are, they don't have a chance to defend themselves against us, and only a coward would take advantage of someone who can't fight back.

"I believe that you found out Galen had imprisoned the mortal, and when you did, it went against your innate sense of justice," he went on. "I further believe that your conscience demanded you speak out, and Galen banished you for it."

Again Griffith regarded him in belligerent silence. When it became evident that he had no intention of responding, Lucien said, "Griffith, you may want to believe that Galen won't harm the mortal, but I'm sure you're aware that he's practicing the Old Ways. If he can do that, knowing that if the council finds out they'll destroy the entire coven, don't you think there's a chance that he might harm the mortal?"

Griffith was silent for several minutes, but then he rose from his chair with a heavy sigh. Walking to the window, he stared out it.

"It's my fault," he said in a defeated voice. "I knew it was wrong to teach Galen the Old Ways, just as I knew it was wrong to learn them from my father. The council had banned them, and it was our duty to obey that law. But I was seduced by the thought of being able to do something that the Morgrets couldn't do. Can you understand that?"

"Yes," Lucien replied. "You felt that your family

should be leading the coven, and knowing something we didn't know took away some of the sting."

He turned away from the window to face Lucien. "Did you know that my family petitioned the council for a challenge after your sixth birthday?"

"No," Lucien answered, astonished.

"Well, we did," he answered bitterly. "We weren't questioning your grandfather's right to the high priesthood. We were, however, challenging your and your father's right to ascend to the position. Your father had defiled our race by mating with a mortal. Worse, he'd sired a son who had to use a crystal endowed with mystical powers to fully function as a warlock. We felt that neither of you was deserving of the position."

"What happened with the petition?" Lucien questioned, feeling dazed. Why hadn't his grandfather told him about this? If he'd known, he would at least have been prepared for Galen's challenge after his grandfather's death.

"The council turned us down," Griffith replied. "They said that there was an experiment underway, and until they had time to fully consider its potential, they would not sanction a challenge."

"What did they mean that there was an experiment underway?" Lucien asked, bewildered.

"They didn't explain it," Griffith replied stiffly, "and it wasn't our place to ask."

Lucien raked a hand through his hair as he absorbed the information. But even when he had, it didn't do him any good, because it still didn't give him any answers.

"So, when my grandfather died, you decided to file another petition, and this time the council granted their permission," he said.

"Yes," Griffith answered. "We were elated, to say the least."

"I'm sure you were," Lucien replied without rancor. "Did you know Galen was going to cheat?"

"So you did figure that out," Griffith said, with another sigh. "Yes, I knew he planned to cheat, and I'm ashamed to say that I encouraged him to do so. If it means anything, it wasn't personal, Lucien. I truly felt that a full-blooded warlock should be in charge of the coven. I also knew that even if you did have to use a crystal, there was a good chance that you would beat Galen. You may be a half-breed, but your magic is some of the most powerful I've ever encountered."

Lucien was thoroughly stunned by the compliment. Griffith continued, "We agreed that Galen would use some minor spells from the Old Ways that would interfere with the crystal's mystical properties during the challenge. Because the Old Ways were no longer practiced, we felt that he could get away with it without being detected."

"You were right," Lucien noted dryly.

"Yes, but what I didn't expect was that Galen would become so enamored of his newfound power that he would continue to use the Old Ways to make himself even more powerful. When I recognized what he was doing, I tried to reason with him, but he refused to listen to me. I had vowed my allegiance to him, so there was nothing I could do to stop him. All I could do was pray that he would come to his senses before the council found out."

"But then the mortal entered the picture, and you could no longer maintain your silence," Lucien guessed.

"Yes," Griffith admitted with a frown. "Galen claimed that the mortal was spellbound. After he captured him, he had a fingerprint check run on him and discovered he was a newspaper reporter named Armand Dantes. Galen said he had to keep him until he found out who his spellbinder was, because whoever it was had to be out to destroy him. Since you're here, I suspect that you're that person."

"Yes, I'm the mortal's spellbinder," Lucien admitted. "I was having dreams that suggested Galen had put the coven in danger, so I sent the mortal here to gather information against him. I'd like to say that my only purpose was to save the coven from harm, but that's only partially true. I also hoped to prove that Galen was corrupt so I could be granted permission to come home."

"So you didn't take to the mortal world?"

"I despised it."

"I'm sorry," Griffith said regretfully. "As I said, I have no personal grudge against you, Lucien. I had hoped that because you were part mortal, you would be happy there."

"I may be part mortal, but it's the warlock within me that dominates. The only place I'll ever be happy is with the coven."

"Well, let's hope that you can accomplish your mission and come home."

"Then you'll tell me where the mortal's being held?"

"I'll tell you, but I must warn you that you may not be willing to do what it will take to rescue him."

"He's in this situation because of me, Griffith. I'll do whatever needs to be done to save him."

"Even if it means practicing the Old Ways?" he pressed. "Because that's what it's going to take, Lucien. I'll have to teach you an ancient spell to free him."

Lucien gulped at Griffith's announcement. If he used a spell from the Old Ways, then he, too, would be breaking high coven law and could end up causing the coven's destruction.

But as he stared at Griffith, he again recalled the lecture the warlock had given so many years ago. Only a coward would take advantage of someone who couldn't fight back. Lucien had taken advantage of both Armand and Ariel. He tried to gloss over his actions by saying he was doing it for the sake of the coven. Now he recognized that to use them for any reason, even something as noble as the safety of the coven, was unconscionable.

"If that's what it takes, then that's what I'll do," he declared determinedly.

Lucien was crouched in the trees in front of the crystal cave. According to Griffith, there was a secret room inside the cave, and that was where Armand was being held. He explained that the room had been used during the practice of the Old Ways. Its purpose had been to ensure that during the invocation of spells involving dark forces those forces were contained in a place where they could be controlled. Once the practice of the Old Ways had been banned, the room had been sealed with an ancient spell, and the members of the coven had been instructed to forget its existence. Griffith's family, however, had passed down not only the knowledge of its existence but the ancient spell that would open its door.

"But getting the door open is not your biggest problem," Griffith told him solemnly. "Because the room was specifically used to call up the dark forces, their essence permeates it. The moment you step into the room, they will try to sway you into releasing them. I don't have the time to teach you the spells that will protect you against them, so you'll just have to make sure you don't give in to their temptations or threats, Lucien. Our people are no longer trained to control them, and it would be impossible to defeat them if they were set free."

After having dealt with Galen's demonic spell, Lucien knew exactly what Griffith was talking about. He also understood the danger if the dark forces were unleashed upon the world. Once mankind was seduced or threatened into recognizing them, they would be given life. When that happened, the entire balance of nature would be upset.

But that isn't going to happen, Lucien reassured himself. *I defeated Galen's demon by concentrating on the power of Ariel's love, and I'll rescue Armand the same way.*

Of course, he'd had the crystal when he fought the demon. The fact that he didn't have it now had him on edge, but he refused to give in to his own doubts. Last night he mated with Ariel. He didn't need a crystal to draw on the power of her love, because he carried the very essence of her soul inside him.

Convinced that the cave was unguarded, he ran across the clearing and ducked into the entrance. He had exactly one hour before the first touch of night, to rescue Armand, take him to Griffith, who had promised to guard him, and get back to Ariel.

All his life he'd been awed by the cave, but tonight he barely noticed it as he dug into his charm bag for the two vials Griffith had given him. Opening the one that contained a murky liquid, he threw the contents against the southern wall and intoned the first part of Griffith's spell. Immediately a dark hole opened in front of him. This was the doorway into the room, but he had to give it light to be able to see inside.

Opening the second vial, which was of clear liquid, he tossed its contents into the hole while chanting the second part of the spell. Immediately upon completion of the incantation, the darkness took on a moonlike glow, revealing the secret room.

As he stared into it, he gasped in wonder. The cave

was beautiful with its gleaming phosphorescent interior, but this room went beyond beautiful. It, too, was made of crystals, but they had the sheen of glistening ebony. Where the cave was filled with a peaceful silence, this room was filled with seductive whispers and sighs, like lovers who lose themselves in each other in the middle of the night.

He reminded himself that despite its beauty, it was dangerous and he had to avoid its temptations. When he stepped inside the room, however, his warning seemed absurd. The room seemed to physically caress him, and he was both shocked and enthralled as he became fully aroused. He trembled as he felt an invisible hand stroke his erection while an equally unseen siren breathed erotic suggestions into his ear. It told him that if he would only believe in it, it would fulfill all his fantasies.

If he hadn't given Ariel that same promise the night before, he might have fallen under the room's wicked enchantment. But the words shocked him back to reality. The room evidently sensed it was losing its hold over him, because the siren's whispers suddenly turned into screams as it threatened him with vile forms of death and destruction if he did not give it recognition.

He closed his eyes and focused inwardly until he conjured up an image of Ariel's face. When he had it fixed in his mind, he let his heart and soul open up to her love. As it coursed through him, the room let out one last scream, then fell into a silence so profound it was like standing in a tomb.

He opened his eyes and quickly scanned the room for Armand. At first it appeared that he wasn't there, but then Lucien spotted him lying on the floor. He rushed to him, and as he knelt beside him, he felt a flash of fear. Armand was so still at first Lucien thought he was dead.

Pressing his hand to the side of Armand's neck, he was relieved to find a strong pulse. Either Galen had put him in some kind of trance or the room's violent response to Lucien's rejection had rendered him unconscious. For whatever reason, however, it made his rescue more complicated, because it meant Lucien would have to carry him.

With a curse, he hefted Armand over his shoulder and carried him out of the room. After putting him down on the cave floor, Lucien retrieved two more vials from his charm bag. He opened both and simultaneously tossed their contents into the opening while chanting another spell Griffith had taught him. It would negate the spell Galen used to enter it, and Galen would no longer be able to get inside. Further, Griffith had added a secondary spell. The moment the new spell was cast, both he and Griffith would forget the words, which meant the room would be sealed forever.

When he finished the incantation, there was a brilliant burst of white light. The room must have sensed what was happening, because it let out an enraged scream as the door closed over it for eternity.

It took Lucien's eyes a few minutes to recover from the blinding light. As soon as they did, he hooked his hands beneath Armand's armpits and dragged him through the tunnel.

Outside, he glanced up at the sky. Though it seemed as if he'd spent only a few minutes in the cave, the position of the sun told him he'd been in there for more than half an hour. Time was running out, and with Armand unconscious, there was no way he would get back to Ariel before nightfall. Though he knew he was too far away from the crystal to connect with her, he tried anyway. When the effort failed, he again cursed himself for not increasing their mental link so he could connect with her whenever he wanted. He consoled himself with the fact that at least she wasn't with Galen, because if she was he would have automatically linked with her.

Hefting Armand back over his shoulder, he headed for the boundary, which was nearly five miles away. As he walked, he kept telling himself that he was worrying needlessly about Ariel. He had told her to be home by the first touch of night, and he was sure she'd follow his instructions. He was just being overprotective again.

Unfortunately, that didn't quell the feeling that if he didn't get to her before nightfall, something terrible would happen.

Ariel paced the kitchen. It was growing dark, and she walked to the back door and stared out at the woods for what seemed like the millionth time. Instinct told her that when Lucien returned, this would be the entrance he'd use. Assuming, of course, that he did return. She was beginning to think that he was gone for good.

Knowing that that train of thought would only make her crazy, she returned to the table and sat down. To while away time, she had spent the afternoon making notes of everything that had occurred between her and Lucien.

Now, looking at her relationship with him in black and white, she realized how stupid she'd been. Everything he'd said and done had been geared toward keeping her from asking Galen questions—or anyone else in Sanctuary, for that matter. His "rules" proved that. Don't take any gifts. Don't go out at night. Don't issue any invitations. Don't trust anyone, not even the children.

What really amazed her was how he managed to manipulate her into trusting *him*. So much so that she even let him cast a love spell over her—assuming, of course, that there was such a spell. It was possible that he just used the sexual attraction she had for him to exploit her even further. But spell or no spell, the reality was that she had given him her virginity. Worse, even after recognizing that he'd duped her, she still had strong feelings for him.

Agitated by her thoughts, she returned to the back door. As she watched the sun set, it suddenly dawned on her that soon all the shops in Sanctuary would be closed. That meant Galen would be gone, and she had no idea where he or anyone else lived. If she needed his help, she wouldn't know how to find him!

Was that why Lucien hadn't returned? Did he know that she'd figured out his scheme? She had to admit it was possible. He did, after all, read her mind. If he also knew that she planned to seek Galen's help if he didn't take her to Armand, it would make sense for him to stay away until the shops were closed, thereby ensuring that she wouldn't be able to find Galen.

Her conclusion made too much sense to ignore, and she hurried to the table to get her purse and car keys. She was going to go into Sanctuary and find Galen. If she waited, it might be too late.

Even as she made her decision, there was a part of her that urged her to wait and give Lucien a chance to explain himself. There was a possibility that she was wrong about him.

"Sure, and tomorrow I'll win one of those ten-million-dollar magazine sweepstakes," she said, as she headed for the front door. "There is no way I'm going to risk my twin's life on the unlikely chance that I'm wrong about Lucien."

When she pulled open the door a minute later, she

let out a startled gasp. Galen was standing on the stoop, his arm raised, as though ready to knock.

"I'm sorry, Ariel," he apologized quickly taking a step back. "I didn't mean to scare you."

Ariel regarded him uneasily. Though she had just decided to go into town and find him, discovering him on her doorstep made her wary. "What are you doing here, Galen?"

He stuffed his hands into his pants pockets and gave her a rueful smile. "I came by to apologize for this afternoon. After you told me off, I realized how arrogant I sounded, and I deserved everything you said about me. I just wanted you to know that, and to tell you that I won't bother you anymore. I hope you enjoy the remainder of your stay here, and if there's anything I can do to help you, please feel free to come to me. And, with that, I'll say good-bye."

Before Ariel could reply, he turned and walked down the steps. She felt torn as she watched him go. One part of her—the part she had come to think of as the spellbound part—insisted that she let him go and wait for Lucien. But the part of her that was connected to her twin pointed out that if Galen truly was the threat, then why was he saying good-bye and walking away from her? For Armand's sake, she had to try to find out if she could trust him.

"Galen, wait." When he turned to face her, she raked a hand through her hair and asked, "Did you mean what you said about helping me?"

"Of course. What do you need?"

"Some information. Will you tell me about the man who owns this house? I think his name's Lucien Morgret?"

"Why in the world would you want to know about Morgret?" he asked, looking baffled.

"It was something Shana said," she ad-libbed. "I understand he was in . . . some kind of trouble?"

He nodded. "He's a very dangerous man with serious psychological problems."

"What kind of psychological problems?"

"I don't know the correct medical terminology, Ariel. I just know that he has a tendency toward violent behavior and he's paranoid. When his grandfather died, there was some suspicion that he may have been involved in his death. The police wanted to question him, but before they could, he disappeared. That was about two and a half or three years ago, and no one's seen him since."

Ariel shook her head, not willing to believe what he was saying. Regardless of her doubts about Lucien, there was no way she could accept that he had been involved in his grandfather's death. That inferred that he was a murderer, and even with a love spell, there was no way she could fall in love with a murderer! Of course, she hadn't wanted to believe he kidnapped Armand, either, and now it was evident that he had.

"Ariel, you haven't seen Morgret, have you?" Galen asked, startling her out of her emotional reverie. She was surprised to see that he had climbed back up the steps and was standing in front of her "If you have, you must tell me. I'm not kidding when I say he's dangerous."

Oh, God, how should she respond? she wondered as she stared up at him in indecision.

"You have seen him, haven't you?" he said in astonishment. "Ariel, can I come in? We really need to talk about this."

She blinked at the question, because Lucien had specifically instructed her that she was never to invite anyone into the house. Of course, he'd also told her that if she gave Galen any form of an invitation he would use it against her. That had already proved false, because she invited him to walk her to her car today and nothing happened. Besides, she'd already determined that Lucien's rules were nothing more than tricks to make sure she didn't talk to anyone and learn the truth.

"Yes, please come in, Galen. You're right. We do need to talk about this," she said, stepping aside so he could come in. After closing the door, she said, "Let's go into the kitchen."

Once they were settled at the kitchen table, she told Galen everything, from how Lucien had first approached her brother to how he'd persuaded her to come with him. The only thing she left out was the love spell. She knew it was pride, but she would never be able to tell anyone about that humiliation.

When she was done, Galen frowned at her in concern. "And you don't know where he is now?"

"No," she answered with a weary sigh as she dropped her gaze to her hands, which rested on the table. "He was gone when I came home this afternoon. I feel like such a fool."

"Don't chastise yourself," he said, reaching out to catch her hand. He gave it a reassuring squeeze and said, "Lucien is a very persuasive man. Don't worry, Ariel. We'll save Armand."

Ariel's head shot up at his words. Regarding him suspiciously, she asked, "How did you know that was my brother's name?"

He gave her a confused look. "You told me his name."

"No, I told you that you knew him as Adam Douglas."

"Ariel, you had to have told me his name. How else would I know it?" he questioned with a nervous laugh.

How else, indeed? she wondered as she stared at him

in growing alarm, because she knew that no matter how hard she tried, she couldn't say Armand's name.

Suddenly she knew in her heart that she'd just made a terrible mistake. Everything Lucien had told her about Galen was true, and she'd walked right into his trap. Even worse, now Lucien would be walking into it.

She tried to reassure herself that Lucien could handle Galen, but as much as she wanted to believe it, she was filled with doubt. Galen was practicing the Old Ways. Lucien had said he barely managed to defeat the demonic spell Galen had turned loose in the house because he wasn't trained to fight against the Old Ways. Indeed, he said that the only chance he had of defeating Galen was if he got him off coven land. Now, because of her, they were all going to die.

But she wasn't going to let that happen, she told herself firmly. She was with Galen, which meant Lucien's mind was connected with hers. All she had to do was tell him to stay away. She had gotten herself into this predicament, and she would get herself out of it.

"I guess you're right," she told Galen. "I must have told you his name without realizing it. Would you like some coffee while we wait?"

"That would be nice," Galen said so pleasantly that she was convinced she had appeased him.

As she walked to the stove, she surreptitiously touched the crystal and thought, *I know you're connected with my mind, Lucien, so you know you're in danger. Stay away from here and save yourself and Armand. Somehow, I'll find a way to save myself.*

Lucien didn't respond, and that worried her, because she suspected his silence meant he was ignoring her. She also recognized that his warlock pride wouldn't let him even consider leaving her in Galen's clutches. *Damn!* Why hadn't she trusted him in the first place?

Because to do that, she would have had to follow her heart, and knowing that Lucien had every intention of breaking her heart, she had refused to listen to it. She had made herself think instead of feel, and now Lucien was going to suffer for it.

I mean it, Lucien! Stay away. I can take care of myself!

When he still didn't respond, an apprehensive shiver crawled down her spine. Lucien was nearby. She could feel him, and her instincts told her that disaster was only a heartbeat away.

Chapter Twenty

The game is up.
—William Shakespeare, *Cymbeline* 3.3.107

L UCIEN arrived at the outcasts' cabin just as the sun set. Though carrying Armand for five miles had been physically taxing, he hadn't even stopped to rest. The feeling that something was wrong with Ariel was growing stronger by the minute, and he was determined to get back to her.

When he crossed back onto coven land a short time later, he stumbled to a stop and gave a disbelieving shake of his head. The moment he stepped into the circle, his mind connected with Ariel's. During the short time he'd been absent, she'd gotten together with Galen. What stunned him was that she was not only telling Galen about him, she'd invited Galen into the house! How could she betray him like this after they'd mated?

Because she's a mortal, and you haven't met a mortal yet you can trust. Even your mother turned her back on you. Why would you expect anything different from a mate?

His first impulse was to project his outrage into her mind, but, thankfully, logic surfaced before he could do that. If he communicated with her now, Galen might be able to connect with him through her. His next impulse was to simply turn around and walk away from her, but he knew he couldn't do that. He had involved her in this situation, and he was morally obligated to try to get her out of it. Besides, she was his mate, and

even though she could turn her back on him, he was incapable of doing that to her. He was compelled to rescue her or die trying.

He'd just reached the house when Ariel realized that
she'd made a mistake by trusting Galen. When she
touched the crystal and warned him to stay away, his
pride was somewhat mollified, even if her concern was
too late.

He slipped in through the front door. When he
reached the kitchen, he saw Ariel standing at the stove,
her back to him. At the sight of her, all the primitive
emotions of protectiveness and possessiveness he felt
toward her surged through him. She had betrayed him,
and yet the power of the love spell still bound him to
her with an intensity that was almost frightening.

He turned his gaze to Galen, who sat at the table
watching her, and said, "Hello, Galen. It's so nice of
you to stop by."

Ariel spun around and cried, "Lucien! Get out of
here!"

Lucien ignored her and focused on Galen, who
leaped to his feet and sneered, "Well, I see the atrocity
of nature has finally arrived."

"I have," Lucien answered, stepping into the room.
"Your father sends his regards. He asked that I tell you
that he forgives you."

"Forgives *me*?" Galen repeated with a harsh laugh.
"He should be begging for *my* forgiveness. He's a fool
who refuses to see the future."

"And what's the future?" Lucien asked, edging
along the wall so that Galen was forced to turn his
back on Ariel. He wanted to order her to run, but if
Galen recognized that he was concerned about her, he
would use her in this battle. Lucien was determined to
keep that from happening.

"As I told your grandfather, I will return our race to

the greatness we once enjoyed!" Galen answered, his eyes taking on a crazed sheen.

A dreadful suspicion began to uncoil within Lucien. "When did you tell this to my grandfather?"

"The night he died," Galen answered. "He followed me to a special place of unbelievable beauty and enchantment that had belonged to us until a bunch of old, senile fools like him denounced the Old Ways and stripped us of our greatest magic. I'm proud to say that my ancestors were enlightened enough to recognize the wrong they had done to us. They knew that the day would finally come when our family would ascend to the position of high priest. They made sure that when that happened, we'd be prepared to right the wrong."

As Galen talked, Lucien recognized that the "special place" he was referring to had to be the secret room in the cave. Since he had found his grandfather's body in the cave, he now knew that Galen had been responsible for his death.

"What did you do to my grandfather?" he demanded.

Galen's lips lifted into a taunting smile. "I didn't have to do anything to him, Lucien. I simply left him in the special place overnight. When I returned in the morning, he was dead."

At the thought of his grandfather being trapped in the secret room with the dark forces overnight, anger surged through Lucien. He had been in that room, had experienced the overwhelmingly evil force of it firsthand. His grandfather had been one hundred and twelve years old, and though his mind had been sharp, his heart had been weak. He probably hadn't lasted an hour, but Lucien was sure that he'd suffered excruciating torture before his heart had finally given out. That he should die so indignantly filled Lucien with fury.

He released it in a savage wind that whipped around

the room like a tornado, and then he drew on every
ounce of power he possessed. When he had it focused,
he mentally projected it at Galen.

Galen let out a bellow of rage as he was suddenly
lifted off the floor and thrown across the room. He hit
the wall and slid down it, but he was on his feet in an
instant. His golden eyes glittered like fire, and his own
maelstrom wind joined Lucien's as he retaliated by
mentally flinging his power at Lucien. As Lucien was
lifted off the floor and propelled backwards, he caught
a glimpse of Ariel. She was still standing beside the
stove, her extraordinarily long hair whipping around
her body and her eyes wide with fear.

He wanted to tell her to get out. Before he could
form the thought, he hit the wall with such force that
it took all his concentration just to remember how to
breathe.

Ariel felt as if she were in some kind of living nightmare as she watched Lucien and Galen battle each
other. It seemed impossible that they were throwing
each other around the room without ever coming into
physical contact.

Within minutes it became obvious to her that Galen
was more powerful than Lucien. He seemed able to
levitate Lucien higher and throw him farther, and she
knew she had to do something to help him. In a normal
situation, she might try to sneak up behind Galen with
one of the cast iron frying pans and give him a good
bop on the head. But the wind in the room was so
strong she had to cling to the kitchen counter to stay
on her feet. There was no way she could sneak up on
him.

Instead, she remained beside the stove, railing at
herself for bringing this about. She loved Lucien, for

God's sake! How could she have done this to him? If anything happened to him . . .

She wouldn't let herself complete the thought, because she wasn't going to let anything happen to him.

Instinctively she pulled the crystal out from beneath her blouse. Lucien had said that the only chance he had of defeating Galen was to draw on the power of her love. Clutching the crystal in her hands, she began to chant, "I love you, Lucien. I love you."

Lucien's strength was waning, and he knew it was only a matter of time before Galen won. But then he felt a sudden surge of power, greater than anything he'd ever experienced.

He had been so focused on Galen that for a moment he couldn't figure out where the strength was coming from. But then he heard Ariel's chant, and a quick glance toward her revealed that she was channeling her love to him through the crystal.

He was momentarily stunned, because he knew that the only way Ariel could be helping him through the crystal was if she truly loved him. But that was impossible, because if she did love him, she would never have been able to betray him in the first place.

Now, however, was not the time to be debating the issue, he recognized, and returned his attention to Galen. Whether or not her love was real, it was giving him incomparable strength.

Galen must have read his mind, because he suddenly said, "She can't help you, Lucien."

As he spoke, he dug his hand into the right front pocket of his pants. When he drew it out, Lucien felt as if his legs had just been knocked out from under him. Galen was clutching half a dozen black crystals from the secret room.

"Ariel, get the hell out of here!" Lucien bellowed as Galen tossed the crystals to the floor.

The words were hardly out of his mouth when there was a fiery explosion and the room filled with a stench so strong that it stole the breath from his lungs. A moment later, six small demons like the one he had faced in Ariel's bedroom were crouched in the center of the room. The difference between these and the other one, however, was that Galen had given them reality. There was no way he would be able to defeat them.

"Ariel, get out!" he bellowed again, as Galen murmured some indistinguishable words and three of them raced toward her, while the other three came toward him.

But his warning came too late. She was cornered against the stove, her eyes wide with horror and her face chalk white as she stared down at them.

Lucien wanted to rush to her aid, but he had his own demons to battle. Two leaped upon his legs, biting viciously through the denim of his pants, while the third sprang into the air and lunged for his throat. He balled up a fist and hit it with such force that it somersaulted through the air three times. At the end of the third rotation, however, it righted itself and came flying back at him, its teeth gnashing. He waited until it was almost upon him, and then he ducked. As it flew past him, he smashed his fists against the other two, knocking them off his legs. Then he ran toward Ariel.

One of the demons clung to her leg while the other two were tangled in her hair. What amazed him was that she wasn't even fighting them. She had closed her eyes tightly and was clutching the crystal desperately and repeating over and over, "I love you, Lucien."

He could feel his own demons snapping at his heels when he reached her. He ignored them as he kicked the one off her leg and then knocked the other two out of her hair. He pushed her behind him and turned so that he confronted all six demons.

"So, what are you going to do now, Lucien?" Galen jeered as he stood behind the demons, his legs spread apart and his arms akimbo. "You can't defeat them, and once you're gone, she's theirs. Would you like me to tell you what they're going to do to her?"

"Lucien, don't listen to him!" Ariel said as she wrapped her hand around his upper arm and stepped to his side. "We can defeat them!"

"Defeat them?" Galen echoed with a boisterous laugh. "Only a mortal could be so optimistic, but you know the truth, don't you, Lucien?"

"Yes," Lucien answered calmly as he again focused upon the power of Ariel's love. "We can defeat them and you, Galen, because Ariel is my mate. We have love on our side. You only have evil."

"No!" Galen yelled in outrage, as he levitated Lucien off the floor and propelled him across the room. "No!"

Even as Galen sent him flying, Lucien focused on Ariel's love, gathering every ounce of power he could from it. The moment he fell to the floor, he mentally projected all that love into Galen's mind.

Galen's eyes widened in horrified surprise, and his mouth flew open as though to scream. But before he could utter a sound, he crumpled to the floor, and when he did, the demons disappeared.

Lucien painfully climbed to his feet and limped to where Galen lay. He didn't bother to check his vital signs, because he knew he was just unconscious. Love could never kill.

"Oh, God, Lucien! Are you all right?" Ariel cried as she rushed to his side and tried to put her arms around him.

Lucien would have liked nothing more than to pull her into his arms, hold her close, and lose himself in the love he could feel radiating from her. But as he

stared at her tear-streaked face, he knew that her love
for him wasn't real. If it had been, she wouldn't have
been able to betray him in the first place.

Catching her arms, he pushed her away from him,
tersely saying, "I'm fine, and so is your brother, whom
I was rescuing while you were double-crossing me
with Galen. So get your things together so I can take
you to him. The sooner the two of you are out of my
life the better."

"Lucien, I know you're angry with me, and you
have every right to feel that way," Ariel said, devastated by his rejection, but she knew that after what
she'd done she couldn't expect more from him. He was
right, she had betrayed him. "What I did was wrong,
but as I watched you fight Galen, I realized how much
I love you, and I think you love me, too. Can't you
find it in your heart to forgive me and give us a
chance?"

"Forgive you?" he repeated disparagingly. "I mated
with you, Ariel. I shared the very essence of what I am
with you, and you *betrayed* me."

"I know," she said, tears welling up in her eyes.
"But if you'll just let me explain what happened, I
think you'll understand why I did what I did."

He gave an angry shake of his head. "Don't you understand? It doesn't matter why you did it. The fact is
that I cast a love spell over you, and it didn't work any
better on you than my father's did on my mother.
You're a mortal, and your love can't be trusted!"

"Well, what did you expect from me?" she demanded, growing angry herself. "Even before you cast
the spell you told me you were going to abandon me,
and you were going to do it for no other reason than
that I'm a mortal. If you want to be able to trust in
someone's love, then you have to give them a reason to
trust you in return. And I hate to break this to you,

Lucien, but I don't think the promise of abandonment would inspire trust in a witch or warlock any more than it does in a mortal.

"It's also unfair for you to judge me based on your mother's actions," she continued vehemently. "That would be the same as me saying that since Galen is bad, therefore all warlocks are bad. That's bigotry, Lucien, and you, of all people, should understand how wrong that is!"

"Are you through?" he asked, his expression one of fury.

She stared at him for a long moment, recognizing that nothing she said was going to make a difference. Even if she hadn't betrayed him, they would still be having this confrontation. His problem didn't have to do with her. It had to do with his mother.

"Yes, Lucien, I'm sorry to say I am," she said wearily. "I've already packed, and my suitcase is in the car. I would appreciate it if you would take me to my brother, because I, too, feel that the sooner you get out of my life the better."

With that, she turned and walked out. Lucien stood staring at the empty doorway, feeling angry, frustrated, and oddly enough, confused.

He jumped when someone said behind him, "For a mortal, she sure makes a lot of sense."

Lucien spun around and frowned warily when he saw Sebastian Moran leaning against his back door. "How did you get in here without an invitation? Or has she betrayed me to you, too?"

Sebastian arched a brow as he drawled, "Family never needs an invitation to enter."

Lucien blinked at him, sure he'd misunderstood. "Family?"

He nodded. "We're cousins, Lucien. Albeit very distant cousins, but we are related. We'll discuss that later. While you take the mortal to her brother, I'll make sure that Galen is properly handled."

"What will you do with him?" Lucien asked, glancing down at Galen.

"For now, I'll just make sure that he's rendered powerless. His fate will be determined at a later date. Take care of the mortal and come back. Then we'll talk."

"I won't be able to do that, Sebastian. I'm an outcast, remember? In order to come back on coven land, I need an invitation from someone who resides here."

"I reside here, and I'm issuing you an invitation."

"What about the other outcasts? Will you issue them an invitation, too?"

Again Sebastian arched a brow. "They won't be able to go to their homes, and their families and friends will still shun them."

"They can stay here," Lucien said, knowing firsthand that even if you were shunned, being on coven land was better than being off it.

"Then, by all means, tell them that they are also invited."

Lucien nodded. "You'll be here when I get back?"

"If I'm not, wait for me. I'll get here as soon as I can."

"And you'll tell me everything?"

"Yes, Lucien, I'll tell you everything," Sebastian said as he hefted Galen off the floor and onto his shoulder.

Ariel knew that she hadn't been in the car for more than five or ten minutes, but it seemed as if hours passed before Lucien joined her.

When he finally climbed into the passenger seat, she sighed inwardly in relief. She needed to get away from him as soon as possible, because she knew that if she didn't, she was liable to beg him to let her stay. Unfortunately, she also knew that that would only result in another rejection, and she simply couldn't handle another one from him.

Except for the directions Lucien gave her, they didn't share a word. When they finally arrived at a cabin, he announced, "Armand is inside."

Ariel jumped out of the car and ran toward the cabin. Lucien followed her. The door was opened by an old woman, who eyed her cautiously.

"It's all right, Myrna. She's the mortal's twin sister," Lucien said behind her.

"A *twin*?" the old woman echoed, staring at Ariel as though she were some alien life form.

Ariel gave her a weak smile. "May I see my brother?"

"Oh, of course!" she replied, stepping back.

The moment she did, Ariel saw Armand sitting at a table.

"Armand!" she cried.

"Ariel?" he gasped in surprise, rising unsteadily to his feet. "What are you doing here?"

"Looking for you," she said, tears running down her cheeks as she ran to him and threw herself into his arms. "Oh, Armand, I've been so worried about you!"

"Oh, God, Ariel," he said, hugging her tightly. "I don't know what's going on. I feel like I've been lost in some kind of a void. I don't know what day it is, what time it is, or even what year it is!"

"Don't worry about that now. I'll fill you in on everything later," she promised, sniffing as she cradled his beloved face between her hands. "God, I love you, and if you ever scare me like this again, I'm going to wring your neck!"

"Ariel, you're embarrassing me," he mumbled,

catching her wrists and pulling her hands away. "We'll talk about this later, okay?"

"Yeah," she said, grinning. "Let's go home."

He gave her a puzzled look. "I might as well. I can't remember why I was here in the first place."

"You go out to the car. I'll be there in a minute," she told him.

When he walked out of the cabin, she turned to face Lucien, who was leaning against the fireplace mantel. She glanced around the room, noting that everyone else had disappeared.

Returning her attention to Lucien, she asked, "Is there a problem with his memory, or did you cast a spell to make him forget?"

"It's a little of both," Lucien answered. "He's confused right now, but when his memory returns, he'll think that he was here on a wild goose chase."

Ariel was quiet as she let that sink in. When it had, she asked, "And what about me, Lucien? Will I also forget why I was here?"

"Do you want to forget?" he countered, a strange tautness to his voice.

"No," she answered softly, cursing the new tears that welled up in her eyes. She quickly glanced down at the floor so he wouldn't see them. When she felt she had her emotions under control, she looked back up at him. "I know you don't think you can trust me, but I swear to you that Sanctuary's secret is safe with me. If, however, you feel you need to cast a spell over me to make me forget, I'll understand. I also want you to know that I don't regret what happened between us, and I want to thank you for saving my brother."

When he didn't respond, she impulsively raised on tiptoe and pressed a kiss to his cheek. As she pulled away, she gave him a sad smile and whispered, "Good-bye, Lucien. I hope that someday you'll find the peace and happiness that you deserve."

She turned and hurried out of the cabin, knowing that if he said one word to her, she would burst into tears.

As she steered the car down the road a few minutes later, she glanced into the rearview mirror. A man's dark shape was framed in the cabin's lighted doorway, and she knew it was Lucien. It was as if he sensed that she'd seen him, because he abruptly closed the door.

Ariel's heart shattered at the finality of that simple act. It was over. She would never see Lucien again.

Lucien had been home for more than an hour, and there was still no sign of Sebastian. He'd spent a good portion of that hour getting Boyd, Myrna, and Roan settled in. Griffith had refused to come with them. He said that after the part he played in Galen's downfall, he didn't deserve to set foot on coven land. Lucien hoped that Griffith would eventually change his mind, because as far as he was concerned, Griffith should be here. The coven needed Griffith's type of moral strength to guide them.

Now, as he collapsed into a chair in front of the fireplace and stared at the pentagram, he acknowledged that he had defeated Galen and saved the coven from destruction. So why did he feel as if the world had come to an end?

Because Ariel's gone.

He closed his eyes against the sharp pain that shot through him at that acknowledgment. She was gone and he would never see her again. He'd known it would hurt, but he hadn't realized it would be an excruciating agony that sank all the way to the marrow of his bones.

"The mortals are safely on their way home?"

Lucien's eyes flew open. Sebastian was leaning against the front door, his arms crossed over his chest.

"Didn't anyone ever tell you that even if you are family, you're supposed to knock before entering someone's home?" Lucien grumbled.

"I did knock," Sebastian replied. "I guess you were too preoccupied to hear me. Anything you'd like to talk about?"

"All I want to talk about is you," Lucien muttered. "Are you finally going to tell me exactly who you are and why you're here?"

Sebastian walked across the room and sat in the chair beside him. "It's a long story. Are you sure you want to hear it tonight?"

Lucien scowled at him. "Yes, I want to hear it tonight, and you aren't going to put me off, Sebastian. Are you really related to me?"

"Yes," he answered, "but don't expect me to give you the genealogical particulars. All I know is that some relative of mine married a relative of yours before your family emigrated to this country. When the high council decided to send someone here to investigate Galen, they chose me, because they knew that Galen couldn't ban someone from the coven who had had familial ties here."

Lucien's heart skipped a beat as Sebastian confirmed his worst fear. "The high council sent you here?" When he nodded, Lucien shot to his feet and began to pace. "*Damn!* It was all for nothing, wasn't it? The council knows about Galen, and they're going to destroy the coven!"

"They are not going to destroy the coven, Lucien."

"But high coven law says . . ."

"I know what high coven law says," Sebastian interrupted impatiently. "Why don't you sit down and hear me out instead of jumping to conclusions?"

Lucien eyed him suspiciously. "You're sure the coven isn't in danger?"

"I swear to you that at this moment, the coven isn't in any danger."

It wasn't exactly the reassurance Lucien wanted, but he decided that if Sebastian was lying to him, there wasn't anything he could do about it. The council was all-powerful, which meant the coven was at their mercy.

He sat back down and said, "All right, I'll listen."

Sebastian leaned back in his chair and folded his hands over his stomach. "A few weeks before your grandfather died, he sent a message to the council saying that he had a serious problem to discuss with them. He said it wasn't a matter that could be discussed through traditional forms of communication, and he called for a formal council meeting. As you're aware, the council meets telepathically, so this involves a lot of preparation. It takes days for them to perform the necessary trance spells that will enable them to communicate collectively. A date was set and they all began preparing. Then, three days before the meeting was to take place, your grandfather died. During the past year, the council has come to believe that the reason your grandfather called for the meeting was because he'd discovered that Galen was practicing the Old Ways."

Lucien gave a confused shake of his head. His conversation with Galen had confirmed what Sebastian was saying. Without even realizing he was speaking aloud, he murmured, "Why didn't Grandfather come to me for help? Together we could have handled Galen."

"But he would have been risking your life, and you were the last of your family," Sebastian pointed out. "If you died, then the family died with you. You know as well as I do that preserving the family is critical, but it's even more crucial in your case."

"Why is it more crucial in my case?" Lucien asked, baffled.

"It's not up to me to give you the details," Sebastian replied mysteriously. "You'll have to go to your mother to learn them."

"My *mother*?" Lucien gasped in disbelief. "I don't even know if she's alive!"

"She's alive," Sebastian assured, "and before I leave here, I'll tell you how to find her. But let me get back to my story."

Lucien was too bewildered to do anything but nod.

"As soon as the council learned of your grandfather's death, they thought that was why he'd called for a council meeting. They figured he knew he was ill and wanted to get permission to send you to your mother."

"What do you mean, get permission to send me to my mother? And why would he want to send me to her in the first place?" Lucien demanded, becoming more bewildered.

Sebastian shook his head. "Again, these are things you can hear only from her. All I can tell you is that when your grandfather died, there was a lot of dissension among the council about letting you lead the coven. They felt that because you were a half-mortal, you might have split loyalties between the coven and the mortal world."

"That's ridiculous!" Lucien declared, incensed.

"They didn't believe it was ridiculous," Sebastian replied calmly. "Remember, Lucien, you're unique. There has never been another half-breed in our history. No one knew what to expect of you. That's why the council agreed to the challenge when Galen disputed your right to the high priesthood. They wanted to see if you were capable of performing as a full-blooded warlock. When you lost, they felt that it was in the best interest of the coven to let Galen take your place."

"Except that Galen cheated in the challenge," Lucien stated tightly.

"At the time the council believed it was a fair fight, and when you refused to accept defeat and chose to be a shunned outcast, they felt they'd made the right decision. They were sure that you were unable to give Galen your loyalty because of your ties to the mortal world."

"I can't believe this!" Lucien declared. "I devoted my entire life to the coven, and they made arbitrary decisions about my loyalty based on nothing more than the fact that my mother was a mortal?"

"I know it sounds unfair, but again, you're unique, and therefore, an unknown quantity," Sebastian defended. "They had to consider the welfare of the coven first, and they simply didn't know what to expect from you. That's why they've kept track of you all these years."

"They've been *spying* on me?"

"I think monitoring would be a better description."

Lucien muttered a vile curse. "I'm surprised they didn't strip me of my powers, since they considered me so untrustworthy."

Sebastian shifted uncomfortably in his chair. "Actually, I understand there was some discussion about doing just that, but it was decided that until you proved you were a threat you would be left alone."

"How lucky for me that I was given the benefit of the doubt," Lucien drawled sarcastically.

Sebastian frowned. "Look, Lucien, I know that what happened to you was unjust, but try to put yourself in the place of the council members. Our entire existence depends upon loyalty and secrecy. The needs of one person don't matter when compared to the security of the covens."

Lucien wanted to argue with him, but he couldn't. He had made the same decision when he cast the love spell over Ariel, thereby sacrificing both her and himself for the coven.

It still grated, however, and he said, "So when did the council figure out that Galen was a rogue warlock?"

"They started becoming suspicious when he made his father an outcast. When they asked him why, he claimed that his father was jealous of him and trying to interfere with the inner workings of the coven. Since a warlock is completely devoted to his child, the possibility of jealousy simply didn't ring true. The council decided to send me in to investigate, and it didn't take me long to figure out that Galen was using the Old Ways."

Lucien opened his mouth to speak, but Sebastian held up his hand. "Let me finish, Lucien, and then I'll answer your questions. As I said, I figured it out, and I knew that under high coven law the coven was doomed. I also knew that the annihilation of the coven meant the beginning of the end of our entire race. We're seriously on the brink of extinction, Lucien. Your coven has fared better than most, because you didn't live through the destruction of two world wars during this century. We can protect ourselves from mortals, but we can't protect ourselves from the weapons of war, particularly bombs. We suffered as badly as the rest of Europe, and many of our people were lost."

"So the rumors of extinction are true?" Lucien asked.

"Truer than you'd want to believe," Sebastian replied grimly. "Anyway, I was able to determine that

Galen hadn't involved the coven in the practice of the Old Ways, so he was the only real threat. Unfortunately, they had all sworn their allegiance to him, so they couldn't fight him. The council couldn't do anything on their behalf, because the high priests are banned from interfering in the internal affairs of any coven but their own."

"I'd think that under circumstances like Galen, they'd lift that ban," Lucien noted dryly.

Sebastian shook his head. "It's critical that each coven maintain its own autonomy. Galen was dangerous enough, but can you imagine what would have happened if he had been able to interfere in and possibly take over other covens? The only way to keep that from ever happening is never to lift that ban under any circumstances."

"You've made your point," Lucien allowed, shuddering at the thought of Galen's being able to draw upon the power of several covens. It would make him invincible.

Sebastian nodded. "The only way the coven could possibly be saved was if there was a warlock who had ties to the coven, but didn't owe Galen his loyalty. You were the only warlock who fit that bill, because the other outcast warlocks had sworn their allegiance to him before their banishment. As I said earlier, the council had been monitoring you, and it was obvious that you were no threat to the coven's security. I persuaded the council to let me give you premonitory dreams that the coven was in danger and see what you would do."

"*You* caused my dreams?" Lucien questioned in surprise.

"Yes," Sebastian replied. "I figured that you'd recognize that Galen was placing the coven in danger, and if your loyalty was with the coven, you would try to find a way to stop him. You proved me right. You sent Armand Dantes here. That's when the council decided to see if you could defeat Galen, and if you could, then they would spare the coven."

"So the coven truly is safe?"

"It's safe from annihilation because of Galen's actions. You have my word on that."

"Thank the gods for that," Lucien said, collapsing back into the chair and brushing a hand over his eyes in relief.

"The gods didn't have anything to do with it, Lucien. You're the one who saved the coven, and because you did, you're now going to be faced with an ever harder task."

Lucien regarded him in bewilderment. "What task?"

"You'll have to learn the details from your mother," Sebastian reiterated. "If, after listening to her, you're willing to take on the responsibility, then you'll become the coven's high priest. The council wants you to know, however, that if you decide that they're asking too much of you, someone else will become high priest. But you needn't worry about your future. Regardless of your decision, you will be allowed back into the coven with all the rights and privileges you enjoyed before becoming an outcast."

Lucien raked a hand through his hair. "Why are you making this sound so mysterious? And why in hell do I have to talk to my mother, of all people? She walked out of my life thirty years ago. She *abandoned* me!"

"She didn't abandon you, Lucien," Sebastian denied. "At least not in the way that you think. But again, it's not my place to tell you the details. You'll have to learn them from her."

He stood, pulled a slip of paper out of his shirt pocket, and laid it on the table between them. "This is the address where she works. Ironically, the entire time you were in Philadelphia, you were only a few miles away from her. When you're ready, find her and talk with her, but don't wait too long, Lucien. The coven needs a leader, and if it isn't going to be you, then the council will have to arrange for a challenge. I'm personally hoping that when I leave here, you'll be giving me your blessing as high priest."

"What's your stake in all of this?" Lucien asked curiously. "Why is it so important to you that I do whatever it is I'm supposed to do?"

For a moment Sebastian didn't look as if he would answer, but then he said, "It's important to me because we are the last of our family, Lucien. When I decided to accept the position of the council's emissary, which is a position I'm now committed to until age forces me to retire, I made a decision not to mate. I'll be a troubleshooter, traveling all over the world. It's a dangerous existence, and I didn't feel that it was right to ask a witch to live a life in which her mate could be killed at any moment."

Lucien understood Sebastian's choice not to mate, but he was disturbed by his acceptance of the position in the first place. He suspected that it wasn't a job Sebastian had wanted as much as it was one that family loyalty had demanded he take.

He decided to confirm his suspicion. "Would you have accepted the position of emissary if you hadn't been related to me?"

"No," Sebastian answered. "But when the council explained to me how important you were, I couldn't turn them down."

"Dammit, Sebastian, you're doing it again," Lucien groused. "*Why* am I so important?"

"You'll understand as soon as you talk to your mother. Do it soon, Lucien. It's important to all of us."

With that, Sebastian left. As the door closed behind

him, Lucien looked down at the paper that told where his mother was. As he read the words "Dr. Elaine Baker-Morgret," thirty years of bitterness surfaced. Regardless of what Sebastian said, she had abandoned him. He leaned back in the chair, closed his eyes, and let himself wallow in resentment. If nothing else, it shut out the memories of Ariel. Unfortunately it didn't alleviate the crippling sense of loss.

Chapter Twenty-one

Love conquers all things; let us too surrender to Love.
—Virgil [Pubilus Vergilius Maro] *Eclogues,*10.1.69

LUCIEN frowned at the door to his mother's apartment. He knew she was inside. He had watched her walk into the building and had been startled by the changes in her appearance. Her dark-brown hair was almost completely silver. She was also much thinner than he remembered. Of course, thirty years had passed since he'd last seen her, and changes were to be expected. He couldn't help wondering what she would think when she saw him. Would she be pleased with the way he'd turned out? Disappointed? Or worse, not care one way or the other?

The last possibility was almost enough to make him walk away, but he knew he couldn't do that. For the past two weeks Sebastian had been hounding him daily to come see her. Though he was using that as an excuse to be here, he admitted it wasn't the real reason.

The simple fact was, he missed Ariel so badly that it was a constant ache that worsened with each passing day. He kept telling himself he had to forget her. She'd betrayed him. Then again, as she said, if he wanted to be able to trust in someone's love, then he had to give that person a reason to trust him in return. She'd also asked him to give them a chance. For the past several days he'd begun to realize that he wanted that chance. He'd seen the future without her, and it was an empty, aching existence. The problem was, he knew he couldn't live in the mortal world, and he didn't know if Ariel could be happy in his.

That was why he finally gave in to Sebastian's badgering. He knew that his mother had left the coven because she'd been unhappy there, and he wanted to know why. If he did decide to build a life with Ariel, he didn't want her so unhappy that if something happened to him, she would abandon their child. Not that he believed Ariel could do something like that. As she had proved with her brother, she was fiercely loyal to those she loved.

Still, it was important that he know if his mother's unhappiness at the coven was inherent to all mortals or simply a personal problem. He had already condemned Ariel to an unhappy, solitary life, but at least in her world she would have her family and friends. His family was gone, so in his world all she'd have would be him and the child they would conceive together, and it might not be enough to make her happy.

Drawing in a deep breath, he knocked on the door. When his mother opened it a few seconds later, her expression was irritated. But then she looked at him, and all the color drained out of her face as she hoarsely whispered, *"Lucien!"*

Lucien stared at her face, which had changed very little over the years. There were a few lines around her eyes and mouth that he didn't remember, and her face was a little thinner. But it was still the face of the woman who used to read him ridiculous fairy tales about sleeping princesses and jealous fairies.

"Hello, Mother," he said.

At that, she promptly burst into tears. Lucien was just as rattled by her weeping as he'd been by Ariel's. He also had no idea what he should do. With Ariel, he'd had to kiss her to calm her, and that certainly wasn't an alternative in this instance.

Luckily he didn't have to come up with a solution, because she quickly pulled herself together. She gave him a watery smile as she said, "You have the same dumbfounded expression your father used to get whenever I'd cry. Please, come in. I promise that I'll try not to shed any more tears."

Lucien supposed he should say something in response to her statement, but he didn't, because he had no idea what was appropriate. His time in the mortal world had been spent behind the bar of the Witches' Brew, and he hadn't had to deal with crying women. Did you tell them it was okay to cry? Or did you encourage them not to do it?

"Can I get you something to drink or eat?" she asked, as she led him into a small, tastefully decorated living room.

"No, I'm fine," he answered as he sat down on the sofa. She sat in the chair across from him. "If my visit's inconvenient, I can always come back."

"Lucien, no visit from you would ever be inconvenient," she said, new tears welling into her eyes. "Your grandfather promised he'd send you to me when it was time for you to know the truth about your birth, but I'd begun to believe that I would never see you again. I know he didn't approve of me and . . .

"Well, now's not the time to get into that," she said, with a dismissive wave of her hand. "You've come to learn about yourself. How much has your grandfather told you?"

"Actually, he never told me anything," Lucien answered.

"Nothing at all?" she questioned in disbelief. Wh he shook his head, she said, "You mean, he here with no information at all?"

"He didn't send me," he explained. "G died three years ago."

"Oh, Lucien, I'm sorry!" she declared sincerely. "Your grandfather and I had our problems, but I did respect him. I'm sure you are just as wonderful a high priest as he was."

Lucien shifted uncomfortably on the sofa. "I'm afraid I'm not the high priest. There were some . . . complications after Grandfather's death, and someone else assumed the position."

"What kind of complications?" she asked, her eyes narrowing. Before he could answer, she said, "It was because you're half mortal, right?"

"Yes."

"Damn!" she muttered, rising to her feet and beginning to pace. "I told your father that something like that would happen, but he wouldn't believe me. He was such a kind, decent man that he didn't see the arrogance that plagued the coven. I kept telling him that they considered mortals beneath them, but he argued that I was just oversensitive. He saw you only as the answer to the future, and he was so caught up in the dream that he couldn't see the hell the others were putting you through."

She suddenly stopped pacing and gave a sad shake of her head. "I'm sorry that you've been treated so badly, Lucien. Maybe if your father had lived, it would have been different. Maybe he could have made them see the future as he saw it, but, quite frankly, I'm not sure he could have."

"You don't like my people, do you?" Lucien noted.

"*Your people,*" she repeated ruefully. "That's the attitude I'm talking about, Lucien. It's true that your race is superior in many ways, but it's also true that you're human beings, just like me or any other mortal. It was that racial attitude of superiority, however, that created 'uper race that now stands on the brink of extinction. *people* were so exclusive that they limited their blood lines, and genetics caught up with them more than a thousand years ago."

"You're talking about our limited procreation?" Lucien guessed.

"Yes," she answered. "Your father recognized the problem, and that's when he sought me out."

"Sought you out?"

"You really don't know anything, do you?" she murmured in amazement. "Your grandfather never told you I was a geneticist?"

"No," Lucien said, stunned. "I knew you were a doctor, but I thought you must be in the medical profession."

She collapsed back into the chair and rubbed a hand against her temple. "I guess I'd better start from the beginning, or none of this is going to make sense to you. As I said, your father recognized the problem within your race, and the rumors of extinction had him concerned. He started reading up on genetics, and he came to the conclusion that if your race mated with mortals, the problem would be solved. He recognized, however, that there would be dissension against such a proposal. That's the problem with elitism. You become so intent on maintaining your exclusiveness that you lose sight of the real problems."

She paused, leaned her head back, and stared up at the ceiling, as though lost in memory. "Your father decided that the best way to prove his theory was to have a complete genetic workup, and that's where I came in. He had studied some papers I'd written and was impressed by them." She suddenly glanced toward Lucien and grinned. "Or at least that's what he told me. He probably came to me because I was the nearest geneticist."

"And that's how you met?" Lucien asked, fascinated by her story.

She nodded. "I have to admit that at first I thought your father was a nut. I was a scientist, and I knew there was no such thing as real witches and warlocks. But then your father showed me a few of his tricks, and I was convinced that he was exactly what he said he was. I agreed to do a genetic workup on him. A couple of months later I discovered that your race has an additional gene that the rest of us don't have. I believe that it's this gene that gives you your powers. It also appears to be dominant, which means that even if you mate with mortals, your powers will be passed on to your children. It's true that the power will be somewhat weakened, as happened with you. But when you get down to the bottom line, that weakness is inconsequential when compared to the fact that interracial children will be able to have as many children as their mortal counterparts. And that was your father's dream. You were to be the new beginning for your race."

"Are you saying that you and Father mated just to . . . create me?" Lucien asked, aghast.

"Oh, no!" she objected with a laugh. "Your father and I mated because we fell in love, although if he hadn't fallen in love with me, I'm sure he would have looked for another mortal he could love. He was devoted to the coven, and he was determined to see your race survive. His master plan was that we would raise you in the coven. Then when you were eighteen, we would send you to a mortal university and encourage you to seek a mortal spouse. He was sure that once the coven realized that you could have more than one child, other witches and warlocks would be willing to seek spouses outside the coven. I estimate that if even three or four people from the coven would do this, within a few generations, the threat of extinction would be nonexistent."

She sobered suddenly and gave another sad shake of

her head. "But then your father died, and his dream died with him. Your grandfather made it clear that he wasn't willing to support it, and apparently the majority of the high council felt the same way. Without your father there to fight on your behalf, you became a failed experiment in their eyes."

The word "experiment" made Lucien recall Griffith's story about the Morgan family's petition for a challenge that the council had turned down. They had told the Morgans that there was an experiment underway, and until they had time to fully consider its potential, they would not sanction a challenge.

"Is that why you left the coven and never tried to contact me?" he asked her. "Because I was a failed experiment?"

She stared at him in horror. "Of course, not! I knew I couldn't stay at the coven without your father. Everyone, including your grandparents, considered me a second-class citizen and treated me with insulting condescension. When I told your grandfather I wanted to leave I had every intention of taking you with me, but he said I had to give you a choice. If you wanted to go, I could take you. If you decided to stay, however, I had to cut all ties with you until he felt it was time for you to learn the truth about your birth. He said that when that time arrived, he would send you to me, but he didn't want you any more confused than you already were.

"When you refused to go with me, it nearly killed me," she confessed, again growing teary-eyed, "but I knew your grandfather was right. You were confused and angry and unhappy. If one of us was going to suffer, it was only fair that it be me. I was the adult. You were just a little boy—or rather, a little warlock. I remember how you hated it when I called you a boy."

"So you walked away and never looked back," he

stated, hating the embittered tone in his voice but unable to stop it.

She bolted upright in her chair and vehemently denied, "You're wrong, Lucien! I looked back every day, and after a few months had passed I missed you so badly that I decided I'd rather be miserable than be without you. But when I contacted your grandfather and asked to come back, he refused. He told me there was no place for a mortal within the coven and insisted that I uphold our agreement. He reiterated that when he felt it was time for you to hear the truth he'd send you to me. Until then he wouldn't let me write or even send you a birthday present. Now that I know he died without telling you about me, I suspect that he had no intention of ever letting you hear the truth," she finished bitterly.

Distressed and not sure what to say, Lucien glanced down at his hands. He believed her story. He had loved his grandfather dearly and would have done anything for him, but he also knew that when the old man's mind was made up about something, he couldn't be swayed. He also had to agree with her premise that his grandfather had never intended for him to learn the truth about his birth. If he had, he would have sent him to her years ago. Instead, he always let Lucien believe that she had abandoned him.

He looked up at her and said, "I'm sorry. What Grandfather did was wrong."

She gave a fatalistic shrug. "I was as wrong as he was, Lucien. I never should have left in the first place."

Lucien didn't know how to respond to that, so he said, "Well, I've heard your story. Now would you like to hear mine?"

"Lucien, I would give away ten years of my life to hear everything that has happened to you since I left the coven," she told him with such sincerity that he was deeply moved.

"After you hear what I have to say, you might not feel that way," he stated dryly.

"Well, tell me anyway."

Over the next hour, he told her everything that had happened since his grandfather's death, including the mating spell he had cast over Ariel.

"So you can see my dilemma," he stated at the end. "By casting the mating spell over Ariel, I forced her to fall in love with me. Now I don't know what to do. I'm dying without her, but is it fair to ask her to come to the coven and build a life with me? What if she ends up being as miserable there as you were?"

"Oh, Lucien, I can see that warlocks haven't become any less egotistical during the past thirty years," she stated wryly. "You couldn't have forced Ariel into falling in love with you. The mating spell wouldn't have worked on her if she wasn't capable of giving you the type of pure love you expect from a mate.

"As for her being happy with you, its obvious that the council has decided that if you're willing to fulfill your father's dream, they're willing to give it a chance. You'll be the high priest, Lucien. You can teach tolerance to the coven, and as more members intermarry, the stigma will lessen. In the meantime, find ways to make her feel productive within your society. And most important of all, reassure her daily that even though she doesn't have the powers of a witch, you love her with all your heart."

"So you think I should ask her to build a life with me?"

"I think that you'll be the biggest fool that ever lived if you let another day pass without going after her. But before you leave, I would like to give you a piece of advice. You've lucked out with your Ariel, but as other members of the coven seek mortal mates, they must proceed carefully. Society is not ready to accept a race of people with extraordinary powers, so it is critical that you continue to maintain your secrecy."

"But how can we maintain our secrecy and still intermarry?" he asked with a frown.

"You must emphasize to the coven that such unions must be made out of profound love," she replied. "They'll know that love when they find it. That is one aspect of your society that you can be proud of. Love has reached its purest form within your race. That's why once you've mated, you can never mate with anyone else, and any mortal who experiences that kind of love will never betray the coven. I'm living proof of that.

"Now go and get Ariel," she urged, as she rose to her feet. "Love her and cherish her and make lots of babies with her. Make your father's dream come true."

"Will you visit us?" he asked, rising also.

Again tears filled her eyes. "If the invitation is sincere, I'll visit so often that you'll get sick of seeing me."

"I would never get sick of seeing you," he said gruffly, as he pulled her into his arms and hugged her. "I'm sorry Grandfather kept us apart for all these years, but we'll make up for them. I promise."

"I know we will," she said, pulling away with a sniff. "Now, get out of here before I start crying."

He rolled his eyes toward the ceiling. "I guess that's one aspect of having a mortal mate that I'll have to get used to. Why do mortal women cry at the drop of a hat?"

"Damned if I know," she said with a laugh.

* * *

"Ariel, are you all right?" Jean asked in concern.

"Of course," Ariel answered, turning away from the window in their office. "Why do you ask?"

"Well, gosh, I have no idea," Jean muttered facetiously, as she dropped some paperwork on her desk. "Maybe it's because you haven't said more than a few dozen words in the last two weeks, and you spend nearly all your time staring out that window. Something's been wrong with you ever since you and Armand returned from the vacation you took together. Did you two have a fight or something?"

"No," Ariel said, turning back to face the window. "We got along fine."

She had been shocked when she returned home and discovered that Jean hadn't been worried about her. She thought Ariel had gone on vacation with Armand. Obviously Lucien had done more spell casting than just keeping her from calling home. In some ways she was glad. She wouldn't have wanted to answer Jean's questions. At the same time, however, it made things difficult, because there was no one with whom she could share her heartbreak, not even her twin, and she'd always been able to share everything with him.

When Lucien had asked her if she wanted to forget, she'd said no, but now she was wondering if it wouldn't have been a blessing if he had made her forget. All she could do was stand by the window and wait for the first touch of night to steal across the sky. Then she would hurry home and stare at the walls until bedtime. Only when she was in bed and asleep was she happy, because every night Lucien came to her in her dreams and they made mad, passionate love.

Sadly, however, she knew that her nights of lovemaking were nothing more than fantasies. When she awakened, they didn't have the feeling of reality they'd had when Lucien had really made love to her in her dreams.

"Ariel, please tell me what's wrong," Jean pleaded, joining her at the window. "I'm your best friend, and I'm worried about you."

"There's no reason for you to be worried," she reassured, giving her friend's shoulders a squeeze. "I just have the pre-winter blues. I'll be back to my old self in a few days."

Jean's expression told her she didn't believe her, but thankfully the bell rang in the shop and she let the subject drop and went to check on the customer.

Tomorrow, I'll do better, Ariel promised herself. Of course, she'd been making that same promise ever since she'd come home, and every day seemed to be worse than the last. When Lucien had said her life would be empty and lonely, he hadn't been exaggerating.

With a sigh, she returned to her desk and tried to concentrate on the mail that had piled up during her absence. When she found herself reading the same letter for the third time and still not knowing what it said, she set it aside and buried her face in her hands. She was going to have to do something about this depression. If she didn't, she would end up in an institution.

"Ariel, you have a customer," Jean announced. "Do you want me to send him in or tell him to come back another time?"

Ariel's first instinct was to have Jean tell him to come back, but she knew she had to pull herself together and get on with her life. She still had bills to pay and a business to run. Brooding over Lucien wasn't going to change that.

She lifted her head and said, "Send him in."

"Good girl," Jean said with a wink.

Ariel rose to her feet and tucked her blouse into her slacks. She'd just raised her hand to smooth her hair when Lucien walked into the room. She froze and stared at him in shocked disbelief.

She was imagining him. He wasn't really standing in front of her! But as her gaze traveled from the top of his head to the tips of his scuffed black boots, she knew he was real.

Excitement flared inside her. She wanted to run to him and throw herself into his arms, but her fear of rejection held her back. Instead she slowly returned her gaze to his face. Did he really look thinner? And had the lines in his face really deepened? Was it possible that he'd been suffering as much as she had? Had he come after her?

Even as hope stirred inside her, she warned herself to ignore it. She was still a mortal, and Lucien despised mortals. She had to remember that at all costs.

"Lucien? What are you doing here?" she asked, her voice sounding oddly breathless.

He stuffed his hands into his pants pockets and shrugged. "I was in the area and thought I'd stop by and see how you and Armand are doing."

"I see," she said, her heart sinking. She was right. He hadn't come after her, and she'd been foolish to think he had. Tears burned the back of her eyes, and she glanced down at the floor, blinking them back. She was not going to cry in front of him. *She wasn't!*

When she had her emotions under control, she looked at him and said, "Armand's doing fine. He's getting ready to take off on another investigation."

"And how are *you* doing?" he asked softly.

Awful! she wanted to wail. *I love you, and I'm dying without you!*

Aloud, she said. "Okay. And you?"

He shrugged again. "So much has been happening in my life that I haven't really had time to assimilate everything."

She wanted to ask him what had happened, but she refrained. The longer he stayed, the greater the chance that she would burst into tears. Why had he come here? Did he want to torture her? "Well, I'm sure you'll figure it all out soon."

He nodded and glanced around the room. When he returned his gaze to her, he whispered, "Are you happy, Ariel?"

"Happy?" she repeated hoarsely, blinking frantically as tears again threatened. She considered lying, but then her temper began to stir. She decided that if he was callous enough to come here and torture her like this, then he deserved to hear the unadulterated truth.

"No, I'm not happy," she said, giving up on her battle with her tears. As they began to roll down her cheeks, she continued, "In fact, I'm even more miserable than you told me I'd be. I spend all day thinking about you, and then I spend all night dreaming about you. I can't stand it, Lucien."

He regarded her for a long, solemn moment before asking, "Do you want me to cast a spell that will make you forget me, Ariel?"

"No!" she answered so quickly and vehemently that she surprised herself. Even more surprising, however, was that she realized it was the truth. Just the thought of not remembering him was more than she could bear. "I'd rather be miserable than forget you."

"In that case, would you be interested in coming back to Sanctuary and building a life with me?" he asked.

If she'd been disbelieving when she saw him, she was now completely flabbergasted. She sat down on her chair before her legs could give out. "Don't joke with me, Lucien."

"I'm not joking, Ariel," he replied. "I'm miserable too."

"You really want us to be man and wife?"

"Well, we call it being mates, but the premise is the same. But before you give me your answer, there are some things you should know."

Ariel stared at him in wide-eyed wonder as he explained about his mother and father and how he was the new beginning of his race.

He concluded, "So, as you can see, now that I'm going to be in charge of the coven, I'm going to be faced with great challenges in helping my people find mortal mates. If you agree to come back with me, I'll be relying on you to help us understand the mortal mind so that they can make good choices.

"But it's not going to be easy," he warned, "and I can't guarantee that everyone within the coven will accept you. What I can guarantee is that if you'll give me a chance, I'll give you everything you want that's within my power. And I'll never abandon you, Ariel. Never. I promise you that."

Ariel wanted to run to him, throw herself into his arms, and scream yes to his proposal. She'd been dreaming about this, but now that the dream was within her grasp, she found her innate cowardice surfacing. Could she handle the life he was offering? More important, could she be the kind of mate he needed—*deserved*? Would he be better off with a witch who shared his powers and his past? Would her love be enough?

"Could I ask you some questions?" she said, knowing she was avoiding answering his question, but she needed some time to think about accepting his proposal. She had to know that if she agreed, it was because she felt it was best for Lucien and not for herself. She loved him too much to make the wrong choice.

"Ask away," he said.

"I know the coven doesn't practice Satanism, but just what do you believe in?"

He gave her a wry smile. "We are followers of nature, and always have been, even when we practiced the Old Ways."

"Just what are the Old Ways?" she questioned next. "Black Magic?"

"Yes and no," he answered. "There are what we call light forces and dark forces, and we believe that both must exist for nature to be in perfect balance. The dark forces, however, are dangerous, and can turn into evil if they're handled improperly. That's one of the reasons the council of high priests banned the practice of the Old Ways. You must be very devout to reject their temptations, and I'm afraid that some of my people were seduced by them and used their power inappropriately. It was those uses that started the witch hysteria."

Ariel considered what he said. She had other questions about the Old Ways, but she had enough information to satisfy her for now. "I have another question. Why do you call yourself a warlock? I understand it's an insulting term to most practitioners of witchcraft."

"It is," he agreed, "and that's exactly why we use it. Eons ago there were some rogue members of the coven who refused to obey our laws. They became sorcerers and were cast out of the coven. They retaliated by turning us in to our enemies, which made them warlocks—betrayers. Since we are not allowed to harm another human being, not even to save our own life, many of our people died because of their betrayal. The council of high priests decided that it was critical that we remember the consequences of their perfidy. They concluded that the best way for us to remember was to call ourselves warlocks. I know the reasoning sounds bizarre, but it's been in effect for more than a thousand years, and maybe way back then it made sense."

Ariel had to agree with him. It did sound bizarre, but so did a dozen other things that had happened since she'd known him. "You say that you're not allowed to harm another human being, but what about Galen? What he did to my brother was harmful, and he definitely tried to harm both you and me. Was he the exception to the rule?"

"Yes, he was the exception, Ariel."

"And what's happened to him?" she asked.

"He's been stripped of his powers and all but the rudimentary parts of his memory. He's like a child now, and like a child, he'll be trained to live the exemplary life that a warlock is supposed to live."

Ariel decided she liked the sound of that. It was a civilized punishment that could truly rehabilitate Galen and turn him into a productive member of his society.

"I have one last question. Why does everyone in the coven have a last name that begins with the letters M-o-r?"

He chuckled, and Ariel was delighted at the sound. It was the first time she'd ever heard it. "It's a little complicated, but I'll try to explain it. The letter 'M' is simple to understand. It's the thirteenth letter in the alphabet, and symbolizes the original thirteen covens. 'O' is the fifteenth letter, and 'R' is the eighteenth letter. When you add thirteen, fifteen, and eighteen together, you come up with a total of forty-six. Add the four and the six together, and you come up with ten. The zero is automatically canceled out, which leaves you with the number one. That is symbolic, because it means that everyone in the coven is united as one. Did you follow all of that?"

Ariel didn't answer. Instead, she stared at him, unable to tear her gaze away from his face. She loved him, and he was offering her a life with him. Was she capable of being the kind of wife he needed to fulfill his destiny? Would her love for him be enough?

Yes, an inner voice whispered. *Yes!*

At that moment she knew that she couldn't walk away from him if she wanted to. He was as essential to her as air and sunlight. Without him she would shrivel up and die. As for being good enough to be his wife? Well, if she failed, it wouldn't be from a lack of trying.

"I don't know if I understood it," she said, "but I suppose you'll have plenty of time over the years to repeat it until I finally do understand."

He grew very still and stared at her warily. "Was that a yes, Ariel? Are you willing to come back to Sanctuary with me? Do you want to be my mate and bear my children?"

"Yes!" she said, as she rose from her chair, ran to him, and threw herself into his arms. "And if you ever walk away from me again, Lucien Morgret, I'll hunt you down and put a curse on you."

He laughed—truly laughed—for the first time in her presence, and the sound was so rich and beautiful that it brought tears to her eyes.

"I love you, Lucien."

"Ah, Ariel, I love you, too," he whispered as he lowered his lips to hers and ran his hands down her body in a loving caress. When they came together over her abdomen, he jerked away from the kiss and gaped at her. "You're pregnant! With twins! There has never been a set of twins in the history of witches and warlocks!"

"Lucien, you have to be crazy," Ariel objected. "Even if I were pregnant, I wouldn't be far enough along even for an over-the-counter pregnancy test to confirm it."

"A warlock is always the first to know when his

mate carries his child, Ariel. Believe me, we're going to have twins."

"How do you feel about that?" she questioned nervously.

"Wonderful," he murmured, and then proved it by kissing her deeply.

"Let's go home," she whispered when he finally let her come up for air. "We have a lot to do if we're going to get the coven started on looking for mortal mates, and do you know who I think our first experiment should be?"

"Who?" he asked indulgently.

"Shana."

"Shana?" he repeated skeptically. "I don't know, Ariel. Shana is a rebel. I'm not sure the mortal world is ready for her."

"Oh, believe me, it's ready for her, Lucien. Mortal men like nothing better than a challenge, and Shana will definitely be a challenge."

"I'll think about it later," he said, dropping another kiss on her lips. "For now, all I want to do is concentrate on the beautiful mortal who has agreed to be my mate and bear my children."

His head shot up, and he stared at her in disbelief. "Ariel, do you know that I may be the first warlock ever to have uttered those words?"

"What words?"

"My children." Not *child*, Ariel. *Children!*"

⬥T⬥ TOPAZ (0451)

DANGEROUS DESIRE

☐ **FALLING STARS by Anita Mills.** In a game of danger and desire where the stakes are shockingly high, the key cards are hidden, and love holds the final startling trump, Kate Winstead must choose between a husband she does not trust and a libertine lord who makes her doubt herself.
(403657—$4.99)

☐ **MOONLIGHT AND MEMORIES by Patricia Rice.** A lovely young widow and a handsome, wanton womanizer make a bargain that can only be broken—as this man who scorns love and this woman who fears passion come together in a whirlpool of desire that they both cannot resist.
(404114—$4.99)

☐ **TO CATCH THE WIND by Jasmine Cresswell.** Between two worlds, and across time, a beautiful woman struggles to find a love that could only mean danger.
(403991—$4.99)

Prices slightly higher in Canada

Buy them at your local bookstore or use this convenient coupon for ordering.

PENGUIN USA
P.O. Box 999 – Dept. #17109
Bergenfield, New Jersey 07621

Please send me the books I have checked above.
I am enclosing $_____ (please add $2.00 to cover postage and handling).
Send check or money order (no cash or C.O.D.'s) or charge by Mastercard or VISA (with a $15.00 minimum). Prices and numbers are subject to change without notice.

Card #_____ Exp. Date _____
Signature_____
Name_____
Address_____
City _____ State _____ Zip Code _____

For faster service when ordering by credit card call **1-800-253-6476**

Allow a minimum of 4-6 weeks for delivery. This offer is subject to change without notice.